'A heatwave of a novel, scorching and powerful. This extraordinary debut, perfect for readers of the magnificent Jane Harper, seared my eyes and singed my heart. Don't miss it.' **A.J. Finn, #1** *New York Times* **bestselling author of** *The Woman in the Window*

'Hammer has travelled back roads and inland waterways. His depictions are unsentimental, without false cheer, but never dismissive. He is nonetheless assaying a part of Australia that is dying, slowly and fatalistically. Thus threnody blends with crime drama in one of the finest novels of the year.' **Peter Pierce,** *The Australian*

'This sprawling and explosive outback thriller is a masterpiece. Strap yourself in for a wild ride as Aussie crime fiction doesn't get much better than this. Verdict: polished gold.' *Herald Sun*

'The epic novel about rural life in Australia that we need right now . . . it sits right up there with Peter Temple's *The Broken Shore*, Garry Disher's *Bitter Wash Road* and Jane Harper's *The Dry,* even as it extends their focus and reach . . . A rural crime novel with remarkable breadth and depth.' **Sue Turnbull,** *The Age/Sydney Morning Herald*

'So does *Scrublands* earn its Thriller of the Year tag? Absolutely. Is it my favourite book of the year so far? Well, it's only June but since you're asking, at this very moment, yes it is . . . Deliberately paced and wound tight, this book will keep you awake until you've finished the final page. And maybe even after that. It's relentless, it's compulsive, it's a book you simply can't put down.' *Written by Sime*

'Brilliant and unsettling, *Scrublands* stands at the junction of Snowtown and *Wake in Fright*, that place where Australia's mirage of bush tranquillity evaporated into our hidden fears.' **Paul Daley, journalist and author of** *Challenge*

'A superbly drawn, utterly compelling evocation of a small town riven by a shocking crime.' **Mark Brandi, author of** *Wimmera*

'A clever, intricate mystery . . . a complex, compelling story deeply rooted in its small-town setting. Highly recommended.' **Dervla McTiernan, author of *The Rúin***

'*Scrublands* kidnapped me for 48 hours. I was hopelessly lost in the scorching Australian landscape, disoriented but completely immersed in the town and people of Riversend, as the heat crackled off the pages. I was devastated when it was time to go back to the real world. This book is a force of nature. A must-read for all crime fiction fans.' **Sarah Bailey, author of *The Dark Lake* and *Into the Night***

'A brilliant read. A thriller that crackles and sweats and a powerful portrait of a small town on the edge.' **Michael Brissenden, journalist and author of *The List***

'Stellar . . . Richly descriptive writing coupled with deeply developed characters, relentless pacing, and a bombshell-laden plot make this whodunit virtually impossible to put down.' **Starred review, *Publishers Weekly US***

'Hammer's portrait of a dying, drought-struck town numbed by a priest's unimaginable act of violence will capture you from the first explosive page and refuse to let go until the last. His remarkable writing takes you inside lives twisted by secrets festering beneath the melting heat of the inland, the scrub beyond waiting to burst into flame. *Scrublands* is the read of the year. Unforgettable.' **Tony Wright, Associate Editor and Special Writer, *The Age* and *Sydney Morning Herald***

'A compulsively page-turning thriller where the parched interior looms as large as the characters.' **Katharine Murphy, *Guardian Australia***

'A narrative of uncommon sophistication.' **Geordie Williamson, *The Australian*, Books of the Year**

'Immersive and convincing . . . This will be the novel that all crime fiction fans will want . . . a terrific read that has "bestseller" written all over it.' ***Australian Crime Fiction***

'One of the most powerful, compelling and original crime novels to be written in Australia.' **Better Reading**

'Chris Hammer's powerful debut *Scrublands* establishes his place among the handful of thriller writers who understand the importance of setting as character, deftly weaving the story of a landscape burned dry and a town whose residents are barely hanging on with a complicated mystery that could only happen in this place in exactly the way Hammer tells it. Fresh and hypnotic, complex and layered, *Scrublands'* gorgeous prose swept me up and carried me toward a conclusion that was both surprising and inevitable. I loved every word. Highly recommended.' **Karen Dionne, international bestselling author of *The Marsh King's Daughter***

'. . . desolate, dangerous, and combustible. A complex novel powered by a cast of characters with motives and loyalties as ever-shifting as the dry riverbed beneath them, Hammer's story catches fire from the first page.' **J. Todd Scott, author of *High White Sun***

'A novel's opening moments are there to rivet readers' attention; this one begins with a dazzler . . . we're hooked.' **Booklist**

'There is a very good reason people are calling *Scrublands* the "thriller of the year". This impressive debut is a powerful and compulsively readable Australian crime novel.' **Booktopia**

'As one bookseller commented, *Scrublands* is another sign we are in a Golden Age of Australian crime. Reading it is a pulsating, intense experience, not to be missed.' **Better Reading**

'The twists in the tale helter-skelter but the ride is intoxicating, and there's no questions that this debut novel introduces another intriguing new voice to the Aussie crime landscape.' **Australian Women's Weekly**

'Much like the bushfire that flares up in the mulga, *Scrublands* quickly builds in intensity, until it's charging along with multiple storylines, unanswered questions and uncovered truths. It is a truly epic read.' **Good Reading**

Chris Hammer was a journalist for more than thirty years, dividing his career between covering Australian federal politics and international affairs. For many years he was a roving foreign correspondent for SBS TV's flagship current affairs program *Dateline*. In Canberra, his roles included chief political correspondent for *The Bulletin,* current affairs correspondent for SBS TV and a senior political journalist for *The Age*. During the summer of 2008–09, at the height of the millennial drought, Chris travelled extensively throughout eastern Australia researching his non-fiction book, *The River*, published in 2010 to critical acclaim. The drought, his journey through the Murray–Darling Basin and time spent in the New South Wales Riverina inspired the setting for *Scrublands*. Chris has a bachelor's degree in journalism and a master's degree in international relations. He lives in Canberra.

CHRIS HAMMER

SCRUBLANDS

ALLEN&UNWIN
SYDNEY · MELBOURNE · AUCKLAND · LONDON

This edition published in 2019
First published in 2018

Supported by

Allen & Unwin
83 Alexander Street
Crows Nest NSW 2065
Australia
Phone: (61 2) 8425 0100
Email: info@allenandunwin.com
Web: www.allenandunwin.com

A catalogue record for this book is available from the National Library of Australia

ISBN 978 1 76087 552 7

Map by Aleksander J. Potočnik
Set in Granjon by Bookhouse, Sydney
Printed in Australia by McPherson's Printing Group

10 9 8 7

FOR TOMOKO

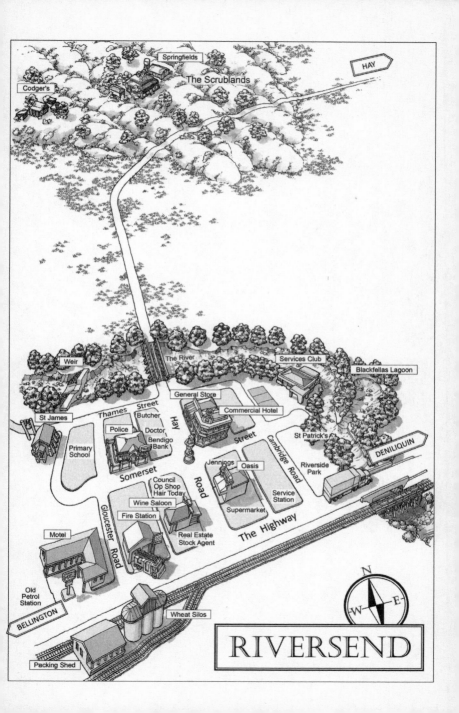

PROLOGUE

THE DAY IS STILL. THE HEAT, HAVING EASED DURING THE NIGHT, IS BUILDING again; the sky is cloudless and unforgiving, the sun punishing. Across the road, down by what's left of the river, the cicadas are generating a wall of noise, but there's silence surrounding the church. Parishioners begin to arrive for the eleven o'clock service, parking across the road in the shade of the trees. Once three or four cars have arrived, their occupants emerge into the brightness of the morning and cross the road, gathering outside St James to make small talk: stock prices, the scarcity of farm water, the punitive weather. The young priest, Byron Swift, is there, still dressed casually, chatting amiably with his elderly congregation. Nothing seems amiss; everything appears normal.

Craig Landers, owner and manager of Riversend's general store, approaches. He's going hunting with his mates, but they've stopped by the church so he can have a few words with the

1

priest beforehand. His friends have tagged along. Like Craig, none of them are regular churchgoers. Gerry Torlini lives down in Bellington and doesn't know any of the parishioners, so he returns to his four-wheel drive, but local farmers Thom and Alf Newkirk mingle, as does Horrie Grosvenor. Alf's son Allen, surrounded by people more than three times his age, joins Gerry in the cab of his truck. If anyone thinks the men look incongruous in their shooting gear, a strange mix of camouflage and high-vis, no one says so.

The priest sees Landers and walks over. The men shake hands, smile, exchange a few words. Then the priest excuses himself, and enters the church to prepare for the service and don his vestments. Having said his piece, Landers is keen to leave, but Horrie and the Newkirks are deep in conversation with some farmers, so he walks towards the side of the church, seeking shade. He's almost there when the babble of conversation abruptly ceases; he turns to see the priest has emerged from the church and is standing at the top of the short flight of steps. Byron Swift has changed into his robes, crucifix glinting as it catches the sun, and he's carrying a gun, a high-powered hunting rifle with a scope. It makes no sense to Landers; he's still confused as Swift raises the gun to his shoulder and calmly shoots Horrie Grosvenor from a distance of no more than five metres. Grosvenor's head ruptures in a red cloud and his legs give way. He falls to the ground like a sack, as if his bones no longer exist. Conversation stops, heads turn. There's a silent moment as people struggle for comprehension. The priest fires again, another body falls: Thom Newkirk. There is no screaming, not yet, but there is panic, silent desperation as people start running. Landers bolts for the corner of the church as another shot goes screaming out into the world. He rounds the end of the wall, gaining momentary safety. But he doesn't stop running; he knows it's him the priest most wants to kill.

one RIVERSEND

MARTIN SCARSDEN STOPS THE CAR ON THE BRIDGE LEADING INTO TOWN, LEAVING the engine running. It's a single-lane bridge—no overtaking, no passing—built decades ago, the timber milled from local river red gums. It's slung across the flood plain, long and rambling, desiccated planks shrunken and rattling, bolts loose, spans bowed. Martin opens the car door and steps into the midday heat, ferocious and furnace-dry. He places both hands on the railing, but such is the heat of the day that even wood is too hot to touch. He lifts them back, bringing flaking white paint with them. He wipes them clean, using the damp towel he has placed around his neck. He looks down to where the river should be and sees instead a mosaic of cracked clay, baked and going to dust. Someone has carted an old fridge out to where the water once ran and left it there, having first painted a sign on its door: FREE BEER—HONOUR SYSTEM. The red gums along the banks don't get the joke; some of their branches are dead, others support sparse clumps of khaki leaves. Martin tries lifting his sunglasses, but the light is dazzling, too bright, and he lowers them again. He reaches back into the car and cuts the engine. There is nothing to hear; the heat has sucked the life from the world: no cicadas, no cockatoos, not even crows, just the bridge creaking and complaining as it expands and contracts in thrall to the sun. There is no wind. The day is so very hot, it tugs at him, seeking his moisture; he can feel the heat rising through the thin leather soles of his city shoes.

Back in the rental car, air-conditioning straining, he moves off the bridge and down into Riversend's main street, into the sweltering bowl below the levee banks. There are cars parked here. They sit reversed into the kerb at a uniform forty-five-degree angle: utes and farm trucks and city sedans, all of them dusty and none of them new. He drives slowly, looking for movement, any sign of life, but it's like he's driving through a diorama. Only as he passes through the first intersection a block on from the river, past a bronze soldier on a column, does he see a man shuffling along the footpath in the shade of the shop awnings. He is wearing, of all things, a long grey overcoat, his shoulders stooped, his hand clutching a brown paper bag.

Martin stops the car, reverses it assiduously at the requisite angle, but not assiduously enough. He grimaces as the bumper scrapes against the kerb. He pulls on the handbrake, switches off the engine, climbs out. The kerb is almost knee-high, built for flooding rains, adorned now by the rear end of his rental. He thinks of moving the car forward, off the concrete shoal, but decides to leave it there, damage done.

He crosses the street and enters the shade of the awnings, but there's no sign of the shuffling man. The street is deserted. Martin regards the shopfronts. The first has a hand-painted sign taped to the inside of the glass door: MATHILDA'S OP SHOP AND ANTIQUES. PRE-LOVED CLOTHING, KNICK-KNACKS AND CURIOS. OPEN TUESDAY AND THURSDAY MORNINGS. This Monday lunchtime, the door is locked. Martin inspects the window display. There's a black beaded cocktail dress on an old dressmaker's mannequin; a tweed jacket with leather elbow patches, hem a little frayed, held aloft on a wooden clothes hanger; and a garish set of orange work overalls draped across the back of a chair. A stainless-steel bin contains a collection of discarded umbrellas, dusty with disuse. On one wall there's a poster showing a woman in a one-piece swimming suit luxuriating on a beach towel while behind her waves lick at the sand. MANLY SEA AND SURF, says the poster, but it has sat in the window too long and the Riverina sun has leached the red from her swimmers and the gold from the sand, leaving only a pervasive pale blue wash. Along the bottom of the window is an array of shoes: bowling shoes, golf shoes, some well-worn riding boots and a pair of polished brown brogues. Dotted around them like confetti are the bodies of flies. *Dead men's shoes*, Martin decides.

The shop next door is empty, a yellow and black FOR LEASE sign in the window, the outline still legible from where the paint has been stripped from the window: HAIR TODAY. He takes out his phone and snaps a few photos, visual prompts for when he's writing. The next store is entirely shuttered: a weatherboard façade with two small windows, both boarded up. The door is secured with a rusty chain and brass padlock. It looks as if it's been like that for a lifetime. Martin takes a photo of the chained door.

Returning to the other side of the road, Martin can again feel the heat through his shoes and he avoids patches of oozing bitumen. Gaining the footpath and the relief of the shade, he's surprised to find himself looking at a bookstore, right by where he's parked his car: THE OASIS BOOKSTORE AND CAFE says a sign hanging from the awning, the words carved into a long slab of twisting wood. A bookstore. Fancy that. He hasn't brought a book with him, hasn't even thought of it until now. His editor, Max Fuller, rang at dawn, delivering his brainwave, assigning him the story. Martin packed in a rush, got to the airport with moments to spare, downloaded the clippings he'd been emailed, been the last passenger across the tarmac and onto the plane. But a book would be good; if he must endure the next few days in this husk of a town, then a novel might provide some distraction. He tries the door, anticipating it too may be locked. Yet the Oasis is open for business. Or the door is, at least.

Inside, the shop is dark and deserted, the temperature at least ten degrees cooler. Martin removes his sunglasses, eyes adjusting to the gloom after the blowtorch streetscape. There are curtains across the shopfront's plate-glass windows and Japanese screens in front of them, adding an extra barricade against the day. A ceiling fan is barely revolving; the only other movement is water trickling across slate terraces on a small, self-contained water feature sitting atop the counter. The counter is next to the door, in front of the window, facing an open space. Here, there are a couple of couches, some slouching armchairs placed on a worn rug, together with some book-strewn occasional tables.

Running towards the back of the store are three or four ranks of shoulder-high bookshelves with an aisle up the middle and aisles along either side. The side walls support higher shelves. At the back of the shop, at the end of the aisle, there is a wooden swing door of the type that separates kitchens from customers in restaurants. If the bookshelves were pews, and the counter an altar, then this might be a chapel.

Martin walks past the tables to the far wall. A small sign identifies it as LITERATURE. A wry smile begins to stretch across his face but its progress is halted as he regards the top shelf of books. There, neatly aligned with only their spines showing, are the books he read and studied twenty years ago at university. Not just the same titles, but the same battered paperback editions, arranged like his courses themselves. There is *Moby Dick*, *The Last of the Mohicans* and *The Scarlet Letter*, sitting to the left of *The Great Gatsby*, *Catch-22* and *Herzog*. There's *The Fortunes of Richard Mahony*, *For Love Alone* and *Coonardoo*, leading to *Free Fall*, *The Trial* and *The Quiet American*. There's a smattering of plays: *The Caretaker*, *Rhinoceros* and *The Chapel Perilous*. He pulls out a Penguin edition of *A Room with a View*, its spine held together by adhesive tape turned yellow with age. He opens it, half expecting to see the name of some forgotten classmate, but instead the name that greets him is *Katherine Blonde*. He replaces the book, careful not to damage it. *Dead woman's books*, he thinks. He takes out his phone and snaps a photograph.

Sitting on the next shelf down are newer books, some looking almost untouched. James Joyce, Salman Rushdie, Tim Winton. He can't discern any pattern in their arrangement. He pulls one out, then another, but there are no names written inside.

He takes a couple of books and is turning to sit in one of the comfortable armchairs when he is startled, flinching involuntarily. A young woman has somehow appeared at the end of the central aisle.

'Find anything interesting?' she asks, smiling, her voice husky. She's leaning nonchalantly against a bookshelf.

'I hope so,' says Martin. But he's nowhere near as relaxed as he sounds. He's disconcerted: at first by her presence and now by her beauty. Her hair is blonde, cut into a messy bob, fringe brushing black eyebrows. Her cheekbones are marble, her eyes sparkling green. She's wearing a light summer dress and her feet are bare. She doesn't belong in the narrative he's been constructing about Riversend.

'So who's Katherine Blonde?' he asks.

'My mother.'

'Tell her I like her books.'

'Can't. She's dead.'

'Oh. Sorry.'

'Don't be. If you like books, she'd like you. This was her shop.'

They stand looking at each other for a moment. There is something unapologetic about the way she regards him, and Martin is the first to break eye contact.

'Sit down,' she says. 'Relax for a bit. You've come a long way.'

'How do you know that?'

'This is Riversend,' she says, offering a sad smile. She has dimples, Martin observes. She could be a model. Or a movie star. 'Go on, sit down,' she says. 'Want a coffee? We're a cafe as much as we're a bookshop. It's how we make our money.'

'Sure. Long black, thanks. And some water, please.' He finds himself longing for a cigarette, even though he hasn't smoked since university. A cigarette. Why now?

'Good. I'll be right back.'

She turns and walks soundlessly back down the aisle. Martin watches her the whole way, admiring the curve of her neck floating above the bookshelves, his feet still anchored to the same spot as when he first saw her. She passes through the swing door at the back of the store and is gone, but her presence lingers: the cello-like timbre of her voice, the fluid confidence of her posture, her green eyes.

The door stops swinging. Martin looks down at the books in his hands. He sighs, derides himself as pathetic and takes a seat, looking not at the books but at the backs of his forty-year-old hands. His father had possessed tradesman's hands. When Martin was a child they had always seemed so strong, so assured, so purposeful. He'd always hoped, assumed that one day his hands would be the same. But to Martin they still seem adolescent. White-collar hands, not working-class hands, somehow inauthentic. He takes a seat—a creaking armchair with tattered upholstery, tilting to one side—and starts leafing absent-mindedly through one of the books. This time she doesn't startle him as she enters his field of vision. He looks up. Time has passed.

'Here,' she says, frowning ever so slightly. She places a large white mug on the table beside him. As she bends, he captures some coffee-tinted fragrance. *Fool*, he thinks.

'Hope you don't mind,' she says, 'but I made myself one too. We don't get that many visitors.'

'Of course,' he hears himself saying. 'Sit down.'

Some part of Martin wants to make small talk, make her laugh, charm her. He thinks he remembers how—his own good looks can't have totally deserted him—but he glances again at his hands, and decides not to. 'What are you doing here?' he asks, surprising himself with the bluntness of his question.

'What do you mean?'

'What are you doing in Riversend?'

'I live here.'

'I know. But why?'

Her smile fades as she regards him more seriously. 'Is there some reason I shouldn't live here?'

'This.' Martin lifts his arms, gestures at the store around him. 'Books, culture, literature. Your uni books over there, on the shelf below your mother's. And you. This town is dying. You don't belong here.'

She doesn't smile, doesn't frown. Instead, she just looks at him, considering him, letting the silence extend before responding. 'You're Martin Scarsden, aren't you?' Her eyes are locked on his.

He returns her gaze. 'Yes. That's me.'

'I remember the reports,' she says. 'I'm glad you got out alive. It must have been terrible.'

'Yes, it was,' he says.

Minutes pass. Martin sips his coffee. It's not bad; he's had worse in Sydney. Again the curious longing for a cigarette. The silence is awkward, and then it's not. More minutes pass. He's glad he's here, in the Oasis, sharing silences with this beautiful young woman.

She speaks first. 'I came back eighteen months ago, when my mother was dying. To look after her. Now . . . well, if I leave, the bookshop, her bookshop, it closes down. It will happen soon enough, but I'm not there yet.'

'I'm sorry. I didn't mean to be so direct.'

She takes up her coffee, wraps her hands around her mug: a gesture of comfort, of confiding and sharing, strangely appropriate despite the heat of the day. 'So, Martin Scarsden, what are *you* doing in Riversend?'

'A story. My editor sent me. Thought it would be good for me to get out and breathe some healthy country air. "Blow away the cobwebs," he said.'

'What? The drought?'

'No. Not exactly.'

'Good God. The shooting? Again? It was almost a year ago.'

'Yeah. That's the hook: "A year on, how is Riversend coping?" Like a profile piece, but of a town, not a person. We'll print it on the anniversary.'

'That was your idea?'

'My editor's.'

'What a genius. And he sent you? To write about a town in trauma?'

'Apparently.'

'Christ.'

And they sit in silence once more. The young woman rests her chin in one hand, staring unseeing at a book on one of the tables, while Martin examines her, no longer exploring her beauty, but pondering her decision to remain in Riversend. He sees the fine lines around her eyes, suspects she's older than he first thought.

Mid-twenties, maybe. Young, at least in comparison to him. They sit like that for some minutes, a bookstore tableau, before she lifts her gaze and meets his eyes. A moment passes, a connection is made. When she speaks, her voice is almost a whisper.

'Martin, there's a better story, you know. Better than wallowing in the pain of a town in mourning.'

'And what's that?'

'Why he did it.'

'I think we know that, don't we?'

'Child abuse? An easy allegation to level at a dead priest. I don't believe it. Not every priest is a paedophile.'

Martin can't hold the intensity of her gaze; he looks at his coffee, not knowing what to say.

The young woman persists. 'D'Arcy Defoe. Is he a friend of yours?'

'I wouldn't go that far. But he's an excellent journalist. The story won a Walkley. Deservedly so.'

'It was wrong.'

Martin hesitates; he doesn't know where this is going. 'What's your name?'

'Mandalay Blonde. Everyone calls me Mandy.'

'Mandalay? That's something.'

'My mum. She liked the sound of it. Liked the idea of travelling the world, unfettered.'

'And did she?'

'No. Never left Australia.'

'Okay, Mandy. Byron Swift shot five people dead. You tell me: why did he do it?'

'I don't know. But if you found out, that would be a hell of a story, wouldn't it?'

'I guess. But if you don't know why he did it, who's going to tell me?'

She doesn't respond to that, not straight away. Martin is feeling disconcerted. He'd thought he'd found a refuge in the bookstore; now he feels as if he's spoilt it. He's not sure what to say, whether he should apologise, or make light of it, or thank her for the coffee and leave.

But Mandalay Blonde hasn't taken offence; she leans in towards him, voice low. 'Martin, I want to tell you something. But not for publication, not for repetition. Between you and me. Are you okay with that?'

'What's so sensitive?'

'I need to live in this town, that's what. So write what you like about Byron—he's past caring—but please leave me out of it. All right?'

'Sure. What is it?'

She leans back, considering her next words. Martin realises how quiet the bookstore is, insulated against sound as well as light and heat. He can hear the slow revolving of the fan, the hum of its electric motor, the tinkling of the water on the counter, the slow breath of Mandalay Blonde. Mandy looks him in the eye, then swallows, as if summoning courage.

'There was something holy about him. Like a saint or something.'

'He killed five people.'

'I know. I was here. It was awful. I knew some of the victims; I know their widows. Fran Landers is a friend of mine. So you tell me: why don't I hate him? Why do I feel as if what happened was somehow inevitable? Why is that?' Her eyes are pleading, her voice intense. 'Why?'

'Okay, Mandy, tell me. I'm listening.'

'You can't write any of this. Not the stuff about me. Agreed?'

'Sure. What is it?'

'He saved my life. I owe him my life. He was a good man.' The distress eddies across her face like wind across a pond.

'Go on.'

'Mum was dying, I got pregnant. Not for the first time. A one-night stand with some arsehole down in Melbourne. I was thinking of killing myself; I could see no future, not one worth living. This shitty town, that shitty life. And he saw it. He walked into the bookstore, started his banter and flirting like usual, and then he stopped. Just like that. He looked into my eyes and he knew. And he cared. He talked me around, over a week, over a month. Taught me how to stop running, taught me the value of things. He cared, he sympathised, he understood the pain of others. People like him don't abuse children; how could they?' There is passion in her voice, conviction in her words.

'Do you believe in God?' she asks.

'No,' says Martin.

'No, neither do I. What about fate?'

'No.'

'That I'm not so sure about. Karma?'

'Mandy, where is this going?'

'He used to come into the store, buying books and drinking coffee. I didn't know he was a priest at first. He was attentive, he was charming and he was different. I liked him. Mum really liked him. He could talk about books and history and philosophy. We used to love it when he dropped by. I was disappointed when I learnt he was a priest; I kind of fancied him.'

'Did he fancy you?' Looking at her, Martin finds it difficult to imagine a man who wouldn't.

She smiles. 'Of course not. I was pregnant.'

'But you liked him?'

'Everyone did. He was so witty, so charismatic. Mum was dying, the town was dying, and here he was: young and vital and unbowed, full of self-belief and promise. And then he became more than that—my friend, my confessor, my saviour. He listened to me, understood me, understood what I was going through. No judgement, no admonition. He'd always drop by when he was in town, always check on how we were doing. In Mum's last days, at the hospital down in Bellington, he comforted her, and he comforted me. He was a good man. And then he was gone as well.'

More silence. This time it's Martin who speaks first. 'Did you have your baby?'

'Yes. Of course. Liam. He's sleeping out the back. I'll introduce you if you're still here when he wakes up.'

'I'd like that.'

'Thank you.'

Martin chooses his words carefully, at least he tries to, knowing they can never be the right words. 'Mandy, I understand that Byron Swift was kind to you. I can readily accept he wasn't all bad, that he was sincere. But that doesn't equal redemption, not for what he did. And it doesn't mean the allegations aren't true. I'm sorry.'

His words do nothing to persuade her; she merely looks more determined. 'Martin, I'm telling you, he looked into my soul. I glimpsed his. He was a good man. He knew I was in pain and he helped me.'

'But how can you reconcile that with what he did? He committed mass murder.'

'I know. I know. I can't reconcile it. I know he did it; I don't deny it. And it's been messing me up ever since. The one truly decent human being I ever met besides my mother turns out to be this horror show. But here's the thing: I can believe he shot those people. I know he did it. It even rings true, feels right in some perverse way, even if I don't know why he did it. But I can't believe he abused children. As a kid I got bullied and bashed, as a teenager I got slandered and groped, and as an adult I've been ostracised and criticised and marginalised. I've had plenty of abusive boyfriends—almost the only kind of boyfriends I ever did have; narcissistic arseholes capable only of thinking of themselves. Liam's father is one of them. I know that mentality. I've seen it up close and nasty. That wasn't his mentality; he was the opposite. He cared. That's what's fucking me up. And that's why I don't believe he abused children. He cared.'

Martin doesn't know what to say. He sees the passion on her face, hears the fervour in her voice. But a mass murderer who cared? So he doesn't say anything, just looks back into Mandalay Blonde's troubled green eyes.

two | **THE BLACK DOG**

MARTIN FINDS HIMSELF STANDING BACK IN THE STREET, AS IF WAKING FROM a dream; he hasn't bought a book; he hasn't asked directions to the hotel. He checks his phone, thinking of accessing Google Maps, but there is no service. Christ, no mobile phone. He hadn't thought of that. He regards the town as he might a foreign land.

The early start, the long drive and the heat have drained him, leaving him feeling hazy. If anything, the day has grown hotter, the glare beyond the shop awnings more dazzling. Nothing moves, except the shimmering heat haze rising from the street. The temperature must have hit forty, without a breath of wind. He walks into the brightness. Touching the roof of his car is like touching a skillet. Something moves in the stillness, a shifting at the edge of vision, but when he turns he can't see anything. No—there, in the centre of the street: a lizard. He walks across. It's a stumpy tail, still as death. Bitumen is seeping through cracks in the road and Martin wonders if the lizard has become stuck. But it scurries away, blood quickened by the heat, rushing under a parked car. Another sound. A spluttering cough. Martin turns, sees the man shuffling along under the awnings on the other side of the road. The same man, in his grey overcoat, still clutching the bottle in the brown paper bag. Martin walks across to greet him.

'Good morning.'

The man is stooped. And apparently deaf. He keeps shuffling, not acknowledging Martin's existence.

'Good morning,' Martin repeats more loudly.

The man stops, looks up and around, as if hearing distant thunder, locating Martin's face. 'What?' The man has a grizzled beard, streaked with grey, and rheumy eyes.

'Good morning,' Martin says for a third time.

'It's not good and it's not morning. Whatcha want?'

'Can you tell me where the hotel is?'

'There is no hotel.'

'Yes, there is.' Martin knows; he read the clippings on his laptop during the flight down, including Defoe's award-winning piece describing the pub as the heart of the town. 'The Commercial.'

'Shut. Six months ago. Good fucken riddance. There it is, over there.' He waves his arm. Martin looks back the way he drove into town. How did he miss it? The old pub, the only two-storey building on the main street, stands at the intersection with its signage intact and an inviting wraparound verandah, looking not so much shut down as closed for the day. The man

SCRUBLANDS

pulls the top of the bag back, unscrews the bottle and takes a swig. 'Here. Want some?'

'No thanks. Not right now. Tell me, is there anywhere else in town to stay?'

'Try the motel. Better be quick, though. Way things are turning to shit round here, it might be next.'

'Where can I find it?'

The man regards Martin. 'Which way you come in? From Bellington? Deni?'

'No, from Hay.'

'Fuck of a drive. Well, head down here, the way you were going. Turn right at the stop sign. Towards Bellington, not Deniliquin. Motel's on the right, on the edge of town. About two hundred metres.'

'Thanks. Appreciate it.'

'Appreciate it? You some sort of fuckin' Yank? That's how they talk.'

'No. I just meant "thank you".'

'Goodo. Piss off then.'

And the derro continues on his shambling way. Martin extracts his phone and takes a snap of his receding back.

Getting into the car is no easy task. Martin wets his fingers with his tongue, so he can grab the doorhandle for long enough to swing it open, inserting his leg to stop the slope swinging the door shut again. Inside, the car is like a tandoori oven. He starts the engine, cranking up the air-conditioner, which does nothing more than pump hot air around the cabin. There's an ugly smell, the residual vomit of some former hirer, lifted from the fabric seats by the baking heat. The seatbelt buckle has

21

been sitting in the sun and is too hot to handle; Martin goes without. He drapes the once-damp towel around the steering wheel so he can hold it. 'Fucking hell,' he mutters.

He navigates the few hundred metres to the motel, swings the car into the shade of a carport by the entrance and gets out, chuckling to himself, spirits revived. He extracts his phone, takes a couple of photos. THE BLACK DOG MOTEL, says the peeling sign. VACANCY. And best of all: NO PETS ALLOWED. Martin laughs. Gold. How did Defoe miss this? Maybe the smooth bastard never moved from the pub.

Inside reception, there's still no respite from the heat. Martin can hear a television from somewhere deep inside the building. There's a buzzer on the counter, a doorbell adapted for the task. Martin presses it and hears a distant chirping off in the direction of the television. While he waits, he checks out a handful of brochures in a wire rack hanging from the brick wall. Pizza, Murray River cruises, a winery, a citrus farm, gliding, go-karts, another motel, a bed and breakfast. A swimming pool with water slides. All of them forty minutes away, in Bellington, down on the Murray. On the counter itself are a handful of takeaway menus printed in red ink. *Saigon Asian—Vietnamese, Thai, Chinese, Indian, Australian meals. Services Club, Riversend*. Martin folds one and puts it in his pocket. At least he won't starve.

A blowzy woman in her fifties wafts out from behind a semi-mirrored swing door, bringing with her an ephemeral gust of cool air and the smell of cleaning products. Her shoulder-length hair is two-tone: most of it's blonde, but the inch or so closest to her scalp has grown out into a doormat weave of brown and grey. 'Hi, love. After a room?'

'Yes, please.'

'Quick kip or overnight?'

'No, probably three or four nights.'

She takes a longer look at Martin. 'Not a problem. Let me check our bookings.'

The woman sits down and kicks an ageing computer to life. Martin looks out the door. There are no other cars, only his, under the carport.

'You're in luck. Four nights was it?'

'Sure.'

'Not a problem. Payment in advance, if that's okay with you. Day by day after that if you stay longer.'

Martin hands over his Fairfax company credit card. The woman looks at it, then up at Martin, placing him in context.

'You're from *The Age*?'

'*Sydney Morning Herald*.'

'Not a problem,' she murmurs and runs the card through the EFTPOS handset. 'Okay, love, you're in six. Here's your key. Wait a tick, I'll get you some milk. Turn your fridge on when you get in, and make sure you turn the lights and air-con off when you leave the room. Power bills are killing us.'

'Thanks,' says Martin. 'Do you have wi-fi?'

'Nup.'

'And no mobile reception?'

'Did before the election. Now the tower's down. Expect they'll fix it in time for the next vote.' Her smile is a sardonic one. 'There's a landline in your room. Worked last time I checked. Anything else I can help you with?'

'Yeah. The name of your motel. It's a bit strange, isn't it?'

'Nup. Not forty years ago it wasn't. Why should we change it just because some bunch of losers like the sound of it?'

——

Martin's room is soulless. Having read Defoe's piece, he'd been looking forward to staying in the pub: beers with the locals, a flow of information from candid bar staff, a counter meal of local steak and overcooked vegetables, a short climb up the stairs to sleep. Perhaps a midnight stagger down the corridor to the communal toilet for a piss, to be sure, but an old building with some character, oozing stories, not the utilitarian blandness of this dogbox: a bare fluorescent tube for a light, a sagging bed with brown spread, the chemical stench of air freshener, a grunting bar fridge and a clanking air-conditioner. There's a phone and a bedside clock, both decades old. Better than sleeping in the car, but not much. He calls the news desk, gives them the motel's number, warns them that his mobile is out of action.

Martin strips off, goes into the bathroom, flushes the dead flies that have accumulated in the toilet bowl, relieves himself, flushes again. He runs the tap at the basin, fills one of the tumblers. The water smells of chlorine and tastes of river. He gets the shower going, not bothering with the hot tap, scowls at the flaccid water pressure, then steps under the flow and lets the water fall across him. He stands there until it no longer feels cool. He holds up his hands, examines them. They've turned white and puffy, wrinkled by the water, like a drowned corpse. When did his hands begin to look so foreign to him?

His body cooler, the room reluctantly cooling, he dries himself and climbs into the bed, throwing off all but the sheet. He needs to rest. It's been a long day: the early start, the flight, the drive, the heat. The heat. He sleeps. Awakens to a room growing darker.

He dresses, drinks more of the abominable water, looks at his watch: seven-twenty.

Outside, behind the motel, the sun persists in the January sky, hanging large and orange above the horizon. Martin leaves the car and walks. The Black Dog Motel, he realises, really is on the edge of town. There's only a derelict service station between it and the empty paddocks. Across the road, there's a railway line and a set of towering wheat silos, glowing golden in the setting sun. Martin takes a snap. Then he walks past the abandoned petrol station to where the entrance of the town is marked by the obligatory signs: RIVERSEND, says one; POPU-LATION 800, says another; LEVEL 5 WATER RESTRICTIONS NOW IN PLACE, says a third. Martin climbs a low ridge running perpen-dicular to the highway, not more than a metre high; he frames the signs with the abandoned service station on the left and the wheat silos on the right, the setting sun sending his shadow across the road behind the signs. He wonders how long ago the population was eight hundred, what it might be now.

He walks back towards town, feeling the power of the sun on his back even this late in the day. There are houses aban-doned and houses occupied, houses with drought-dead gardens and houses boasting bore-water verdure. He passes the green corrugated-steel shed of the volunteer fire brigade before pausing at the junction with Hay Road, with its shops sheltering beneath their joined awnings. Another photograph.

He continues east along the highway, past a deserted supermarket, its sun-bleached CLOSING DOWN SALE banners still plastered to its doors; past the Shell service station, its owner giving him a friendly wave as he closes up for the night; alongside a park, green grass with more signs—BORE WATER ONLY, a band rotunda and a toilet block for motorists, all sitting below a levee bank. And another bridge, two lanes and concrete, stretching out across the river. Martin draws a map of Riversend in his mind: a T-junction fitted snugly into a curve in the river, with the levee bank cosseting the town to the north and east. Martin likes the layout; there is something considered and self-contained about it. Adrift on the vast inland plain, it anchors Riversend to some sense of purpose.

He scrambles up the side of the levee bank beside the bridge, finding a foot track running along its ridge. He stands and looks back along the highway, wiping sweat from his brow. The horizon is lost in a haze of dust and heat, but he feels he can see the curvature of the earth, as if he's standing on a headland looking out to sea. A truck thunders across the bridge and past him, heading west. The sun is setting, turned angry and orange by dust, and he watches the truck until it is first contorted, then swallowed whole by the haze.

Martin leaves the road, walking on top of the levee bank. Beside him the riverbed, glimpsed through the gums, is cracked bare mud. He's thinking the trees look healthy enough, until he comes to a dead trunk, looking as solid as its neighbours, just devoid of leaves. A flock of cockatoos passes overhead, their raucous calls awakening the sounds of other birds and creatures in the twilight. He follows the path until he reaches a curve in the riverbed. Above it, on a natural rise, sits a yellow-brick building, the Riversend Services and Bowling Club, its lights shining out through plate-glass windows above a steel-form deck, like a cruise ship beached at low tide.

Inside the club, the air is cool. There's a counter, with temporary membership forms and a sign instructing visitors to sign themselves in. Martin complies, tearing off a guest slip. The main room is large, with long windows looking out across the river bend, the trees almost imperceptible in the dusk outside the brightly lit room. There are tables and chairs, but no patrons. Not a soul. The only movement is the lights flashing garishly from poker machines standing beyond a low partition at the far end of the room. A barman is sitting behind the long bar reading a book. He looks up as Martin approaches.

'G'day there. Get you a beer?'

'Thanks. What've you got on tap?'

'These two here.'

Martin orders a schooner of Carlton Draught, asking the barman if he would like one.

'No thanks,' says the barman. He begins to pull Martin's beer. 'You the journo?'

'That's right,' says Martin. 'Word spreads fast.'

'Country towns. What can you say?' says the barman. He looks like he's in his early sixties, face red from a life of sun damage and beers, white hair combed and plastered in place by hair oil. His hands are large and marred by liver spots. Martin admires them. 'Come to write about the shooting?'

'That's right.'

'Good luck finding anything new to say. Seems to me everything has been written three times over.'

'You could be right about that.'

The barman takes Martin's money and deposits it in the till.

'You don't have wi-fi here, by any chance?' asks Martin.

'Sure do. In theory, anyway.'

'What does that mean?'

'Doesn't work half the time. And, when it does, it's like drought relief: comes in dribs and drabs. But give it a whirl, there's no one else here, so it mightn't be clogged up.'

Martin smiles. 'What's the password?'

'Billabong. From back when we had one.'

Martin succeeds in logging in on his phone, but his emails won't load; there is only a spinning wheel of computational indecision. He gives up and puts the phone away. 'I see what you mean.'

He knows he should ask about the killings, how the town is reacting, but he feels somehow reluctant. So instead he asks where everyone is.

'Mate, it's Monday night. Who's got money to drink on a Monday?'

'How come you're open then?'

''Cos if we're not open, we're shut. And there's too many places shut around here.'

'They can still afford to pay you, though?'

'They don't. Most days, we're volunteers. Board members. We have a roster.'

'That's impressive. Wouldn't happen in the city.'

'It's why we're still open and the pub is shut. No one's going to work in a pub for free.'

'Pity to see it go, all the same.'

'You're right there. Bloke who ran it was decent enough—for an outsider. Sponsored the local footy team, bought local produce for his bistro. Didn't save him from going out of business, though. Talking of bistros, you looking for something to eat?'

'Yeah. What have you got?'

'Nothing here. In the back, there's Tommy's takeaway, Saigon Asian, good as anything you'll get in Sydney or Melbourne. But be quick, last orders at eight.'

Martin checks his watch: five to eight.

'Thanks,' he says, taking a long draught of his beer.

'I'd let you sit here and eat it, but I need to be closing up myself. Only customers we get on a night like tonight—people having a quick one while they wait for their takeaway. But we're open every night 'cept Sunday. And lunchtimes every day except Monday. Want to take any drink with you?'

Martin imagines drinking by himself in his room at the Black Dog Motel. 'No thanks,' he says and drains his beer. He thanks the volunteer barman and extends his hand. 'Martin,' he says.

'Errol. Errol Ryding,' says the barman, taking Martin's hand in his own impressive mitt.

Errol, thinks Martin. *So this is where all the Errols have gone.*

———

In the blackness Martin tries to stretch out and finds he can't. His legs can't straighten. Dread descends like a curtain, smothering him in claustrophobia. Tentatively he reaches out, fearful of what his fingers will find and knowing already the resistance they must encounter. Steel. Unbending, unforgiving, unrelenting. Fear is wrapping itself around his neck, stifling his breathing. He holds his breath, lest someone hear his slightest expiration. That noise—what is it he can hear? Footsteps? Come to free him, come to kill him? More noise. The distant crump of artillery, the soft percussion of impact. Martin no longer wants to stretch. He folds himself tighter, foetus-like, and puts his fingers in his ears, fearing the donkey bray of an AK-47. And yet there is a noise, a rumbling, a clanking. He removes his fingers, listens in hope and fear. A tank? Could it be a tank? He strains to hear the rumble of the engine, the clank of the tread. It must be close. The Israelis, invading? Come to rescue him? But do they know he's here? Will they simply run the tank over him, crush him in his prison, unaware of his existence? Should he yell? Should he not? No. The soldiers would never hear him. Others might. And now. That roaring. Coming closer. A real roaring. An F16? One missile, one bomb, no one will ever know he was here, what became of him. The roar, closer and closer. What are they doing, coming in so low?

A louder clank, and he's awake, gulping air, tearing at his blanket. The lights from the passing truck penetrate the flimsy curtains of the Black Dog Motel as it roars its way east. 'Fuck,' exclaims Martin. The growl of the truck recedes, leaving only the tank-engine whir of the air-con. 'Fuck,' says Martin again, extricating himself from the blanket, turning on the fluoro strip light. The bedside clock says 3.45 am. He sits up and gulps down a tumbler of pungent water, but his mouth is still dry and salty from the takeaway. Perhaps he should have brought some grog back after all. He considers the pills in his travel bag, but he's not going back there. Instead, he begins the long wait for dawn.

three | **BLOODY SUNDAY**

MARTIN WALKS OUT BEFORE THE DAWN, THE AIR COOL AND THE SKY MUTED, finding his way through deserted streets to the epicentre of his story: St James. He stands before the church as the sun lifts from the horizon and sends shafts of golden light through the branches of the river red gums. He's seeing it for the first time, but the building is familiar nevertheless: red brick and corrugated-iron roof, raised ever so slightly above the surrounding ground, half a dozen steps leading up to a utilitarian oblong of a building, its purpose suggested by the arch of its portico, the pitch of its roof and the length of its windows, and confirmed by the cross on its roof. A rudimentary belltower stands to one side: two concrete pillars, a bell and a rope. ST JAMES: SERVICES FIRST AND THIRD SUNDAYS OF THE MONTH——11 AM, says the sign, black paint on white. The church stands alone, austere. There is no surrounding wall, no graveyard, no protective shrubs or trees.

Martin walks the cracked concrete path to the steps. There is nothing to indicate what occurred here almost a year ago: no plaque, no homemade crosses, no withered flowers. Martin wonders why not: the most traumatic event in the town's history and nothing to mark it. Nothing for the victims, nothing for the bereaved. Perhaps it's too soon, the events still too raw; perhaps the town is wary of sightseers and souvenir hunters; perhaps it wants to erase the shooting from its collective memory and pretend it never happened.

He examines the steps. No stains, no marks; the sun has bleached the cement, sterilised the crime scene. On either side of the path, the grass looks dead, killed off by the sun and lack of water. He tries the door, hoping the interior might prove more forthcoming, give some insight into the town's reaction, but finds it locked. So he walks around the building, searching for some useful detail, but there is nothing to see. St James remains impervious to scrutiny, surrendering nothing to journalistic inquiry. He takes some pictures he knows he will never look at.

A longing for coffee is building inside him; he wonders what time the bookstore opens. His watch says six-thirty. Not yet, he guesses. He follows Somerset Street south, St James on his right, the primary school to his left. The road curves. He can see the rear of the motel behind a wooden fence. He passes the police station and arrives back at Hay Road, the main street. In the centre of the intersection, standing on a pedestal, head bowed, is the life-size statue of a soldier dressed in the uniform of the First World War: boots, leggings, slouch hat. The soldier is standing at ease, his gun by his side. Martin looks up, regarding the dead bronze eyes. There are white marble slabs mounted on the plinth listing the locals who died for their country: the Boer War, the world wars, Korea and Vietnam. Martin looks again into the face of the bronze digger. This town is not new to trauma and the traumatised. But perhaps war is easier to memorialise than mass murder; war has some point to it, or so its widows are told.

A ute makes its way down from the highway, its driver flicking the ubiquitous finger of acknowledgement to Martin, who awkwardly returns the gesture. The vehicle continues on its way, heading up onto the bridge and out of town. It's Tuesday morning. Martin recalls Mathilda's Op Shop opening only on Tuesday and Thursday mornings. Were other businesses the same, the ones still surviving, their owners conspiring to concentrate their meagre earnings into a couple of hours each week, townspeople and farmers doing their best to support them? A town circling the wagons against drought and economic decline? If so, Martin knows he needs to make the most of it, introducing himself to people while they're out and about, canvassing their views and probing their feelings, judging how much life is left in Riversend. He walks across to the bank. Sure enough: open Tuesday and Thursday mornings. It's the same at the dry goods store, Jennings, diagonally opposite, but the Commercial Hotel, freshly painted, will remain closed no matter what the day of the week. Next to the pub, closer again to the bridge, is Landers' General Store and Supplies. Open seven days. Martin makes a mental note: Craig Landers was one of those killed in the shooting. Who is running the store now? His widow? Mandalay had mentioned her name, Fran, said they were friends.

For a moment he's distracted by what sounds like distant thunder. He searches the sky for confirmation, but there's not even a wisp of cloud, let alone a thunderhead. The thunder comes again, persists, grows closer. Four bikies appear, coming down Hay Road from the highway, riding two abreast, faces unsmiling. Their machines throb and pulsate, the sound bouncing off the buildings and reverberating in Martin's chest. They wear matte black helmets, sunglasses, beards and moustaches. They aren't wearing leather jackets, just their colours on thin denim with cut-off sleeves: *Reapers*, with a silhouette of the grim reaper and his scythe. Their arms bulge with muscles and tattoos, their faces with attitude. The men pass, seemingly oblivious of Martin. He takes a photo with his phone, then another, as they continue on their way, heading up onto the bridge. A minute or two later, the thunder is gone and Riversend returns to torpor.

It's half an hour before another vehicle appears. A red station wagon turns in from the highway, passes the soldier and parks outside the general store. As Martin approaches, a woman emerges from the car, springs the boot and picks up a small bale of newspapers. She looks about his age, with short dark hair and a pretty face.

'Can I give you a hand?' offers Martin.

'Sure,' says the woman. Martin reaches into the back of the car, pulling out a tray with a dozen loaves of bread in brown paper wrappers. The bread is warm and the smell enticing. He follows her into the store and sets the tray on the counter.

'Thanks,' says the woman. She's about to say something else, but stops, her mouth contracting from a flirtatious smile to a puckered scowl. 'You're the journalist, aren't you?'

'Yes. That's right.'

'You're not that Defoe man, are you?'

'No. My name is Martin Scarsden. Are you Mrs Landers? Fran, isn't it?'

'I am. But I have absolutely nothing to say to you. Or to any of your ilk.'

'I see. Any particular reason?'

'Don't be obtuse. Now, unless you want to buy something, please leave.'

'All right. Message received.' Martin makes to leave, then thinks better of it. 'Actually, do you sell bottled water?'

'Down the end there. Cheaper by the dozen.'

At the end of the aisle there's a stack of generic brand one-litre bottles of mineral water held together in half-dozens by cling wrap. Martin picks up two, one in each hand. At the counter he selects one of the loaves of bread.

'Look,' he says to the widow, who is cutting free the news-papers, 'I really don't want to intrude—'

'Good, then don't. You people have done enough damage.'

A retort comes to mind, but he thinks better of it. Instead, he takes the two Melbourne newspapers, the *Herald Sun* and *The Age*, plus the *Bellington Weekly Crier*, pays and leaves. LABOR RORTS, yells the *Herald Sun*; ICE EPIDEMIC'S NEW WAVE, warns *The Age*; DROUGHT DEEPENS, weeps the *Crier*. Outside, he desperately wants to break open one of the sixpacks of water, but realises that once the cling wrap is compromised, the bottles will be all but impossible to carry, so he heads back towards the Black Dog. On the way he checks the Oasis, but the bookshop and its coffee machine are not yet operating.

At quarter past nine, having feasted on bread, bottled water and instant coffee amid the Black Dog's cigarette butt-strewn car park, Martin is at the police station. It's a converted house, not a purpose-built station; a solid-looking little red-brick affair supporting a new grey steel roof, dwarfed somewhat by its large blue-and-white sign, sitting on the corner of Gloucester Road and Somerset Street, next to the bank and opposite the primary school. This is the one interview he was able to organise in advance, calling through on his mobile from Wagga the morning before. Inside, working at the counter, is Constable Robbie Haus-Jones. Ever since the shooting he's been hailed as a hero, but to Martin he looks like a teenage boy, with acne and an unconvincing moustache.

'Constable Haus-Jones?' asks Martin, extending his hand. 'Martin Scarsden.'

'Martin, good morning,' says the young officer in an unexpected baritone. 'Come on through.'

'Thank you.'

Martin follows the slight young man through to a plain office: desk; three grey filing cabinets, one with a combination lock; a detailed map of the district on the wall; a dead pot plant on the windowsill. Haus-Jones sits behind the desk; Martin takes one of the three chairs arranged in front of it.

'Thank you very much for agreeing to speak to me,' says Martin, deciding to skip the normal small talk. 'I'd like to record the interview for accuracy, if that's okay with you, but just let me know if at any stage you want to go off the record.'

'That's fine,' says the policeman, 'but before we start, can you run me through what you're after? I know you explained yesterday, but I was a bit distracted. To be honest, I was being polite; I didn't think the interview would be approved.'

'I see. What changed?'

'My sergeant down in Bellington. He urged me to do it.'

'Well, I must thank him if I see him. The idea for the story isn't to dwell on the shooting as such, although that's the starting point. The idea is to report on how the town is coping a year later.'

The young officer has let his eyes drift to the window as Martin is speaking, and he leaves them there as he replies. 'I see. Okay. Fire away.' His eyes return to Martin, not a hint of irony in them.

'Good. As I say, the shooting won't be the focus of the story, but it makes sense to start there. Am I right to think this is the first time you've spoken to the media on the subject?'

'First time for the city press, yes. I gave a few quotes to the *Crier* early on.'

'Good. So let's start.' Martin activates the voice recorder on his phone and places it on the desk between them. 'Can you take me through what happened that morning? Where you were, what happened next—that sort of thing.'

'Sure, Martin. It was a Sunday morning, as you probably know. I wasn't rostered on, but I'd come into work to clear up a few things before going to church.'

'At St James?'

'That's right. I was right here, sitting at my desk. It was a warm morning, not as hot as today, the window was open. Perfectly normal day. It was about ten to eleven. I was just finishing up. Didn't want to be late for church. Then I heard what must have been a shot, then another, but I thought nothing of it. Cars backfiring, kids with crackers, something like that. Then I heard a scream, and a man shouting, and then two more shots, and I knew. I wasn't in uniform, but I got my gun from the locker and went outside. There were two more shots, in rapid succession. There was a car horn, more screaming, all coming from the direction of the church. I saw someone sprinting up to the corner of the primary school grounds, heading this way. There was another shot and the man fell. To be honest, I didn't know what to do. It was real but not real, like I'd been dropped into a bucket of madness.

'I went back inside, rang Sergeant Walker at home in Bellington and alerted him, put on my body armour and went back outside. I ran along Somerset Street to where the body was lying in the road. It was Craig Landers. Dead. A single shot through his neck. There was a lot of blood. A lot of blood. I couldn't see anybody else; I couldn't hear anybody. The screaming had stopped. Everything was completely silent. There was one car parked outside the church on Somerset, more around the front, parked under the trees in Thames Street. I had no idea how many people might be there. There was no cover between me and the church. I was completely exposed. I thought about running back to the station, getting the vehicle, but then I heard another shot. So I started walking up the road towards the church.

'When I got a bit closer, I ran to the back of the building, taking cover, and then worked my way up the side wall, gradually moving forward. When I got to the corner of the church and looked around I could see the bodies. Three on the lawn, another shot through the windscreen of a car. They were all dead, there was no question about that. And sitting on the church step, holding a rifle, its stock on the ground, was the priest, Reverend Swift. He was sitting perfectly still, looking straight ahead. I proceeded around the corner with my pistol trained on him. He turned and looked at me, but otherwise he didn't move. I told him to release the rifle and raise his hands. He didn't move. I took a few more steps forward. I'd decided that if he tried to raise the rifle I would shoot him. I thought the closer I got, the more chance I would have of hitting him.'

The policeman is looking at Martin as he speaks, his voice unemotional.

'Did he speak?' asks Martin.

'Yes. He said, "Good morning, Robbie. I wondered when you'd get here."'

'He knew you?'

'Yes. We were friends.'

'Really?'

'Yes.'

'Okay, what happened next?'

'I took a couple of steps forward. Then . . . it was very fast. A car came through, along Thames Street, past the front of the church. I tried not to look at it, but it distracted me, and he had his gun on me before I knew it. He smiled. I remember the smile. He seemed calm. And then he fired, so I fired. I closed my eyes

40

and fired twice, opened them and fired twice more. He was down, bleeding. He'd let the gun drop. I went to him, kicked it further away. He'd kind of crumpled, there on the steps. I'd hit him twice in the chest. I didn't know what to do. There wasn't a lot I *could* do. I held his hand while he died. He smiled at me.'

There's silence in the small office. The policeman is looking out the window, his face tight, a slight frown creasing his young forehead. Martin lets the silence linger. He hadn't been expecting this level of candour.

'Constable Haus-Jones, have you recounted these events to anyone else?'

'Of course. Three police inquiries and the coroner's office.'

'I mean, any other journalists or public forums?'

'No. But it will all come out in the inquest anyway. It's on in a month or two. Sergeant Walker suggested I tell you what I know, provided that it's not contentious and that it's based on fact.'

'So you didn't speak to my colleague, D'Arcy Defoe?'

'No.'

'Okay. The day of the shooting, what happened next?'

'Next? Well, I was alone for quite a while. I guess people were still hiding. I went into the vestry and called through to Bellington on the church phone. Called my sergeant, called the hospital. Then I went outside and checked the bodies. Gradually people came out from behind cars and trees. But there was nothing we could do. The men were dead, all shot through the head, except for Gerry Torlini, who was in his car; he'd been shot through the chest and through the head.'

'Which shot killed him?'

'Whichever hit him first. Either would have killed him instantly.'

'For the record, were the victims all locals?'

'Local enough. Craig Landers ran the general store here in Riversend. Alf and Thom Newkirk owned adjacent farms just out of town. Gerry Torlini ran a fruit shop in Bellington and an irrigation orchard down by the Murray. Horace Grosvenor was a sales rep who lived in Bellington. So all from here or Bellington.'

'All regular churchgoers?'

'I'm sorry, Mr Scarsden, I think you might be drifting from your brief. Are you investigating the shooting, or writing about Riversend?'

'Sorry. It's just that what you're saying is intriguing. But you're quite correct. Tell me, though: you said you considered the priest, Reverend Swift, a friend. How so?'

'Is that relevant?'

'I think so. In writing about the impact of the shooting on the town, one of the things I'll be looking at is attitudes towards the perpetrator.'

'If you say so. I don't quite see it myself, but you're the journalist. Yes, I'd thought we were friends. I thought Byron was a good man. I thought he was something special. How stupid is that? He'd come up once a fortnight to conduct a service, but when I told him I was having trouble with some of the young blokes around town he helped set up a youth centre. We used to run it together. He'd come up every Thursday afternoon, then later on Tuesdays as well. We held it in one of the demountables at the school, one that had been vandalised in the past.

One of the things we did was fix it up. We did sport: footy and cricket on the oval. He'd take them swimming in the river, down at the weir, when we still had a river. The boys and girls never thought much of me, I was always the town copper, but they thought the world of him. He was very charismatic, had them eating out of his hand. Used to swear and smoke and tell dirty jokes. They loved it. Every now and then he'd slip a bit of God into it, but he was never heavy-handed. They thought he was cool.'

'Did you?'

The policeman offers a sardonic smile. 'Yeah, I guess I did. A town like this, isolated out on the plain, there's not a lot for the kids. Parents under pressure, no money, hot as Hades. They get bored, and when they get bored they can get nasty. Picking fights, picking on each other. Big kids bullying little kids. And then Byron turned up and changed the dynamic. He was, I don't know, kind of a Pied Piper figure. They'd follow him about.'

'That's impressive,' says Martin. 'But you know what was written about him after he died—that he abused some of those kids. What do you reckon?'

'Sorry. That's the subject of ongoing police inquiries. I couldn't possibly comment.'

'Understood. But could I ask if you ever witnessed anything to cause you to become concerned?'

Robbie considers his position before answering. 'No. I never saw or heard anything like that. But then again, I'm a police officer. He would hardly be telling me, would he? More likely he saw me as a perfect cover.'

'You resent that?'

'If it's true, of course I resent it.'

'You say he was your friend. You say you admired him. What do you think of him now?'

'I detest him. Forget the child abuse, that doesn't come into it. He killed five innocent people and forced me to kill him. He destroyed families and ripped a hole in a respectable town. He offered hope and then wrenched it away again; set himself up as a role model for the youngsters, and then left them a terrifying example. Our town is now synonymous with mass murder, Mr Scarsden. We're the Snowtown of the Riverina. It's with us for good. I can't begin to tell you how much I detest him.'

When Martin emerges from the police station half an hour later, he knows he has a red-hot story: a terrible story, a compelling story, a front-page story. He can already see the red EXCLUSIVE stamp: the police hero talking for the first time, his harrowing account of looking death in the eye, of shooting his friend dead, of holding his hand while he died. 'Like being dropped into a bucket of madness.' It would reignite the whole saga, fire the imagination of the public.

Martin looks back at the police station, enjoying the surge of adrenaline the interview has given him. He has no idea why Robbie Haus-Jones agreed to talk now and talk to *him*, and he has no idea why the senior man down in Bellington had encouraged him. But he is so glad that he did. This will show the doubters; Max will be proud.

four **GHOSTS**

MARTIN WANTS TO TAKE ANOTHER LOOK AT THE CHURCH, TO RETRACE THE constable's steps, but first there are more pressing concerns: coffee. It's ten-thirty and he's yet to have a decent cup. But when he gets to the Oasis, there's a sign on the door, GON OUT, BACKSON, with a picture of Pooh Bear and Piglet. Whimsy, Martin decides, would be more appealing post-coffee than pre-coffee. Maybe the petrol station offers something approximate, or maybe the services club is open? Or he could return to the Black Dog and brew up another cup of bottled water, Nescafé and long-life milk. He opts for abstinence.

He turns from the bookshop and spies the shuffling man progressing slowly down the other side of the road. Martin figures the day has already climbed into the thirties, shaping as a repeat of yesterday's scorcher, yet there the old fellow shambles, grey overcoat apparently surgically attached. Martin looks up and down Hay Road. There's a woman using the ATM at the bank opposite the pub, and a couple emerging from a car and entering the general store, getting their supplies before the heat of the day really kicks in. Martin looks back, but the shuffling man has vanished. He should have progressed only another twenty metres or so, not out of sight. A car? Martin crosses the road. There are a couple of empty cars, but no sign of the old man.

The op shop is open, a rack of clothes placed out on the pavement. Martin enters. There's an elderly woman sitting behind a desk doing a crossword. She nods at Martin and goes back to her puzzle. It's a small shop, smelling of mothballs and old sweat, with racks of second-hand clothes, pre-loved toys and chipped kitchenware. No books, though, and no shuffling man. 'Thanks,' he says as he heads towards the door.

'Nine letters, between heaven and hell,' says the old woman without looking up.

'Purgatory,' says Martin.

The old woman harrumphs, but fills in the spaces anyway.

On the street Martin is still perplexed. Where has the old bastard gone? He walks past the hair salon and regards the abandoned building next door, chain and lock intact. Further along the real estate agent has placed a sandwich board on the pavement, declaring she's open for business. Martin is thinking he'll check it out, however unlikely it is that the old man is in the market for property, when he discovers a narrow lane, less than a metre wide, running between the abandoned store and the real estate agent. 'Bingo,' he mutters. Then he stops. What's he doing? Why isn't he engaging the crossword woman: 'How's business? More people donating than buying? Leaving town, dropping stuff off?' Or the real estate agent: 'Foreclosures up? Why? Drought or mass murder?' But he has plenty of time for that. After all, he has Constable Robbie Haus-Jones captured for posterity on his phone; the rest will just be colour.

The alley runs between the two buildings, brick walls on each side. It's littered with newspapers and plastic bags, and reeks of cat piss. The far end appears to be blocked off by sheets of corrugated iron. Martin progresses slowly, careful where he puts his feet. There is a small, barred window to his left with frosted glass. The real estate agent's toilet, at a guess. Further down, recessed into the wall on the right, there's a wooden door, red paint flaking. Martin tries the knob. The door opens, hinges complaining, and he enters a room from another time. It's dark after the glare of Hay Road, light coming through where one of the boards across the front windows has been prised loose. There are several holes in the ceiling, and through one a shard of sunlight pierces the room, illuminating a slowly whirling cloud of dust. It's a large room: floorboards broad and twisted, two tables, a few chairs, some benches along the far wall. The tables and chairs are pressed wood, cheap furniture from some distant decade in the middle of the last century. And sitting on a stool at what could be a counter, or what could be a bar, is the shambling man, with his back to Martin. The brown paper bag is on the counter, the neck of the bottle protruding, the lid removed.

'Good morning,' says Martin.

The man turns, seemingly unsurprised. 'Oh, it's you. Hemingway.' And turns back.

Martin walks across to the counter. There's a second stool beside the old man. On the counter are two small glasses half full of something dark and viscous. The shuffling man has his hand resting on one. Martin looks around. There is no one else in the room. He sits on the second stool.

The wino looks up from his drink. 'Well, this time you're half right.'

'How's that?'

'This time it's morning.'

'Who are you drinking with?' asks Martin.

'No one. You. Ghosts. Does it matter?'

'I guess not. What is this place?'

The man looks around then, as if only now realising where he's sitting. 'This, my friend, is the Riversend wine saloon.'

'Seen better days.'

'Haven't we all.' If the man is in any way inebriated, he doesn't show it. Drunks sometimes don't. Or maybe it's still too early in the day. His hair is shoulder-length, unwashed and straggly, streaked with grey. His face is weather-beaten where it isn't covered in a matted beard. His lips are cracked, but his blue eyes are canny and not so bloodshot.

'I've never heard of a wine saloon,' says Martin.

'Of course you haven't. The country's full of ignoramuses; why should you be any different?' The man's voice is half tetchy, half amused.

Martin is unsure how to respond, looks at the glass in front of him.

'Go on, take a sip. Won't kill you.'

Martin complies. It's cheap port, overly sweet and cloying. He nods his appreciation, raising a wry smile from his host.

'You asked about the Commercial across the way?' the man asks. 'Seen plenty others like it, right? Your quintessential Aussie pub. You could put it on a fucken postcard, send it to yer Yankee friends. List it on the National Trust. Well, not this place. This is the history that doesn't get told.'

'I don't follow.'

'Jesus. Bright young bloke like you. Don't they teach you any history in those universities?'

Martin laughs.

'What's so funny, Hemingway?'

'I did history at university.'

'Jesus, ask for yer fucken money back.' But once the old coot has chuckled he grows serious. 'It's like this, young fella. In the old days, when it was still a going concern, the Commercial had three bars. There was the lounge bar: you could take the family, have a meal. There was the saloon bar: ladies allowed, but blokes needed to be dressed proper. Shirt with a collar, long trousers or shorts with long socks. Extremely classy, I can tell ya. And then there was the front bar, the workers' bar. That's where the shearers, the silo workers and the road crews could go for a beer without needing to wash, where they could swear and get pissed and leer at the barmaid. Pretty rough places, those front bars.'

'And what was this place?'

'This place was for those who weren't good enough for the front bar.'

'You serious?'

''Course I'm fucken serious. Do I look like a clown?'

'So who came here?'

'You're a smart fella. Know anything about post-traumatic stress disorder?'

Martin nods. He's not about to confess the condition largely remains a mystery to him, even after a year of counselling.

'Yeah, well, there was a time when this country was flooded with it. Flooded. Except it wasn't called PTSD back then. It was called shell shock, if it was called anything at all. Thousands of men, tens of thousands. Back from the Western Front; later on, back from fighting Hitler and Tojo. Some missing legs, or arms, or deaf or blind. Some full of syphilis and clap and tuberculosis. Some much more fucked up than that. Ugly, violent, alcoholic men. Drifting round the countryside, swarms of 'em during the Depression, moved on from place to place like sheep sent down a stock route. Except instead of heading towards the abattoir, they were coming back from one. You seen the memorial down at the crossroads, outside the pub? Fucken joke, isn't it? They cast 'em in bronze, raised 'em high, called 'em heroes. But some of those names, some of those very names carved on that memorial, some of them would have ended up here or in places like this. They were all over the place, these wine saloons, in the bush and in the cities. Every country town had one. It was different in those days. No Medibank, no Medicare, no cheap medicine. They self-medicated. It weren't no table wine they served in wine saloons, it was plonk: flagon port and cooking sherry and home-stilled spirits. Nasty, cheap and effective. This is where they came, the walking ghosts who weren't welcome in the Commercial fucken Hotel.'

'I never knew,' says Martin. 'Are you a veteran, then? Vietnam?'

'Me? Nah. Not of any war, anyway.'

'So why come here? Why not the pub? Or the club?'

'Because, I'm a bit like those old fellas. I'm not welcome in the front bar. Besides, I like it here. No one's going to bother me here.'

'Why aren't you welcome in the front bar?' Martin persists.

The old man takes a slug of his drink. 'Pub's shut. You want some more?'

'Bit early in the day for me.' Martin hears a scrabbling noise. Over against the wall, under a bench, a mouse moves furtively along the skirting board.

'I'm not so popular round here,' volunteers the man. 'Don't live up to the civic standards. You're the first living person I've spoken more than three words to for a year.'

'So why stay?'

'I grew up here. This is where I'm from. So fuck 'em, I'm staying.'

'What did you do? To get everyone so offside?'

'Nothing, to tell you the truth. Or not much. But ask around, see what they say. They'll tell you I'm a crook, that I've spent half my life in Long Bay, or Goulburn or Boggo Road. It's bullshit, but people believe what they want to believe. Can't say I care. That's their problem.'

Martin regards the face, the slightly bulbous nose, veins showing, and the grizzled beard. The face is lived in, but in the muted light Martin can't guess its age. Anywhere between forty and seventy. On the back of the man's hands and wrists are the blurry blue lines of prison tattoos. Yet the eyes are alert; Martin feels the old tramp assessing him. 'Well, nice to meet you. I'd better get going. What's your name?'

'Snouch. Harley Snouch.'

'Martin Scarsden, Harley.' The men don't shake hands.

Martin turns to leave, but the old man isn't finished. 'The priest. Don't believe everything you're told. People believe what they want to believe; doesn't mean it's true.'

'How do you mean?'

'He was a charmer, mate. Could charm the pants off a possum. People liked him, don't want to admit they got him wrong.'

'In what way?'

'The kids. What your mate wrote in the paper. It was dead right. But lots of people don't want to believe it, don't want to admit it was going on under their noses.'

'So you believe it?'

'Sure. I seen him with those kids, giving them hugs and whatnot. Swimming with them down at the weir. All over 'em like a rash.'

'Did you tell anyone? The police?'

'Mate, I don't talk to the police. Not if I can help it.'

'What about Swift himself? Did you ever talk with him?'

'Sure. Plenty. Man of the cloth, guess it was his duty, ministering to the likes of me. He'd come in here for a drink on occasion. Could put it away, too. Not a pissant like you. Tell his dirty jokes and filthy stories.'

'What? He alluded to abuse?'

'Yeah, alluded. That's a good way of putting it. Checking me out, no doubt, looking for an accomplice. Once he realised he had the wrong bloke, he backed off. But, mate, I'm the invisible man. I walk round this town and people don't see me. Doesn't mean I don't see them.'

'So what did you see? Did you see Swift engaged in anything criminal?'

'Criminal? No, I wouldn't say that. But I saw him with those kids and I listened to his unsavoury jokes. All I'm saying is don't believe everything you're told.'

'Okay. Thanks.'

'Don't mention it. In fact, don't mention me. Leave my name out of that shit sheet of yours.'

'See what I can do.'

'Fucken journo.'

Back on the main street, the day is growing heavy with heat, but the air smells of nothing more dishonest than dust and the sun has an antiseptic sting to it. Martin crosses the road towards the Oasis. He wonders if the invisible man is watching him through the boarded-up window, but figures Harley Snouch is still at the bar conversing with his ghosts. Martin stops in the middle of the road, turns back and snaps a photo, but suspects the contrast is too great—the wine saloon's facade is too dark against the shattering brightness. Martin squints, but can't even make out the screen on his phone. He walks back under the awning and takes a closer shot of the rusting chain and its padlock.

At the Oasis the Pooh Bear sign has been removed from the door. Martin enters, is surprised to see a couple of customers, two elderly ladies drinking tea at one of the tables. In a clear space in the centre of the rug, next to a playpen, a baby is rocking gently up and down in a lightweight bassinet, sucking on a bottle.

'Good morning,' says Martin.

One of the women beams in affirmation. 'Isn't it?'

Mandy appears, pushing through the swing door at the back of the shop, carrying a tray with scones, jam and cream. She offers Martin a smile, replete with dimples. 'Wouldn't you know it? Peak hour. Let me finish up with the sisters.'

A few minutes later she's back, having delivered morning tea to the old women. 'Hi,' she says. 'Hope you haven't come to chat. Liam's been a little shit this morning. Can I get you something?'

'He looks jolly enough.'

'Yeah. Wait till he's finished his bottle.'

'A large flat white then, biggest you've got. Double shot if it's big, triple shot if it's bigger.'

'Done. You want takeaway?'

'Might have it here, if that's okay?'

'No problem. Get a book while you're at it. You forgot yesterday.'

Martin does what he's told, but not before making some unconvincing cooing noises at the baby, who studiously ignores him and concentrates on the bottle instead. He's a chubby little fellow, dark brown eyes and a mop of curly brown hair. The old women regard him indulgently.

By the time Mandy returns, Martin has picked out a couple of worn paperbacks, one a detective book, the other a travel story, both by unfamiliar authors. She is carrying a Bavarian beer stein, complete with a conical metal cap. Martin laughs. 'Are you serious?'

'Largest I've got.'

'Thanks.'

Martin enjoys his coffee, flicking idly through his books. The old ladies finish their morning tea, thank Mandy and pay, their demeanour relentlessly cheerful. Mandy clears their plates, taking them out through the back of the store. It's a curious setup. If the money comes from coffee and cakes, there's no sign of it. No tables and chairs, just the old armchairs and occasional tables. No coffee machine, no urn, not even a display case of cakes or a jar of biscuits. Everything out the back, as if the cafe occurred accidentally one day and Mandy and her mother never got around to doing it properly. Maybe it had to do with licensing, or health regulations.

Mandy reappears and plucks the baby from his bassinet, pulling all sorts of faces and making all sorts of noises, culminating in a raspberry blown against the child's stomach. The boy chortles with delight. Her love for him, her delight in him, is evident. She holds him close as she sinks down into one of the armchairs.

'So, Martin, how's the story progressing?'

'Not bad, considering I've been here less than a day.'

'Yeah, I heard you spoke with Robbie. He say anything interesting?'

'Yes. He was most forthcoming.'

'But he doesn't know why Byron did it either, does he?'

'No, not really.'

Mandy becomes more serious. 'What did he say about the allegations of child abuse?'

'Not a lot. Said he never saw any evidence of it.'

She smiles. 'Told you so. No one believes it.'

'Some people do.'

'Like who?'

'Harley Snouch.'

Her face changes. The smile is no more; she is scowling, almost sneering. 'So you found him, did you? Lurking over there in his lair.'

'The wine saloon? Yeah. You know about that, then?'

'Of course. He sits over there, perving at me through those boarded-up windows. He thinks I don't know, but I do. Awful old bastard.'

Martin regards the Japanese screens arranged in front of the shop windows, recognising his misconception: he'd thought they were there simply to block out the heat and light. 'Why's he spying on you?'

'He's my father.'

Martin's amusement vanishes. 'What?'

'He raped my mother.'

Martin opens his mouth to say something, but there are no words. Mandy is looking at him. He feels the weight of her eyes, as if she is judging him. 'Jesus,' he says; finally, lamely. 'How can you bear it? Why don't you leave?'

'Fuck that. He destroyed my mother. He's not going to destroy her bookshop. And he's not going to destroy me.'

—

Outside, Martin stands in the shade, flips up the little tin cap and takes a sip of what remains of his coffee. It's lukewarm now, no bad thing given the heat of the day. He stares across at the wine saloon, squinting against the glare, the once-anonymous building grown sinister. Is Snouch looking at him, peering out through the gaps in the boarded-up windows, or have the phantom soldiers corralled him? There is no way of knowing. Martin considers returning to the wine saloon, confronting Snouch, but to what purpose? To articulate his disgust? How would that help Mandy? And how would it help his story?

He abandons the idea and instead walks back towards the scene of the shooting, giving the Anzac statue a once-over as he turns left into Somerset Street, walks past the bank, the police station and the primary school. He stands on the bend in Somerset, where it turns ninety degrees to run up alongside the church. This is where Craig Landers died, shot through the neck as he fled from the church. Martin can see St James clearly enough, a good hundred metres or so away. Hell of a shot for a preacher man. Martin looks for evidence of where exactly Landers fell, but there is none. He continues on, imagining what it might have been like for Robbie Haus-Jones on that day. No cover at all; a police-issue armoured vest and a pistol, up against someone with a rifle, across seventy-five metres of open ground. Haus-Jones might look like a teenager, but there can be no doubting his guts. Martin pulls out his phone and snaps a photo. He can almost hear the descriptive passage writing itself in his mind, imagining the young policeman's trepidation.

Martin carefully places his coffee stein on the ground, gets out his phone and opens up the voice recorder app, locating that morning's interview. He flicks backwards and forwards through the recording erratically, missing the simplicity of his old tape recorder, and eventually finds the relevant section. He replays the policeman's matter-of-fact recollection, counting shots as he listens:

'*It was a warm morning, not as hot as today, the window was open. Perfectly normal day. It was about ten to eleven. I was just finishing up. Didn't want to be late for church. Then I heard what must have been a shot—*' one '*—then another—*' two '*—but I thought nothing of it. Cars backfiring, kids with crackers, that sort of thing. Then I heard a scream, and a man shouting, and then two more shots—*' three, four '*—and I knew. I wasn't in uniform, but I got my gun from the locker and went outside. There were two more shots, in rapid succession.*' Five, six. '*There was a car horn, more screaming, all coming from the direction of the church. I saw someone sprinting up to the corner of the primary school grounds, heading this way. There was another shot—*' seven '*— and the man fell. To be honest, I didn't know what to do. It was real but not real, like I'd been dropped into a bucket of madness.*

I went back inside, rang Sergeant Walker at home in Bellington and alerted him, put on my body armour and went back outside. I ran along Somerset Street to where the body was lying in the road. It was Craig Landers. Dead. A single shot through his neck. There was a lot of blood. A lot of blood. I couldn't see anybody else; I couldn't hear anybody. The screaming had stopped. Everything was completely silent. There was one car parked outside the church on Somerset, more around the front, parked under the trees in Thames Street. I had no idea how many people might be there. There was no cover between me and the church. I was completely exposed.

I thought about running back to the station, getting the vehicle, but then I heard another shot.' Eight. *'So I started walking up the road towards the church.'*

Martin closes the audio app and puts the phone away. It's too hot here. The school should plant some trees. He picks up his stein and moves towards the church; perhaps some shade might be found there. Eight shots. Craig Landers through the neck at a hundred metres. Three more victims shot through the head. Gerry Torlini shot through the head and the chest. Eight shots, six direct hits. And yet, when Constable Haus-Jones confronted the priest from just a few paces away, close enough to kill him with two shots to the chest from a police-issue pistol, the minister had fired first and missed. It made no sense. Was it possible the priest had deliberately aimed and missed, had forced the policeman to kill him? A moment of clarity after his rampage?

Martin gets to the church and switches his thoughts to the young constable, trying to imagine what might have been going through his mind. Holding his stein as Haus-Jones might have held his gun, Martin walks the length of the church, pauses for a moment, takes a deep breath and steps around the corner. 'Shit.'

'What?' says the boy sitting on the church step.

'Sorry,' says Martin. 'Didn't expect to find anyone here.'

'That's obvious,' says the boy. He's dressed in shorts, t-shirt, a bucket hat and thongs. 'What's that?'

'This? A German beer stein. Containing coffee.'

'Does it taste better like that?'

'No, but it's big.'

'You must like coffee.'

'Yes. I do.'

The boy is thirteen or so, just hitting puberty. Martin walks up to him, looks around and sits on the side of a large planter box. There's nothing growing in it, just hard-packed dirt. 'My name's Martin. What's yours?'

'Luke McIntyre.'

'Whatcha doing here, Luke? Isn't it a school day?'

The boy frowns. 'You don't have kids, do you?'

'Why do you say that?'

'It's January. Middle of school holidays.'

Martin recalls the deserted school grounds. 'Of course it is.'

'Isn't it a work day?'

'Yeah, good point. Even so, it's a strange place to be on your holidays, on a hot day, sitting in the sun.'

'You're not going to give me the skin cancer lecture, are you? I'm wearing a hat.'

'No, I promise—no lectures. But I am interested in what you're doing here.'

'Nothing. I'm not doing anything wrong. I just come here to sit. No one ever comes here. It's peaceful.'

'It is now. But you know what happened here, I guess.'

'Yeah. The shooting. He was sitting here, you know, when the cop shot him. One moment he was alive, breathing, the next he was dead. Shot dead. Two bullets in the chest. One got him in the heart.'

Martin frowns. There is a faraway quality in the boy's voice. 'Is that why you come here?'

'Don't know.'

'Did you know him? The priest?'

'Reverend Swift? Sure.'

'Can you tell me about him? What was he like?'

'Why do you want to know?'

'I'm a journalist, writing a story. Trying to figure out what happened.'

'I don't like journalists. You're not D'Arcy Defoe, are you?'

'No, I'm not. I told you, my name's Martin. Martin Scarsden. I don't want to quote you; I won't write your name or anything. I just want to know what happened.'

'I don't know.'

'Look, Luke, if you think the other journalist was wrong, here's your chance to help me get it right.'

Luke considers this for a moment, then places his palm flat on the step beside him, eyes shut, as if seeking guidance. Or permission. 'Okay,' he says. 'What do you want to know?'

'Well, just what sort of guy Reverend Swift was.'

'Byron. He told us to call him by his first name. He was awesome. He looked out for us kids, stopped the big kids from bullying us. Got us to do shit together. Taught us how to be friends. We'd go down there, across the road to the weir, go swimming, camping, light campfires. A couple of times he hired a bus, took us to Bellington, to the water park or go-karting. Paid for it himself. And he taught us cool stuff. How to light fires without matches, how to track animals, what to do if you are bitten by a snake. All the stuff my old man could never be fucked doing. And we played sport: footy, cricket, basketball. He wasn't like other grown-ups.'

'And the policeman, Constable Haus-Jones? He helped out too, didn't he?'

'Yeah. But I don't think he really gave a shit about us kids.'

'How do you mean?'

'The big kids said he had the hots for Byron.'

Martin smiles, despite himself. 'What do you reckon?'

'Nah. They're full of shit.'

'You obviously thought a lot of Reverend Swift. And he must have thought a lot of you. Tell me, did he ever . . .'

'Oh, shit. Here we go. Not like the other reporters? Bullshit. Here's the bit where you ask if he ever touched me. Or if he asked me to touch him. Whether he showed me his dick, or asked me to kiss it. Or if he ever fucked me in the arse. Well, fuck you. You news people, and the teachers, and the fucking cops and even me own mum. No, he never did any of those things. Not to me, not to anyone else. I was a kid. I was twelve. I didn't even know what those things were, that they even existed. And then you come along, you know-it-all adults, and want to know whether he did this or did that. And he was dead, fucking shot dead, and none of you gave a shit about that. Shit. Shit, shit, shit.' The boy has tears in his eyes and tears on his cheeks. 'And you come here, right where he was killed, and ask me again? You know something? You're a cunt, Martin Scarsden.' The boy stands and runs off, across the road, past the trees and up the levee, before disappearing down the embankment towards the river.

'Shit,' says Martin. He sips his coffee, but it no longer tastes so good.

five | **THE PLAIN**

MARTIN SITS IN HIS ROOM AT THE BLACK DOG AND ASKS HIMSELF WHAT THE fuck he is up to. He's all too aware that his editor, Max Fuller, his old friend and mentor, has gone out on a limb to give him this assignment, that there are plenty back in the newsroom who reckon he isn't up to it. And now he's doing his best to prove them right. It's a straightforward assignment: how is the town coping? More in the writing than in the reporting, right up his alley. But instead of asking the barman at the club, or the woman at the op shop, or chasing down the real estate agent, all he's done is talk to a criminal in a wine saloon, lust over a bookstore keeper still mourning her mother and traumatise an already traumatised kid. And count gunshots like some half-baked conspiracy theorist on a grassy knoll. *What a fucking joke.*

He walks into the bathroom and takes a piss. The urine is bright yellow as it streams into the bowl. *Dehydrated*, thinks

Martin. No bloody wonder; wandering around town like Sherlock Holmes instead of doing his day job, seizing this chance Max has orchestrated for him. He washes his hands, splashes water onto his face, regards his reflection in the mirror. His eyes look puffy and bloodshot from lack of sleep, the nascent sunburn unable to disguise his skin's underlying pallor; there's a general sagginess to his flesh, revealing the first suggestion of jowls. Forty years old and looking older, the handsome pants man left behind somewhere in the Middle East. Mandy Blonde must be laughing herself sick. *How miserable, how pathetic.* The kid was right: he is a cunt.

He decides he's had enough. He's not up to it. Not anymore. Not up to another three nights fighting insomnia in the Black Dog, not up to another three days wading around in the grief and trauma of an entire town, stirring it up. For what purpose? A nicely written piece for the fleeting entertainment of the suburbs; a nicely written piece likely to go off like a grenade among the denizens of Riversend just as they're finally putting their lives back together. By which time he would be long gone, back in Sydney, well clear of local distress, being congratulated by colleagues, getting one of those proforma herograms from management. He thinks again of the boy, seeking solace on the church steps, sent running, crying, down to the empty riverbed. By him. But enough. Time to leave. Time to find something else to do between here and oblivion.

At the counter, the proprietor is unsympathetic. 'Sorry, love. No refunds. We're like the Hotel California. You can check out, but you can never leave.' She laughs at her own joke. Martin doesn't.

'Okay, I won't check out, but I am leaving.' He takes the key back off the counter. 'I'll post it to you. Don't let anyone into my room.'

'Your choice. Send us the key by the end of next week or it's another fifty off your credit card. Have a good drive.' Her smile is as convincing as her hair colour.

Outside, the sun is overhead, slamming down like a hammer on the anvil of the car park. Just like when he arrived the day before, except today a gusty wind has come up, blowing hot air, bellows-like, in from the desert. Thankfully, the hire car is in the shade of the carport. Martin loads his overnight bag into the boot, pops his daypack on the back seat with the remaining bottles of mineral water, takes a long swig out of the bottle he's already opened and places it on the passenger seat.

He starts the car, drives to the edge of the highway. He doesn't know where he's going. He's made no flight booking, made no calls to Max Fuller or anyone else. But he's not staying, that's the main thing. On a whim, he turns right, heading towards Bellington and the Murray. There will be coffee and phone reception and internet. And a river with water in it.

The road is dead straight and deserted, save for the roadkill deposited by last night's trucks. He watches in fascination in his rear-view mirror as the bottoms of the receding wheat silos begin to dissolve in the heat haze, leaving only their upper halves to float eerily in the sky. Martin stops the car, steps out. The mirage is still there. He takes a final snap with his phone. Riversend disappearing up itself.

He's just getting the car back up to speed when the ute appears from nowhere. One moment he's alone—earth, sky, road and nothing else—the next moment there is the blaring of a horn. He jerks involuntarily, almost leaves the road. Then the ute is alongside, the bare buttocks of some yob stuck out the passenger-side window not two metres away, accompanied by raucous laughter and screeched profanities. He brakes, and the ute accelerates away, fingers gesturing obscenely from both driver and passenger sides. There's a red P-plate on the back of the vehicle.

'Shit,' mutters Martin, feeling shaken by the suddenness of the incident. He considers pulling over, but continues on his way. Out here, there's not a lot of difference between sitting in a stationary car and one doing a hundred and ten kilometres an hour. In his mind he constructs the event as a narrative, rehearsing it, as if still intending to write his piece.

The ute has dissolved into the liquid distance and he's once again isolated on the flat and featureless plain. He searches it for a dark line of trees, but Riversend's river is too far behind him and the Murray is still more than half an hour away. There is nothing but stunted saltbush, dirt and the flatness. The car is alone on the highway, speeding from the illusory past to the insubstantial future. He feels as if he is aloft, orbiting a revolving earth. Deliberately he embraces the illusion, persuading his mind that it's not the car that is moving, but the earth spinning underneath its wheels. For a long moment the illusion holds but it's brought to an abrupt halt by a rapidly approaching curve in the highway. Back in control, Martin slows ever so slightly and navigates the bend, speeding past a woman waving her arms frantically beside a red car on the verge.

He hits the brakes; the car takes forever to slow. He makes a U-turn, speeds back to the woman. She races across to him as he stops, lowers his window. It's Fran Landers, the woman from the general store. 'Help me,' she gasps. 'Help them. They've crashed. Over there.'

Martin is out of the car, quickly taking in the situation. It's the ute. It's failed the bend, coming off the outside. It's a hundred metres away across the field. Martin runs through the gap it's ploughed through the roadside fence.

There is something crumpled on the ground up ahead. A person. Not moving. A young man, pants still around his knees, thrown clear when the ute rolled. The angle of his neck tells the story. Dead. Martin hears the gasp of Fran Landers behind him.

'C'mon,' he says.

They sprint the remaining distance to the ute. It's standing right way up on its wheels, facing back towards the highway, but the windscreen is missing and the roof is partially caved in. In the driver's seat, unconscious, with blood seeping from a gash across his scalp, a young man is slumped forward onto a deflated airbag. His face is white and his lips are blue.

'Jamie!' gasps Fran. 'My God. It's Jamie. It's my son.'

Martin reaches through the missing window, feeling for a pulse, finding one.

'Don't touch him,' Fran shrieks. 'His spine. Don't move him. For God's sake, don't move him! You'll cripple him.'

Martin ignores her. She screams as he reaches in, places one hand under the boy's chin, another supporting the back of his head, and gently tilts the head back against the headrest, allows the mouth to fall open. He puts his fingers into the open mouth, wishing the woman would stop screaming, and pulls the tongue forward from where it has lodged. It comes loose, with a wet pop, like a cork from a bottle, followed by an awful rattling gasp as the youth resumes breathing. Martin leans back from the window and stands up. Some muscle in his back is in spasm and he stretches. The woman is silent, no longer frantic, no longer moving. A single tear escapes her right eye, runs down her cheek and drips onto the parched earth. She's staring at Martin.

'Your son,' he says.

She looks away from him then, towards her son. The colour is coming back into his face, the blue lips growing pink again. She regards her boy, reaches in, dabs at his bleeding brow.

'Will he be okay?' she asks.

'I'd say so. He'll live. But we need to get help. I'll drive back to Riversend. They can call Bellington. You stay here. Look after your son. If he comes round, and he can move, then he can get out and lie down. Give him water, but nothing to eat. If he's still unconscious, place a wet towel over his head. Keep him in the shade if you can.'

Martin walks back, checks the other boy to make sure, but the young man remains resolutely dead. There's a bad smell and the flies are gathering. Back at the highway, Martin checks inside the red car. On the back seat there is a reflective wind-shield protector, glistening foil decorated with Disney characters. He pulls it out, walks back, and drapes Mickey and Goofy over the body. Even the dead deserve shade. He uses his phone to take a picture of the scene.

—

The services club is almost, but not quite empty. There's a barman, not Errol, a different bloke; Martin, sitting at the bar drinking a schooner of light beer; and a couple sitting at a table sharing a carafe of house white while they put away a feed of Asian. Martin notes absent-mindedly that they're eating with knives and forks. Is there some invisible border, a latter-day Goyder's Line, beyond which chopsticks are prohibited and knives and forks mandated?

Robbie Haus-Jones walks in, still in uniform. The two men shake hands.

'How you doing?' asks the constable.

'Been better. Any news on the boy?'

'Yeah, he'll be fine. In hospital in Bellington for observation. Bruising from the seatbelt, mild concussion and a couple of cracked ribs, but nothing permanent.'

'That's good.'

'Quick thinking by you. Fran Landers told me all about it. How did you know what to do?'

'Hostile environment training. Did it before I went to the Middle East. It's one of the few things I remember from the training, people asphyxiating in accidents. Can I get you a drink?'

'Yeah, thanks, I could do with one. I'll have a Carlton.'

Martin orders the beer.

'I'll need to get a formal statement from you in the next day or two. No hurry. Fran's statement pretty much covers it all.'

'No problem. Who was the dead kid?'

'Allen Newkirk. Local lad.'

'Newkirk? Not related to Alf and Thom?'

'Alf's son. He was at St James with his dad and the others on the day. He was sitting in the car next to Gerry Torlini. Saw it all. Got covered in gore. Fucked him up completely. Never got over it. I've been out at the farm, breaking the news to his mum.'

'Jesus. How did she take it?'

'How do you reckon? She's coming apart. Her husband dies at St James and Allen survives, then ends up dead in a mindless car accident. How fucked is that? Still, it would have been worse if you weren't there.'

'Then how come I feel so lousy?'

The cop has no answer to that and the two men sit quietly for a few minutes, drinking their beers. It's the young officer who breaks the silence. 'I read some of the reports about what happened to you in the Middle East. It sounds awful.'

'It was.'

'What happened?'

Perhaps it's the alcohol, perhaps it's the events of the day, but to Martin's surprise, he finds himself answering.

'I was based in Jerusalem, but every now and then I'd go into the Gaza Strip. Part of the job. The Israelis have cut it off, built a wall around it. Israelis aren't allowed in; most of the Palestinians aren't allowed out. But foreign journalists, aid agencies, diplomats and the like can get access. From time to time the Israelis will shell the place or launch a strike from a helicopter or F16, but it's not as dangerous as you might think. Not most of the time.

'I'd been in there for three days when it all went pear-shaped. There'd been some sort of riot at a prison on the West Bank, over near Jericho, where the Israelis had locked up some hardcore radicals. To the Israelis they were terrorists; to the Palestinians they were political prisoners. You know the story. Anyway, the Israelis sent in the army and half-a-dozen Palestinians were killed before order was restored. Gaza ignited. I was interviewing an official in Gaza City when my driver interrupted, said we had to go. We were heading for Erez, the border crossing back into Israel, in his old Mercedes. I saw militia on the streets, knew the situation was volatile. The driver got a call; there was a roadblock ahead. He pulled off, drove in among some buildings. He thought he might be able to get around the roadblock, but we decided I should get into the boot of the car, just to be on the safe side. So I got in. He was going down back alleys and tracks, and I was getting bumped around something awful, feeling carsick. And then we stopped. It was muffled, but I could hear the driver talking in Arabic. Then someone was yelling, there were a couple of shots, a quick burst from an AK. I just about shat myself. I heard the driver yelling, 'Okay, okay.' I think he was trying to let me know he was alive, but I could hear the voices fading. He was being led away somewhere—to someone in authority, I hoped, where he might be able to sort it. He was well connected, a member of an influential clan. Perhaps he would be able to pay a bribe or call in a favour or simply convince them to let him go on his way. It all depended on the men with the guns, what clan they belonged to and where their loyalties lay.'

Martin pauses, takes a slug of his beer.

'What happened next?' asks Robbie Haus-Jones.

'Nothing happened next. That was the problem. I was in the car boot for three days and nights, not knowing what would happen to me. I figured they weren't about to shoot me, but you never know. I could be held hostage. It's happened before. And as time went by, it occurred to me that something might have happened to the driver and no one knew I was there. That was the worst moment: realising that I could die there, in the boot of the car, from starvation. I had water—we always carried bottled water in the boot—and it was winter, so cold at night and not so hot during the day. It's possible I could have lasted weeks.'

'Another drink?' asks Robbie.

'Sure.'

The policeman orders two more beers. 'So how did you get out?'

'Eventually, the driver came back. Jumped in the car, drove off. Went somewhere safer and opened the boot. He had a bandage on his head. He asked if I was okay, said he thought we should still try to get to Erez, but that I had to stay in the boot. It seemed to take forever. When we got there, he opened the boot a fraction, asked for all my cash and my passport. Then he closed the boot again. It must have been an hour at least, then we were driving again, just a short distance. He got the car as close to the Palestinian end of the crossing as possible and opened the boot, got me out and to the gate as quickly as he could. My legs were cramping, so he was practically carrying me. You can imagine what I smelt like. The guards gave me my passport, nodded me through. The driver helped me down the tunnel—it's this long walkway, hundreds of metres, covered in boarding and corrugated iron. Usually there are people coming and going, but that day it was empty. We were almost to the Israeli checkpoint, halfway along, when a voice came over a loudspeaker telling the driver to stop, saying I needed to come the rest of the way by myself. They made me go through the usual full-body scans, despite my distress. Anyway, I finally got through and the Israelis put me in a little golf buggy thing and drove me to their end of the tunnel. They let me shower, gave me food, clean clothes. They asked me what had happened, so I told them. Then they released me to the care of an Australian diplomat and I was free.'

'I remember the story. I saw you on the news.'

'Yeah. I got shit-canned for that. Can you believe it? I gave an interview to the ABC correspondent, a mate of mine. My foreign editor was furious, wanted to know why I hadn't kept it all for the paper. Terrific, hey?'

The men sit in silence. Martin feels relieved he's been able to recount the bones of the story in such a matter-of-fact way. He feels a little numb, but not so bad.

'Martin, about the shooting—you know there's not a lot I can tell you. I'm not part of the investigation. A priest shoots five people dead, they don't give the job to a constable, especially not one who was involved. It's run out of Sydney. Sergeant Herb Walker down in Bellington is the local contact. You should speak to him.'

'Herb Walker. Thanks. I'll do that.'

'I was investigated, of course. God, if you unbutton your holster, you need to write a report; pull out your gun and there's a full-on inquiry. But I was cleared pretty quickly. He'd already shot five people dead, after all. And there were witnesses.'

'Does it still bother you, shooting him?'

'Of course. Every day. Every night.'

'Counselling?'

'More than you can imagine.'

'Do any good?'

'Not much. Maybe. I don't know. It's the nights that are worst.'

'I know what you mean. Didn't they offer you a transfer?'

'Yeah. Of course. But I want to get it out of my system here. Leave it all here, then move on. I don't want to take it with me.'

More silence.

'Robbie, why do you think he did it?'

'Truthfully? No idea. But there are things that bother me about it. All the obvious "what if" and "why didn't I" sort of things, they haunt me, but there are other things as well.'

'Like what?'

'There were a lot of people gathering outside the church. Maybe two dozen. He shot some and spared others. All the witnesses say the same thing: he didn't go berserk. He was calm, methodical. He could have killed a lot more.'

'You think he targeted those he killed, that it wasn't random?'

'Don't know. No idea. But he didn't shoot any women.'

'And he was a hell of a shot, wasn't he? Dropping Craig Landers from that distance.'

The constable doesn't respond immediately and the men are left looking at their beers. Neither of them has been drinking; the once-frothy heads have flattened out.

'Martin, there's an old bloke who lives out in the Scrublands called Codger Harris. Go and see him. He can tell you about Byron and his guns.'

'The Scrublands? What's that?'

'Shit country. Mulga scrub. Hundreds of square kilometres of it. Starts about ten clicks north of town. Here, I'll draw you a map of how to get to Codger's.'

Robbie takes a napkin and sketches out a route, warning Martin of pitfalls and wrong turns.

Directions completed, the constable drains his beer and nods at Martin. 'I'd better get going. See you round. And don't be so hard on yourself; you saved a kid's life today.'

six | SCRUBLANDS

THE HEAT IS WORSE. YESTERDAY'S WIND HAS TURNED HOT AND UGLY, GUSTING in from the north-west, propelling fine particles of dust and carrying the threat of fire. The very country Martin is driving through looks sick: anaemic trees, spindly shrubs and, between them, more dirt than grass. He's driven from the black soil of the flood plain into the Scrublands, a huge peninsula of mulga scrub where there is no soil, just the red granular earth, like an oversized ants' nest. The land is elevated ever so slightly above the flatness of the plain, just a few metres or so, with its own rises and falls. The track is hard, corrugated and unforgiving, runnelled by long-ago storms and scattered with large stones; periodically the tyres throw one up to thump into the car's floor. A track for four-wheel drives, farm trucks and hire cars. Martin takes it easy; Robbie Haus-Jones has warned him that not many come this way, that it's easy to get lost among the erratic tracks and the featureless landscape; break an axle and it will be a while before anyone finds you. So Martin nurses the car and remains patient.

He's not entirely sure what he's doing here. The impetus to leave town has withered, the insensitive exchange with the boy Luke already losing its potency, already fading, soon to be consigned to some seldom-visited storeroom of his memory, to sit alongside his collected regrets and misgivings. Robbie Haus-Jones still wants a formal statement on the ute crash and Allen Newkirk's death, but that only explains why Martin remains in Riversend, not what he's doing out here, in this hellish landscape, on this godforsaken day, chasing the tendril of a story. Not the story he was assigned, something more elusive, more intriguing. Perhaps that's it: the journalistic instinct is too ingrained, too much a part of him, compelling him onwards, even if he's no longer sure he has the stomach for it. Perhaps it's all he has left.

He passes through a fence line, rattling across a cattle grid. A pole on either side of the opening is adorned with the bleached skull of a cow, one rocking back and forth, animated by the punishing wind. Martin is pleased to see the skulls; he's on the right track. He stops, takes a photo. Next he comes to a fork in the road, takes the left track. Another kilometre or so, and he reaches a five-bar gate. HARRIS, says the top sign. NO SHOOTING, NO TRESPASSING, NO FUCKING AROUND, says the lower sign. Martin climbs out, into the blast-furnace wind, opens the gate, drives through, closes the gate. Not much further.

It's not really a farm, rather a semi-coherent collection of scattered structures, arranged as if dropped like marbles into a ring by some lumbering giant. The building material of choice is corrugated iron, crudely wired to wooden poles. The most rational structure is a cattle yard, roughly square, made of locally milled wood interspersed with some rusted iron fencing. The cattle yard is empty, of cattle and grass and any other living thing; even the flies have abandoned it. Martin steps out of the air-conditioned car, expecting the heat, not expecting the cacophony: the corrugated-iron sheets bang and squeal and shriek in the wind. 'Jesus Christ,' mutters Martin, wondering where to start.

He walks towards the largest structure, eyes narrowed against the wind-blown sand. It's a crude sawmill, not used for years by the look of it. To the mill's left is a more complete structure, albeit standing at a dangerous tilt and swaying in the wind. It's a garage. The two wooden swing doors stand open, hanging from their hinges, digging into the dirt and holding the structure erect, like a house of cards. Inside the garage, its bonnet missing and its whitewall tyres flat, rests the carcass of a Dodge, its once-black paint turned grey and powdery, splotched with patches of rust like a pensioner's hands. There's a bitch with a litter of pups splayed across the back seat of the old car. The pups are suckling, but the mother is unconscious, imitating death.

Martin finds the house, largely indistinguishable from the other structures littering the bush block, except its walls are marginally more upright, the windows are shuttered, the roof boasts eaves overhanging the walls. And the door is shut. It's a green door, paint flaking, wood exposed, patina emerging.

He knocks, noting the futility of the effort amid the thunderous day; the polite forms of society out of place in the Scrublands. The door has a brass knob. He twists it, shoves the door open and yells into the gloomy interior. 'Hello? Anyone home? Hello?'

He steps inside. The light diminishes, the noise diminishes, the smell increases. It hits him as his eyes are adjusting to the gloom: sweat, dogs, rancid fat, farts, urine. An olfactory assault, even with the wind whistling in through gaps in the walls.

'Who the fuck are you?' There is an old man, naked, slouched in a chair, hand wrapped around his swollen member. Martin has interrupted him mid-stroke.

'Shit—sorry,' Martin stammers.

But the old bloke doesn't seem at all fazed. 'Don't go. I'll be done in a mo.' And resumes his pumping.

Martin can't bear it. He retreats outside, glad of the metallic racket, if not the heat. *What a shithole.*

A minute or two later, the man emerges, still naked, his shrinking penis red and dripping. 'Sorry, mate. Caught me off guard. Come in, come in. Codger Harris, how are you?' He extends his hand.

Martin looks at the man's hand, looks at the man's face. He doesn't shake hands. 'G'day,' he says instead. 'Martin Scarsden.'

'Yeah, right,' says the old bloke. 'C'mon in anyway, Martin.'

Martin follows him into the hovel, looking anywhere but at the man's sagging buttocks.

'Sorry about the clothes-free zone. Too bloody hot for 'em. Pull up a pew.' The old man flops back into the hammock-like chair, canvas stretched between a rough wooden frame, where he'd been pleasuring himself when Martin first entered.

Martin looks around, can't immediately find anywhere to sit, grabs a milk crate, up-ends it, sits opposite the old man.

'Shit, Martin, begging your pardon. Not used to visitors, forgetting me manners.' And Codger Harris is back on his feet, remarkably nimble given his appearance. 'What d'ya want to drink?' He crosses to a bench, picks up a flagon and a couple of old Vegemite jars. Martin wasn't aware that flagons still existed. 'Not that there's much choice. Chateau Scrublands, that's about it. Care for a glass?'

'Bit early for me. And a bit hot.'

'Bullshit. Can't come all this way and not sample the local produce. You like wine, Martin?'

'What sort of wine is it?'

'This? Shit, this isn't wine, this is dynamite. But d'ya know anything about wine?'

'A bit.'

'So you know about terroir?' The man has the French pronunciation correct.

'Yeah. Good wine contains something of the land where the grapes are grown. That's it, isn't it?'

'Spot on. Top marks. Take a slug of this then, the terroir of the Scrublands, liquefied.' He half fills a Vegemite jar and hands it to Martin, pouring a full jar for himself.

Martin takes a sip, half gags, swallows anyway. It tastes like raw alcohol, except worse, like it's stripping the enamel from his teeth.

'Whatcha reckon?'

Martin coughs. 'Yeah, you've captured the Scrublands all right. Note perfect.'

Codger Harris laughs, an easy amiable laugh, takes a slug, not flinching, and grins at Martin. 'Truly shitful, isn't it?'

'You can say that again. What is it?'

'Moonshine. Make it out the back. Got a still.'

'Christ. You could sell it to NASA for rocket fuel.'

The old man grins with pride, takes another slug. His teeth are yellow stumps. 'You prefer some weed? I got piles of it out back. Or tobacco. Got a bit of that as well. Cunt of a thing to grow—needs plenty of water, plenty of compost. Weed's better. Grows anywhere. Even out here. Works better, too.'

'No, I'll stick to the terroir, thanks all the same.'

'Goodo.' And the old fellow drains his Vegemite jar, letting out a satisfied sigh, followed by a satisfied fart. 'So what can I do for you, Martin? Reckon you haven't come here for the grog.'

Martin smiles. Codger Harris is truly appalling, but the old man possesses an element of inexplicable charm. As if to underline the point, Codger reaches down and scratches his scrotum. Inexplicable is right. 'Codger, I'm told the priest, Byron Swift, visited you sometimes?'

'Oh yeah, the preacher. Fine fellow, fine fellow. Good lookin' bloke, bit like yourself, only younger. Used to come out here a fair bit. Was very upset when I heard what happened, what he did. Never would have guessed it, not for a moment. Seemed a real gentleman. Who told you he used to come out here? Thought it was our secret.'

'Does it matter who told me?'

'No, guess not. You're not a copper, are you?'

'No. A journo. I'm writing a story about Riversend.'

'Shit. That the truth? Christ. I could tell you a few stories. Make your hair curl.'

'Please do.'

'Shit no. I know your sort. Come out here, ply me with grog, get me to spill me guts. Next thing I know, paparazzi everywhere.' There is a huge grin on Codger's face, teeth stumps spread like tractor treads. He gives his balls a tug as if to emphasise the absurdity of his claim. Martin grins as well, inadvertently taking a sip of moonshine. He gags again; it's no better the second time around. Codger hoots with glee.

'So he did visit from time to time?'

'Sure.'

'How come?'

'Dunno. For me wit and insight, probably. Maybe he wanted to save me soul.'

'Seriously, Codger. What did he do out here?'

'Sometimes we'd shoot the breeze. Drink moonshine, smoke weed. Mostly he used to go shooting.'

'Shooting? Really?'

'Yep. He liked shooting.'

'And drinking and smoking dope? Doesn't sound very priestly.'

'You got that right. Bit of grog in him and he swore like a trooper, too. But a nice bloke. And he'd never drink or smoke when he was shooting, only afterwards.'

'That's interesting. Did you shoot with him? Was it targets or what?'

'No. I went with him one time, but he preferred to go alone. He shot rabbits mostly. And sparrows. Saw him pick off a few sparrows.'

'Sparrows? Shit, he must have been a hell of a shot.'

'Fucken oath, Martin, you got that right. A natural. Never seen anything like it. Those guns, they would become like a part of him. You shoulda seen it. He'd go into the zone and *pap, pap, pap*. Shoot the wings off a fly. He had a twenty-two. You know what that is? Small calibre. Said it made it more difficult. Never shot roos or scrub wallabies; reckoned it was too easy.'

'How many guns did he have?'

'Dunno. Three or four. The twenty-two. A hunting rifle. A high-powered marksman's rifle with sights. A shotgun. I tell you, it didn't matter: he was good with all of them.'

'How did he learn to shoot like that?'

'I think he grew up on a farm, but he didn't like talking about his past.'

'Why's that?'

'Dunno.' Codger Harris is thinking, remembering. 'He used to come out sometimes, go bush, camp out overnight. Said he liked the solitude. This bush, the Scrublands, it goes a long way, thirty or forty kilometres, back to the hills. My place goes for ten k, after that it's Crown land. Too shitty for farming, too shitty for a national park, too shitty for logging. Just shitty all round. But excellent for solitude.'

'When you were drinking together, what did he talk about?'

'Oh, you know, the usual. Philosophy, religion, politics. Girls with big tits. Racehorses.'

'Codger, maybe you can help me. I'm having trouble reconciling the idea of Byron Swift as a priest and a pillar of the community with someone who drinks hooch, smokes dope and goes round shooting small birds. I can't imagine a priest like that.'

'Well, that was him all right.'

'Sounds like you were impressed.'

'Too right I was. Most handsome man I ever saw. Tall, square-jawed, could have been in the movies. But that was only half of it. The way he moved, the way he carried himself, the way he spoke. He made you feel special just being with him. No wonder the sheilas liked him.'

'Did they?'

'So they say.'

'So why did he want to be a priest?'

'Well, I dunno, do I? But he had religion all right. Had it bad. Believed Jesus died for all of us, for all us sinners. It was no act.'

'Really?'

'Oh, fuck yeah. He didn't talk about it often, but when he did, it came from the heart. He never tried to convert me or anything, but for him it was real, like only part of him was in this world and part of him was somewhere else. He used to say a little prayer before he started shooting and a little prayer afterwards, for the animals he killed. Sounds strange, but there was something holy about him, something not of this world.'

'In what way? Can you explain it?'

'Nup. Not really. Just an impression. But he would have made a great Catholic, a great confessor. I told him things I'd never told another living being. In a way he saved me, got me to re-engage with people. Up until then I'd been a hermit.'

'Why do you think he shot those people at the church?'

Codger's half-amused affability falls away. He becomes serious, looks lost. 'I don't have a clue. And don't think I haven't thought about it. Lots of time to ponder the shit out of things in the Scrublands. I wish there was something I could have done to help him, to help prevent it.' Codger takes a slug of moonshine, cracks a toothy smile. 'That's what I do out here: live in the past, drink grog and have an occasional wank. Not much of a life, is it?'

'What do you think of this assertion that he was molesting local boys?'

'Bullshit. Absolute bullshit.'

'How can you be sure?'

'Sometimes, when we was in our cups, we'd talk about it, doing the business. He had some good stories, I can tell you. But they were all about sheilas. He was into sheilas, not kids.'

'How can you be sure?' Martin repeats.

'Well, I can't be, can I? But tell a story like those he told and you get a gleam in your eye. You can't fake that.'

Martin considers this for a moment as a searing gust of wind shakes the shanty. He looks around the one-room house: the makeshift kitchen with its piles of unwashed pans, the unmade bed with its yellowing sheets, the old books and random objects stacked in haphazard piles.

'Why do you live out here, Codger?'

'That's my business. I like it.'

'Can you make a living?'

'You can. Not much of one, but you can. Running bush cattle. There's a lot of them out there in the scrub. Have a big muster, make a fair old quid. But not now, not in this drought. They'd be skin and bones and chock-a-block with parasites. But come the rains and I'll get a crew in, make a few bucks.'

'And it's just you out here, you and the Crown land?'

'Nah, there's a few of us dotted round the place. There's an army vet and his sheila down the track a bit. Nice enough bloke, Jason, but not quite right upstairs. Keeps to himself. No idea why the woman stays. Harley Snouch is over the other side at Springfields, and there's a few shacks and caravans here and there. People come out hunting from time to time.'

'Harley Snouch? He has a bush block? Do you see much of him?'

'Not if I can help it. Not after what he did. Bastard.'

'What did he do?'

'Raped that beautiful girl. Fuckin' animal.'

—

Driving back into town on the road from Hay, crossing the long and rattling bridge above the flood plain, wind gusts bucking the car, Martin descends into Riversend and, on impulse, turns right towards the church, thinking he might chance upon Luke, the lad he'd upset the day before. But there's no sign of him.

Reversing in under the trees, he faces the church across the road. This must be where Gerry Torlini, the fruiterer from Bellington, collected his two bullets—one in the head, one in the chest—while Allen Newkirk cowered beside him. Martin looks at the church steps, maybe thirty metres away. An easy shot for a marksman like Byron Swift.

He climbs out. The church stands aloof and unadorned, tenuously connected to the outside world by an overhead power cable and a phone line. The entrance has double doors, shaded by a portico. Today, one door is ajar. Martin climbs the fatal steps and pushes through the door, wondering if Luke might be sheltering inside.

It's darker and cooler, much quieter, out of the wind. The boy is not here. Instead, up near the front, in the second line of pews, a woman is kneeling, perfectly still, praying. Martin looks around, but he can see no memorial to the shooting inside the church, just as there is none outside. He sits in the back pew, waiting. He recognises the woman's piety, her supplication, but can't remember how. How long is it since he felt anything remotely similar, experienced anything approaching grace? Codger thinks there was something holy about the priest, as does Mandy. How could that be, a man who shot things, who killed small animals and murdered his parishioners? How could that be when Martin, who just the day before had saved the life of a teenage boy, feels so much like a husk? He looks at his hands, places the palms together as if to pray, and stares at them. They don't seem to belong to him, and the gesture does not belong to them, and he does not belong in this place.

'Mr Scarsden?' It's the praying woman. He hadn't noticed her rise and walk towards him. It's Fran Landers. 'Sorry,' she says, 'were you praying?'

'Not exactly.'

'Well, sorry to interrupt. I just wanted to thank you for what you did yesterday. If you hadn't been there, I would have let him . . .' And she shudders.

Martin is on his feet, reaching out, touching her shoulder. 'Don't trouble yourself with that. He survived, that's the main thing. The only thing. It's all you need to know.'

She nods, accepting his words.

'How is he, anyway?'

She looks up at him, gratitude shining in her eyes. 'Oh, he's good. I spent the night with him down in the hospital in Bellington. He's all shaken up. Concussion and cracked ribs and a twisted back. But nothing serious. He just needs to take it easy. They'll keep him there for a couple of days just to make sure. I came back to town this morning to open the store. A friend is minding it for me. I just wanted to come in here and offer thanks. I'm glad you're here too. So I can thank you and apologise for being so rude when you came into the store.'

'Were you?'

'It felt like it.'

'Fran, excuse me for saying so, but it strikes me as a little odd that you would come here, to this church, to pray, to offer thanks, given what happened here.'

'How do you mean?' Fran looks unsettled.

'This is where your husband was shot.'

'No,' she says. 'Not here, not inside. But I see what you mean. It is a little strange, I guess. I tried the other church, the Catholic church, but it didn't seem right. I've been coming to St James ever since we moved here. It's okay once I'm inside.'

'I'm sorry to ask this, but you know the allegations about Reverend Swift—the ones that were in my paper . . .'

'I *don't* believe them,' she interjects before he can finish.

'Why not? How could you know for sure?'

'Because I knew Byron Swift. That's how.'

'You knew him well?'

'Well enough.'

'I thought he wasn't up here in Riversend that often.'

'Often enough.'

'So what was he like?'

'He was kind. And generous. And decent. Not the monster *your* paper made him out to be.'

For a moment, Martin is lost for words. He can hear the fondness for Swift in her voice, see the indignation in her eyes. Defending the man who killed her husband.

Fran fills the silence, her passion dissipating. 'But it doesn't matter one way or the other now, does it? He's dead. Robbie Haus-Jones shot him through the heart out there on the step.'

'So your son never said anything? About him abusing children?'

'No. Not to me. Now, I'm sorry, but I have to get back to the store.'

'Of course. But, Fran, I would like to talk to you. Conduct an interview for the piece I'm writing. It's all about Riversend, how the town is coping a year on. Would you be able to help with that?'

Her eyes betray her reluctance, but her indignation ebbs and she nods. 'Of course. I owe you everything. You saved my son.'

'Thank you. And I'm sorry for being so intrusive.'

'That's okay. I understand. It's your job. All the killing, all the death. It's what you do. But if it wasn't for you, I'd have nothing left. Better you than D'Arcy Defoe.'

seven **THE DRAGON**

MARTIN DRIVES THE SHORT DISTANCE BETWEEN ST JAMES AND THE OASIS. HE reverses back carefully so his rear bumper is close to the precipitous gutter but not touching it. This time he gets it just right, and feels the better for it. He's got the beer stein and the travel book he bought the day before. He's scrubbed out the stein. He's only halfway through the book. It provided some distraction in the witching hours when he couldn't sleep, but searching for a replacement will allow him to spend some time in the bookstore and escape the heat of the day.

The shop's door is unlocked, but it's empty of customers. The smell is good, though: coffee and home cooking. As if on cue, Mandalay Blonde appears from the door in the back of the store and glides down the central aisle towards him, her baby astride her jutting hip, held in place with a casual arm. To Martin, it makes her look simultaneously maternal and sexy.

'Afternoon, Martin. I hear you're quite the hero.'

'Yeah. Something like that.'

'Well, good for you. There's enough people leaving town as it is; we don't need them dying as well. Can I get you something?'

'Yes.' He holds out the stein. 'Another coffee, if I may. And what is that smell?'

'Muffins. Apple and cinnamon or blueberry. Homemade.'

'One apple and cinnamon, please.'

'And you've brought back one of your books? Very good. Pop it on the counter and you can have fifty per cent off your next one. Give me a hand first, though, will you?'

Martin follows her down the aisle and through the door, passing from an office-cum-storeroom into her home. Doors lead off either side of a corridor, a nursery on one side, her bedroom on the other, offering a fleeting glimpse of an antique brass bed, strewn with books, clothes everywhere. At the end of the corridor the kitchen is large and light, with a big wooden table and two stoves, an electric range placed close by the original wood stove.

'Grab those, will you?' she asks, pointing to the boy's playpen sitting on a quilt in the middle of the floor. 'Take them down to the shop.'

Returning to the bookstore he lays out the quilt on the Persian rug, in the same place it was the day before, and unfolds the playpen. Mandy's with him shortly, baby held close. She puts her son down in the pen. 'Keep an eye on him, Martin. Coffee and muffin on their way.'

Martin sits in one of the old armchairs and considers the child. He is lying on his stomach, straining to lift his head, doing a kind of baby push-up. There's a small furrow on his brow, as if he is concentrating hard. Martin smiles.

Mandy returns with a tray. The coffee stein is there, a muffin on a plate with a pat of butter and a cup of coffee of her own—just as he'd been hoping. She places the tray on an occasional table beside him, her proximity exhilarating, taking her coffee and sitting opposite. Martin wonders anew at her beauty.

'So, how goes the work, are you getting what you need?' she asks.

'Yes. Pretty good, actually. As well as Robbie Haus-Jones, I'll now be able to interview Fran Landers.'

'Yes, I can imagine. The man who shot down the rampaging priest, plus the grieving widow. Very good. And who else have you been talking to?'

'I went out to the Scrublands this morning. Talked to an old fellow out there, Codger Harris.'

'Codger Harris? What did he have to say?'

'You know him?'

'No, but I know what happened to him. Everyone does.'

'What's that?'

'It's an awful story. Happened years ago—before I was born, I think. Codger was the bank manager down in Bellington. I forget his real name; it's something like William. Anyway, one afternoon his wife and little boy were playing in the park by the river, right in the middle of town, when a truck went off the road; the driver had a heart attack or something. Killed Codger's wife outright. Their son, just three or four years old, lasted in hospital for a day or so. And that was it for Codger. He held it together for a few months and then fell apart spectacularly. Went crazy. They institutionalised him, gave him shock therapy, filled him up with drugs. He was never the same again. When he came back, he moved out to the Scrublands. Old Man Snouch gave him some land and he's been there ever since. More or less a hermit, eccentric, but wouldn't harm a fly. No one says anything, but people look out for him. Take him stuff. That sort of thing.'

'Old Man Snouch? Who's that?'

'Harley Snouch's dad, Eric. Died a few years ago. My grand-father, if what my mother says is true.'

'You don't sound so sure.'

'Oh, I'm sure. Mum never lied about anything, let alone something as serious as that. But when I was a kid, before I was old enough to know the truth, I knew there was this man called Harley out there somewhere who was my father. I used to dream about him returning to Riversend and he and my mother getting back together and us being a real family. We'd lead an idyllic life. And all those shitty kids would shut up and pick on someone else.'

'The bullies? Is that why they targeted you?'

'That was at the heart of it. Snouch was in jail, but there were plenty of people who took his side. They accused my mother of making it up, or of leading him on, or of being a slut. You know kids: they shout in public what their parents whisper in private. Mum had to tell me in the end, what really happened, so I knew why they were calling me names.'

Before Martin can respond, the door of the shop bursts open. It's Robbie Haus-Jones dressed in fluoro-orange overalls. He stops abruptly just inside the door, nods awkwardly to Mandy, speaks to Martin.

'Saw your car. Glad you're here. C'mon. We've got a bushfire.' And he turns and walks out.

Martin looks at Mandy, she shrugs, and Martin follows Robbie outside, leaving the muffin but taking the stein. The smell of wood smoke is in the air, as benign as a campfire, carried on the gusting wind. Robbie climbs into the police four-wheel drive; Martin climbs into the passenger side. 'You realise I know bugger-all about fighting bushfires, don't you?' he says.

'You'll be right. Stick close, we'll look out for you. But we need all the help we can get. We're down more than half-a-dozen from last year.'

'How's that?'

Robbie frowns at Martin before turning his attention back to the road. 'What do you reckon? Byron Swift, Craig Landers, Alf and Thom and Allen Newkirk, Jamie Landers, the pub owner. Plus a few more driven off by the drought.'

Robbie turns right onto the highway, pulls into the drive of the fire station. The doors are open and there's a new fire tanker out front, with three men and two women in high-vis bent over a map spread on the bonnet of a car. 'Brought you a ring-in, skipper,' says Robbie, smiling, as he and Martin climb out.

'Good lad. Hiya, Martin. Welcome to the team.' It's Errol, the barman from the services club, callused skin abrasive as they shake hands. 'Robbie, we're going to get going. Get Martin kitted out and we'll see you out there, at the turn-off.' The crew starts piling into the tanker truck as Robbie leads Martin into the shed and finds him fluoro-orange overalls, leather gloves, a hard hat, goggles. A few moments more are lost as they hunt for some leather boots to replace his city shoes. Then they're off, turning back into the main street, Hay Road.

'Where we heading?' Martin asks.

'The Scrublands. Fire from out on the plain. Into the trees now. It'll go through like a dose of salts. We'll try to hold it at the highway until the crews from Bellington get here.'

'What about the scrub?'

'Who cares? Shit country.'

'And the people who live there?'

'Yeah, we'll get 'em out if they're stupid enough to still be there. Know anything about bushfires, Martin?'

'I told you: nothing.'

'No worries, there's not much to know. First thing, only thing: don't get killed. You know what kills people in bushfires?'

'Smoke inhalation?'

'Nup. That's house fires. City fires. In bushfires, it's heat, pure and simple. The fire front will generate temperatures of hundreds of degrees. If it catches you in the open, it'll cook you alive. So whatever you do, don't get in front of the fire. You hear stories of people sheltering in swimming pools, farm dams, water tanks. Won't help. Water keeps 'em from burning, but the air is super-heated so they can't breathe—burns their lungs out from the inside. We attack from the flanks, not from the front.'

'How do you tell the front from the flank?'

Robbie laughs. 'Look at where the fire is, where the smoke is coming from, which way the wind is blowing it. Work out which way the fire is travelling, don't get in front of it.'

'Sounds simple enough.'

'It is, unless the wind changes. A fire can have a one-kilometre front and fifteen-kilometre flanks. Wind changes ninety degrees and you have a fire with a fifteen-kilometre front and a one-kilometre flank. Heading straight at you.'

'Terrific.'

'Don't worry. Shouldn't happen today. The weather bureau says it's north-westerlies all day. If you're caught in the open, seek shelter. People have survived lying on the floor of their cars, covered in woollen blankets. Provided the windows are shut and don't shatter, you can be lucky. The fire front will pass in five to ten minutes and the temperature will drop again. Get through that, and you'll live.'

'Great. Anything else?'

'Yeah: look up. Avoid burning trees, even ones that look like they've been put out. Falling branches don't issue warnings. And drink lots of water, more than you think you need. Don't wait to get thirsty: dehydration is dangerous.'

They're crossing the bridge now, and from the slight elevation Martin can see the eruption of grey smoke on the north-west horizon, pumping up into the clear blue sky. It's a long way off, but it's huge.

Ten kilometres further north and the Scrublands begin, the sickly mulga extending both sides of the road. They come to the turn-off into the scrub, the same turn-off that Martin had taken a few hours earlier when he sought out Codger Harris. The tanker has stopped, and Errol and a solid-looking woman from his crew are standing there talking with some locals. Robbie and Martin jump out of the four-wheel drive.

'Shit, did ya have to bring him?' A man with a long thin ponytail streaked with grey flicks his head in Robbie's direction. He's wearing a tattered t-shirt, an oily bandana, a denim jacket, torn jeans, boots. There's a ferocious-looking tattoo crawling up one side of his neck and a chunky gold earring. Next to him is a small woman in a t-shirt and jeans, arms tattooed, and next to her a motorbike, a chopper with extended forks, and a pile of bags.

'Give it a break, Jase,' says Errol. 'He's here to help.'

'Well, he doesn't get onto my place without a warrant, fire or no fire.'

'Fine by me,' says Robbie.

Errol shakes his head, ploughs on. 'Anyway, smart leaving early. Is Codger still in there?'

'Yeah. Me and Shazza stopped by to warn him, but couldn't fit him onto the bike. You blokes should get in and get him out.'

'First priority. What about Snouch?'

'What about him? He's got a car. He can look after himself.'

Errol turns to Robbie. 'Can you get Codger? Take Moxie. Don't muck about. Grab him, what he can carry, leave the rest.'

'And no going onto my place,' interjects the man with the motorbike.

'Fuck off, Jason,' retorts Robbie, 'or I'll search those bags over there.'

Jason shuts up.

Robbie and Moxie head off, and Martin gets a quick briefing. He's assigned to help a taciturn young bloke called Luigi. Luigi will direct one of the fire tanker's two hoses; Martin will follow a few metres behind him, helping to manoeuvre the canvas tube. A farm tanker pulls up, full of water to replenish the fire truck's pumps. A light aircraft flies over, Errol communicating via the radio in the tanker's cab. And all the time the smoke cloud is spreading lower and wider, the pale blue retreating south-east. In front of him, not twenty metres away, a mob of forty or fifty roos comes hurtling out of the scrub and across the road. For a moment the wind dies and the first ash starts to fall, like black snowflakes.

'All right, gather round,' yells Errol. 'It'll be with us in about fifteen minutes; the Bellington crews will be here in about twenty. It's moving quick, but the front is still narrow. We'll try and flank it on the road, stop spotting. The Bellington crews will head straight into the bush along Glondillys Track, east of the highway, and start back-burning. Once we've done what we can here, we either join them, or move round the back of the scrub and stop it escaping onto the plain. Questions?'

There's silence; soldiers before a battle. The wind is up again, stronger than ever.

Robbie's police truck comes barrelling out of the bush, emergency lights flaring brightly, skidding to a halt in the gravel beside the tanker. He's out of the car in a flash. 'Has Snouch come out?'

Errol shakes his head. 'Nup. Sure he's not in town on the piss?'

'No, he's in there all right. Old cunt. Saw him drive past this morning.' It's Codger Harris, climbing out of Robbie's four-wheel drive to join them, dressed in a mishmash of ill-fitting clothes.

'Fuck,' says Robbie, looking at Errol.

'Fuck,' says Errol, looking at the ground, hand kneading his brow. 'Fuck.'

'He's got a car. Leave him.' It's Jason's partner, Shazza.

Robbie is shaking his head. 'Nup. Can't do it. I'll get him.' And he's running back to his four-wheel drive. And running after him, not knowing why, is Martin. He gets the passenger door open, climbs in as Robbie fires the engine. 'Martin, get out. Get out now.'

'No. I'm coming.'

'You're a fucking idiot then. Hold on.' Robbie guns the engine, swings the truck around, hurls it down the dirt road into the bush. 'We get him, throw him in the back, and get the hell out, okay?'

Martin grunts assent, and then the two men are silent, lost in their internal remonstrations, while the world around them grows increasingly apocalyptic, the sky closing in, the light fading, ash falling, some of it glowing orange at the edges. Robbie pushes the four-wheel drive through the bends of the dirt road, his face intent, driving as fast as he can, their safety inconsequential. They round a curve; two wallabies are standing in the road. Robbie mows them down, not braking before, not braking after, one animal thundering off the roo bar, the other crushed beneath the wheels. Martin holds on, his knuckles white; Robbie staring through the gloom, a man possessed. The sky is almost black, and the cloud of smoke is so low it's almost down to the roof of the speeding vehicle. Day has gone, there is no light left, they're driving through night, headlights piercing smoke as they might mist. Another bend, and they burst into a clearing. Martin takes it in: an old Holden, up on a jack, one wheel off. A farm shed. A garage. The banks of a farm dam. The house. Snouch, with a garden hose trained on the house, turning as they burst into his existence.

Robbie and Martin are out of the car as one, Martin keeping abreast of the younger man.

'In the truck now! We're going!' yells the policeman.

But Snouch is shaking his head. 'Look,' he says, pointing up.

Martin looks up, through the blizzard of ash: the clouds that just a moment ago were black as coal are turning blood red, brighter and brighter as he watches, as if glowing from within, bathing the yard in orange light. And he can hear something in the distance, above the wind: a roaring, like a freight train heading straight towards them.

'Into the car!' yells Robbie. 'We'll drive into the middle of the dam!'

'No!' shouts Snouch above the roaring. 'The house. Brick and stone. It won't go up straight away!'

Robbie nods, and the men sprint for the house, the policeman first, the journalist second, the old crim not far behind. The roaring is almost upon them. Martin can hear explosions, like cracking whips or gunshots, and as he gains the verandah he can glimpse it through the scrub, the licking orange tongues of death. Last through the door is Snouch, pulling the hose after him, water pouring from its nozzle. Down a wide central corridor they go, rooms off either side, the house dark save for the glow before them.

It's Snouch's house, and it's Snouch who takes control. 'I've soaked the back of the house as much as I can, shuttered the windows. But the verandah is wood, goes all the way around.

It'll catch for sure. Roof's tin, but some embers'll get under sooner or later. The walls are stone and brick, though, thick as buggery. Gives us a fighting chance. Here.' And Snouch turns the hose on them, soaking them, sticking the nozzle down inside their overalls, giving them dripping towels to put under their hard hats. 'C'mon. We'll start at the back, fight it, retreat as we have to. Cover your mouths, stay low if there's smoke. We'll go back out the way we came in, but leave it late as you can, okay?'

And the freight train smashes into the back of the house, engulfing it in orange and red mist, like a dragon devouring its prey. Snouch pushes forward, as if against a tide, hose spraying out in front of him like a shield, followed by Robbie and Martin. They're in a kitchen, like a room in a nightmare, conjured from hell. *It's out there*, thinks Martin, *and it wants to come in and eat us*. It's alive: a serpent, a dragon. The sink is full of water; there are buckets of water on the floor. Snouch has prepared. The heat is unimaginable, overwhelming.

Robbie heads into a room off the kitchen with a bucket of water. The policeman is steaming. Steaming. Martin looks down at himself. Steam is pouring off him too. How hot is it? He's hit by water from the hose again, lets it cover him. He looks up; Snouch has turned it on himself, then on Robbie as he comes back with the empty bucket. Martin grabs a bucket, heads into a room running off the other side of the kitchen, sprays the water across the curtains, hoping like hell he doesn't shatter the glass behind them. There are shutters on the window, protecting it, but they appear transparent, as if the fire is an X-ray, penetrating the wood as easily as the glass of the window and the cloth of the curtains. A quick look around: a tidy room, a baby's cot, a cedar dresser, paintings on the wall in gilded frames. Then he's back in the kitchen, holding his arms wide for the kiss of Snouch's hose.

There is smoke now, seeping in through the windows and doors, smoke from the scrub, smoke from the verandah. A wooden shutter bursts into flames. Snouch sprays water onto the window frames. Another shutter erupts, a cruel orange flaring. Snouch is into one side room then the other, spraying water quickly before retreating. The room is starting to fill with smoke. The men move back towards the corridor: Martin then Snouch, who soaks the kitchen side of the door, and finally Robbie, who closes it.

Snouch hoses the corridor side of the door, then turns the hose on Robbie, sticking it down his overalls, down Martin's, down his own, shouting above the thunderous roar. 'It'll go from the kitchen into the roof. We go right to the front of the house. Don't want to be under a collapsing roof.' He's about to say something more, when the hose coughs once and stops. The men exchange grim looks. Martin can feel heat pumping through the closed kitchen door. 'Fire's got to the pump house. Front's moving past us, fifty metres at least.'

They withdraw down the corridor. Robbie goes ahead, running to the front door, slamming it closed on the flaccid hosepipe. Snouch moves more slowly, looks into each room off the corridor, as if saying farewell, before closing their doors tight. For the first time Martin has a moment to pause, to consider the house: its foot-thick walls, high ceilings, kauri pine floors, wraparound verandah. No bush hut, no corrugated-iron improvisation, but a nineteenth-century homestead. He glimpses a formal dining room, a large polished wooden table, a dozen seats, a huge sideboard. A crystal decanter, cut-glass tumblers, a chandelier. And a burning shutter. The door closes. Another room. A study, broad mahogany desk, covered in papers, calligraphic pens and ink pots, rulers and markers and a magnifying glass. A computer and printer on a side table. Antique maps on the walls. Snouch slams the door shut.

They gather by the front entrance. Martin removes his glove, places his hand against the door. It's hot, possibly burning on the other side. But it's solid hardwood. The corridor is starting to fill with smoke.

'Listen,' commands Snouch.

Martin tries to hear above the roaring fire, his own panting and the pounding of blood. 'What?'

'It's not as loud. The front is passing.'

The three men again exchange glances, still desperate but tinged with hope. Not much longer. The dragon is moving on, safety beckons. They may get through this yet. But now, as if to incinerate hope, a huge crash comes from the back of the house. Martin realises it's the kitchen starting to disintegrate, the ceiling coming down. Another crash and the kitchen door bursts open, like the gates of Hades. The heat hits Martin in the face like a punch through the billowing smoke.

'In here!' barks Snouch. He leads them through a side door, slamming it behind them. The room is some sort of parlour, furniture covered in sheets. 'We can't stay long. The roof'll come down. The corridor will go up in no time. Floorboards are a hundred and thirty years old. We judge by the side window, the corridor. When the shutter lights, or the door, we go out this front window. Okay? The verandah on the front here is paved, but the awning may be on fire. Run as fast as you can into the drive and go face down on the dirt, away from the cars and the house and anything else that's burning. Got it?'

Robbie and Martin nod.

The house is yelling now, screaming in its extremity: screeching steel, exploding timber, roaring fire, drowning out the sound of the receding dragon. Martin is soaking inside his overalls but his face feels paper-dry. He looks at the others, their faces red as if sunburnt. He watches as the shutter on the side window begins to smoke and burn, slowly, almost apologetically. Smoke is gushing in under the corridor door. Martin begins to cough uncontrollably, his throat raw.

Snouch rips away the curtains covering their escape route. He removes his glove, touches the glass for a split second, touches it for a moment longer, places his palm firmly upon it. He turns and nods encouragement. 'When I get the window open, the draught will draw the fire. We'll need to be quick. Bash the shutters open. The clasp will give easily enough. Robbie first, Martin next. Ready?'

They nod.

Snouch is about to pull up the sash windows when he pauses. He scurries across the room, returns with a leather ottoman, places it under the window. He looks about to say something when there's a terrible shrieking of tortured wood and metal followed by the thunderous noise of another section of roof caving in. He yanks at the window. For a moment it's stuck. Robbie and Martin move instantly to help, but Snouch yanks again and the sash window lifts. Robbie leans through and smashes the shutters open with the heel of his hand. There is nothing to see—just a wall of roiling smoke gashed with orange. Robbie swings one leg up into the cavity, leans on Martin to get his other leg clear. He grimaces, limbos his way through the window and is gone. Martin is quick to follow, standing on the stool, stepping onto the sill, lowering himself as he shimmies forward, scraping his back as he drops, half falls, onto the verandah. Then he runs into the smoke, still coughing uncontrollably. He gets two metres, three, and then goes sprawling off the edge of the verandah, momentum carrying him through the top of a smouldering bush and onto the dirt of the drive. He pushes his face low, sucking in breath, trying to stop coughing. He gets some air, though his lungs feel as if they're burning. He gathers himself, runs in a low squat, the world through his goggles becoming clearer. The police truck is on fire. He goes round it, gets to open ground and throws himself onto the gravel, lying flat with his face in his gloved hands. All around is noise and light and smoke; he lies unmoving, too scared to think.

⌣

Robbie Haus-Jones is drunk, swaying on his chair at the Riversend Services and Bowling Club, slurring his words. Sitting next to him, Martin Scarsden, by contrast, feels stone-cold sober, despite having matched the younger man drink for drink. The first beers had all but evaporated, they disappeared so quickly, and after that there has been no stopping them. Not that anybody is about to try; those who cheat death are entitled to drink their fill. And besides, the rest of the fire crew are more than holding their own. Errol, as captain, has ordered them here for debriefing and Errol, as club president, has authorised free booze for the heroes of the Scrublands. Initially, the drinking had been quiet and reflective, but now it's growing raucous as the fear of the afternoon is washed away by the ebullience of survival.

'Jeez, I thought you blokes were goners for sure,' says Moxie for the umpteenth time, shaking her head. 'When the front hit the road and you weren't back, I thought that was it, game over.' She's not really talking to anyone anymore, and no one is really listening to her anymore, but she repeats the story anyway. 'I'll never forget that sight, when we drove up to the house and there you were, the three of you, just sitting there, waiting. I'll never forget it. Who says there ain't no miracles?'

Robbie leans across, wraps his arm around Martin's neck, holds his beer aloft with his free hand. 'Here's to Martin bloody Scarsden. He's come to save us all!' He laughs at his toast and slurps down more beer, spilling some as he does so. Some other crew members raise their glasses, laughing as they drink. Martin reckons he'd get the same reaction if he toasted herpes; tonight, everyone is drinking, no one is judging.

The crew is sprawled around a couple of tables, still wearing their fire-retardant overalls, with hard hats, gloves and goggles discarded here and there. There are others as well, townspeople compelled by the drama of the day. Codger Harris is sitting by himself, not one of the fire crew, not one of the townspeople, quietly sipping on a large glass of whisky. He appears to be weeping. A man gives him a reassuring pat on the back as he walks by, but doesn't stop to talk.

A roar goes up, and through the entry comes one of the Bellington crews. The Riversend firefighters stagger upright.

Hands are shaken, backs are slapped, smiles and laughter are exchanged, the reek of wood smoke overpowering. Tables are moved together, chairs pulled up. Errol is at the bar, ordering jugs for the newcomers; Moxie has started up again: 'Jeez, I tell you, I thought those blokes were goners for sure . . .'

Martin gazes through the windows overlooking the empty river; somehow it has turned to night outside despite being late afternoon just a moment before.

The newcomers drain schooners, relate their own battles. Martin learns that the fire was slowed by the highway, that the Riversend crew narrowed the flanks, that the Bellington crews got to Glondillys Track in time to back-burn, to stop the front there and get into the scrub to take care of most of the spotting. A second crew is mopping up, another will guard the fire during the night; he's told it could smoulder for weeks unless there's rain.

Martin finds himself leaning on the bar next to Robbie, needing its support after all. 'You reckon we should have left him out there overnight?'

'Sure. Up to him. Could have come into town if he wanted. You heard him.'

'Yeah. Even so. He's lost everything.'

'That's true.'

'What's the story with his house? Did you notice? It was quite the grand affair.'

'True. I knew he had the place. Springfields, it's called. Didn't know it was like that. You'd have to ask a local.'

'Aren't you a local?'

'Fuck no.' Robbie laughs. 'I've only been here four years. Takes at least ten. Double for coppers.'

Martin smiles. 'Double again for journos.' He reaches for a jug on the bar, refills their glasses. 'He certainly knew what he was doing, though, don't you think? The way he took charge? Pretty together for an old derro.'

'Yeah. I wonder about that sometimes.'

The two men turn to face the bar rather than watch the revellers.

It's a long moment before Robbie speaks again, in a low voice. 'Why did he do it, Martin? Why did he shoot those people? I still can't understand it.'

'Neither can I, Robbie; neither can I.'

'Do you think we ever will?'

Martin sighs. 'Probably not.'

They stand in silence, no longer drinking, lost in contemplation. Martin looks across at the policeman. He seems so young staring down into his beer. He *is* so young. Martin wishes there was something he could do, but he decides against interrupting the other man's thoughts.

Finally Robbie turns to Martin. He no longer looks drunk. 'He said something, Martin.'

'Who?'

'Byron. Before I shot him.'

'You told me. Something like he'd been waiting for you.'

'Not just that. There was something else.'

'Go on.'

'You can't quote me or say it came from police sources, but it will come out at the inquest in a month or two. And there are other people in town who already know. You're going to find out one way or another.'

Martin waits.

'Just before he lifted his gun and fired, he said, "Harley Snouch knows everything."'

'"Harley Snouch knows everything"? Knows what?'

'Can't tell you; I don't know. He's been questioned, I know that. Extensively. But like I said, I'm not part of the investigation.'

'What do you think he meant?'

'Search me. If he knows, he's not telling me or anyone else. It keeps me awake at night wondering, but I really don't know. No fucking idea.' The young policeman stares at his beer, but Martin can think of nothing to say.

A hush falls upon the room, and Martin turns to look. And there, standing just a few feet from them, regarding them, is Mandy Blonde. She is wearing a white blouse and jeans, her cleanliness accentuated by the dirty, sooty, smelly fire crews surrounding her.

'Hello,' says Martin.

'Hello, Martin,' says Mandy.

Robbie turns at the sound of her voice.

'Hello, Robbie.' And she steps over to them, kisses Robbie full on the mouth, and then does the same to Martin. She steps back, one hand holding Martin's hand, the other holding Robbie's. 'Thank you. Thank you for saving him.'

Martin looks over her shoulder to where Codger is sitting looking at them, but not really at them. He appears to be checking out Mandy's arse.

'Not Codger, Martin,' says the constable. 'Harley Snouch.'

eight **STALKER**

MARTIN IS BACK IN THE BOOT OF THE MERCEDES IN GAZA. BUT THIS TIME IT'S warm and dark and secure, and somehow it smells good. Outside, a baby is crying, wailing against the injustices of the world, but inside his cocoon Martin feels safe. He turns over, floating in his sleep, when abruptly, without warning, he's hit in the ribs. He's awake in a flash, fear coursing, but not before another kick hits him in the stomach. Even with his eyes open, it takes him a second to realise where he is: in bed, a large bed. Mandy is looking at him, laughing.

'What the—?' he begins, as another blow lands. He pulls back the covers. Between the two of them is a baby, flailing chubby legs.

Mandy laughs again. 'Liam. He comes in with me most mornings.'

Martin rubs his ribs. 'Christ. He's got a kick like a mule.'

'That he has.'

Later, as they eat breakfast at the kitchen table, Martin's mind reluctantly kicks into gear. He feels wrung out: exhausted from fighting the fire, hazy from all the beer, exhilarated from sleeping with Mandy. He nurses the coffee, savours the muffins, swallows some painkillers to fend off an embryonic hangover. He just wants to sit, enjoy the moment, let his stomach settle, but he can't prevent the thoughts from coming. 'Mandy, about last night . . .'

'Complaints?'

'No. Of course not. Shit no.' She's smiling, teasing him. He realises he's at a disadvantage; the disadvantage of an older man entangled with a beautiful and self-possessed young woman. But he pushes on. 'I don't understand.'

'About what?'

'Harley Snouch. I thought you hated him. But last night you seemed grateful that Robbie and I had saved him.'

Mandy says nothing for a long time. Her eyes grow moist, the tiniest frown creases her forehead. 'I know. It doesn't make sense, does it?'

'No, not really.'

'It's just, sometimes, I wish things were different. Like I dreamt about when I was a girl.'

'Mandy, you're no longer a girl.'

'I know. What do you think I should do?'

'Seriously?'

'Seriously.'

'I think you should leave town. If Snouch did what your mother claimed, he's no sort of grandfather for your boy. You have Liam to think about.'

Mandalay Blonde says nothing.

———

As soon as Martin leaves the bookstore, the hangover kicks in with a vengeance. He squints into the scolding brightness of Riversend and his head pounds; he steps into the oven of Hay Road and his stomach churns. The town stinks of wood smoke, no longer benevolent. He climbs into his car, parked where he'd left it the day before. Thankfully, it's sitting in the morning shade of the shop awnings and has cooled overnight. There's a bottle of water on the front seat. Martin takes a swig. The water feels good in his throat and rebellious in his stomach.

Back at the Black Dog he stands in the shower, under the streaming water, trying to cleanse himself of the persistent smell of smoke, washing it away with the chlorinated swamp water of Riversend. He tries to wash his hair with the cheap motel shampoo. It takes three attempts to work up a semblance of lather in the bore water. He looks at his hands, unsurprised to see how quickly his fingertips have wrinkled. But somehow, despite the hangover, despite his fatigue, he is feeling more alive than he has for a year. The interview with Robbie, saving Jamie Landers, surviving the fire, sleeping with Mandy. Somehow, in this dried-out town, he can feel his blood beginning to course once again. He dries his face, evaluating what he sees in the mirror. His eyes are bloodshot from the smoke and the grog, but the sun has returned the colour to his face and the stubble covering his budding jowls lends definition to his jawline. He tries smiling, likes what he sees, and smiles for real. Perhaps not the dashing young foreign correspondent of yesteryear, but perhaps not quite a washed-up hack yet. Maybe, just maybe, Mandy's affection is motivated by more than just gratitude.

He considers his article, the story he has been commissioned to write: profiling Riversend a year on. He's thinking he can do better, that it can be more focused. Not just a traumatised town recovering, but a town divided over the memory of its priest, a mass murderer and accused paedophile, yet a man remembered fondly by some. The interview with Robbie Haus-Jones will still be the cornerstone, or at least the first half, and who knows what Fran Landers may volunteer now she has agreed to be interviewed? It's intriguing: Swift shot five people dead, yet there are still those who say what an admirable guy he was: Codger, the boy at the church, Mandy. And those ready to condemn him, like Harley Snouch and Robbie.

And yet Martin can't get a grip on it; he has no idea what caused the priest to turn homicidal. Had it been a psychotic episode, or had it been an attempt to silence those about to accuse him of abusing children, or had it been something entirely different? A gregarious young man, popular and giving of himself. Who also liked shooting, drinking and smoking dope. And, according to the award-winning piece by D'Arcy Defoe, a man who abused children. Defoe might take the occasional liberty, but he wasn't about to make up something like that. It must have been well sourced. So, a young man living a lie. Yet neither Mandy nor Codger nor Luke believes the accusation. What then? Why did Byron Swift say: 'Harley Snouch knows

everything' just before Robbie shot him? What did Harley
Snouch know? If Snouch knew about the priest's abusive behaviour, why shoot his five accusers, then with his final words point
the policeman towards the old man? None of it makes sense.

Martin looks at his watch: nine-thirty in the morning, the
whole day ahead of him. His mind is alive, but his hangover
is becoming oppressive and his fatigue is rising in pace with
the temperature. He swallows two painkillers and climbs into
bed, knowing he needs to rest.

He wakes at eleven feeling marginally better, but the day is
feeling increasingly worse. Outside the wind is low, too mild
to fan an outbreak of fire, but it's just as hot, just as dry, just
as smoke-filled. The cloud from the Scrublands fire is being
fanned across the town, yet it provides no shade, no filter: the
sun's heat feels more intense, not less. The car is hot and stifling
when he climbs in, despite being parked in the shade of the
motel's carport. He drives back onto the highway, turns left
and drives the length of the main street, where the smattering
of shops have opened for their twice-weekly trade. He smiles
at the bookstore as he passes, before steering up across the
long bridge.

Ten minutes later, he gets to the turn-off where the fire crew
gathered the day before. The dirt track winds off north-west
into the bush, past a motley collection of mailboxes. To the right
of the track, the bush is black and smouldering, to the left it
is largely untouched. This is where the firefighters controlled
the flank of the fire. He stops the car, takes some photos with
his phone, then resumes his journey.

Soon, the bush is burnt out on both sides of the track, and he wonders if it's wise to be out here alone; he tries to reassure himself that there's nothing left to burn. The smoke is all around him, swirling. The night before, at the club, someone told him that the mulga scrub could smoulder for weeks, even months, that the roots could burn away underground with little sign of it above ground. The only thing that would put the fire out once and for all would be soaking rain and plenty of it. Martin glances up at the pallid sky; the Second Coming seems more likely than a cloudburst. The fire has stripped the woodlands of any vestiges of shade; black stumps stand smoking, devoid of foliage.

He reaches the cattle grid. One pole stands untouched, the bleached skull intact. The other pole is nothing but a blackened stump, skull nowhere to be seen. He realises this is the way to Codger's place—he's taken a wrong turn—but he climbs out to photograph the crossing. The smell hits him immediately; a barbecue gone wrong. He sees what he didn't see from the car: cattle carcasses trapped against the fence line, burnt and bloating in the sun, flies swarming. He walks towards them, thinking to sanitise the pile of death by photographing it, but his stomach revolts and he throws up into the sand and ash. He retreats towards the car, vomits again, and climbs back into his air-conditioned sanctuary. He rinses his mouth with water from the bottle, spits out the door, executes a three-point turn with great care, not wanting to get stuck here, of all places. His headache, subdued by the sleep at the Black Dog, is back and insistent.

He locates the fork in the road that leads to Snouch's place, Springfields. He drives slowly, carefully, along the track Robbie had navigated at such speed less than twenty-four hours before. There is evidence of the progress of the fire crew that extricated them; a fallen tree chainsawed and dragged from the road. The landscape is monochromatic: black stumps, grey smoke, white ash. Even the sky, with its wash of smoke, is more grey than blue.

Martin arrives at Snouch's homestead, or what remains of it. Off to the right are the embankments of the dam and a metal machinery shed, unaffected by the maelstrom, but elsewhere is a scene of devastation. He parks close by the burnt-out carcasses of the police four-wheel drive and Snouch's old Holden, its charred chassis still held aloft by a jack. The house is a smoking ruin: the stone steps stand, as do three brick chimneys, their fireplaces exposed to the elements. The brick and stone walls largely remain, testament to their solidity, although some sections have crumbled and collapsed. A scene from a war.

Martin walks the perimeter. There is an iron stove towards the rear, in the kitchen where Martin, Robbie and Snouch made their initial stand, but anything that isn't steel or stone or brick has been incinerated. Pieces of curled and twisted corrugated-iron roofing lie scattered about, some inside the confines of the ruin, some distributed randomly around the yard, the confetti of the apocalypse. There is the sound of the wind and the rattling of corrugated iron; apart from that the day is silent.

'Snouch?' yells Martin, walking back towards the machinery shed.

He finds him inside, spanner in hand, leaning into the innards of an old Mercedes, its bonnet up. The car is at least forty years old, but its deep blue paint is in good repair. The tyres are flat.

'Oh, it's you.' Snouch straightens, hand feeling his lower back as he stretches.

'How are you?' asks Martin.

'Pretty fucking ordinary, to tell you the truth. Got any water on you?'

'Yeah. Sure.' Martin goes to his car, returns with three large bottles of mineral water, gives them to Snouch.

'Thanks,' says Snouch, opening a bottle and slugging down half of it. 'Thanks. That's better. Dam's full of ash.'

'Nice car.'

'Will be if I can get it going.'

'How long since you've driven it?'

'Dunno. Thirty years. It was my father's. He died five years ago.'

'Well, you'll need help then. Battery will be shot. It'll need new engine oil, same for the gearbox and diff, I'd imagine. New tyres.'

'Yeah. I know. I was just killing time. Waiting for someone to show up. Don't have any tobacco, do you?'

'No. Don't smoke.'

'No one fucken does anymore.'

The two men move away from the car. Snouch sits on the rim of a tractor tyre; Martin pulls up an old wooden fruit crate. Snouch takes another slug of water. He's still wearing the clothes he was wearing the day before and reeks of smoke and body odour. His face is blackened and grimy, his eyes red and streaked. He looks awful.

'Thanks for coming out.'

'No problem.'

Martin again wonders how old Snouch is; it's difficult to determine. He looks like he's in his sixties, but fighting the fire he'd moved with the assurance of a much younger man.

'What will you do now?' Martin asks.

'Dunno. Camp out until the insurance comes through.'

'You're insured?'

'Yeah. Does that surprise you?'

'Yeah, it does.'

An old vagrant, an alcoholic, reputedly a former felon, cast out by the townspeople. Who lives in a beautiful old homestead, well maintained and insured, who drives a beaten-up old Holden but has a Merc in the machinery shed. Martin looks around him. The shed is no dusty relic. There's a workbench, with tools mounted on a shadow board. Some are old and rusting, but others look well used and well cared for.

'The house, Snouch—your house—it was really something.'

'Yeah. Gone now, though.'

'It was your family's?'

Snouch contemplates Martin, takes a swig of water and responds. 'That's right. Springfields. Settled in the 1840s. House built in the 1880s. Built to last. It was vacant when I got back here; I've been restoring it. My fault it's gone. Should have cleared the trees back further. Might still be standing.'

'Is this where you grew up?'

'Some. Here and Geelong.'

'But why keep it? Why not sell, move on?'

'Why should I? It's what I have left. What I *had* left. All I had to pass on.'

'Pass on? To whom?'

'Who do you think?'

Instead of answering, Martin broaches the issue he came here to discuss. 'Last night, at the club, I was talking to Robbie Haus-Jones. He was pretty drunk.'

'Can't blame him for that. Wouldn't mind getting a skinful myself. All the grog went up in the fire. Probably what blew the roof off.'

'He recounted what happened the day Byron Swift died. His last words, before Robbie shot him: "Harley Snouch knows everything."'

'Yeah, so the coppers claim.'

'What did he mean by it?'

Snouch breathes in deeply through his nose, lips compressed, clearly annoyed, before answering. 'No fucken idea. I've been over it a thousand times with the filth, with that fat fuck Walker from Bellington and with the Sydney dicks. No fucken idea. Did me no favours though, I can tell you that much for free. Cops investigating me for interfering with kids, of all things. Took ages for them to believe I was innocent and didn't have the foggiest what Swift meant.'

'You knew him, though—Reverend Swift?'

'Yeah, a bit. Like I told you the other day in the saloon.'

'So why would he implicate you like that, say you knew everything?'

'Dunno. Spent the past year thinking about it. Still don't have a clue.'

Martin ponders that for a moment. He's not making much progress. 'Okay, so what did you tell the cops? How did you get them off your back?'

Snouch laughs at that. 'You don't know much about coppers, do you, Hemingway?'

'How do you mean?'

'They get paid to solve crimes and catch crims. But in this case, the crime was solved and the crim was dead. Case closed.'

'Case closed? A massacre of five people?'

'Sure. The coroner will still want to know the ins and outs of a cat's arse, but not the coppers. They don't give a shit. Case closed. The fucker's dead, shot through the heart by the town sheriff. *High Noon.*'

Martin regards Snouch's face. It looks ravaged, covered in ash and grime, his eyes bloodshot and watery. But when he looks down at the man's hands, resting in his lap, Martin sees that they are perfectly still. Not a tremor to be seen. 'Harley, tell me something: is Mandy Blonde your daughter?'

'No, I don't believe she is.'

'She thinks so.'

'Yeah, I know. That's what her mother told her. Katherine claimed that I raped her and young Mandalay was the result. It's horseshit, all of it, but you can't blame the girl for believing her mother.'

'If she's not your daughter, why are you holding this place in trust for her?'

Something passes over Snouch's eyes—pain, perhaps?—and he closes them for a moment. When he opens them, Martin can see sadness written there.

'None of your business, son.'

'But you fixed the place up. I saw it. It was magnificent. Why would you do that if you didn't care?'

'Jesus H. Christ. I got you wrong. You're not Hemingway, you're Sigmund fucken Freud.'

'And if she's not your daughter, why are you stalking her?'

'Stalking her? Is that what she said?'

'Said you spy on her from the wine saloon.'

'Is that right?'

'Well, *is* that right? Why would you do that if she wasn't your daughter?'

'You're the psychoanalyst, Sigmund—you tell me.' Snouch looks directly at him, challenging him to respond.

'Okay, Harley, here's what I think. I think you are a profoundly sad and twisted old fuck. And I think from here on in you can stop perving at her from the saloon and give the girl a chance. Got it?'

Snouch's first response is anger, Martin can see it flashing in his eyes; enough for Martin to fear, for just a moment, that the old man may lash out. But the anger vanishes almost as quickly as it appeared and the intensity fades. Snouch nods his assent. Martin feels good for a moment, his threatening tone vindicated, at least until he sees the tears well in the old man's eyes and spill over, tracing clear lines through his soot-coated cheeks.

Martin shakes his head, stands to leave. 'Shit, Harley. Give it a break. I'll bring some grog out for you tomorrow. You don't have to cry. If she's not your daughter, you should just leave her in peace.'

'That's not it. That's not why I watch her.'

'Why then?'

'You wouldn't understand.'

'Try me.'

'Because she's the spitting image of her mother.'

'Katherine?'

'Yes, Katherine.'

Martin is lost for words. Either Snouch is an innocent man yearning for his lost love, or a guilty man overcome with what he has wrought. Martin looks long and hard and finds himself unable to divine the cause of Snouch's tears. Yet he knows full well that Snouch and Mandy can't both be telling the truth about her conception.

nine **BELLINGTON**

MARTIN STOPS BY THE BOOKSTORE ON HIS WAY BACK THROUGH TOWN, BUT THE GON OUT, BACKSON sign is on the door, so he continues on his way, turning right at the T-junction, past the fire station, the wheat silos and the Black Dog, accelerating as he heads out of town onto the long flat plain between Riversend and Bellington. The car seems to enjoy the straight empty road, no longer constrained by the speed limits of Riversend or the rutted tracks of the Scrublands. Martin pushes it up to a hundred and twenty-five kilometres an hour, well above the limit. Who's to know? Who's to care?

He does slow, if only slightly, as he reaches the curve in the road, the scene of the ute accident. The hole in the fence is still there, but the ute has been removed. He considers stopping to take a photo or two, but the car carries him past; it's not as if he's about to forget the details.

The road stretches towards infinity. There are no clouds, just a milky greyness from the bushfire receding behind him. Out on the shimmering horizon, the sky has turned liquid, leaking down into the plain. There are no trees; the only animals are dead ones, killed by the night trucks ploughing their way between Adelaide and the east coast. There aren't any crows; even roadkill is powerless to lure them into the midday sun. The thermometer in the dash gives an outside temperature of forty-two degrees.

He thinks of Riversend and all its tragedies, large and small: Codger Harris and his dead wife and child; Harley Snouch professing love for the woman he's accused of raping; Mandy, unable to close her mother's bookstore and move away; Robbie Haus-Jones, haunted by St James and killing his friend; Fran Landers mourning her husband; the boy, Luke, unable to comprehend the horror that has split his young life apart. It makes Martin wonder about himself, why the experience in Gaza has left him so gutted, why the damage lingers. After all, he has lost no one, suffered no enduring injuries. Compared to the people in Riversend, he has got off lightly. He is unable to formulate a satisfactory answer and his mind wanders into a daydream, an imagined utopia: he and Mandy living in a shack on the coast, watching winter squalls blowing in off the ocean, Liam playing peacefully nearby.

Bellington emerges from the plain in a rush. The earth's flat browns turn an almost iridescent green: grapevines and citrus orchards, irrigation-nourished verdure. And then the town itself, stretched out along the Murray River. He pulls into a park, has a piss in the public toilet, then wanders down to look at the river. It's flowing between high banks, a green-glass mass, its intent unperturbed by the imperceptible fall of the land. Martin has heard somewhere that the flow is artificial, governed by some huge dam, high in the mountains. He doesn't care; its existence is reassuring after the parched riverbed of Riversend. A pair of kookaburras herald his arrival with a raucous cackle; cockatoos squawk somewhere in the distance. He extracts his phone, relieved to see its signal bars. Civilisation.

He sits at a picnic table in the shade and collects messages. There are a couple of texts and a voicemail from his editor, Max. 'Hiya, soldier. Wondering how you're travelling. Heard you're out of mobile range. Call us when you can, let me know how you're going. Cheers, mate.' He thinks of calling, but texts instead: *All well. Story progressing. Cracker interview with local cop. More to come. Will call soon.*

He powers up his laptop, using his phone to connect to the net. He finds the number of the local cop shop quickly enough and calls, asking for Sergeant Herb Walker. He's told Walker is out of the office but will be back soon; Martin leaves his number. He knows Walker encouraged Robbie to agree to an interview and hopes the sergeant might now be as forthcoming himself. He finds the number and address for Torlini's Fruit Barn, on a side road off the main street, plus a residential number for Torlini. He checks it out on Google Maps. It's just outside town, not far from the river, possibly the family farm. He looks out at the Murray. What were Gerry Torlini and Horace Grosvenor doing at the church in Riversend? Simply accompanying Craig Landers and the Newkirks? Having just traversed the unforgiving plain, Martin can't understand anyone doing it without a reason. He searches for Horace Grosvenor's address and finds he is sitting across the road from his house. It seems like fate. He packs up his laptop and notebook and walks towards Grosvenor's home, passing the playground and a low plaque. He's almost past it when he realises its significance. He backtracks and snaps a photo with his phone. *In loving memory, Jessica and Jonty. So sorely missed.*

The house is solid and respectable red brick, with a healthy garden full of hydrangeas and a BORE WATER ONLY sign. Martin takes a snap: bore water just a hundred and fifty metres from Australia's biggest river. He rings the doorbell; a singsong chime answers from somewhere inside.

The door opens and Mrs Janice Grosvenor is revealed as a large woman wrapped in a floral print dress, presenting somewhat like a sofa with legs. Martin explains himself and the story he is writing. Mrs Grosvenor looks unwilling. Martin persists. Mrs Grosvenor reluctantly lets him in, apparently concerned that it would be impolite to refuse. And once he's seated, she insists on making tea for her unwelcome guest. He waits in the living room, seated attentively on the edge of a sofa just as floral and only marginally less mobile than Mrs Grosvenor. It has antimacassars to safeguard its fabric from the oleaginous heads of friends and family. Along the mantelpiece are framed photographs. Children and grandchildren; a black-and-white wedding shot of a far younger and slimmer Mrs Grosvenor and her groom; a more recent colour shot of a ruddy-faced man, laughing at the camera: Horace Grosvenor. Through open double doors Martin can see the dining table: sturdy wood, boasting two huge vases of hydrangeas, one bunch blue, the other pink.

Mrs Grosvenor returns with a tray supporting a teapot dressed in a crocheted red-and-blue cosy, cups, saucers, cut-glass sugar bowl, milk jug. There is a plate of homemade slice: date and walnut. Martin leaps to his feet, separating a nest of tables, placing one before himself and another before Mrs Grosvenor. Mrs Grosvenor plays mother, pouring tea, offering slice; Martin plays child, accepting tea and slice with gratitude. Formalities complete, the two sit facing each other, sipping tea.

'Mrs Grosvenor, I realise this is difficult, especially me dropping in so unexpectedly, but I would be grateful for any insights you could give me. It's likely that this will constitute just a small part of the final story.'

Janice Grosvenor nods assent.

Martin asks permission to record the interview.

Another nod of assent.

And he begins, asking innocuous and inoffensive questions. What sort of man was Horace?

A wonderful father and good provider.

What has the community response been like?

Wonderful, most supportive.

After twenty or so minutes he has established an incontrovertible impression of Horace and Janice Grosvenor as decent, respectable and utterly boring. That Horace could come to such an exotic end, shot down in cold blood by a murderous priest, belies the monotony of his previous sixty-four years.

'Mrs Grosvenor, do you have any idea why Reverend Swift might have wanted to harm your husband?'

'Don't think he did. Think he was having an episode. Poor Horrie was in the wrong place at the wrong time. All there is to it.'

'Yes, so it seems. Do you know why your husband was there, as you say, in the wrong place at the wrong time? Did he go to Riversend to attend church?'

'Doubt it. Be a first if he did.'

'So why was he there?'

'Couldn't say. Sorry.'

'Did he go to Riversend often?'

'From time to time. But not to church.'

'Did he know any of the other men who were killed?'

'Yes. All of them.'

'All of them?'

'All of them.'

'How was that? I thought three of them were from Riversend.'

'Yes. But he certainly knew them.'

'How?'

'They were fishing mates. Fishing and hunting. Called themselves the Bellington Anglers Club. Here, I'll show you.' And with a great deal of effort, ham-hock forearms pushing down on the arms of the chair like pistons, accompanied by a bellows-like exhalation of breath, Mrs Grosvenor lifts herself out of the chair that has been so snugly encompassing her. Martin feels an absurd pang of guilt at having induced such an effort. But soon enough Mrs Grosvenor is on her feet and off into her home's hinterland, returning some moments later with the impressively large head of a Murray cod, stuffed and mounted, mouth agape at the imposition. She hands it to Martin, who examines the fish with some disquiet. Deep down a small rebellion flares in his stomach, a last stand of the morning's hangover.

'A big one,' he says, not knowing what else to say.

'Plenty more in the garage. One of Horrie's hobbies. Used to have some in the house, but I took them down after he passed. Hope he doesn't mind.'

'I'm sure he would understand.'

'Hmmph. Maybe.'

'Mrs Grosvenor, this club—what did you call it again?'

'The Bellington Anglers Club.'

'The Bellington Anglers Club. Was it a formal club, or just a group of men who went fishing together?'

'And hunting. But yes. Just men who were friends. They'd go a couple of times a year. Long weekends down to Barmah forest, fishing and camping. Horrie loved it.'

'And when they weren't fishing and hunting? They still socialised?'

'Not really. Horrie and Gerry Torlini would see each other at the bowls club, but not the fellows from Riversend so much. Horrie and I were better friends with the members at the club. Some of those men were part of the angling club too. But they weren't at Riversend on the day of the shooting. If you want to know more, you can ask for Len Harding at the bowls club. He's there most days, holding up the bar. But I'm not sure how any of this would help with your story.'

'Quite right, Mrs Grosvenor, quite right. I should be more focused with my questions. My editor is always telling me that. But just a final question or two, if you would indulge me.'

'Can't stop you asking.'

'You mentioned hunting. Did your husband and his friends ever go shooting in the Scrublands?'

'Is that up near Riversend?'

'That's right. It's bushland, mostly Crown land, just outside of town.'

'Yes. That's why he was up there: to go hunting. They'd been out on Saturday, were going again on Sunday. What he was doing at the church I have no idea. Wait here. There's some mounted possums in the garage, they might be from up there.'

Martin is quickly on his feet. 'No, Mrs Grosvenor, that's not necessary. Please. I assure you. You've been too kind. But one last question. Was Reverend Byron Swift a member of the Bellington Anglers Club?'

'I don't think so. If he was, Horrie never mentioned his name.'

⁓

At the Sioux Falls Cafe, Martin sits directly under the air-conditioner and eats a hamburger with the lot and downs a six-hundred-millilitre carton of iced-coffee-flavoured milk, and feels much the better for it. The last vestiges of nausea surrender, overwhelmed by superior force. He wipes grease from his chin, turns on his laptop and opens the files containing the newspaper clippings. He finds Defoe's award-winning piece and quickly scans it. The relevant section is not hard to find:

> *It's understood the five victims knew each other. In all likelihood, one or more of them had learnt of Byron Swift's perversions; police believe this may have led to their deaths. One theory is that Swift shot them to silence them.*

So Defoe had made the connection; he just didn't dwell upon how the men knew each other or how they came to be at the church. Fair enough; the article was about the priest, not his victims. Martin had overlooked the reference as he skimmed through the clippings on the plane trip to Wagga, back when his assignment was all about the present, not the past. He's searching Defoe's article for anything else he might have missed when his mobile rings. He unlocks it, smearing the screen in the process. It's the local policeman, Sergeant Herb Walker. He tells Martin to come right over.

Harley Snouch had called Herb Walker 'that fat fuck'. He's right about one thing: the police sergeant is only slightly less corpulent than Mrs Grosvenor. Walker looks to be in his mid-fifties, a face of putty features sitting below a bouffant Elvis haircut turned snow white. He sits behind his desk, hands folded on his belly, nicotine-stained fingers entwined. From time to time he separates his hands and pats his gut appreciatively, giving him a self-satisfied air. As their conversation proceeds, Martin realises it's something of a tell; Walker pats his belly with alternate hands when thinking, and with both hands when he's pleased with himself or to emphasise a point. He'd want to be less obvious testifying in the witness box.

'I've been expecting your call,' he says to Martin. 'Sooner or later you were bound to end up here.' Double belly pat.

'Well, I certainly owe you a debt of gratitude.'

'How's that?'

'Constable Haus-Jones told me that it was you who encouraged him to talk to me. Thank you for that.'

'You're welcome. Was he of any use?'

'Yes. He was most forthcoming. He has a very clear recollection of the day of the shooting.'

'Burnt into his memory, I should imagine. And he spoke on the record?'

'Yes. He was most helpful.'

'He tell you Byron Swift's last words?'

'"Harley Snouch knows everything"? Yes, he did. What does it mean?'

'Don't know. Yet.' Walker has a rather pained look on his face, as if something is bothering him. 'He tell you about the woman hiding in the church, behind the door? The one who heard everything?'

'No. Who is she? Can I talk to her?'

Walker shakes his head. 'No. Sorry. She'll testify at the inquest, but I can't reveal her identity against her wishes. And don't go asking around—she was visiting from interstate.'

'Did she talk to Swift? Inside the church?'

'No. She was just coming out of the toilet as the shooting started.'

'So why tell me about her?'

'You're right. It's not relevant.' Walker lifts his hands from his belly and makes an apologetic gesture. 'Let's move on. I hope, like the constable, I too can be helpful. But you must understand that this conversation is totally off the record. No quotes, no references to police sources. Use the information as you see fit, but it absolutely cannot be traced back to me in any way, understood?'

'Absolutely.'

'Very good.' Double belly pat.

'Would you mind if I recorded the conversation, nevertheless, to ensure accuracy?'

'Yes, I would mind. You may not record it. Unlike young Robbie Haus-Jones, I am actively involved in the investigation. I trust you to protect your sources; otherwise I wouldn't be talking to you. But recordings go astray: they turn up in police searches, they find their way onto the internet. So no recording. Take notes, and if you need something clarified later, just ring me. Agreed?'

'Agreed.' Martin has sufficient faith in his notebook, pen and shorthand. 'Shall we start?'

'I thought we already had.' Double belly pat.

'Sergeant Walker, the story I came to write was how Riversend is coping a year after the shooting. That's evolved a bit. I'm also interested in what the locals think of Byron Swift. I've been surprised to find that some people remember him rather fondly. Does that surprise you?'

'When you've been a policeman as long as I have, nothing surprises you.'

'What about yourself? Did you know Swift?'

'No, not well. I would meet him on occasion. I know old Reverend Samuels was very pleased to have him here.'

'Who is Reverend Samuels?'

'He was the local Anglican minister here for fifty years or so. But he was getting too old to run the parish by himself, so they sent Swift to do the legwork for him. Seemed to work well, from what I can tell. But I'm not the one to ask. Not a churchgoer, you'll understand.'

'Is Reverend Samuels still in town?'

'No, they retired him pretty soon after Swift died. He couldn't cope with the workload by himself and I guess they didn't have any more young priests to send to help. There's a new man here now, Vietnamese fellow, Thieu. You can look him up, but he's only been here about four months. There was another bloke filling in for a few months in between.'

'I see. You say you didn't know Swift very well, but did you have any impression of him at all?'

'Back then I thought he was a very conservative, well-mannered, well-presented young man. Now I know different.' Double belly pat.

'How do you mean?'

'Okay, now we get to the guts of it. Remember, off the record, not attributable.'

Martin nods, watching the policeman drum his gut, considering his words.

'Byron Swift was a murderer. You know that. He was also a paedophile. You know that too. But what you won't know is that he was also a man without a past. And he was protected by powerful and influential people.' The hands are still, the eyes are locked on Martin's.

Martin holds the gaze for a moment before transcribing the comments into his notebook. His hands are a little shaky, but it's nothing to do with his hangover. *Shit*, he thinks, *he's going to tell me everything.*

'Okay,' he says aloud, 'let's take those one at a time. Murderer. He shot five people dead at St James. Is there any evidence that he killed before?'

'Evidence? That's a precise word. Maybe not evidence, but a strong suggestion.'

'Can you take me through it?'

'Sure. After the shooting, the investigation started looking at his past. At first glance it was straightforward. He was sent up here about three years ago, not long after he was ordained. He'd come from Cambodia, where he'd been working for a Christian charity. Before that, he was training in Perth, including a theology degree at Murdoch University that he didn't finish. Before that, another half-finished uni degree; before that, state school in Western Australia. An orphan, a ward of the state.'

'And?'

'And it's bullshit. There really was a Byron Swift born near Perth. He was an orphan and a ward of the state; he did go to school in Perth, living with various foster families. He went to uni for a while, before dropping out and travelling overseas. He worked for the charity in Cambodia all right, where he died of a drug overdose aged twenty-four. Except there is no record of that. None. The record of the death has been expunged from official records. Expunged. Officially, Byron Swift died last year from bullet wounds in Riversend.'

'How do you know then?'

'Sorry, can't say. Take my word for it.'

'Okay. Go on.'

'What else can I tell you?'

'If the man Robbie Haus-Jones shot dead wasn't Byron Swift, who was he?'

'I can't say for sure, but if I had to guess, I'd say a former soldier. He had a tattoo that indicated he'd been in Afghanistan.

Special forces. SAS. A couple of us on the investigation were thinking of exhuming the body, getting DNA.'

'Where's he buried?'

'Here. Just down the road, in the town cemetery.'

'Do you think it'll happen? The exhumation?'

'I doubt that very much.'

'Why not?'

'Because we've been warned off. That part of the investigation has been ruled out of bounds.'

'By whom?'

'No idea. Way up the food chain. Understand, I'm just local liaison; the investigation is being run out of Sydney. And there's not a lot of appetite for digging into this, if you'll pardon the pun.'

'A cover-up?'

Walker considers his response, but not for long. 'I think so. Although there would also be pragmatists who simply don't see the point of investigating any further. We know who the perpetrator was and what happened to him. Case closed. A coroner's inquest to tie up loose ends, but no criminal case.'

'That's strange. Someone else said almost exactly the same thing to me this morning.'

'Wise person. Wouldn't have been young Robbie, by any chance?'

'No, it wasn't. But let me ask you this: if all the police are interested in is solving crimes and catching crims, why are you still interested in what happened?'

Walker sighs. 'Because it happened on my patch. I mightn't be much of a copper, but I run a good town here. And I don't like how he was protected. I don't like people fucking with my patch.'

'Protected? Swift?'

'Yes.'

'What do you mean by that?'

'It happened like this: two days before the shooting in Riversend, I got an anonymous phone call. It was from the phone booth in Riversend. It was a boy. He told me that Reverend Swift had sexually abused him and another lad.'

'Shit. What did you do?'

'I arrested him.'

'Swift?'

'Yep. Put him in the cells.'

'On what charge?'

'No charge. Just wanted to deliver him a message. Then I drove up to Riversend to see if I could find anything out. Constable Haus-Jones tell you about that?'

'No. No, he didn't.'

'Yeah, well, that's not a surprise. He didn't believe any of it. Anyway, I get back here, intending to release Swift, having given him the message, so to speak, but he was already out. The constable told me the order had come down the line from Sydney. I rang to check and I was told in no uncertain terms that investigating Reverend Byron Swift was most definitely a no-go.'

'Who told you that? Can you remember?'

'I can, but I'm pretty sure they were just relaying a message. I don't know where it originated, but somewhere high up, I can tell you that much.'

'Shit. So what happened next?'

'Well, I kept at it. If they hadn't sprung him and ordered me off, maybe I would have let it go, but that got my back up.'

Martin feels a chill as a piece of the puzzle falls into place. 'What did you do?'

'Robbie had told me the names of some of the lads in their youth group. I rang a couple of the fathers that night, ones I knew, to warn them not to trust the priest around their kids.'

'Shit. Let me guess: you rang Craig Landers and Alf Newkirk. On Friday night. The next day, they went shooting with Thom Newkirk, Gerry Torlini and Horrie Grosvenor. And on Sunday morning, realising that Byron Swift would be in Riversend, they decided to confront him.'

Sergeant Herb Walker pats his belly with alternating hands before answering. 'Lots of ifs and buts and maybes in that lot, son. But I don't know anything that says you're wrong.'

Martin sits and thinks it through for a while. 'This allegation about child abuse—it first came out in an article about the shooting by my colleague D'Arcy Defoe.'

'So I believe.'

'You spoke to Defoe?'

'Martin, you don't reveal your sources, I don't reveal my contacts. But let me say that I was disappointed in Defoe's article. It was all sizzle and no sausage.'

'How so?'

'Well, it had all the stuff about Swift being a rock spider, but nothing of the cover-up, nothing of him getting sprung from jail by powerful people. In the end, it made it look like I'd fucked up; that there was evidence he'd been a kiddie fiddler, and me and Robbie Haus-Jones had ignored it. I was right pissed off.'

'And still are.'

'Too fucking right.'

'Let me get this straight. You lock Swift up and he gets released. And this is, what, two days before the shooting at St James?'

'That's right.'

'So afterwards, were you ever able to establish that he did abuse children? Or was it just that one anonymous phone call?'

'No, it stood up, all right. Two young fellows, in separate interviews, told me to my face. Your mate D'Arcy was right on that score: Swift was a paedophile.'

'Who were the boys?'

'Martin, I can't tell you that. It's child abuse. I can't release the names of victims without a court order.'

'Were they from Riversend?'

'Yes, I can confirm that much.'

'Thanks. Tell me, did you inform D'Arcy about Cambodia? Or that Swift may have been someone else, ex-SAS?'

'Martin, let's get this straight, I never said I spoke to your colleague, okay? But to answer your question, I didn't know any of that at the time D'Arcy Defoe wrote his stories. That only came to light months later.'

'What about Robbie? Does he know that Swift might not have been who he claimed to be? He told me they were friends.'

Walker nods his head, as if in appreciation of the question, before answering. 'No, not until recently. I asked him about it just a few weeks ago. He seemed genuinely shocked.'

'You think he believes it?'

'To be honest, I think it's rattled him. You should ask him.'

'I probably should.'

Martin is having trouble ordering his thoughts, speculation sparking unbidden in a dozen directions at once. 'Sergeant Walker—Herb—why are you telling me this? And why did you encourage Robbie to talk to me?'

'Why? Because this stinks to high heaven. It's about time the truth came out.' Emphatic belly pat.

After the interview, sitting outside in his car, oblivious to the heat, Martin's mind churns. Herb Walker and Harley Snouch believe Swift was abusing children while Codger Harris and Mandy Blonde don't believe it. But the police sergeant's information puts it beyond doubt: two boys had confirmed it was true. But that isn't what's exciting Martin. D'Arcy Defoe had already exposed the priest's sickening appetites. Martin has found a new, unreported story: Swift was an imposter, a former special forces soldier who was being protected by people high up in the police force. Was it possible that Swift was part of some sort of paedophile ring?

———

Bellington Hospital is single-storey, brick from the ground to floor level, weatherboard from there to its corrugated-iron roof. It sits above a curve in the Murray River, two buildings joined together by a covered walkway. A couple of elderly patients in wheelchairs sit outside, smoking and contemplating the water easing past. Martin enters through sliding electric doors into the foyer. It's quiet, there's the antiseptic smell of hospitals everywhere, and the linoleum floor has the comfortable give of a long-settled building. There's a bored-looking woman at reception half-heartedly working her way through a sudoku.

Martin approaches the desk. 'Jamie Landers, please?'

'Down there, third on the left,' she replies, not even looking up from her puzzle.

Martin feels vaguely foolish; he's been concocting various tales to get past reception, none of them necessary.

It's a pleasant-enough room, with high ceilings and big windows. There are four beds; only two are occupied: Jamie Landers sitting up staring at his phone, an old man sleeping in the opposite bed.

'G'day, Jamie.'

'Who are you?'

'My name's Martin Scarsden. I helped your mum at the accident scene.'

'You the guy who saved my life?'

'Something like that.'

'Well, what about Allen? Why didn't you save him?'

Martin is not sure what he was expecting—gratitude, perhaps—but not this. Jamie is looking at him with the surliness of a chained dog.

'Nothing I could do, Jamie. He broke his neck when he was thrown clear of the car. He would have died instantly.'

'Yeah, well, how fucked is that?' The tone is accusatory, as if Martin possessed some power to alter the course of events. He's tempted to point out the obvious—that it was Jamie Landers who was driving the car—but he restrains himself and takes a seat.

'How you feeling?'

'Shithouse. I cracked a couple of ribs on the steering wheel. They hurt like fuck, but these lousy shits are skimping on the painkillers. Probably pocketing them.'

'I'll have a word to them, see what I can do,' Martin lies.

But Jamie Landers sneers. 'Bullshit. As if. What do you want?'

'I'm a journo. I'm writing about Byron Swift.'

'That cunt. What about him?'

'Was he a paedophile? Did he sexually abuse children?'

'I know what a paedophile is. I'm not a fucking moron.'

'Was he?'

'Of course he was. He was a priest, for God's sake. He lived in Bellington, yet he sets up a playgroup for schoolkids forty minutes away in Riversend. Of course he was going the grope. Join the dots, Sherlock.'

'Did you ever witness anything?'

'Nah, nothing graphic. He was too smart for that. But he was all over those kids, pretending to be their friend, giving them hugs and pats on the bum. He was grooming them.'

'Did he ever try it on with you? Or with Allen?'

A look of disgust, of disdain, writes itself on Landers' face. 'Me? Of course not. I'm not a fucking kid. He wouldn't have dared. We'd have sorted him out.'

'How's that?'

'We would have beaten the shit out of him.'

'Right. I see. So this allegation that he was a paedophile, did you guys report that to Sergeant Walker here in Bellington?'

'Not me, mate. I don't talk to coppers.'

'But your dad knew. I know Walker warned him that Swift might be interfering with kids. Theory is that your dad went to St James to warn him off, to tell him to stay away from you and the other young people.'

Jamie Landers' laugh is one of contempt. 'Fuck, I don't know why the old man went to the church, but it sure as shit wasn't to protect me.'

———

The sun is setting, a huge ball turned blood red by the residual smoke of the Scrublands fire, as Martin visits the Bellington cemetery. The day is tired, drained by the heat, the air burdened by smoke and dust, leaves drooping from the trees, shrubs shrinking from the sky, not reaching towards it. Martin finishes a bottle of mineral water, carrying the empty plastic container with him.

Byron Swift's grave is at the end of a row, a simple black headstone. *Reverend Byron Swift. 36 years. Known unto God.*

Martin looks at it for a long moment, not quite believing the inscription. *Known unto God*: the epitaph reserved for unidentified soldiers. Yet here it is, on the tombstone of a parish priest, lending credence to Walker's allegation that Swift was indeed a former soldier. And that's not all. Lying atop the grave, wilted by the heat but surely placed there this very day, a posy of sky blue flowers. Someone is mourning the dead priest, or mourning whoever he actually was. Martin takes out his phone, records the image.

It's all he can do to get back to Riversend in one piece. In the twilight and gathering gloom, kangaroos emerge from nowhere to nibble at what little grass can be found on the highway's verge, their eyes glowing white in the headlights.

Befuddled by the brightness, they break first one way, then the other, bounding perilously close to the path of the oncoming car.

Martin slows, and slows some more, only to be flooded by the lights of a B-double, thundering through the encroaching night. The passing truck almost blows him off the road. When the next truck approaches, he pulls off the road altogether and lets it pass, lesson learnt.

He's been thinking of visiting Mandy Blonde, of telling her what he's uncovered, or not telling her anything and moving straight back into the previous night's sex. But he can hardly keep his eyes open. The Black Dog is all he can manage. He falls into bed, the clanking air-conditioner providing more noise than relief. And as he falls asleep, a final sum. Almost a year ago, Byron Swift shot dead five people outside St James church in Riversend. And on the same day, on the other side of the world, Martin Scarsden climbed into the boot of an old Mercedes and let his driver shut him away.

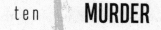

ten **MURDER**

MARTIN IS BACK IN THE BOOT OF THE MERCEDES, BUT THIS TIME AROUND HE'S not terrified, he's bored. 'Christ. Not this again,' he sighs, before the significance of the *again* insinuates itself into his rising consciousness, and he realises that he's not really marooned in the boot of an ancient German limousine somewhere on the Gaza Strip, but dreaming. That adds a level of pique to his boredom. There had been a time when he'd considered himself borderline creative, capable of thinking outside the square, but here he is, confining himself even in his dreams to the inside of a very small square. Boring and annoying.

Somewhere in the distance he can hear the *crump crump* of Israeli artillery, but even that is probably a ruse. Maybe it's not artillery; maybe it's someone hammering on the lid of the car boot. Cripes. He should either fall back into a deeper sleep or wake up completely; these boot dreams are turning into a drag. *Crump crump.*

What the fuck is that?

Martin emerges from sleep, slipping the bonds of the Mercedes to enter another day. It's Friday, four days since he arrived in Riversend. The air-conditioner is clanking away, some failing metal gizzard thumping its protest: *Crump crump crump.*

Martin is fully awake; it's someone pounding on the door of his room at the Black Dog. 'All right. All right!' he yells. 'Coming!'

Out of bed, in boxers and t-shirt, he opens the door to an explosion of sunlight, engulfing Mandy Blonde in its glare.

'Shit. What happened to you?' she asks.

'What? Nothing. You woke me up.'

'Really? Remind me to avoid middle age.'

'Thanks. Lovely to see you too.'

'Can I come in?'

'Of course. Excuse the middle-aged mess.'

Mandy enters, and it's only once she's inside out of the razor-blade sun that Martin can see her properly. Her eyes are puffy and red. He's about to deliver a rebuke along the lines of 'pot calling the kettle black' when he thinks better of it. 'Are you okay?'

'I thought you might come round last night.'

'So did I. But I went to Bellington, got back late. Long day, I was buggered. Is that why you're crying?'

'Dream on.' She manages a small smile of derision, with only the suggestion of a dimple.

Martin waits. It's coming, he knows. Crying people don't seek out others and then not tell them why they're crying.

'Martin, they've arrested Harley Snouch.'

'What? Why?'

She doesn't answer straight away as she fights to control her emotions. A tear swells into the corner of her eye. Martin thinks he's never seen someone so beautiful in all his life, and then thinks what a turd he is for thinking such a thing. Then she bites her lip, and Martin thinks she's even more beautiful again.

'What's happened?' he asks.

'They're saying awful things. That he's killed someone, out at Springfields.'

'Who's saying?'

'People. Everyone.'

'Who's he killed?'

'They're saying he called an insurance inspector, for the fire damage. The inspector found bodies. Greedy fuck. Can you imagine that? Killing people, then calling in an insurance clerk because you want money?'

A small sob escapes her and Martin steps forward, holds her, tries to comfort her, saying it's just gossip, that it might not be true, all the while wondering if it is and what it might mean.

'Martin?' she whispers.

'Yes, Mandy?' he replies, gently wiping a tear from her cheek with the pad of his thumb.

'Martin, have a shower. You stink.'

—

Freshly showered and, thanks to a brief stopover at the bookstore, freshly caffeinated, Martin is back behind the wheel of the rental. Mandy is in the passenger seat, biting nervously at her lip, as he

147

drives them across the clanking bridge above the flood plain that never floods. The town is behind them, Liam being cared for by Fran at the store, and soon enough the beige and tan fields fall behind as well as they enter the monochromatic world of the Scrublands, still smoking two days on. Martin finds his way first time, but as they approach Snouch's place, Springfields, they are brought to a stop by a police car parked sideways across the road. As they pull up, Robbie Haus-Jones steps out of the car, and they join him amid the smoke and lifted ash.

'Nice car, Robbie,' says Martin by way of greeting.

'On loan from Bellington. Hi, Mandalay.'

'Robert.'

'I'm sorry, but you can't go any further. That's my job. Keeping guard.'

'Who's in there?' asks Martin.

'Herb Walker and Constable Greevy from Bellington. And that bastard, Snouch. The sarge thought'd be best if I waited out here. He's not wrong there.'

'Why's that?'

''Cos otherwise I might kill the old fuck.'

Martin steals a glance at Mandy, but her emotions are in check and her face is impassive.

'Jesus wept, Martin, we risked our lives for that bastard in that bloody fire. And all the time, he had all these bodies in his dam. No wonder he didn't want me to drive the car into it. Murderous old pervert.'

It's Mandy who speaks, her voice eerily calm. 'How many bodies?'

'At least two. Probably more.'

'You sure?'

''Course I'm bloody sure.'

'Christ,' says Martin, not knowing what else to say. The three of them stand there, held still by the enormity of the situation, transfixed by intertwining fates, like three pillars of salt. Finally, Martin says, 'So what's the theory?'

'I'll tell you what I think,' Robbie replies, face haggard and eyes moist. 'I reckon it was the two of them. The old perv and the priest. Byron fucking Swift. My friend, Byron Swift. Shooting rabbits at Codger's? Bullshit. Out shooting kids more like it. "Harley Snouch knows everything." Too right he fucking knows. And to think . . . And to think . . .' He can speak no more, sobs welling up from deep down, shaking his body. It's Mandy who steps forward and wraps her arms around him.

Fuck me, thinks Martin. *Victims comfort victims. What a town.*

The embrace is broken by the sound of an approaching helicopter. Robbie snaps back, as if afraid some binocular-wielding observer might spy him in his moment of weakness. They watch the PolAir chopper circle the property before easing in to land. 'That's homicide, from Sydney,' says Robbie. 'You'd better go.'

Back in the rental, driving towards Riversend, Martin glances across at Mandy, who is staring straight ahead, her eyes glassy. 'You okay?'

'No. I'm not. It's all messed up; *I'm* all messed up. And it's not getting any better.'

Her voice is despairing, fatalistic, enough for Martin to pull the car over, coming to a stop among smouldering stumps. Ash, disturbed by the wheels of the car, rises from the ground, surrounding them before billowing away with the wind.

'Mandy, listen—this is not you, this is them. You can't blame yourself for what they've done. It doesn't work that way.'

'Doesn't it? I feel as if everything I touch turns to shit.' Mandy is looking straight ahead, staring at the devastated landscape. 'What sort of idiot am I? Byron Swift kills five men, yet somehow I end up defending him, telling you he was a good man. A good man? And Snouch. My mum accused him of rape, wouldn't have a thing to do with him. And yet when you and Robbie save his life, I feel grateful, like I'm still that stupid kid wishing for my parents to reconcile. I'm trying so hard, trying so hard to get it right, but it always turns out the same; no matter what I do, I end up being the victim. I'm sick to death of it. Maybe you're right—maybe I should just leave town.'

'Maybe you should.'

'But how? Go where? I promised my mum I was getting my shit together. She was so worried about me, having the baby and all. She had this thing, that you had to be settled into yourself by the time you turn thirty. She said it all the time, that it didn't matter what you did in your early twenties, you could write that off, but after thirty it became harder and harder to change. It was her way of telling me to grow up, but sometimes I feel so lost, like I'm going backwards, like I'm still a teenager.'

'Well, there's plenty of time. How old are you?'

'Twenty-nine.'

Martin is surprised; he would have guessed she was twenty-five at most. He scrutinises her face; there are fine lines around her eyes, but even in her distressed state she looks as if she could be twenty-one: young and vulnerable.

'Don't be so tough on yourself, Mandy. You've endured some awful shit. And you're making a good fist of it, running the bookstore, caring for Liam. That can't be easy. I think your mum would be proud of you.'

Mandy turns to look at him at last, and he takes it as a minor win, as if he has reached her through her despair.

'I'm not so sure about that. She would have seen me turning into her. And that wouldn't have made her happy,' Mandy says.

'So, perhaps it is time to move on. Before you're thirty.'

She turns away from him again, brow furrowed, pondering her options. Martin feels helpless, surprised by the intensity of his concern for her. She stares out at the ruined landscape for some minutes before she shakes her head decisively and turns back to him. 'No, Martin. That's not the answer. I've had enough of being pushed around by events, taking the line of least resistance. I've done that my whole life. I've got to take a stand. For me. For Liam. I've got to ditch my romantic notions and see the world for what it is.'

The despair in her voice has been replaced by resolve. Martin takes it as a good sign; he starts the car and puts it into gear.

———

Back in Riversend, the phone on the counter at the Oasis is ringing as Mandy lets them in. It stops just as she is about to reach for it. She turns, shrugs, is about to say something when it starts ringing again. She answers, listens for a moment, then hands the receiver to Martin. 'It's for you.'

'Hello, it's Martin Scarsden.'

'Where the fuck have you been? We've rung half the numbers in Riversend.'

'Hi, Max. Nice to talk to you, too.'

'Cut the bullshit. We're hearing someone's been murdered down there.'

'Two someones. On a property outside town. I've been out there, just got back.'

'Really? You're on top of it? Good man. Good man. Knew you would be. What can you tell me?'

'Two bodies in a dam. Chief suspect an old felon, an alleged rapist, name of Harley Snouch.'

'Terrific. This is huge. Riversend: murder capital of Australia. Front page. At this stage it's an exclusive, no one else knows. Can you file?'

'Yeah. What do you need?'

'Everything. File everything. What's the best number? This one?'

'Yes, probably. If I swap back to the motel, I'll let you know. It's called the Black Dog.'

'Is that a joke?'

'No.'

'Good then. Bethanie Glass is on the case up here. You two tick-tack okay? Terri is coordinating. I'll give them this number. This guy Snouch, when was he convicted? We'll pull the file.'

'Long time ago. Twenty-five years at least, more like thirty. Details are sketchy on that. He denies it.'

'Of course he does. Don't they all? We want something up online before the cops tell the competitors. Get cracking.' And the editor hangs up.

Martin looks at Mandy. 'Sorry, I should have asked you first, but is it okay if I work out of here for a while? They want me to file.'

'So I gathered. If you have to, you have to,' she says, looking troubled. 'Go through to the back; you can use the office. There's a computer and a phone. Internet's slow; okay for email but not much more. I'm going to pick up Liam.'

Martin can see she's upset, dreading the news he's about to send hurtling out across Australia, but the story has him in its grip and by the time he gets to her office he can think of nothing else.

———

The rest of the day is a blur; the first story hitting the web in time for the lunchtime peak. Martin filing what he's gleaned from Robbie—the fact that homicide has choppered in from Sydney, plus some background on Snouch—with the Sydney police reporter Bethanie Glass pulling it together with information she has garnered from headquarters and the clippings file. No sooner has he filed than Bethanie is on the phone. She's got a fresh line from a police source. So far there are two bodies, almost skeletal, in the farm dam. Police are working on the theory they're German hitchhikers, Heidi Schmeikle and Anna Brün, last seen getting into a blue car in Swan Hill about a year ago. Martin asks for the date, does his calculations. Mid-January. A Tuesday, five days before Byron Swift lost it and started shooting his parishioners. *What the fuck does that mean?* It doesn't matter, it's going in the paper: let the readers speculate.

Martin files again, including Swift in the main story, then knocking out a side piece, speculating wildly about Swift's potential involvement, setting out the dates of the abduction and murder and of the St James massacre. He includes Robbie's theory that the priest and the alleged rapist Harley Snouch were in it together, attributing the information to police sources, joining the dots for the readers in a flurry of inspiration, indignation and righteousness. And as he writes, it feels good to purge himself on the computer screen, to vent his anger at the two perpetrators, one living, one dead; one a rapist, the other a mass murderer, both of whom had somehow inveigled him into doubting their guilt. Now, in his copy, the ambiguities of the real world are banished, all is black and white, there are no shades of grey. The words flow in a torrent, almost writing themselves: the evidence, the summation, the conviction. Guilty as proved. He attaches the copy to an email and clicks the send button with a self-satisfied sigh.

He starts work on a third piece: a feature about a once-proud town, ravaged by drought, besieged by bushfire, where good people fight to retain honour and dignity against unfair odds. He describes how their efforts have been undermined by atrocity and murder, how the town will forever be inextricably linked to unspeakable evil: 'the Snowtown of the Riverina' as one local now calls it. He writes of how deeply the townspeople feel betrayed, people like Constable Robbie Haus-Jones, who had worked with the priest at a youth centre, and who eventually cleansed the town by shooting Swift. He shamelessly includes the story of Robbie and himself putting their lives on the line to rescue Snouch just two days before his arrest. He reworks it, puts the fire at the top, making the contrast between the good cop and the twisted criminal all the stronger, understating his own heroism, but making sure it's included. It's better than a good yarn, better than a strong narrative; it's a real cracker. Defoe will be spewing, Max will be elated, the newsroom sceptics will be silenced. He gets it away by mid-afternoon, feeling vindicated. It's Saturday tomorrow, the biggest paper of the week. Talk about good timing. Front page, man on the spot, sidebar on the Byron Swift connection, plus a feature in News Review. Some of the old electricity is back, some of the old nervousness, something he hasn't felt since before Gaza.

He rings Bethanie. She's happy, confident they have demolished the competition, says the editors are arguing over what to put online and what to hold for the splash. They agree to watch the television news, see if there is anything they need to add. Martin mentions that he's working on a follow-up for the Sunday papers about Byron Swift's mysterious past, making sure he stakes his claim lest Bethanie get wind of the story through her Sydney police contacts. Then he takes a break, stretching his back as he stands. It's been a while since he's spent so many uninterrupted hours on a keyboard.

Mandy is in the kitchen. Liam is in some sort of harness, attached by springs to a doorframe, and is bouncing up and down, chuckling to himself. Mandy is cutting beans, as if hypnotised. There is a huge pile beside her on the bench. Martin sits at the kitchen table, breathes, allows a moment for the thoughts tumbling through his head to subside, re-entering the here and now. Mandy continues cutting beans.

'Mandy, there's no way you could have known.'

'Really? You think? What sort of idiot am I? Just when I start to forgive him, this happens. Always getting fucked over, always the victim, always these fucking men stomping all over me.'

Martin doesn't know what to say, so he steps up behind her, placing his hands on her shoulders, a gesture of comfort, but she shakes him off.

'Don't, Martin. Don't walk up behind me when I'm holding a knife.' There's real anger in her voice.

'Right,' says Martin. He returns to his seat at the table. Mandy continues cutting beans. He wonders what he's doing here, in this woman's kitchen, a woman so cruelly treated by the fates. What will he do when the story is finished? After he has his front pages and his feature articles? Drive back out of town, leaving her here? Isn't that what she wants, what she expects? He's starting to regret sleeping with her. There was the euphoria of surviving the bushfire, her own willingness, but even so. He's about to say something when he notices the blue flowers in the vase on the windowsill above the sink. 'Nice flowers. What are they?'

'What?'

'The flowers.' He gestures.

'What the fuck, Martin? They're swamp peas. Fran gave them to me when I picked up Liam. She sells them down at the store.'

Fran Landers? Martin remembers her praying in the church, the widow defending Swift. What had she said? Something about Swift being kind and decent.

He's about to ask Mandy more, but is interrupted by a buzzer. 'What's that?'

'Someone in the store. I forgot to lock up. Keep an eye on Liam, I'll be right back.'

Martin looks at the chubby child, who is now rocking gently back and forth in his harness, dark eyes gleaming up at him. Martin puts out a hand, extends a finger. The child takes it, wraps his tiny fist around it. So small, so pink. A blank hand, with none of life's transgressions inscribed upon it.

Mandy returns. 'It's someone for you,' she says. 'Some television reporter.'

'Shit, that didn't take long.'

'No. They've parked their choppers on the school oval. They're prowling around town filming anything that moves, knocking on doors, trying to find someone to interview.'

Martin thinks about it for a moment, then walks out into the store. He doesn't know the man, but recognises him from television: Doug Thunkleton. The TV man recognises him, strides towards him, hand outstretched, greeting him like an old friend. 'Martin Scarsden. Wonderful to see you.'

The man has a rich baritone, even deeper in reality than it sounds on the news. He's wearing a tie, no jacket, his shirtsleeves rolled up. His face is make-up smooth with no sign of sweat.

Doug doesn't muck about. 'Martin, we're almost on deadline. We need to chopper out to Swan Hill to feed. Any chance of an interview? As the reporter who broke this story?'

Martin feigns reluctance, but agrees. Max will love it: his man and his paper on the evening news.

Doug has a car, an old Ford, hired with television's magic chequebook from some local. There's a baby seat still bolted into the back and the interior smells of blue cheese. Martin wonders how much he's paying.

The TV reporter drives them to St James, where his camera crew is filming. They stand Martin in front of the church, bounce the sun into his eye with a large white disc, and Doug gets going, not so much questioning him as prompting him, like two colleagues colluding. And collude they do: Doug dons the voice of television authority, his demeanour suitably serious, while Martin wraps himself in the mystique of the investigative reporter, a man with covert sources and deep knowledge. He lets slip that he has been researching the story for a considerable amount of time, states that it's a *Sydney Morning Herald* investigation, hints at police contacts. He mentions at least a half-a-dozen times that the full story will be in tomorrow's paper. Five minutes and they're done, Doug attempting to wheedle a little more information out of his interviewee as the crew picks up some editing shots. Martin doesn't add anything, other than to imply that he has the trust of the police, that they're grateful for his insights. Martin leaves the crew scrambling to get Doug's new piece to camera recorded. The last thing he hears is the cameraman saying, 'Fantastic. That'll fuck the ABC.'

When Martin gets back to the Oasis, he finds the door locked. There's no GON OUT, BACKSON sign. He knocks, but there's no answer. He glances at his watch. It's twenty minutes to five. The Channel Ten chopper lifts off from the primary school oval and heads south, followed shortly after by the ABC. Martin feels a little surge of satisfaction. They're here to follow up *his* story.

He walks down to the general store.

Fran Landers gives him a smile when he enters. 'Hello, Martin. Need some more water?'

It occurs to him that he does, so he walks to the end of the aisle and picks up two sixpacks of one-litre bottles, wishing he'd driven the car down from where he had left it outside the Oasis. He walks back down a different aisle, confirming that he and Fran are the only ones in the store, and places the water on the counter.

'You heard about the police at Springfields?' he asks, as a way of initiating conversation.

'I've heard of nothing else. The town's abuzz. Television reporters like blowflies. Awful people.'

'Indeed,' says Martin.

'You are as well, of course,' says Fran, smiling. 'Although in your case, you're forgiven.' There's something flirtatious in her manner. Martin wonders if she's coming on to him.

'That's nice to hear. What are people saying?'

The coquettish smile drops away and she sighs. 'That there are bodies in Harley Snouch's dam. At least half-a-dozen. Discovered by a power company linesman, or an insurance inspector, or a firefighting helicopter refilling from his dam. They've already flown Snouch to Sydney to interrogate him. Awful man. He should never have been allowed back into town.'

Martin considers this, decides there's not much point in pursuing town rumours, that Robbie Haus-Jones and Herb Walker will be more reliable sources of information. Instead, he indicates the bunches of pale blue flowers standing in a small white bucket at the end of the counter. 'Nice flowers. Swamp peas, aren't they?'

'That's right. Very good. Would you like a bunch?'

'Not right now. Can't carry them. Do they grow around here?'

'Most years. Great swathes of them around Blackfellas Lagoon on the other side of the river. Beautiful. Not in the drought, though; no water. I pick them down near Bellington. Even on the Murray, they're almost impossible to find. But I know a billabong where they still grow. It's very pretty down there first thing in the morning as the sun is rising.'

'Long way to go for flowers.'

'Not really—I go every day to get the papers, bread and milk.'

'And to put swamp peas on Byron Swift's grave.'

Fran stops moving, expression draining from her face. Martin thinks of her praying in St James. Praying for whom?

'It's okay, Fran. I'm not going to put your name in the paper. Not like that.'

'Like what, then?'

'Explain it to me. Why are you mourning Byron Swift?'

'He was a good man.'

'He killed your husband.'

'I know he did. It was awful. Unforgiveable. But you didn't know him from before all that. He was a kind man. So gentle.'

Martin nods, grits his teeth, concluding it's better to be blunt. 'Were you having an affair with him?'

The shopkeeper doesn't answer immediately, but he can see the confirmation in her wide eyes, in her open mouth, in the way she involuntarily takes a small step backwards.

'Are you going to put that in the paper?'

'No. And I won't mention your name if I do. Besides, I've got my editor on my back. They want everything they can get on Springfields and the bodies in the dam. The anniversary of the shooting at St James has very much taken a back seat.'

'I see.'

'Fran, what can you tell me about Harley Snouch?'

'Is this for your paper?'

Martin nods. 'But I won't use your name.'

The woman sighs, relieved at the change in topic. 'Okay. I guess I owe you, after all, for saving Jamie. But please don't write about Byron and me. Jamie has been through so much. He doesn't need that.'

Martin nods. 'I promise I won't mention you. Not by name.'

Fran looks unsure, eyes unhappy. 'What do you want to know about Snouch?'

'I'm not sure. Everything, I guess.'

'Well, there's not that much to tell, really. He turned up a while back, maybe two years ago, moved into his family's place, Springfields, but only after his father died. He was a lovely old fellow, Eric. A true gentleman. People said he had banished Harley, wouldn't allow him to step foot in the house while he drew breath. First time he came into the store, I didn't know who he was. Seemed nice enough, but there was something strange about him, something out of kilter. Then I found out who he was. After that, I didn't talk to him, no more than I had to. I wouldn't refuse him service, but I didn't encourage it. He was pretty much ostracised. I see him wandering around, wearing that awful old coat, always drunk.'

'What did he do that was so terrible?'

'Didn't Mandy tell you?'

'Not really,' he dissembles. 'It upsets her too much.'

'Yes, well, that's true.'

'You're friends, aren't you? You and Mandy?'

'Yes. She was really nice after Craig died. Helped me a lot. And I look after Liam for her sometimes.'

'You're right, she is nice. But you were telling me about Harley Snouch. Why was he ostracised?'

'Well, it was before my time, before Craig and I came back here. The story is that Harley was the most eligible bachelor in town, only child of the Snouches of Springfields. He'd been away to boarding school, then university somewhere. He came home over the summer break and met Katie Blonde, who was the daughter of a local truck driver. Smart, though, and very good-looking; Mandy is her spitting image apparently. Katie had been to university too, at Bathurst or Wagga or somewhere, which was fairly unusual in those days, a girl from a working-class family. Harley and Katie were an item, engaged to be married. Then they were gone, back to university. No one knew anything had gone wrong until a year later. She came back again, with a degree and a baby. But there was no Harley Snouch.

'It was only later that people learnt she'd accused him of rape, that he'd gone to prison. Everyone was horrified, of course. His mother, poor woman, died of shame. The old man became a recluse, sold off parts of the property. Gave a lot to the government for a national park that never happened, gave land to war veterans and ne'er-do-wells and to poor old Codger Harris. Thank God he's dead—Eric, I mean. Imagine the shame of these latest murders. Anyway, by the time Craig and Jamie and I got here, it was all a bit like a town legend. And then Harley

Snouch turns up out of the blue, released from prison. And then Mandy came back to look after Katie and he's wanting to know her. Ugly man.'

Martin's mind is alive with possibilities. 'So when did the old man die?'

'Not sure. Maybe five years ago.'

'So Harley Snouch only turned up well after his father had died?'

'Oh yes. Like I said, the old man had banished him. Never wanted to see him again.'

'But left him the farm, nevertheless?'

'I wouldn't know about that. I guess so. He lives there.'

'Yes—up until Wednesday, anyway.'

Martin considers what Fran has told him. Such a strange story. Two young people: bright, good-looking, engaged to be married. Then they disappear, ostensibly back to their respective universities. A year later the woman returns with their baby, while he's been sentenced to prison for raping her.

'Is there anything else?' Fran asks. 'I need to be closing up, preparing for tomorrow.'

'What's tomorrow?'

'The funeral. For Allen Newkirk.'

'The boy in the ute?'

'Yes.'

Martin pays for his mineral water and hefts it from the counter, then pauses to ask one more question. 'Fran, when you were praying in St James the other day, giving thanks for Jamie being spared, did you say a prayer for Craig as well?'

She takes offence at that. 'Yes, of course I did. He was my husband.'

'Thanks, Fran. Thanks for helping.' And carrying his water, he leaves.

Parking at the Black Dog, he discovers he's no longer the only guest. There are three cars parked outside rooms in the motel's solitary wing. Two are police cars; the other looks like a rental. Lounging against the front of the rental in the shade of the carport is a thin man smoking a cigarette. He's wearing the remains of a suit: the coat has gone, the white shirt is smeared with charcoal, the tie is at half-mast. His city shoes are caked with mud.

'Tough day,' says Martin, getting out of his car.

The man looks unflinchingly into Martin's eyes. 'Who are you?'

'Martin Scarsden. *Sydney Morning Herald.*' Martin offers his hand, but the man merely looks at it, declining to shake it.

'Didn't take you long to get here,' he says, a disparaging tone to his voice.

'I've been here for a few days.'

'Why's that?'

'Writing a piece on the anniversary of the shooting by the priest. Do you think there's a connection between the two?'

'The two what?'

'The two shootings. The priest at the church and the bodies in the dam.'

'What makes you think they were shot?'

'Weren't they?'

'You tell me.'

Martin realises his run of luck with the police has come to an end; this is a fully-fledged homicide officer, not an academy graduate like Robbie or a small-town powerbroker like Herb Walker. The detective is not about to volunteer anything. The best Martin can hope for is confirmation or denial. 'We're running a story in tomorrow's paper saying there were two bodies found in the dam by an insurance inspector. We're saying you think they were German backpackers, abducted a year ago from Swan Hill. That you've arrested Harley Snouch.'

The cop considers him, as if deciding whether or not to engage. He takes a final drag on his cigarette, drops the butt to the ground, grinds it under his shoe. 'I look forward to reading it. Nice to meet you, Mr Scarsden.' And he walks past Martin into room number nine.

eleven | **NEWSBREAKERS**

THE OASIS IS OPEN, BUT MANDY IS CLOSED. SHE SELLS MARTIN A COFFEE, but makes it clear she doesn't want to talk, muttering something about feeding Liam. Martin barely notices; he's on a high. He takes his coffee and proceeds to the general store. Fran isn't there, but the Saturday papers are. He buys them and takes them outside to relish—not the Sydney papers, but their Melbourne cousins. No matter, the front pages are just as good. BUSHLAND MURDERS screams the rival tabloid, the *Herald Sun,* but its copy is a mishmash of information cribbed from the *Sydney Morning Herald*'s website and the television news. He smirks as he reads a verbatim quote, lifted from the interview he gave Channel Ten, attributed to 'an informed source'. The *SMH*'s Melbourne cousin, *The Age*, does it better: EVIL STALKS TOWN OF DEATH and the subheading *Massacre Priest Linked to Backpackers' Murder.* The splash has a red EXCLUSIVE banner above their by-lines: *By*

Martin Scarsden in Riversend and Bethanie Glass, Senior Police Reporter. There's an aerial shot of the property, police cars and figures in white overalls by the farm dam, courtesy of Nine News. And his second piece, under the headline MASSACRE PRIEST'S NEW HORROR, has his dinkus photo, the red EXCLUSIVE stamp and is branded as *A Herald Investigation*. Martin smiles with satisfaction: the holy trinity.

He scans through the stories quickly, picking out where Bethanie or the subeditors have inserted facts or cleaned up his copy. He discards the front section, moving through to News Review. The graphic artists and layout subs have done his copy proud, dressing his tale of a dying town with suitably bleak images; if they'd taken a week they couldn't have done a better job. And there's more to come: he's already written half of the follow-up, THE PRIEST WITH NO PAST, having woken early in his motel room, unable to sleep. It will make the perfect follow-up for the Sunday papers, the *Sun-Herald* and *The Sunday Age*. Max Fuller was right; coming to Riversend was exactly what he needed.

He's just about finished admiring his work when the bell starts pealing. His watch says nine-thirty; he thought the funeral wasn't starting until ten. Dumping the papers in a footpath rubbish bin, he heads towards St James. He walks down the centre of Hay Road, feeling the sting of the sun on his face. He likes the sound of the bell: armed with his front-page exclusives it makes him feel like Clint Eastwood, striding, spurs jangling, through some frontier shithole, heading fearlessly into a showdown, the lone gunman imposing order through a blend of gunpowder, resolve and integrity. Even now, fearful townsfolk could be peering out from behind shutters under the awnings of Hay Road as he paces towards his destiny. The daydream lingers for a moment before being brought crashing down by the blare of a car horn immediately behind him. He jumps involuntarily. 'Get off the road, you tosser!' yells the driver.

The bell is no longer ringing as he approaches St James. He's surprised by the size of the media throng that has coalesced across the road from the church: camera operators with tripods arrayed four abreast; stills photographers lounging, nursing huge lenses attached to cameras and monopods; a couple of radio reporters looking lost. They're standing where the cars were parked when Byron Swift opened fire, where Gerry Torlini died. Doug Thunkleton is back, holding court among a small gaggle of television reporters, including a man in his fifties and three pretty young women, blonde hair bouffant, their faces familiar. Doug has an earpiece clipped to the back of his jacket; Channel Ten must have some sort of live feed capacity set up.

Martin realises it's a very big story for a very small town. He of all people should have realised it would be like this: the dearth of news in Australia in January, a big story breaking in the so-called media silly season. And here he is in the middle of it.

One of the stills photographers, a compact young woman wearing cargo pants and a khaki vest full of pockets, peels off and greets him as he approaches. 'Martin? Hi, I'm Carrie O'Brien. Drove up from Melbourne last night. Anything in particular you want?'

'Not really, just get as much as you can from this. It's not really part of the story. Just a kid who died in a car accident, but I might file something on it. I witnessed the accident.'

'Shit. Really?'

'Yeah. I might even have a shot on my phone. I'll give it to you later.'

'Okay.'

'In the meantime, try to get lots of faces. We may be able to pick up some people shots that will be useful later for the other stories. And do you have a phone that works?'

'Yeah. I've got a sat phone in the car to file with. You can use it if you're desperate.'

'Have you been out to the property?'

'Not yet. The *Herald* hired a plane and got some aerials yesterday. I don't know why *The Age* didn't use them. Some stuff-up. They're on the website.'

'Sounds about right. Where you staying?'

'Hopefully the same place as you. The Black Dog. I stopped by on my way through. I'm on the waiting list.'

'Good luck with that.' Martin can see where this is heading. Carrie seems nice enough, but he's not so keen on sharing with a photographer, particularly not a room with one bed. And he's not about to assume he can simply shack up with Mandy in order to give his room to a photographer. She was distant and moody this morning. Perhaps he should have talked to her more, explained what he was writing, but what the fuck, this story was growing more legs than a centipede. Maybe he would have to share with Carrie after all. At least the paper hadn't sent a bloke.

The first of the locals are arriving at the church. Robbie Haus-Jones is standing on the steps in his police uniform. Martin saunters across the road, enjoying the jealous regard of his colleagues: the investigative reporter with police contacts.

'G'day, Robbie.'

'Hi, Martin.'

'It's awful, isn't it?'

'What, this? Sure is. Enough dead people in this town without young fellas crashing cars.'

Martin is about to say something when he gets a burst of flashback: laying the Disney character windshield reflector over the body of the dead boy. He looks down at his hands. They don't appear to be trembling.

'You okay?' asks Robbie.

'Fine. Fine. How's the investigation going?'

'No idea. They're not telling me anything. But I know one thing: they haven't arrested Harley Snouch. They've let him go.' There's an edge of anger in Robbie's voice.

'What? How's that possible? Bodies in his dam and they let him go?'

'Lack of evidence. Apparently he found the skeletons, walked all the way to the highway to get word to Bellington.'

'Not to you?'

'No. Not to me.'

A small pit has opened in Martin's stomach. He thinks of his articles in the paper, all but accusing Snouch of murder. Accusing? More like convicting. 'Shit. Did you see the papers this morning?'

'Yeah—we're all over them.'

'Except I wrote that the bodies had been discovered by an insurance inspector. Didn't you mention something like that when we saw you out near Springfields yesterday?'

'Not me. All I knew was that someone had found skeletons. I thought it might have been a chopper pilot, but it was definitely Snouch.'

'Shit.' Martin is suddenly feeling very exposed, out in the burning sun, standing on the church steps away from the shade. He glances back at the media pack; a couple of cameramen are filming him. Shit indeed. Where did he get the insurance inspector from? Mandy? How could he write something like that without double-checking its veracity? Max Fuller will be furious; Martin can hear him repeating C.P. Scott's famous dictum even now: 'facts are sacred'. Then he recalls the slim cop leaning on the car smoking outside the Black Dog. 'Fuck it. You know, Robbie, I mentioned it to this detective at the motel last night, said the bodies had been uncovered by an insurance inspector, that Snouch was in custody. He didn't correct me. Slim guy, receding hair, five o'clock shadow. A smoker. Didn't tell me a thing, but it wouldn't have hurt him to say I was off the mark. What's his name?'

Robbie doesn't reply. Instead, he's looking at Martin with something approximating trepidation.

'What? What did I say?'

'You didn't hear it from me, okay?'

'Sure. What? You can't tell me his name?'

'No, I can't. It's against the law.'

'What? What fucking law?'

'He's not a cop.'

'Not a cop? What the fuck is he then?' Martin recalls the way the man acted, the way he dressed, the way he spoke. All cop. And then he realises what Robbie is saying. Technically, identifying ASIO agents is against the law. 'Holy fuck. A spook?'

'You didn't hear that from me.'

'I sure didn't.' Christ. *A spook*? It made no sense. Bodies in a dam, abducted hitchhikers. Why would ASIO be interested in that? And why so quickly? The guy arrived with the Sydney cops.

Robbie interrupts his train of thought. 'Martin?'

'Yes?'

'Sorry, mate, but I'm going to have to ask you to join your friends across the road. The family has requested no media in the church.'

'Including me? I was there, remember?'

'Yes. So was I. But I'll be staying out here too. Standing on these fucking steps, of all places. But if I let you in, the others will all want in as well. Sorry, Martin; it's the family's call, not mine.'

Martin feels peeved, but realises that Robbie is merely the messenger. 'Fair enough. And thanks for letting me know about the spooks. I'll keep that under my hat for now.'

He walks back towards his admiring colleagues, head down, as if pondering serious new information, when all he's really doing is avoiding eye contact. They won't be admiring him for much longer, not once they cotton on to the fact that he might have falsely accused an innocent man. That studio-bound pedant on *Media Watch*, with his team of acolytes, will be all over him like a rash. And his colleagues certainly won't be admiring him if Snouch starts spraying around defamation writs; most of them have been repeating his allegations as fact. But as he stands in the shade of the trees and starts to think it through, it doesn't make sense to him. It's been a long time since he did his stint on police rounds, but he remembers enough about police methodology to recall that coppers invariably target the most obvious suspects, and for good reason: they're usually proven right. If a woman turns up beaten to death, then the husband or boyfriend is immediately a suspect. The cops will typically lock them up for as long as legally permissible, apply maximum pressure, extract as much information as possible, maybe even a confession, before alibis can be confected. So what was going on? Here, they have a man who, judging by his prison tattoos, has done time in jail, an alleged rapist no less, reporting bodies in his dam—bodies that he knows are likely to be found now that the fires have denuded the place and he's waiting for insurance assessors. Surely he must be the primary suspect. So why were they letting him go? The hole in Martin's stomach grows a little bigger. There's stuff happening here and he has no idea what it is. Or perhaps Robbie has simply got it wrong; maybe they haven't arrested Snouch yet, but it won't be long. 'Helping police with their inquiries' was the usual phrase. Why arrest him and set the habeas corpus clock ticking if he's helping anyway? Martin calms down a little.

More people are gathering outside the church now, and the cameramen and photographers are concentrating on their work, the clatter of camera shutters chattering away like a coded conversation. Herb Walker is there, having a quiet word with Robbie off to one side. Fran Landers arrives, accompanied by

Jamie. The boy stares at the ground, looking as if this is the last place in the world he wants to be. Mandy arrives with Liam in a stroller, ignoring the media completely, and Robbie helps her up the stairs and into the church.

Martin looks about to see if he can spot Carrie; instead a movement catches his eye. Standing behind the media, up on the ridge of the levee bank, wearing a red shirt, is the boy Martin met on the church steps on his first full day in Riversend. What was his name? Luke? The boy is holding a long stick, like a walking stick, and as Martin watches, he lifts it to his shoulder like a gun and points it at Martin. He lowers it a little, mouths the word 'pow', and then he's off, scrambling down the other side of the levee bank, leaving Martin rooted to the spot, breath frozen in the simmering heat of the day.

After the funeral, Martin tries the Oasis first, but there is no chance of a quiet word with Mandy; the place is crawling with journalists. She has wheeled her coffee machine out on a trolley and positioned it next to the shop counter, rigging it up with a jerry can of water. But the boom in business has not improved her mood; she scowls as she serves him a takeaway coffee. Martin guesses she's read his stories—or learnt of them from the swarming reporters—his stories condemning Swift and condemning Snouch. Her manner is distant, almost formal; he decides now isn't the time to broach the subject with her.

He pays for his coffee and makes his way down Hay Road, crossing Somerset, past the World War I digger on his plinth and the locked doors of the Commercial Hotel. If only the pub had held on for another six months; it wasn't just coffee that journalists put away by the bucketload.

At the general store, Fran is back behind the counter, still wearing her church finery. Jamie is helping, scowling at the mix of locals and media browsing among the aisles as he does so.

'Hello, Mr Scarsden,' says Fran. 'I was wondering when you'd be back. You've been selling a lot of papers.' Today there are no smiles, no suggestion of flirtation.

'So I see,' says Martin, regarding the vacant space where the papers usually sat in small piles. 'You're not happy about that?'

'Happy to sell papers, not so happy with you implicating Byron in the deaths of those girls.'

'Fran. Is there somewhere we can talk? In private?'

The storekeeper considers the throng of customers. 'I guess so.' She turns to her son. 'Jamie, can you mind things for a moment while I talk to Mr Scarsden out the back?'

Jamie grunts his assent and Fran leads Martin past the customers and through a door at the back of the store. She turns on the lights; fluorescent tubes hanging in banks from the ceiling flicker to life, casting a hard-edged light. The room is nothing like Mandy's home at the back of the Oasis; this is one big space, windowless and full of shelving, much of it empty, with cardboard boxes containing various products here and there. There are spiderwebs on the higher shelves, but otherwise the storeroom is well kept. In one corner, to the left of the door, there's a desk with a computer monitor that looks a decade out of date. Fran brushes at the seat behind the desk with her hand, protective of her church clothes, and sits. Martin takes the seat on the other side of the desk.

He doesn't bother with niceties, but picks up the conversation where they'd paused it at the counter. 'You don't think Byron was involved in the death of the girls in the dam?'

'No. Do you have any proof? Do the police?'

'Not yet. But they're investigating.'

Fran glowers at him. He decides there's little to be gained in arguing the toss: neither of them can know for sure whether Swift was involved and he risks angering her unnecessarily. He spreads his hands, a conciliatory gesture.

'Fran, I need your help. I've been thinking over the day of the shooting. There are things that bother me, now that I know about you and Byron.'

'I see.'

'He wasn't a regular churchgoer, your husband, was he?'

The question seems to drain the indignation from her. Instead her voice is subdued, her eyes not meeting his as she answers. 'No.'

'Did he know about you and Byron?'

Fran remains still, eyes fixed on the blank computer monitor. Finally, a nod of affirmation.

'Did you warn Byron that Craig was going to the church?'

Another nod.

'What did you fear Craig was going to do?'

She turns to Martin, eyes pleading.

'Tell me, Fran.'

A small sob escapes her, a fragile thing, fleeting. 'I overheard them. Out by our garage. Craig and his friends. The ones Byron shot. They said they were going to kill him. In horrible ways. I knew they meant it.'

'What did they say?'

'Craig said he was going to ram his shotgun up his arse and give him both barrels.'

'Why, Fran? Why kill him? Why then?'

'I don't know. I just heard them saying that's what they were going to do.'

Martin leans back, considers what she's telling him and finds himself not believing her. But why would she mislead him? He decides to be direct. 'I've been told, by a reliable source, that on the Friday night before the shooting the police warned Craig that Swift was molesting children. Are you saying Craig didn't mention that to you?'

'I've already told you: it wasn't true, I didn't believe it.'

'But Craig told you?'

'Yes, I knew.'

'So you warned him? Warned Byron?'

'Yes. I ran to the church. I told him that Craig and the others were coming to kill him. I begged him to leave. He said that he was already going; the bishop had ordered it. He said he wasn't worried about Craig and his friends, that he could handle them. He asked me to wait for him out by Blackfellas Lagoon. We'd gone there together sometimes.'

'You believed him?'

'Of course. I always believed him.'

'So you weren't there when the shooting happened?'

'No, I wasn't. He made sure of that.'

Martin considers that for a moment, before changing tack. 'You say you always believed him. Did you believe he was who he said he was?'

She doesn't answer immediately; Martin sees only confusion on her face. 'What? What do you mean?'

'That he was someone else. An imposter. Maybe a former soldier.'

'No. Never. That's rubbish. Who told you that?' Indignation has replaced her puzzlement.

'How did he seem to you, Fran, that last time you saw him?'

'Fine. He seemed fine. Calm, I would say. Calm and rather happy. Happy to be leaving.' She sobs once more, her eyes moist, indignation superseded by distress. 'I wasn't happy, but he was.'

⁓

Martin walks. The heat of the day has reached its hours-long crescendo, and he's sweating profusely, but he feels a compulsion to walk; sitting still is not an option. The sky is almost white, so leached of colour it seems metallic, with no hint of cloud. There's a faint smell of bushfire and the wind is getting up. Another hellish day in the 'town of death'. How long has it been since there was any rain? How long since an overcast day?

Fran's words replay over and over in his mind. He turns them, examines them, searches them for significance. Was it possible? That a jealous husband, already enraged at being cuckolded by a priest and now informed the priest had abused his only son, decided to take revenge? And that the priest, fore-warned by his lover, acted in self-defence?

No. The men may have spoken of killing him, but they weren't armed; they'd left their guns behind. Perhaps they went to beat him up, but he shot them down without mercy. Gerry Torlini was in his car, Craig Landers was a hundred metres away, running for his life. No, self-defence was out of the question. Defending Fran Landers from potential retribution? That might explain shooting Craig Landers, but not the others. Not respectable Horrie Grosvenor, his widow Janice left uncomprehending in Bellington.

So not self-defence and not defending Fran, but that didn't rule out Herb Walker's call to Craig Landers as the catalyst for the shooting. He'd warned Landers and Alf Newkirk on the Friday night that the priest may have been interfering with their sons. The two men met, along with fellow members of the Bellington Anglers Club, when they went hunting on Saturday, and the men were outraged by the news. Then, on the Sunday morning, they realised Swift was in Riversend to conduct the fortnightly church service. One or more of them spoke of killing the priest, perhaps meaning it, perhaps not. Fran Landers overheard them and raced to meet her lover, believing that her husband was intent on killing him. She told Swift that Walker had talked to Craig, had made the allegation of child abuse. And so Swift shot them. It all made sense. Except it didn't. He didn't have to shoot anyone. He could have simply left town.

By the time Martin gets to the park, up near the bridge on the way to Deniliquin, the sweat is really pouring off him. His shirt is sopping wet and clinging. He tries the bubbler in the park, but either it's not working or has been cut off as a water-saving measure. He climbs the stairs to the rotunda, attracted by the shade. He should be working on his story, the story of the priest with no past, but the clarity of the previous day has deserted him together with the self-confidence of the morning. Byron Swift's connection to the Scrublands murders had seemed so certain, but today he isn't so sure. It was Robbie's theory, concocted in anger and despair, but there is no hard evidence. That wouldn't necessarily prevent Martin writing the story. He had the hook:

One police theory is that renegade priest Byron Swift was also involved in the killings at Springfields. A Herald *investigation can now reveal that Swift was not what he seemed. He was a man without a past.*

Such mystery surrounds his past that elements within the police force want to exhume his body, while ASIO has sent an experienced investigator to Riversend.

It has all the characteristics of a ripping yarn, a perfect Sunday paper read: murder, religion, spooks, sex. Christ, what a combination. So why is he hesitating? Byron Swift is dead, and the dead can't sue. He can write whatever he likes about the priest without fear of blowback. Except maybe from Max Fuller, his editor and long-time mentor. Back when he was just a cadet and Max was chief of staff, all the cadets and cub reporters had lived in fear of him and his insistence on absolute accuracy.

Martin examines his hands. Not working hands, not honest hands. Assassin's hands? Character assassination, not the real thing—not like Byron Swift's hands. Swift could cut a man down at a hundred metres, a bullet through the neck, his hands steady and heart inured; Martin Scarsden could sever a man's reputation from much further afield, from beyond the grave if necessary, hands soft and heart absent. Martin tries to imagine the hands of the young priest. Were they soft and white like his, or had they retained the callused insensitivity of a special forces soldier? Martin looks at the back of his hands, searching for evidence of keyboard atrocities.

'Hello.'

The voice snaps Martin out of his reverie. It's the boy, in his red shirt, still with his stick.

'Hello,' says Martin.

'Sorry,' says the boy.

'What for?'

'The church. I didn't mean to scare you.'

'That's okay,' says Martin. 'You want to sit down?'

'Sure.' The boy sits on the next bench along, up against the side of the rotunda.

'It's Luke, isn't it?' asks Martin.

'That's right,' replies the boy.

'I'm Martin, remember? Martin Scarsden.'

Martin waits. He figures if the boy has sought him out, he must have something he wants to say. But the boy just sits there, occasionally looking at Martin, but nothing more. Maybe he just wants some company. So it's Martin who initiates the conversation. 'Were you there when it happened, Luke?'

The boy looks unnerved. 'Who told you that?'

'No one. Just a guess. This morning—the thing with the stick.'

'I've never told anyone,' says Luke.

'Not even the police?'

'No. They didn't ask. Didn't have to. There were plenty of people there.'

'Tell me what you saw.'

'Why?'

'I want to understand it.'

'Well, I don't understand it.' The boy looks at his stick, balancing it on his hands. 'I was in the main street when I saw his car outside the bookstore. It was Sunday, so I figured he'd come up to do the church service. I walked round there, to the church, and waited. I was there when he drove up. We sat on the steps. He told me that he had to leave, that he didn't want to, but his bishop had ordered him. I said it wasn't fair. He said that life wasn't fair. He said other stuff like that.'

'Can you remember what?'

'Yes, I remember it all.'

'What did he say?'

'He said I was a good boy and I shouldn't worry about God, that God would come to me when I needed him. He said God didn't give a shit about the little stuff, like swearing or lying or playing with yourself. He said God only cared about what was in our souls, whether we were good people or not. That God knew. And when we were faced with hard decisions, then God could help. And if we ever did bad things, then God would forgive us, even for things we couldn't forgive ourselves.'

'What did he mean by that, "bad things"?'

'I don't know. He didn't say.'

'That sounds like quite a grown-up conversation.'

'Yeah. But he was good like that. He didn't talk down to us kids.'

'Did he often talk about God?'

'No, hardly ever. I think it was because he was leaving. I've been thinking about what he said. Maybe I understand a little better now.'

'Did he say anything else?'

'Yeah. He said there were bad men in the world, even in our own town, and that I should play with kids my own age. I'm not sure why he said that. He said that once he was gone, if I had any problems, I should go tell Constable Haus-Jones and he could help me.'

'Do you know what he was talking about?'

'No. Not really.'

'I see. How did he seem to you? Was he agitated?'

'No. He seemed calm. Sort of happy and sort of sad. Does that make sense? I thought he was sad because he was being ordered to leave town.'

'You know, Luke, some people think he must have been crazy to do what he did. Did he seem crazy to you?'

'No.'

'What happened next?'

'We were sitting there talking when Mrs Landers came running up. She seemed really upset, like she was crying or something. They went inside to talk, so I went across the road to the shade of the trees. I was sad he was going. He was a good guy. Mrs Landers left and a little later people started turning up for church. He came out to talk to them. Then some men turned up. Mr Landers from the store and some other men. Allen Newkirk was with them, so I went up the hill above the river, where I was this morning.'

'You didn't like Allen?'

'No. He was a bully.'

'I see. And then?'

'Mr Landers was talking to Byron.'

'Could you hear what they said?'

'No, I was too far away.'

'Were they angry? Shouting?'

'No. Byron looked like he was laughing.'

'Laughing?'

'Yeah, like they were having a joke or something. Then he went back into the church. Allen walked over and got into a car. The others were all talking to other people. Everything seemed normal. Then—then it happened. He came out with a gun and shot them.'

'Just the men Mr Landers arrived with?'

'Yes. The fat man from Bellington first. Then the Newkirks. Then he looked around. He saw me up on the ridge, watching, and he shook his head, waved at me to go away. But I didn't. Couldn't. I couldn't believe it. I could see it all. Byron was still looking around. Then a car started, and he saw it. He fired two more shots, at the car. *Pow, pow*, quick like that. Then people started screaming, but he still seemed very calm. I could see Mr Landers running up the street. I think Byron must have seen where I was looking. It was my fault. He walked to the corner of the church, saw Mr Landers running, and then he lifted the gun and *pow*. One shot. Then he went and sat on the steps and waited. A car drove past, and he stood and raised the gun, fired a shot into the air. He looked at me again and shook his head. I wanted him to run away, but he sat down again. I could see Constable Haus-Jones coming down the street, up behind the church, with his gun. I didn't know what to do. I didn't want to look at him in case Byron saw me and knew he was coming and shot him too. But I didn't want Constable Haus-Jones to shoot Byron. So I hid.'

Luke is looking down at the stick, twirling it absent-mindedly in his hands. He doesn't seem at all upset; maybe replaying the scene constantly in his mind has normalised it.

'What about the other people who were there?'

'They ran away. Some hid behind cars, some ran up over the bank and down to the riverbed. There was no one left, just Byron, with the constable getting closer.'

'Did you see what happened when Constable Haus-Jones confronted Byron?'

'Yeah, they talked for a bit. Constable Haus-Jones was pointing his pistol at Byron. I thought Byron was going to surrender. But he didn't. He lifted the gun, pointed it at Constable Haus-Jones and fired. And then Constable Haus-Jones shot him. Four times. *Pap, pap. Pap, pap.* Byron fell down, dropped the gun. Constable Haus-Jones walked over, moved the gun away with his foot. Then he carefully put his gun down. Then he sat with Byron. He was crying.'

'Jeez, you poor kid.'

'Yeah.'

'Luke, you say they talked for a bit before he was shot. You didn't hear what they said?'

'No.'

'How long did they talk for?'

'Not long. I don't know. A minute maybe, something like that.'

'And when the priest lifted his gun, did he do it quickly?'

'No. He did it really slowly. Constable Haus-Jones wasn't caught by surprise.'

'What do you think of the constable now?'

'I feel sorry for him. He didn't have any choice.'

There's a pause, Martin imagining the scene, Luke reliving it.

'Luke, did anyone else go into the church, before the shooting?'

The boy frowns. 'Yes. Just before. A woman went in.'

'How long before?'

'Maybe a minute or two. Not long. And afterwards, after the shooting, after Byron was dead, she came out again, all shaking, looking really scared.'

'Who was she Luke? Did you recognise her?'

'No. I never saw her before. And not since. She must have been from out of town.'

Martin ponders this, recalling Walker's revelation that a woman visiting from interstate had overheard the final conversation between Robbie and Byron Swift. And Walker's assertion that she hadn't spoken to the priest.

He turns back to the boy. 'Do you have any idea why he did it—why Byron Swift shot those men?'

'No. I think of it every day. I don't know.'

They sit side by side, the newsman and the boy, lost in thought. Again, it is Martin who breaks the silence. 'Luke, I owe you an apology. For the other day, when I first met you outside the church. I didn't mean to upset you.'

Luke nods, saying nothing.

'The police still believe the allegations made against him, you know.'

Does Constable Haus-Jones?'

'No. But two boys told the police it was true.'

'It's not true, Mr Scarsden. It's not. He never touched me and he never touched anyone else.'

The journalists, cameramen and photographers, having swarmed locust-like from the church to the Oasis, have now moved en masse to the services club. They're in the main bar area, drinking Coca-Cola, eating takeaway from Saigon Asian and working away on laptops. Over to one side, by the windows looking out over a steel-form deck and the dry riverbed, sit a group of police officers. Robbie Haus-Jones isn't there, but Herb Walker is, hoeing into a steak and beer, plus a couple of other men, all too easily recognisable as cops in their bad suits or chinos and polo shirts. Homicide detectives.

Carrie detaches herself from a gaggle of reporters and comes over to him.

'Glad you turned up,' says the photographer. 'I've been looking for you. You hear about the doorstop? The cops are speaking out the front at one.'

'Thanks. I didn't know. Want a drink?'

'No, I'm right. I've got one.' And she returns to her friends.

Martin checks the time. Twelve forty-five. Bugger. Not enough time to eat, so he walks to the bar, fills a glass of water from the jug sitting there, downs it and fills another, before moving along to order a drink. Errol is manning the bar. He gets Martin a light beer and a packet of chips, taking Martin's money and shaking his head. 'I don't know what we ever did to deserve this.' Martin assumes he means the murders, not the media.

The police hold their press conference in the shade of a large gum tree. The senior man, wearing a suit, identifies himself as Detective Inspector Morris Montifore from Sydney homicide, spelling his name for the reporters and introducing his colleague Detective Sergeant Ivan Lucic and Sergeant Herbert Walker of the Bellington police. There's a young female constable with a voice recorder, but she doesn't rate a mention. Martin looks about and finds the ASIO officer from the motel car park lurking behind the media, smoking a cigarette. The man winks at Martin and, smirking, mouths: 'Top story.'

Detective Montifore begins. 'We can confirm that two sets of human remains, deceased remains, have been discovered in a farm dam on a property approximately twelve kilometres north-west of Riversend. The property has been designated a crime scene and media are requested not to attempt to access the property at this time. A preliminary search has found no evidence of additional bodies, but that will need to be confirmed by a more extensive and systematic search. I repeat, there is no evidence that there are more bodies out there, contrary to speculation in some sections of the media. The bodies are badly decomposed and we believe they have been there for some time. We are unable to make any positive identification as yet and identification of the deceased may take some days, even weeks. Police are taking this investigation very seriously, but at this early stage we are still collecting evidence at the scene. However, we have already established a number of leads and will be pursuing them vigorously. Questions?'

Doug Thunkleton's booming voice crashes through, drowning out the lesser inquiries of his rivals. 'You describe the property as a crime scene. What makes you certain there is not an innocent explanation for the bodies being there, like a drowning or Aboriginal remains?'

'Yes. We have definitive reasons to believe there has been foul play. I can't go into the details, but there is sufficient evidence to believe we are looking at homicide. Additionally, the remains are not from the distant past. Some articles of clothing, or remnants of clothing and personal effects, have been found. We are using these articles of clothing to help with identification but, as I said, that may take some time.'

Another voice, one of Doug's blonde rivals. 'Who discovered the bodies?'

'The owner of the property. His house and some other buildings were destroyed in a bushfire earlier this week. He was surveying the damage when he made the discovery. Newspaper reports that the remains were found by alternative individuals are not accurate.'

There's a small, smug chuckle from behind Martin.

'Is the property owner under arrest?'

'No.'

'Is he a suspect?'

'No. He is helping with inquiries, but no more than that. Again, media speculation that he is implicated in the killings has no basis in fact and is not sourced from the police.'

Another chuckle.

Doug Thunkleton again: 'Detective, there is also newspaper speculation linking Reverend Byron Swift to these latest murders. Is there any evidence to support that speculation?'

'Not at this stage. Thank you for that question. There is no substantive evidence to link him to these crimes. We'd be interested to hear from anyone with any evidence that does link the two tragedies.'

Another chuckle. Martin can feel his hackles rising, even as his colleagues continue to fire questions.

'Have the bodies been in the dam for more than a year?'

'We can't be sure, but that's possible.'

'Is it possible the bodies are those of the two German backpackers abducted in Swan Hill a year or so ago, as also mentioned in newspaper reports?'

'It's possible, but no more than that.'

Another chuckle.

Martin has had enough. 'Detective Inspector, why aren't the police capable of investigating this crime independently?'

'I don't follow your question. The police are confident we can move quickly to achieve a resolution of the investigation.'

'Then why is ASIO involved, and what is the nature of their involvement?'

This time there is no chuckle.

The detective is caught off guard. 'Um, yes. I'm not authorised . . . I'm not sure of the relevance . . . Ah, yes: I'm here to answer questions on behalf of the New South Wales Police Force. Nothing more.'

It's Martin's turn to chuckle. He looks behind him, but the intelligence officer is nowhere to be seen. A half-finished cigarette lies smouldering on the lawn.

———

'That was fucking terrific!' enthuses Sergeant Herb Walker. 'You shoulda seen the look on his face when you dropped him in it. Dumped his fag and scarpered.' He laughs at the memory, slapping his belly for emphasis. 'Total fire ban. Could've busted him then and there.' The Bellington sergeant has given Martin a lift after spotting him walking away from the services club.

Martin smiles. 'So he is ASIO?'

'Too right he is, superior cunt.'

'What's his name?'

'Goffing. Jack Goffing.'

'What's he doing here?'

'Fucked if I know. As far as I can see, he's not doing anything. Just sits in on interviews, monitors what we're doing, doesn't add anything or make suggestions. Just sits there like he's marking us. Montifore must know more, but he's not telling me.' Walker turns his four-wheel drive into the lane behind the Commercial Hotel and parks halfway along, away from prying eyes. He fishes a packet of cigarettes out of his top pocket and lights up. He leaves the engine going, air-conditioning pulsing, even as he opens his window and blows a stream of smoke out into the heat.

Martin is feeling lucky. Walker is in an expansive mood and obviously delighted Martin has blown the whistle on the ASIO agent. Martin waits until the policeman has taken another long drag on his cigarette before continuing. 'So what's the story with Harley Snouch? Are you going to charge him?'

'Not yet, but he's still in the frame. Lucic wanted to throw him in the can and sweat him but Montifore wants to give him enough rope to hang himself. "Slowly, slowly, catchy monkey."'

'What do you reckon?'

'Me? I'd be very fucking surprised if he wasn't implicated in one way or another. Don't quote me on any of this, by the way.'

'Of course not.'

'What's your angle for tomorrow, Martin? Got anything new?'

'We'll have all the routine stuff from the press conference et cetera, but I'm also doing a feature on Byron Swift and his shadowy past. Whether that was his real name or not.'

'Really?' says Walker. 'This day just gets better and better. What have you got?'

'Most of it's from you, Herb, to be honest. What you told me the other day. How he has no history in the church, suspicions he was a former soldier, the inscription on his gravestone, the suggestion that the real Byron Swift died in Cambodia of a smack overdose. Am I good to go with that?'

Walker takes a long toke of his cigarette as he considers. 'Sure. Just make sure you leave me out of it. Throw in a red herring or two if you can. Cite an ASIO source—that'd put the cat among the pigeons.'

'Maybe. What about the suggestion that he was being protected by someone, that attempts to investigate him by police before the shooting were thwarted?'

'Excellent. Right on the money. That's what that spine-less cunt Defoe should have written in the first place. Stir the possum. But for Christ's sake leave me out of it, Martin. Nothing that can be traced back to me, okay?'

'Absolutely. But there is one thing that intrigues me, something you might be able to help me with.'

'What's that?'

'The day of the shooting. I've spoken to people who say Swift was acting normal that morning at church, that he was outside chatting to people like nothing was the matter. Then he went inside for ten minutes or so and came out a different man, shooting people. It makes no sense.'

'You're telling me. Crazy fucker. Nothing about that morning makes sense.'

'Yeah, but what happened to him in those ten minutes? As far as I can make out he was alone in the church.'

'So? What are you driving at?'

'I'm guessing that he rang someone, and that's what triggered the shooting. Is that something that was followed up in the investigation?'

'I'd be surprised if it wasn't. In one sense it was an open-and-shut case—he shot five people in broad daylight in front of witnesses and then young Robbie shot him dead—so there wasn't that much to investigate. On the other hand, we all wanted to know why he did it. And there was massive public interest, plus pressure coming down from the pollies making sure their arses were covered. I'll tell you what I'll do, I'll see if I can find out. Montifore has all the files with him.'

'Why? Does he think there's a link with the bodies in the dam?'

'Yeah. We all do. Or we suspect it. Or at the very least we'd be stupid to discount it. Those girls disappeared just a few days before the shooting and wound up dead in a dam just outside Riversend. Might be a coincidence, but you'd be mad not to investigate possible links.'

'So it's definitely the German backpackers?'

'Yeah, not much doubt. The bodies aren't much more than skeletons, but we found bits of clothing, some of their belongings. They have to go through formal identification, dental and

DNA and all that shit, as well as doing the right thing by the relatives, but everyone knows it's them.'

'How did they die?'

'Shot through the head. We'll trawl the dam for bullets. If we can link them to Swift's guns, or to Snouch's, that'll be game over.'

'Right. But apart from the timing—the week before Swift went postal—and the location—close by Riversend—there is nothing substantial or conclusive linking Swift with the backpacker murders?'

'Well, nothing conclusive, that's for sure. But there is some new information.'

'Can you share it with me?'

'Let me have a think.' Walker draws on his cigarette, examines it, takes another long toke, then stubs it out on the outside of the door and drops the butt into the laneway. He issues one last stream of smoke through the window and then closes it. 'All right, you can write it, but pretend you discovered it all by yourself. No citing police sources or any of that shit. There's an old coot lives out there who reckons that Swift used to go out shooting in the Scrublands, rabbits and stuff, not that far from where the bodies were dumped. His name is William Harris. People call him Codger.'

'And that's new information?'

'Yeah.'

'How come that wasn't discovered after the church shooting?'

'Good question. As I told you, there were people protecting Swift while he was alive—and who wanted to protect him after he was dead. Anyway, I gotta get going. Where can I drop you?'

'At the bookstore. The Oasis. You know it?'

'Sure. What's happening there?'

'Good coffee.'

'Right. And that hornbag single mum, hey? Wouldn't mind a bit of that myself.'

Martin doesn't respond, and a moment later Herb Walker drops him right outside. 'Good on ya, Martin. I'll see about those phone calls. Just remember, leave me out of it. Give me a ring if you need anything.'

'Absolutely. And, Herb, thanks for your help. I really appreciate it.'

'No sweat, mate. Stir that possum hard.'

Martin jumps out of the four-wheel drive and watches Walker head off towards the highway and Bellington. He turns and mounts the footpath outside the bookstore, wondering how Codger Harris's information has only now reached the investigating officers and why Robbie Haus-Jones had withheld it. Was he part of the conspiracy Walker was alleging, to protect Byron Swift and cover his tracks?

Martin wonders about D'Arcy Defoe. The two have been rivals ever since joining the *Herald* as cadets together. They're like oil and water: D'Arcy in his tailored suits, Martin in his jeans; D'Arcy indulging in fine dining and finer wines on his expenses while Martin lives on takeaways; D'Arcy cultivating the top end of town and currying favour with management, Martin doing his best to ignore them. Their relationship is competitive, respectful and superficially friendly, and has remained so, even as their contemporaries have fallen away onto the editorial back-bench or been lured away by the money and family-friendly hours of public relations. They rose through the ranks together:

Defoe the wordsmith and Scarsden the newshound. There was an evening drinking wine in London when Defoe had declared there are two types of correspondents: 'frontline correspondents and chateau correspondents'. He didn't need to spell out how he saw their respective roles.

But Defoe has always been a good reporter. Martin can't believe he would willingly bury Walker's allegation of powerful people protecting Swift. More likely he'd held off on writing it, searching out confirmation from his high-level contacts in state parliament. That's another of their differences: D'Arcy is adept at playing the long game, storing away facts, leads and contacts only to bring them together weeks or months later in a big reveal. Martin is more like a bull at a gate, anxious to publish and move on to the next story. Perhaps Defoe has never been able to stand the allegations up? Or perhaps he will, now that the story is current once again. Perhaps he's already deploying his company credit card at Sydney's better restaurants, garnering information, preparing a splash to over-shadow Martin's anniversary profile on Riversend. Martin wouldn't put it past him.

The bookstore is open but empty. Martin walks up the aisle and pushes the swing door open. He sticks his head through. 'Hello?' he yells.

'Down here.' It's Mandy.

He finds her in the bathroom off the kitchen, giving her boy a bath. 'Hi there,' he says.

'Hi.'

'All right if I work out of your office again? The police gave a doorstop; I need to file.'

She takes a breath before answering. 'Sure. If you have to.' Permission granted, but her voice is grudging.

'Thanks, Mandy. We'll catch up later, okay?'

'Maybe not. Not tonight, Martin.' She is kneeling beside the bath, her back to him, hands supporting the boy.

'You okay?'

'Sure. Why wouldn't I be? But I've had a long day. I'm zonked.'

'Anything I can do?'

'Tell the truth.'

'What does that mean?'

'Byron. He didn't kill those girls.'

'You can't be sure of that.'

'You can't be sure he did.'

Martin doesn't know what to say. He can hear an edge to her voice, an edge of controlled anger. 'Maybe I should work from the motel.'

'Yeah. Maybe you should.'

twelve | **AN ALLEGORICAL TALE**

MARTIN SCARSDEN IS FEELING DECIDEDLY UNSETTLED AS HE WALKS DOWN HAY Road through the Sunday morning quiet. He heads towards the general store, past the soldier standing vigil outside the empty Commercial Hotel. He feels none of the exuberance or confidence of the previous morning, when the story seemed so obvious and his perspective so clear. He doesn't walk down the centre of the street; instead he hugs the shade of the shop awnings, haunted by doubts. Two backpackers are dead, dead a full year, found by Harley Snouch in his farm dam. The town priest, Byron Swift, and his five victims are also dead, dead and buried twelve months ago. But the rest is elusive. No one can definitively say why Swift shot Craig Landers and his mates in the Bellington Anglers Club, no one knows who killed the German backpackers or why, and no one knows if there is a connection between the two killings. Eight people shot dead and no answers. Or if there are answers, he doesn't know what they are, despite his front-page splashes. Maybe, instead of trying to figure it out by himself, he should be concentrating on those who know more than he does.

He's aware he's been lucky with Robbie Haus-Jones and Herb Walker; both have entrusted him with information they shouldn't be sharing with a journalist. Martin considers this. In Robbie's case, they've formed a bond, first through Martin saving the life of Jamie Landers and then through surviving the firestorm at Springfields together. But possibly through something else. Robbie was friends with Byron Swift and must still be coming to terms with shooting him dead on the church steps, while trying to work out in his own mind why his friend turned homicidal. And just a few weeks ago, Herb Walker had shared his suspicion that Swift was an imposter. Walker said that had rattled the constable.

Who does Robbie confide in? From whom does he draw solace and support? Not from Walker, that much seems clear. How does he bear up, all alone in this town, carrying that weight? As far as Martin knows, he has no partner, no family, no close friends. A real loner. Perhaps Robbie recognises in Martin a kindred spirit. Or maybe he hopes Martin can discover Swift's motivation and determine his real identity. Martin wonders what the constable will make of this morning's papers and his feature on the priest with no past.

Martin gets to the general store, but it's not yet open, despite it being well past nine o'clock. Martin checks the opening hours: 8 am Monday to Saturday, 9.30 am Sunday. Fair enough. He sits on a bench in the shade and waits.

Herb Walker's motivation seems easier to divine. A year ago he was master of all he surveyed, a big fish in a small pond. But then bigger fish from bigger ponds interfered with his investigation into allegations of child abuse against Byron Swift. And after the massacre at St James, he was relegated to being an adjunct to the investigation. So he spoke to D'Arcy Defoe, making sure the child abuse allegations were ventilated in public. Good for him. He didn't stop there, either; he started digging into Swift's past, eventually discovering he wasn't the real Byron Swift, only to hit a brick wall when he suggested the priest be exhumed. And now something similar is happening. Walker can hardly complain about the Sydney homicide detectives; he is, after all, a country cop. But the presence of the ASIO agent, Jack Goffing, must leave him feeling out of the loop, especially if Goffing isn't telling Walker why he's here, sniffing around his patch. Walker is protective of his fiefdom. It explains why he wants to talk to Martin.

Which brings Martin to Jack Goffing. What is ASIO doing here? Walker doesn't know. According to the Bellington cop, Goffing isn't actively investigating anything, he's simply monitoring the police. Martin wonders how Goffing and Montifore are getting along, if they're sitting around at night comparing notes and war-gaming strategies, or whether Montifore is as resentful as Walker. Perhaps Montifore might be willing to talk, if not about his investigation, then maybe about ASIO. Or could the cops have actually called on ASIO for assistance? That seems unlikely; there wouldn't be much the spooks could offer a homicide investigation, at least not this one. In any case,

Goffing arrived in Riversend two days ago, the same day the homicide cops choppered in. Most likely he flew in with them; Martin recalls the mud on the man's shoes and the charcoal on his shirt when he first encountered him in the Black Dog's car park, suggesting he'd been out at Springfields with Montifore, Lucic, Walker and the forensic investigators.

But why? The dead backpackers had been nineteen and twenty, middle-class German students travelling around Australia like so many other young foreigners. They'd come to the Murray to look for seasonal work picking fruit. There was absolutely nothing in their backgrounds, or in their deaths, to suggest any possible security threat to Australia. Besides, if Goffing had flown in with Montifore's team, the identity of the bodies wouldn't have been determined by then. The conclusion is inescapable: Goffing is in Riversend in case the bodies in the farm dam are linked in some way to Byron Swift's rampage at St James. But how? How were the killings at the church and the bodies in the dam connected? Did Swift kill the backpackers and then unleash his violence at the church? And what does the St James massacre have to do with national security? A disturbing thought: is Goffing here to uncover new information about the priest and his murderous spree, or is he here to suppress it? Is that what Walker thinks?

Martin's train of thought is interrupted by the arrival of Fran Landers. She parks her red station wagon with practised skill, reversing in quickly towards the curve before stopping just centimetres short. She gets out, scowls at Martin, then walks to the back of the car to retrieve the milk, paper and bread she has picked up in Bellington.

Martin stands up. 'Morning, Fran. Give you a hand?'

'No thanks, Martin. I think you've done enough.'

'How's that?'

'I don't just sell the papers. I read them as well.'

His feature on the mystery priest. Shit. He steps down from the gutter to stand beside her. 'Fran, I'm sorry, but it's what I do. It's my job to inform people what's happening. But if there's anything in that article that you think is wrong, then tell me. That's all I want to do: tell people what's happened.' Even to his own ears, it sounds ingratiating and insincere.

She regards him with animosity. 'Even if it hurts and harms those who have been hurt and harmed enough already?'

'Look, Fran, you know it's not like that. I found evidence that Byron Swift was an imposter, some former soldier only pretending to be Swift. I asked you about it, remember? Surely you understand I couldn't keep that quiet? It's a big story—people have the right to know.'

'If it's such a big story, why did you have to put in all that stuff about him having an affair?'

'Because it informs the readers what he was really like. Sure, I wrote that he was involved with a married woman, but I didn't say more than that. And it was down in the body of the article; the subs wanted it at the top. I could have named you, but I didn't.'

She looks at him with disgust. 'Well, thanks for nothing. And you still repeated all that rubbish about him being a paedophile. What a lot of garbage.'

'Is it? It was already all on the record. Surely you remember my paper making a big deal of it a year ago. And the police have told me that some boys—boys here in Riversend—confirmed that allegation to them.'

'What police? That fat dopey cop who was so busy persecuting Byron that he couldn't be bothered finding those poor girls?'

'What?'

'Sergeant Walker in Bellington.'

'Yeah, I know who you're talking about, but what do you mean about the girls? He couldn't possibly have known about them a year ago. Their bodies have only just been found. What are you talking about?'

Fran looks at him for a moment, obviously confused. 'Don't you read your own stories?'

'What?' It's Martin's turn to look confused.

Fran leans into the back of the car and retrieves a newspaper, *The Sunday Age*, and hands it to Martin. There's no missing the headline screaming across the front page: COPS IGNORED MURDER TIP-OFF. The story is accompanied by a colour photo of two pretty girls at a cafe table, toasting the camera with broad smiles. The two German backpackers. The by-line hits him in the guts. *By Bethanie Glass, Senior Police Reporter, and Martin Scarsden in Riversend*. Shit. This time, the red EXCLUSIVE stamp incites dismay, not pride.

New South Wales Police ignored information received within days of the disappearance of two German backpackers that the two young women had been murdered and their bodies dumped in a Riverina farm dam.

The anonymous tip was received by Crime Stoppers and passed on to local police in the Murray River town of Bellington, but a search of the dam was never conducted.

A source close to Crime Stoppers has confirmed the tip-off was received three days after German backpackers Heidi Schmeikle and Anna Brün were seen getting into a blue sedan in Swan Hill, and two days before Riversend priest Byron Swift went on a murderous rampage, shooting dead five locals.

Bellington police officer Sergeant Herbert Joseph Walker offered no comment when contacted by . . .

There's more. Much more. But Martin can't bring himself to read it. *Herbert Joseph Walker.* Shit a brick. The use of the policeman's full name was no subeditor's slip; Bethanie had deliberately used it knowing it is the form typically used to identify criminals appearing before a court. Walker would know that too.

Martin turns to Fran Landers, who has been watching his reaction with interest. 'Fran, can I use your phone? It's important.'

Fran nods, perhaps sensing his desperation, fetches her keys from the ignition and unlocks the door of the general store. Martin rushes to the counter and picks up the phone.

'Thanks for giving us a hand,' says Fran, carrying in the newspapers and spreading them out on the low flat areas before the magazine racks, but Martin ignores her sarcasm. He has his notebook out, dialling Walker's office number, but is put through to an answering machine.

'Herb. It's Martin Scarsden. I am so sorry about the story in today's paper. I promise, I didn't know. It was my colleague,

Bethanie Glass. She got it from her sources in Sydney. I'll try your mobile. Hope to talk soon.'

'Shit. Shit, shit, shit,' he mutters to himself as he dials the mobile number.

The call goes straight to voicemail. Martin is forced to repeat his awkward message of denial.

'Shit,' he says to himself, hanging up. He addresses the shop-keeper, who is lugging another load in from the car. 'Thanks for that, Fran. I've gotta run. We'll talk. I'll make it up to you somehow. Promise.'

'Yeah, sure,' she says as he rushes past her and out the door.

Doug Thunkleton and his camera crew are draped over the old armchairs inside the Oasis, drinking coffee and reading the papers, when Martin pushes through the door. One of the camera guys has Liam out of the playpen and is bouncing him up and down on his knee, making vastly stupid faces and eliciting gurgles of joy from the boy.

'Here he is,' says Doug enthusiastically, 'the man of the moment.'

'Hi, Doug,' replies Martin flatly. 'Where'd you get the papers?'

'Bellington. We're in the Riverside Resort and Spa. Swimming pool, bar, wireless. Mobile reception. And there's some okay restaurants down there. You should move down. It's only a forty-minute drive.'

'I'll think about it. Thanks for the tip. Is Mandy about, the owner?'

'Out the back, making toasties. You just missed the coppers. They were just in getting coffee.'

'Bugger. Did they say anything? They doing another doorstop?'

'No, didn't say a lot. Not overly impressed with your piece, though.'

'I guess not.'

'Yeah, well fuck 'em,' says Doug casually, oozing journalistic solidarity. 'We're not here to help. It's a top story. I wish I'd got it. My people are very revved up.'

'Yeah, I can imagine. Did Walker say anything?'

'The Bellington cop? No. I asked him for an interview. You know, giving him the opportunity to put his side of the story. He just looked at me like I was some kind of turd. The old story: when the cops want publicity, they tip us off, but when they fuck up, they brush us off.'

'Always the way,' says Martin, wondering if he should wait for Mandy or go out the back to find her.

'Say, Martin,' says Doug, 'you got time for a quick interview? Your story is driving the news cycle. We could get it out of the way before the day gets messy.'

The last thing Martin wants is to be seen gloating about Bethanie's scoop on television; nothing would piss Walker off more. 'Maybe later on, Doug. There's a few things I need to check out. The story may have moved on by this evening.'

'Really?' says Doug, news antenna twitching. 'You got more coming?'

'We've always got more coming,' says Martin, regretting his smart-arse tone even as he speaks. What is it about these TV types that gets up his nose so much?

The situation is saved by Mandy emerging from the back room carrying toasted sandwiches in brown paper bags. Doug Thunkleton pays, making sure to collect the receipt from Mandy, then distributes the bags to his crew. The camera guy gently returns Liam to his pen.

'We'd better get going,' says Doug. 'Lot to do. Got a few strong leads of my own to follow up. Might catch you later.'

The television team departs, leaving Martin and Mandy in the silence of the bookstore.

'Busy morning,' says Martin.

'Busy morning,' says Mandy. 'Sold a lot of coffee.' Her manner is distant, her smile absent, but at least the quiet anger of the past day or two seems to have dissipated. Perhaps she's accepted he has little choice but to report the story. 'There's a lot of messages for you. Your Sydney journo, Bethanie, left at least half-a-dozen.'

'This morning?'

'Yesterday afternoon and evening. She didn't find you?'

'No. She must have been calling me about today's story.'

'Yeah, I saw it. That slimy TV reporter showed me. That fat cop left a message for you too. They were in for coffee a moment ago. Here.' She gives Martin a piece of folded paper.

Martin takes the paper, opens it up, reads the message: *Fuck you too pal.*

'Not good?' asks Mandy.

'Not good.' He shows her the note, provoking a small smile.

'Couldn't have said it better myself,' she says.

'Yeah, thanks for that.'

'Your story in the paper—it's all wrong.'

'About Walker? It's not my story; it's all Bethanie's work.'

'Not that story.'

'My feature on Swift? What's wrong with it? He *was* a man without a past. And the allegation about preying on children is on the public record and the cops have confirmed it.'

'No. Not that.' Mandy is looking at him calmly, without rancour.

'What then?'

'You all but convict him of killing those girls, the backpackers.'

'That's what the police believe. It's in the article. They say he used to go shooting out in the Scrublands.'

'Yes. That's true.'

'You knew that?'

There's a silence in the bookstore. Martin can hear the tinkling of the water feature on the counter, the slow movement of the ceiling fan. Liam is silent. Mandy is looking at Martin expectantly.

'Mandy, tell me.'

'Byron didn't kill those girls, Martin.'

'So you said yesterday. How can you be so sure?'

'I've checked. That night they were taken, down in Swan Hill, he was here, with me. All night.'

'Christ. You and Byron Swift?' Martin's mind spins, recalibrating, accommodating this unexpected information. 'Are you sure? About the timing, I mean?'

'Yes. I wrote it down. I keep a diary. Sorry.'

'Sorry? Why sorry?'

'Your story. It's wrong again.'

She's right, of course. The day before Martin had all but convicted Harley Snouch and today he has all but convicted Byron Swift. But his immediate concern is for her, not his inaccurate reporting. He takes the few short steps to bridge the gulf between them and puts his hands on her shoulders, half anticipating she will push him away. Instead, she moves closer, allowing him to embrace her. And for a moment that's enough. But only for a moment.

'You know we can't keep this to ourselves, don't you?' he says.

She nods. 'Will you write about it?'

'I'll have to. But first, we need to tell the police. They're working on the theory that Byron Swift was involved in the murder.'

'I guess you're right. I don't have to show them my diary, though, do I?'

'I imagine so. Why not? Are there things you don't want them to read?'

'Yes. Of course.'

'Illegal things?'

'No. Just private things.'

'There are eight people shot dead. They're going to want to see it.'

The discussion is abruptly interrupted—two journalists and a photographer barge into the store, demanding coffee. Martin asks Mandy permission to use the phone. She nods and starts on the coffees as he makes his way back to the office. He rings Bethanie on her mobile. She picks up on the third ring.

'Martin? Is that you?'

'Yeah, it's me.'

'Did you see the story? I was trying to get hold of you all yesterday afternoon and evening. Didn't you get any of my messages?'

'No. I didn't. My fault, but I wish I'd known in advance.'

There's a pause before Bethanie speaks. 'Martin, I'm sorry—if he was one of your sources, I mean. But Max made the call, said we couldn't sit on it.'

'Understood. I should have been checking for messages.'

'Are you still staying at the Black Dog?'

'Yeah. I must have been out walking.'

'Right. Got a better offer, hey?' And she laughs. 'Who's that cute Melbourne snapper again?'

'Yeah, I wish. Listen, we've got a few problems. I've just got hold of some new information that appears to rule out Byron Swift being involved in the killing of the backpackers. Or at least it clears him from being part of their abduction.'

'Shit. Is that from the cops? They're still talking to you?'

'No. It's not from the cops. I'm going to have to tell them, though.'

'What's the problem then?'

'Just the small issue of my article this morning all but convicting Swift of topping the girls.'

'How's that a problem? The guy's dead; he's not going to sue. Plus, he did put five people into an early grave. Go tell the cops and we have our yarn for tomorrow.' Bethanie adopts a mock newsreader voice. 'The *Herald* is again leading the investigation into the murder of two German backpackers in the Riverina, supplying police with vital new evidence,' she says, before returning to her normal voice. 'Just don't tell them until late today, okay? They've got the shits with us; we don't want them handballing it to the competitors.'

Martin can't help but laugh. 'Yeah, good point. I just hate getting it wrong, that's all. Max too. You know what a stickler he is.'

'Yeah, well, on that score I've got good news and bad news.'

'That sounds ominous. What gives?'

'It's like this: on the good side of the ledger, the researchers have been digging away on our behalf. We've spoken to someone who knew the real Byron Swift in Cambodia and says it's not the same person. Your man without a past story is right on the money. That's one of the reasons I was trying to contact you yesterday evening. I'm not sure if you noticed, but we inserted a few pars into your feature, firming it up.'

'Thanks for that. Much appreciated. What's the bad news?'

'The researchers have found no record of a Harley James Snouch ever being charged or convicted or arrested or investigated for rape, not in the past thirty years. Nothing in the court records, nothing in the newspaper archives. In fact, no record of him being convicted of anything. Not in New South Wales or Victoria. We're looking at Queensland and South Australia.'

'Christ, are they sure? He's got prison tats, for God's sake. We've more or less accused him of murdering the girls when the cops haven't charged him, and we've described him as an alleged rapist. Does Max know?'

'Yeah. He's crawling up the wall. You don't want to talk to him.'

'But I told Max at the time that Snouch denied the conviction.'

'Really? You sure? Max told us Snouch had denied the rape, not the conviction.'

'What?'

'I'm sure. He said we were safe to go with it, just to make sure we said alleged until we could confirm it was rape and not sexual assault or something else.' There's a pause before Bethanie speaks again. 'Sounds like you two had your wires crossed.'

Martin feels a hollowness in his core. It looks like he's not only got his facts wrong, but has somehow made Max complicit in his error.

'Fuck it. Hose him down, will you? Snouch has lived with these allegations for years without taking legal action. Shit. And see if you can soften Max up for the next instalment: he's not going to be overjoyed when we put Byron Swift in the clear over the backpackers.'

'Leave him to me, Martin. As long as the *Herald* is leading the way, he'll be fine.'

'Yeah, maybe.'

'Anything else?'

'One thing: your story, the Crime Stoppers tip-off. I assume you got your info from the Sydney cops?'

'That's right. Covering their arses, no doubt. Making sure any blame fell on Walker, not them.'

'Do you know who they are?'

'No. It came through police PR.'

'So an authorised drop, from the hierarchy? Trying to discredit Walker?'

'Probably. But that's strictly between you and me, okay? I can't afford to piss them off.'

'Of course not.'

'Okay. And let's make sure we keep each other up to date from now on.'

'Too right. I'll touch base later in the day. This lack of mobile coverage is starting to give me the shits.'

'Tell me about it.'

They talk for a bit longer, making sure of phone numbers and times to call, then hang up.

Back in the store, the journalists are paying for their coffees. Martin waits for them to leave before speaking. 'You okay?' he asks Mandy.

'Yep. I'll be fine. They told me the police are working out of the Riversend station today, calling in people for interviews. There are TV crews and photographers set up outside.'

'Who are they talking to? Did anyone say?'

'Yeah. People who live out in the Scrublands. Checking if they saw anything.' She pauses briefly, biting her lip. 'Can we leave it until a bit later before we talk to the cops? I don't want to go over while the TV crews are there.'

'Sure,' says Martin, feeling first relief—he and Bethanie don't want her interviewed until later either—and then feeling like a heel for thinking of himself at Mandy's time of need. 'If they're still around later, I'll go by myself, ask the police to visit you over here. Tell them you're looking after Liam.' Martin looks at the boy, lying on his back on the floor, playing with his own hands as if they're toys. Less than a year old. *Christ. Mandy and Byron?* 'Mandy, did Fran know about you and Byron?'

'Yep.'

'And did you know about him and Fran?'

'Yep.'

'Jeez.' Maybe he should think beyond his feature; there has to be a book in this. What a town: either screwing each other or shooting each other. No wonder the population is in freefall. Martin dismisses his thoughts as unworthy. 'I didn't realise that you and Byron Swift were so, you know, intimate. My story today, that he wasn't who he claimed to be, that he was a former soldier, does that ring true to you?'

She nods, looking none too happy as she says, 'Yeah, I guess.'

'Did you know?'

'No. I mean, I guessed he'd been in the military. He had some tattoos. But I didn't know anything about a false identity. I thought Byron Swift was his real name. Are you sure that it wasn't?'

'Pretty sure. We've been able to confirm the real Byron Swift died in Cambodia.'

'Good God. Do you think that's got something to do with why he did it? Shot those men outside the church?'

'I don't know. Maybe.'

They stand in silence then, overtaken by their own thoughts. Martin is imagining Mandy falling under Swift's spell, sleeping with him, knowing that he was also sleeping with Fran Landers. What must Mandy think of Swift now, knowing he was deceiving them both, pretending to be someone he wasn't? Evidently her regard for him endures: she's still willing to defend him, to show her diary to the police, to clear Swift of abducting the backpackers. Is she still in love with him?

'How do you feel about that?' asks Martin. 'That he was an imposter?'

Her forehead furrows, her lower lip quivers, her eyes reveal pain. She shakes her head, as if in disbelief. 'Not good,' is all she says.

Martin takes her hands in his, a gesture of sympathy and support. 'Believe me, I want to work it out, find out why he shot those men. You were right, that first day when I came to Riversend: it would be a hell of a story. Will you help me?'

She nods, her face serious. 'Yes. If I can.'

'Okay. Let's sit down. I'll record it.'

'Of course. You want to do it before the police start questioning me, don't you?'

Martin wonders if his motives are so transparent. 'Yes.'

'Will you write about Byron and me? Byron and Fran? Please don't. If not for my sake, for Liam's.'

Martin looks again at the baby. 'Mandy, is Byron Liam's father?'

She looks up, meets his gaze, unapologetic. 'Yes. But please, Martin, whatever you do, please don't write that. You can't write that. Liam doesn't deserve to be branded with his father's sins. Promise me that and I'll help you.' The look on her face is so sincere, her words so heartfelt, that Martin agrees. How could he not?

They're interrupted again. A radio reporter after coffee. Mandy serves her and then posts the closed sign on the door and locks it. 'Okay, let's get on with it.'

Martin feels torn. Part of him wants to protect her, to shield her and her son; another part wants to interrogate her, to extract what she knows and write the story of the Lothario priest cutting a romantic swathe through the lonely hearts of the

Riverina. It would elevate an already remarkable story to a sensational one. Just add sex and stir. A younger Martin wouldn't have hesitated; he'd have written it all: named Mandy and Fran, revealed Liam as Byron Swift's illegitimate son. He could still do it; by the time the anniversary story went to press he would have left Riversend far behind. He can picture his triumphal re-entry into the newsroom, admired by his colleagues and celebrated by his editors. His career would be back on track; there might even be awards and pay rises. But at what price? The emotional destruction of Fran Landers and Mandalay Blonde. He looks at the baby boy playing happily on his rug, eyes twinkling, and knows he won't do it. Max Fuller's go-to correspondent has gone. Gone for good. There are worse things than being trapped in a car boot.

'What is it?' asks Mandy, sensing his disquiet.

Martin shakes his head. 'Nothing. It doesn't matter. But listen, if I'm going to report this to the public, give an accurate depiction of Byron Swift or whoever he was, how can I leave out that he conducted simultaneous affairs with women in the district? I've already reported he was having an affair with a married woman. I'm going to have to refer to it in some fashion. I won't mention you or Fran by name, and I won't mention Liam at all—I'll put in some obfuscation, like you live in Bellington or something, but I can't see any way around it. What do you think?'

Mandy smiles, an unexpected reaction. 'That's fine. If you can do it like that, then you should include it. Absolutely.'

'Really? Are you sure? I thought you didn't want me to mention it?'

'I don't want you to use our names, but of course you should include it. Don't you see? This was a man who was having regular sex. With me, with Fran, with God knows who else. Does that sound like a paedophile to you? Have you ever heard of a child molester who was so obsessed with women? Who could sustain relationships with grown women? I'm almost thirty; Fran is in her forties.'

Martin returns her smile; his dilemma resolved. 'Point taken. I might use that in my piece.'

'Yes. You should.'

They sit in the armchairs near the front of the bookstore. Martin sets his recorder app going, places his phone atop a pile of books on one of the tables and takes up his notebook, although he suspects Mandy has already imparted her most important information. Mandy scoops up Liam and settles him on her lap, perhaps more for her comfort than her son's.

'Tell me about him, Mandy. What was he really like?'

'Dreamy. At his best he was fun, considerate, charismatic. You just wanted to be with him.'

'Charismatic? That's something.' She's used the term before, so has Robbie Haus-Jones.

'Yeah, but different. Charisma makes you like a person; Byron made you like yourself. Does that make sense? You know, the drought was terrible, and having him in the town, even if only for a day or two a week, made us all feel better. He and Robbie were running the youth centre. I remember how it gave Mum a real lift. She said it was proof that there were still good men in the world.'

Martin shifts a little in his seat. After the charismatic priest and his good works, what could Mandy possibly see in a shell-shocked hack like himself? 'You say that was him at his best. Does that mean there was another side to him?'

'I think so. To be honest, he was very self-centred. I don't mean in an egotistical way. I mean that when he was with you, you had all of him. It was like you were the centre of his universe. He made you feel so special. But when I wasn't with him, I don't think he spared me a second thought. It was his great charm and his great weakness. He lived in the moment, or so it seemed to me.'

'Was he ever violent?'

'No, not towards me.'

'Towards anyone?'

'Possibly.'

'What does that mean?'

'He beat up Craig Landers.'

Martin stops writing. 'What? Why?'

'You'd have to ask Fran.'

'Craig found out? Confronted him?'

'I don't know. Ask Fran.'

'So he beat him up? Her husband? That must have humiliated Craig even further.'

'I guess so.'

'Doesn't sound very priestly.'

'No. I remember Byron felt bad about it. Spent a lot of time praying after he did it, asking for forgiveness.'

'That's interesting; he prayed afterwards. So he was religious then? It wasn't an act?'

'Oh no, he was religious all right. Devout. More than devout—pious. He would stop every now and then, close his eyes, bow his head and say a few words. Just like that. He never tried to convert me. He wasn't a proselytiser. He said God would find me when the time was right; that a life without faith is a life only half lived. He told me God was with him all the time, in actions great and small, that it made him who he was, that it centred him. Those were his words: it centred him. He had a tattoo, here, on his chest, a crucifix—on his heart.'

Martin frowns. 'He sounds like Jekyll and Hyde. One minute he's the pious priest, caring for his flock and looking after the local kids. The next he's drinking, smoking dope and screwing around. And shooting things.'

Mandy is shaking her head even before he's finished speaking. 'No. That's wrong. He wasn't a split personality. He was the same calm, assured person whether he was praying or whether we were getting drunk and screwing. Can you believe that?'

'To be honest, not really. He sounds too good to be true.'

'Maybe he was.'

'You were in love with him?'

'Yes. I was. I knew he wasn't about to marry me, though, or acknowledge me as his partner or anything like that.'

Martin feels unsettled, her declaration of love for Swift so certain, so matter-of-fact. 'And that doesn't bother you? That he wasn't in love with you?'

'No. I mean, I know he didn't love me exclusively, but I think he did have love for me.'

'And with Fran Landers and who knows who else?'

'Yes. Does that bother *you*, Martin?'

He squirms a little at that. 'I guess it does. He was either a complete charlatan or the most saintly man who ever lived.'

Mandy doesn't reply, just looks him directly in the eye. He holds her gaze. What is it he sees there? Defiance? Doubt? He pauses then, trying to nail down in his own mind what Swift must have been like, but finds the man elusive, hard to define.

'Didn't it strike you as incongruous? Here he is, preaching love for all living things, tolerance and forgiveness, and then he's out killing things, shooting animals in the Scrublands. Did you challenge him about it?'

Mandy doesn't say anything for a full ten seconds, just looks deep into Martin's eyes. He doesn't flinch, returning her gaze steadily. Eventually she speaks, quietly, her voice barely above a whisper, as if in confessional. 'He said that it made him feel closer to God, to nature, that it was praying with his body as well as with his mind and soul. He said it was a kind of meditation, a religious experience. He said it made him feel one with himself and one with the universe.'

Mandy bows her head into her hands. Martin looks at her, feeling a chill go up his spine, the hairs on the back of his neck standing stiff. He recalls the story Mandy had recounted to him the day he arrived in Riversend, telling him she'd fallen pregnant in Melbourne, that Swift had saved her life. It was a total fabrication.

'Mandy, did he know you were pregnant?'

'Yes. He called in here the morning of the shooting, before he went to the church. He told me he was leaving, right after the service. That the bishop had ordered him to leave. So I told him, said I wanted to go with him. But he said I couldn't, it wasn't possible.'

'Did he say why not?'

'No. Maybe it had something to do with him not really being Byron Swift, but I didn't know about that until today.'

'And you accepted that? That you couldn't go with him?'

'I didn't have much choice.'

'And how was he? Was there any indication of what he was about to do?'

'None.'

Martin pauses, trying to assimilate this wash of new information. It corroborates what the boy Luke said, that he saw Swift's car at the bookstore.

'Fran saw Byron at the church a little later. She says that he asked her to wait for him out at Blackfellas Lagoon. She seems to believe they were going to leave together.'

'More like he didn't want her to witness what he was about to do.'

'Maybe. You don't think it's possible that he would have taken her with him?'

Her features, so impassive a moment before, grow agitated as Martin's insinuation, that Swift favoured Fran. 'No. Why would he have taken her and not me? I was having his baby.'

There is silence as Mandy composes herself. Martin tries to imagine what was going through the young priest's mind that fateful morning. He'd been accused of molesting children by Herb Walker. So he'd either decided to leave town or had been instructed to go; he was either fleeing from the allegations of abuse or from the fear an investigation would uncover his impersonation of Byron Swift. Was he planning to move elsewhere, drop the Byron Swift identity and reinvent himself as someone else? That would certainly explain why he didn't want to take Mandy with him. But what of Fran?

'Mandy, that story you spun me when I first got here, about Liam's father being some abusive arsehole, what was that?'

She sighs. 'I couldn't tell you the truth. You must realise that. I didn't know you; I'd just met you. You were just another journo hungry for a story. You would have splashed it all over that horrid rag of yours. Made it all dirty and ugly when it wasn't like that at all. I was here after the shooting. I remember the journalists exaggerating any little thing, blowing them out of context. I saw what drives you. You think I'd visit all of that on my son?'

'So why tell me anything at all?'

'Because I wanted your help. I wanted you to find out who he really was. Why he did it.'

'To find out who he really was? So you had guessed that Byron wasn't really his name?'

'No, not that. But there were his tattoos, indications he'd been in the armed forces. And all the contradictions in his personality and how he led his life. Once he was dead and I had Liam, I wanted to know more about him. I thought I might persuade you to find out for me.'

'Persuade? How about manipulate?'

She's growing testy again, unhappy at being challenged. 'Use whatever word you like.'

'And that story about getting pregnant from a one-night stand in Melbourne, you made it all up on the spot, just like that?'

'Of course not. It's what I've told people in the town ever since I got pregnant. I didn't want them to know Byron was Liam's dad.'

'Why not?'

'What do you think? I went through shit as a kid because my father was a rapist; how would Liam fare if the whole world believed his father was a homicidal maniac?'

The rape. Martin can see the passion in her face, see her love and her conviction. But she's about to be interviewed by the police; he might not get another chance for some time. He swallows, pushes on.

'Mandy. The allegation of rape against Harley Snouch. We can't find any record of it. The researchers have been scouring the archives. It looks like there was no conviction.'

She looks shocked, eyes wide with disbelief, before certainty returns. 'It doesn't mean it's not true.'

'No, it doesn't.' He tries to pitch his words as sympathetically as possible. 'You don't think it's possible your mother made it up?'

'Fuck no. Why would she do that?'

'I don't know. Maybe she had good reason. The first time we met, you spun me a story to protect Liam, about you contemplating suicide, Byron saving you, touching your soul.'

'But that's all true in it's own way—I *was* lost before I met him. It's like an allegorical tale.'

thirteen THE HOTEL

MARTIN SITS IN MANDALAY BLONDE'S OFFICE, TRYING TO WRITE, BUT MAKING no progress. The daily story is only half written and his feature on Riversend's attitude towards its homicidal priest taunts him from the screen. He's feeling a swelling anger, a deep anti-pathy towards Byron Swift. A murderer, possibly a paedophile, and certainly a serial exploiter of vulnerable women. Could anyone be more susceptible to seduction than Mandy Blonde, marooned in Riversend caring for her dying mother? Telling poor Fran Landers to wait out at Blackfellas Lagoon when he had no intention of taking her away; telling Mandy, newly pregnant, that she couldn't leave with him. And that was just in Riversend. How many more women had he preyed upon down in Bellington? How many more had he impregnated and abandoned in other country towns? Was that the sordid secret behind his assumed identity: fleeing a series of paternity claims? And yet, even now, the women, the victims, defend him. Jesus wept. What did Swift tell himself: was he honest enough to admit to his predations, or did he rationalise them as giving comfort and succour to those who needed them?

Again Martin is forced to consider his own behaviour: sleeping with Mandy when he has no more intention of taking her out of this town than Byron Swift ever did. And in an hour or two, he'll walk down to the police station and drop her in it. Her diary, her relationship, her boy. No wonder he can't concentrate; the urgency of the daily story, the biggest story in the country, is upon him, yet he can't progress until he informs the police about the diary. He thinks of Mandy, so beautiful and so vulnerable, condemned to become entangled with the Byron Swifts and Martin Scarsdens of this world. Eventually he's had enough of staring at the laptop screen and decides to get out and about.

Outside the heat is waiting. It no longer comes as an affront or a surprise, merely an accepted constant, bearing down like the weight of existence, all that he deserves. He walks in the shade of the shop awnings towards the crossroads where the bronze soldier stands impervious. Two grizzled bikies roar slowly past on their guttural machines, acknowledging no one. A car moves along Somerset Street, heading west, past the soldier, past the bank, moving slowly before coming to a stop, the driver executing a reverse angle park across the road from the police station, joining a number of others. Martin can see a huddle of media gathered in the shade of a tree opposite the station. He'd been thinking of walking down there himself, checking it out, but now he considers turning right and going to the services club for something to eat.

Undecided on which way to turn, he does neither. Instead, he pulls out his all-but-useless mobile phone and takes a photo of the digger on his pedestal. He looks about him. The soldier, standing atop his column, constitutes the centre of Riversend. Looking down at him from behind, from its prime position at the crossroads, is the Commercial Hotel, its facade as fresh as on the day it closed. Across Hay Road from the pub is the Bendigo Bank, and diagonally opposite the Commercial is the red-brick solidity of the old council chambers. The soldier is facing the chambers. The other corner is taken by Jennings Dry Goods, closed on this Sunday morning. Martin walks over and peers through the windows. Clothes, hardware, household goods, small electrical appliances, some toys: everything except food and perishables.

An idea is forming in Martin's mind. Somewhere in his feature there may be room for a descriptive passage on Riversend, capturing the town's decline. It could start here at the crossroads, with the memorial to dead soldiers and the bankrupt pub, then proceed down Hay Road, past the op shop's sad window, past the closed hair salon, to arrive at the wine saloon, with its forlorn interior and its dusty ghosts. Martin walks out from under Jennings' awning into the glare of the midday sun. God it's hot. He quickly takes a photo of Jennings, noticing that above the awning, on the rendered facade below the peaked roof, JENNINGS DRY GOODS 1923 is written in raised letters. Brilliant. He makes a mental note to return on a working day to interview the latest generation of the Jennings family.

He looks at the Bendigo Community Bank on the other side of the intersection and is rewarded by a similar revelation. It's a solid building rendered with concrete, the architrave of its entrance dressed in stone. The building carries the russet and gold livery of the franchise, but above the awning, wrought-iron lettering spells out its origins: THE COMMERCIAL BANK OF AUSTRALIA LTD. The bank is still operating only because locals have formed a community bank under the Bendigo umbrella; the big banks can no longer extract sufficient profit out here.

Martin captures more images; more grist to his mill. He crosses Somerset Street to the council chambers, set slightly back from the street on a large block of land. This time it's a plaque that tells the story: *This building housed the Riversend Council Chambers from 1922 until 1982, when the council was merged into Bellington Shire Council. Unveiled 12 June 1991 by Errol Ryding, Last Mayor of Riversend.* A wry smile and more photos. A sign on the door communicates the building's current purpose: RIVERSEND ART GALLERY AND STUDIO. OPEN TUESDAY AND THURSDAY MORNINGS 9 AM–1 PM. Martin imagines walls covered in gum-tree paintings, shelves of brown-glazed pottery and hand-spun wool, all gathering dust. As a nod to its municipal past, there's a community noticeboard attached to the wall by the door. He reads a council notice setting out draconian water restrictions, a homemade flyer for the Black Dog Motel, a fly-spotted note advertising babysitting services from someone called Gladys Creek. The bottom of the ad has Gladys's phone number repeated on thin fingers of paper designed to be ripped off by prospective customers. None have been taken. Martin collects another photograph. There are a couple of lost pets: a collie called Lassie and a moggy called Mr Puss, both with photos. The owner of Mr Puss is offering a small reward for the cat's return. There are ads for old cars, for a harvesting contractor; a note that the footy team, having missed the finals, will resume practice in March on the primary school oval.

Martin returns to the middle of the intersection, looking again at the bronze soldier. He rather likes the pose. The soldier does not appear heroic. He's not gazing off at some far horizon, towards some glittering future. Instead, his head is bowed, eyes directed downwards, mourning his fallen comrades. Martin steps back a few paces, captures a couple more shots of the memorial, with the old pub in the background.

He's putting his phone back in his pocket when a movement catches his eye, up on the wraparound verandah of the Commercial. He focuses, trying to shield his eyes from the sun. Yes. Movement. A flash of colour, someone in a checked shirt, yellow and black, a fleeting impression as the person moves off the verandah and into the building. Someone is in the old pub. Martin chuckles; maybe Snouch has moved in, qualifying for the front bar at last.

Martin crosses the remainder of the intersection and gains the shade under the verandah. The main door on the corner is locked and padlocked. Above the door is the obligatory sign: THE COMMERCIAL HOTEL. AVERY FOSTER. HOTELIER LICENCE NO. 225631. A red CLOSED notice hangs in the window of the door; no doubt there's a green OPEN sign on its reverse side. Martin walks beside the pub, stopping to press his face to the window, using his hands binocular-style to reduce the glare from the street. He can make out the front bar, with tables and chairs near the window and stools by the bar. There are no bottles behind the bar, but inverted glasses are still arrayed along some shelves. Apart from the missing bottles, it looks as if the place has been shut for the weekend, ready to reopen come Monday. Martin wonders if Avery Foster's licence is still active or whether it's been sold off to some suburban beer barn.

It occurs to Martin he's distracting himself, wasting time, delaying the walk to the police station and the inevitable confrontation with Herb Walker. Nevertheless, he continues. There's a service lane running along the back of the pub, extending the whole block between Somerset Street and Thames Street, where Herb Walker had parked momentarily the day before. Martin walks down the lane to where the fence ends in a pair of five-bar steel gates, chained shut. The gates prevent vehicle entry to a small gravel car park behind the pub, enough for three or four cars. There's a low porch devoid of handrail: a delivery platform designed for reversing trucks. There's a stack of wooden pallets, blue paint faded and peeling. And a car, one rear tyre flat, the other on its way down. He wonders if the closure of the pub might have been a sudden thing, its owner taken ill, leaving his car behind, the hotel left largely untouched.

Martin can see the swing doors to the old cellar, and a wooden stairway leading up to the accommodation on the top floor. He climbs over the waist-high gates, moving as quickly as possible to keep contact with the scalding metal to a minimum. He mounts the concrete stairs onto the delivery platform, finding the door locked. He doesn't bother trying the cellar doors; the padlock looks resolute enough. He climbs down from the platform and walks over to the stairs and starts ascending, past a sign: STRICTLY HOTEL GUESTS ONLY. The green paint on the handrails has wrinkled and bubbled under the solar assault, and Martin keeps his hands to himself.

At the top there is a short landing and a door, its upper half a window. There's a hole punched in the bottom left-hand corner of the window near the handle. Martin tries the door. It's unlocked, opening outwards. Inside, his feet crunch on broken glass as he pauses to allow his eyes to adjust. He's in a short passage, running into another corridor about five metres in front of him. At a guess, the passage between the door and corridor separates two hotel rooms. The air smells stale and musty. Martin moves to the junction with the other passageway. The main corridor is lined by the doors of the hotel rooms, left open with sunlight spilling through them. To the left the corridor goes only a few metres before ending in a closed door with the word PRIVATE in old-fashioned gold paint. The door boasts three serious-looking locks: private indeed. Martin surmises it's the owner's apartment. He walks along, tries the door. It's locked.

Back the other way the doors on the left open onto hotel rooms. At the end of the corridor, where it turns ninety degrees to the right, there is another open door, leading into the best room in the hotel, the corner room. There's a double bed, a washbasin and a small desk, and the room has its own set of French doors opening onto the verandah. Someone has been sleeping on the bare mattress of the bed; there are blankets bundled at its end and an ashtray full of butts on the bedside table. On the floor, next to an empty bourbon bottle, there's a scattering of pornographic magazines. Martin picks one up; he didn't think they still existed in this digital age. There's nothing subtle about the imagery. It's brutal, mechanical, emotionless, the flat lighting leaving nothing to the imagination. He wonders if they belong to the person in the checked shirt.

Exiting the room, Martin follows the corridor around its right-angle corner. It opens out a little where thickly carpeted stairs with brass runners head down on the right to a landing, from where they must continue back towards the front of the hotel. Opposite the stairs a wide passage leads to the verandah. There's an ornate dresser on one side of the passage and a bucolic print depicting an English fox hunt on the other. Martin continues along the main corridor, more open doors to the left. To his right, a door opens onto a guest lounge. An old sofa and lopsided armchairs face a new flat-screen television. Someone has been here as well. Another overflowing ashtray, empty beer cans, dirty coffee cups.

The smell is worse down this end of the hotel, no longer merely musty. There are communal bathrooms at the end of the corridor, one for men, one for women. Martin gives them a miss. There is a final hotel room, this time with the door closed. Martin approaches it, and the smell is coming at him in waves: the smell of death. His stomach turns, from the stench and from the trepidation at what he might find inside the room. He holds his breath, pushes the door open, braces himself.

The place reeks. He pinches his nose shut between finger and thumb and enters, almost afraid to look at the bed. But it's empty. What, then? He walks around the bed and there, lying spread on the floor, is the body of a cat, crawling with maggots and flies. Martin gags. Mr Puss, he guesses; locked in the hotel room with no way out. Poor thing. Martin retreats backwards towards the door, but then stops. He creeps forward again. There. The cat's tail has been nailed to the floor.

———

Martin sits slumped on a bench in the Riversend police station, wondering if Walker will give him the time of day. The pretty young constable behind the counter has taken Martin's name through to the office and returned with the message that if 'sir' would like to wait, Sergeant Walker will talk to him when he has an opportunity. So Martin sits and waits, suspecting Walker will simply leave him stewing all afternoon. There's a wooden rack filled with brochures: Neighbourhood Watch, fire permits, how to get your driver's licence.

Forty minutes later, Jason the army vet emerges from the back rooms and walks out of the station, deep in thought and apparently oblivious to Martin's presence. A minute or two later Herb Walker appears. Martin leaps to his feet. Walker regards him with contempt. 'This better be good, fuckface.'

'Herb. Thanks for seeing me—'

'I didn't come to see you. I came for a smoke. C'mon.' He walks to a door leading out to the car park at the back of the station.

Outside, the overweight police sergeant extracts a cigarette and disposable plastic lighter from a khaki packet, lights up, sucks in a huge lungful of smoke and blows it back out with a long sigh of satisfaction. Only then does he regard Martin. 'That's better,' he says. 'You can't even blow smoke in their faces while you interrogate the fuckers anymore.'

'Herb, I just want you to know I wasn't aware of the article until I saw it this morning—'

Walker has his hand up, palm out, ordering Martin to stop. 'I hope like hell that isn't why you've come here.'

'No, but it's worth saying.'

'Really? And if you had known, would you have pulled the story to help me out?'

'No. But I would have warned you, got your side of the story, and made sure it was written as objectively as possible.'

The policeman takes another long suck of his cigarette. 'So what is it that you desperately want to tell me? Be quick, you're on cigarette time. As soon as I've finished this, I'm back inside.'

'Byron Swift couldn't have killed those girls. At least, he couldn't have abducted them.'

Walker raises his eyebrows. 'That's interesting. How do you know that?'

Martin tells the policeman about Mandy's record of her being with Byron on the night of the abduction, explaining that she's willing to talk to the police, but would prefer not to be paraded before the media.

Walker listens intently, finishes his smoke with another massive toke and grinds the butt beneath his black boot.

'So this is going to be in the paper tomorrow?'

'Yes. There's no reason to hold it, is there?'

'You asking permission to publish?'

'No.'

'No, I didn't think so. You shagging her now, are you?'

'What's that got to do with anything?'

'Not a lot.' Walker offers a leery grin.

'Herb?'

'Yes, Martin?'

'Did you find out? Did he make calls from St James before the shooting?'

Walker looks at Martin as if deciding whether or not to confide. 'Yes. Two calls. One outgoing, then one incoming.'

'You have the numbers?'

'Not yet.'

'Will you tell me when you do?'

'Maybe. If I need your help. If I don't, you can whistle Dixie. But right now, you've had more than your durry's worth. I need to get back in there. Tell Miss Mandalay Blonde we'll be in touch.'

'Before you go, Herb: today's story, Bethanie's story, the tip-off to Crime Stoppers about the bodies in the dam—what happened?'

'Get fucked, Scarsden.'

———

It's only as he's leaving the station that Martin remembers he hasn't told Walker about the dead cat. He'd been intending to, just in case it held any significance. A shiver defies the oppressive heat, running up his spine. There is something wrong with this town, as if the heat has turned it, like milk curdled by the sun.

He sees Carrie the photographer across the road, chiacking with the other photographers and camera crews. Doug Thunkleton's cameraman says 'g'day' as Martin approaches. 'Anything happening?' he asks. 'They doing a doorstop?'

'Not that they're telling me,' replies Martin. 'Where's Doug?'

'He's been looking for you. Wants you for another interview.'

'Is that right? Where is he?'

'Where do you reckon? At the club with the rest of you slack-arse journos.'

'I'll give him your love.' Martin walks away a few metres, followed by Carrie, so they can confer in private.

'I've shot the shit out of it,' says the snapper. 'Unless something happens soon, or unless you've got some requests, I'm pretty much out of ideas. You think we're going to see an arrest?'

'Don't know. The cops are telling me jack shit. But Bethanie and I have another good yarn for tomorrow, so they'll be needing pictures. You got any of the cops?'

'Yeah. Some good ones of them gathered in a huddle talking early this morning. There's a bit of finger-pointing, like they're debating something. The cop cars are in the background with nothing else but trees. They could be anywhere. Crime scene, anywhere.'

'Where were they?'

'Outside the services club. Here, have a look.' She scrolls through the photos using the screen on the back of her camera, but even in the shade the day is too bright to discern much detail.

'Looks perfect. What were they debating?'

'No idea. I was on the long lens, couldn't hear a thing. Probably what to have for breakfast. How much longer do you think I'll be needed up here?'

'Don't know. If they arrest anyone, they'll want to parade them for the cameras, but who knows if that'll happen. Why? You need to get back to Melbourne?'

'Wouldn't mind. Slept in the car last night.'

Martin thinks guiltily of his motel room. 'Shit. That's no good. You could have shared with me.'

'Thanks, Martin—you're not the first to offer,' she says sardonically.

'Listen, the Channel Ten guys are staying at some swish place in Bellington. Why not move down there?'

'You sure?'

'Absolutely. Mobiles work down there. I can always call if there's anything urgent.'

'Done.'

———

When Martin arrives at the services club, he goes straight to Tommy's Saigon Asian. Having explored the confusing menu extensively during the past week, he knows what to avoid, if not exactly what he likes. Today he orders chicken schnitzel and chips, with a side order of stir-fried English spinach. Tommy, a second-generation Vietnamese–Australian with a strine accent strong enough to cut glass, takes his money, says 'No worries, mate' and hands Martin a plastic disc that will light up and vibrate when his lunch is ready. Martin pays and makes his way through to the club proper.

A small group of journos have congealed around a table not far from the bar. Some are trying to work on laptops, swearing at the hypothetical wi-fi, while others are kicking back and chatting.

Doug Thunkleton greets him, his booming voice full of bonhomie. 'Martin Scarsden! The great man! Join us.'

Martin declines with a wave and a smile. 'Maybe later.' He goes to the bar where Errol is again working.

'Hi, mate. What can I get you?'

'G'day, Errol. Schooner of light beer, thanks.'

'Stubby okay?'

'Sure.'

Errol fetches the Tasmanian beer in the familiar green bottle. Martin gives Errol twenty dollars, but Errol doesn't go to the till straight away. 'Anything happening down there?'

'Where's that?' Martin asks.

'The cop shop. Heard they were doing interviews. People from out in the Scrublands.'

'Yeah. Just been down there. All looks pretty routine to me, but they're keeping it tight.'

'Reckon it was the priest, do they?'

'That seems to be the main theory. What do you reckon?'

'Me? Wouldn't have the foggiest. Don't know why you buggers keep asking me. As if I'd know.' And Errol goes to the register and gets Martin his change.

Martin takes his beer and moves towards a table a good distance from the clutch of journalists, but he can see Doug Thunkleton and the others sizing him up. The last thing he feels like is supplying the television bulletins with another talking head, so Martin keeps going, taking his beer and his plastic disc out onto the deck overlooking the river.

The heat is stifling after the air-conditioned interior of the club, almost unbearable, despite the shade provided by a canopy of translucent plastic. He places his beer on a small table and stands with his back to the glass windows of the club, fishing out his sunglasses to guard against the glare. Before him, he can see the long slow bend in the riverbed. No, not slow, stopped;

it's completely devoid of water. The trees hang unmoved by even a whisper of breeze. There's still the smell of smoke in the air, lingering from Wednesday's fire. Somewhere in the far distance he can hear cicadas. He's trying to ascertain the direction when he hears a rattling cough. He's not alone on the deck. Over behind one of the roof pillars, Codger Harris is working his way through a rollie.

'G'day, Codger. Mind if I join you?'

'Free country, son.'

Martin pulls up a seat next to the former bank manager. The older man offers him his tobacco packet, but Martin declines.

'Anything left of your place?'

'Some. Not much to start with.'

'Insurance?'

'A bit. For the fencing and water. The house escaped. Guess the fire reckoned it wasn't worth the effort.'

'What about the cattle?'

'Don't know. Some survived, for sure. But that could be a cruel joke.'

'How do you mean?'

'Well, there was fuck-all feed as it was. What the drought didn't kill off, the fire has. If it rains, after a fire like that, it'll be green as Kent. Fattest cows you ever saw. If it doesn't rain, they'll starve to death. Or I'll have to go shoot 'em.'

Martin examines his beer. There isn't a lot to say.

'Talking of which, it wasn't you who dobbed me in to the coppers, was it?'

'How do you mean?'

'They had me down there half the morning, asking me about Reverend Swift coming out shooting in the Scrublands. Wanted to know all about it. Get that from you?'

'Not directly. It was in an article I wrote, that he went out into the scrub shooting. But I didn't say your place. There are a few people around town who knew about it. I know at least one person told Robbie Haus-Jones.'

'That nice young copper in town here? Wonder why he's coughing up now.'

'Fairly straightforward, I'd think,' says Martin. 'After the church shooting, it was largely irrelevant. Swift was dead. Didn't matter what he'd done beforehand. But once the bodies were discovered in the dam at Springfields, suddenly it's relevant.'

'So covering his arse, then.'

'How do you mean?' asks Martin.

'Well, you know—five innocents dead, plus the priest. "Officer Haus-Jones, was there any warning, any way this could have been predicted or prevented?" "No, sir. Nothing. He lived in Bellington." But then when those girls are hauled out of that dam at Snouch's place, it's time to fess up. "New information, sir. Hope it's useful." It's what I'd do in his situation.'

Martin nods slowly. Codger Harris may look decrepit, but his brain cells are still firing. 'So the police wanted to know about anyone coming out to your place shooting?'

'Yeah, pretty much. Didn't feel too comfortable dobbing on people, but as the cops said themselves, this is murder, not some speeding ticket.'

'So, apart from the priest, who did go shooting in the Scrublands?'

'Couldn't say. It's a huge area. The only ones for sure were Craig Landers and the Newkirks and their mates. They might come out once or twice a year.'

'The Bellington Anglers Club?'

'Is that what they called themselves? Yeah. But they were always well behaved. Always asked before they came on the property. Used to say cheerio when they were leaving, give me a rabbit or two, a couple of ducks one time.'

'No one else?'

'For sure there were others. You could hear the guns going off. Sometimes in the day, sometimes at night. But whoever it was, they didn't come asking permission. Weird cunts, some of them, though.'

'How's that?'

'Sometimes they'd shoot me cows, then butcher them. Drag their guts out, that sort of thing. After the choicest cuts, I'd reckon. Fucking waste, though. Whole cow for a kilo or two of steak.'

'You sure that's what they were doing?'

'What else could it have been?'

'I don't know. Just for kicks. Possible, do you think?'

'Jeez, young fella. You'd have to be pretty sick to do something like that.'

'Well, you'd have to be pretty sick to kill a couple of pretty young backpackers and dump them in a farm dam.'

'Yeah, well, ain't that the truth. Sooner they lock up that bastard Snouch and chuck away the key, the better.'

'You're convinced it's him?'

'Yeah. Probably him killing me cows too. His family used to own all that land. Still thinks it's his. It'd be just like the miserable shit to come killing my cows when he's got plenty wandering around his own land.'

Martin drains the remnants of his beer, already grown tepid in the heat of the deck. 'Where you staying, Codger? Not at the old pub, are you?'

'Me? No. Wouldn't mind, but the place is closed. Errol Ryding's putting me up. Good man, Errol. I'll get the bus down to Bellington tomorrow, see if I can buy a jalopy, then I can get back home.'

'It's just I thought I saw someone up on the pub verandah this morning. Thought it might have been you. I guess not. Might have been the owner, collecting some stuff.'

'I think that'd be pretty unlikely, young fella.'

'Why's that?'

'He's dead. Topped himself. City bloke. Sank his pension into it. Did the place up, tried to make a go of a bistro. Anyway, his wife couldn't stand it and went back to the city, then the drought really kicked in and the money dried up. Didn't really know anyone, didn't have anyone to talk to. Blew his brains out with a shotty. Happens more often than you'd think out here. Don't know why I haven't done it myself.'

fourteen | **BLOOD MOON**

MARTIN ENDS UP WRITING HIS STORY AT THE SERVICES CLUB. HE'S TRIED THE bookstore, but it's shut, with the GON OUT, BACKSON sign hanging on the door. He guesses Mandy is with the cops, getting the third degree about Byron Swift and her diary. Pity. She might have been able to shed some more light on where the investigation is heading. Nevertheless, she's most definitely going to be the top of the story; not much he can do about that.

A Sydney Morning Herald *investigation has broken open the search for the vicious killers responsible for the brutal murder of German backpackers Heidi Schmeikle and Anna Brün, providing vital new information that has again shifted the focus of the police investigation.*

The Herald *has gathered evidence clearing the number-one police suspect, homicidal priest Byron Swift . . .*

Before getting down to writing, Martin has relented, providing commentary for Doug Thunkleton and his rivals, all without revealing his new angle. Thankfully they've disappeared down to the resort in Bellington, leaving him to work in peace at the club. He extracts enough bandwidth from the recalcitrant wi-fi to file, then calls through first to Bethanie and then Max from the phone in the club foyer.

'Yeah, okay, Martin, I've got it now. Looks good. Good stuff. Bethanie's got a couple of minor additions, but it's certainly a new angle.'

'You don't seem too enthused.'

'To be honest, I'm not,' says the editor.

'You're joking, right? The *Herald* out in front of the police? What could be better?'

'You're right. Sorry, champ. I've just been getting a lot of shit on this story. The editorial board have got their knickers in a knot. They're demanding everything be legalled and fact-checked. They're insisting on being kept in the loop.'

'What? Three front pages in a row and they're not happy? We own this story, Max. Look at the TV news tonight. I'm on most of them: the expert from the *Herald*. What more do they want?'

'Accuracy, apparently.'

'Shit, Max. What's that supposed to mean?'

'Well, in no short time we have reported that Harley James Snouch is the primary murder suspect and an alleged rapist. With no substantive evidence of either. Then we all but convict Reverend Swift of the murders. That was in your stories in today's paper, if you'll recall. Today's, Martin. And tomorrow's splash is that Swift is probably innocent. To be honest, some of those upstairs are asking if you're up to it.'

Martin is silent for a moment, taken aback by the allegation, before he feels a surge of defensive anger swelling.

'What do you think, Max? Do you think that?'

'No, I don't. You have my utter confidence and trust.' The reply comes immediately and with conviction.

Martin breathes out, some of the anger dissipating. Good old Max: a journo's journo, an editor's editor.

'Thanks, Max, I appreciate it. But I really am reporting it as it happens to the best of my ability. It's why the cops aren't talking much on the record; they don't know where this is heading either. They'd put all their eggs in the Byron Swift basket before this new info—I was reporting that one hundred per cent accurately. And I know they haven't ruled Snouch out altogether. It could turn out that we were right all along.'

'Well, keep at it. How much longer do you think you'll need to be down there? It's already been a week.'

'What? As long as it takes. It's the biggest story in the country. And I still want to do the feature piece, the original piece. That's for next weekend. The anniversary of the shooting. As for the daily news stuff, who knows? The police investigation might peter out, or it could bust wide open.'

'Fair enough. But, Martin, we've had a good run with it. It doesn't have to be front page every day.'

'What's that mean?'

'That means you don't have anything to prove. Not to me, not to anybody else. You don't have to push the envelope, not on every story.'

Martin stews on that for a moment. 'Are you worried about my judgement?'

'No, champ. Your judgement is fine. However, I do worry about you. How are you holding up?'

'Terrific, actually. I've been feeling more like the old me. You were right; it was good to get out of the office and into the field.'

'Glad to hear it. Ring if you need to sound me out on anything. Let's not give those shits in Mahogany Row any ammunition.'

'Thanks, Max. For everything.'

Martin buys a bottle of white wine at the bar and some takeaway at Tommy's, carrying them down to the bookstore. The store is shut, but when he walks around the block to the back alley he can hear music coming out through the screen door of Mandy's home. He knocks, hears the baby give a joyous gurgle, and then Mandy opens the door.

'Hello, Martin,' she says with a long sigh. She looks bedraggled, exhausted and beautiful. And not so keen to see him.

'I brought a peace offering,' he says, holding up the wine in its brown paper wrapper and the white plastic bag bursting with takeaway.

'You'd better come in then.'

Liam is sitting in a highchair eating some orange mush that's come out of a blender. The highchair is isolated in the middle of the kitchen and Martin can see why; for every spoonful that Liam gets to his mouth or its environs, he sends another dollop flying over the side of the highchair, cooing with delight as it splats onto the lino floor. Mandy frowns at him, shaking her head.

'Thanks for this, Martin. I couldn't bear cooking after today.'

'So it didn't go well?'

'No. You could say that.' There's an irritated edge to her voice.

'Want to talk about it?'

'Want to knock the top off that bottle?'

She fetches some glasses, Martin opens the wine; he takes a sip, she takes a slug. Martin thinks about making some witty toast to lighten the mood, but the only things that come to mind seem lame so he simply raises his glass. Mandy doesn't return the gesture; instead she sets out dishes on the table. Martin starts serving the food, waiting for the dam to burst. It doesn't take long.

'Those fuckwits,' she starts. 'I volunteered this information. I didn't need to, I'm helping them to do their job, and they sit there and judge me. Like I'm the town bike or something.'

Martin says nothing, attempting to project a sympathetic air while dishing out Tommy's eccentric approximation of Asian cuisine. The fried rice appears to contain corn kernels, spam and small cubes of beetroot, all sourced from cans.

Mandy drains her wine and continues. 'I mean, you know a thing or two, right, Martin? I told them what they needed to know, that Byron was here with me the entire night. They asked me how I could be sure, so I showed them the diary. They confiscated it and just laughed when I asked for a warrant. Can they do that?'

'I guess so. It's material evidence in a murder inquiry. You could demand it back, but I'm pretty sure they could get a court order to keep it.'

'Well, it seems like an abuse of power to me.'

'Yes, you're probably right,' Martin dissembles.

'But that's not what really pissed me off. It was all the stuff about my history. You know, how many men have I slept with, how well I knew Craig Landers, how the business is going. How the business is going, for Christ's sake? Who my friends are, who I see on a frequent basis, who looks after Liam when I can't. What's that all about?'

'Covering their arses,' Martin assures her. 'They've ballsed up the investigation, pinned the backpackers' murder on Swift, and then you turn up and demonstrate that they're on the wrong track. So they're trying to make sure they don't miss anything this time around.'

'And will all this come out in court?'

'Can't see why it would.'

'And then all the questions about you. How is that relevant? You weren't even here a year ago. What the fuck could you have to do with any of it?'

'They asked about me?'

'Yeah. The fat cop from Bellington and that skinny one with the five o'clock shadow, the creepy one.'

'Goffing. His name is Goffing. What did he ask?'

'Weird stuff. Like whether you're reliable, whether I feel you're leading me on to extract information from me.'

'And what did you say?'

'Yes. I said you had seduced me. That I'm putty in your hands.'

Martin laughs. 'Really? You told him that?'

'No. I suggested it was unlikely you were hanging around to extract information from me because, until this morning, you didn't know that I had any. I told them you were just another cunt-struck middle-aged loser. They thought that had the ring of truth to it.' She offers a weak smile.

'Gee, thanks.'

'Any time.' The smile vanishes again. Pity; he likes her smiles.

Just then Liam lets go with an audible fart, huge for his size, with a disturbingly liquid quality to it. A few seconds later the smell wafts across the kitchen table like a chemical weapons attack and the remains of Tommy's takeaway lose any residual appeal.

'Nappy time,' Mandy declares with faux levity, and goes to release her boy from his highchair. She cradles him so as not to squash his nappy. 'Martin, I just want to be with Liam tonight. You okay at the motel?'

'Sure.'

She walks over, still holding Liam, and gives Martin a generous kiss on the mouth. The stench is unbelievable.

'And thanks for coming to cheer me up. And for dinner. And for listening.'

Banished, Martin walks out through the store and into the evening calm. The sun is down and the stars are emerging. A blood-red moon hangs in the western sky like the blade of a scythe. Hay Road is deserted, but there's a car parked outside the general store and the lights are on. Martin walks down, hoping to buy water. Instead, he finds Jamie Landers, slouched on the bench outside the store, nursing what looks like a half-bottle of tequila. The boy is staring at the moon.

'Mind if I join you?' asks Martin.

Jamie looks up at him, face blank, the aggression of Bellington hospital nowhere to be seen. 'Sure.'

Martin takes a seat on the bench. Jamie offers him the bottle; he takes a small swig. He was right: tequila.

'Do you think it means anything? The moon?'

From where they are sitting the moon sits in the narrow gap of sky between the bottom of the awning and the silhouetted shopfronts across the road. It looks much larger than it would in the expanse of an open sky.

'It's the smoke haze from the Scrublands, turns it red.'

'I know. But even so.'

They sit in silence for some minutes before Jamie speaks again. 'About the other day, at the hospital. Sorry I was such a little shit. It was Allen, dying like that. I was upset.'

'It's totally understandable.'

'Stupid, isn't it? Pointless. He survived St James. He saw Swift shoot his dad and his uncle. He was sitting next to Gerry Torlini when Swift shot him. He got covered in blood, but he survived. And now he's gone, just like that.' The young man clicks his fingers to emphasise his point. 'Just meaningless. Fucking meaningless.'

Martin says nothing.

'I've been reading your stories,' says Jamie. 'You think you're getting any closer to working it out? Why he went mental and shot everyone?'

'Sometimes I do, I feel that I'm almost there, then the next thing I'm back at square one.'

'Yeah, well, at least the coppers are talking to you. I guess they have to.'

'Why's that?'

''Cos they're not smart enough to work it out by themselves.'

Martin chuckles. 'I'll let you tell them that.'

'Yeah. Sure.'

There's another pause as they consider the moon.

'Hey, Jamie. The day your dad died, the day Byron Swift shot him, had you been out hunting with them the day before?'

'Nah. Allen went; he liked guns and all that shit, not me. They were too boring for me, all those old men.'

'Did you speak to your dad, though? That morning?'

'Yeah. Too right. He was fucking rabid. Said the coppers had told him Swift was a ped. Said if he'd laid a hand on me he'd do for him.'

'Do for him?'

'Shoot him.'

'What did you say?'

'Same as I told you. He never touched me. Wouldn't dare.' There's no anger in the youth's voice, hardly any emotion at all; resignation, perhaps. There's more silence. Martin thinks he can almost see the moon moving, sinking towards the line of shops across the way. He turns back to Jamie, is about to ask him something more, when he notices the teenager's shirt: yellow and black checks.

'Jamie, did you and Allen ever hang out in the old pub? Go upstairs there?'

For the first time since Martin sat down, Jamie Landers turns from the moon and looks him in the eye. 'You found the cat?'

'I found the cat.'

'Fuck. I forgot about that. I should clean it up.'

'What was it? What happened?'

'Oh, it was Allen. Sick fuck. High as a fucking kite on speed.'

'Allen?'

'Yeah. Never the same after the church shooting. It fucked him up big time.' Jamie returns his gaze to the moon, takes a long swig of his tequila. 'Doesn't matter now, though, does it? None of it does.'

'I guess not.'

Martin leaves Jamie to his thoughts and starts walking up Hay Road. He's left his car at the services club, but he decides to leave it there and walk back to the motel. Nothing in this town is very far apart. When he first arrived, Riversend's compact streetscape appealed to him; now it feels almost claustrophobic, so small, overwhelmed by the vastness of the plain, like a Pacific atoll with rising sea levels gnawing at its shores. He's been here for almost a week and is starting to feel as if he knows every building, every face in Riversend. He looks up at the hotel; there is no sign of life. What must it be to live in this town? To be young and live in this town? Every day, the same stifling heat, the same inescapable familiarity, the same will-sapping predictability. Even Bellington, with its water and its services, shimmers with allure, like some mirage out across the flatness. So why is it getting under his skin? Why does he care? It's like those strange adopt-a-road programs. Adopt-a-corner-of-hell. Why not?

Lost in such thoughts, Martin continues along Hay Road, bathed in an eerie orange light, the heat still rising from the road even as the moon shadows extend across it. A farm ute passes him, its headlights yellow, its dodgy muffler loud, enhancing the silence once it gets to the T-junction and turns left, leaving him totally alone once more on the main street of Riversend.

He's back in front of the bookstore, but it's closed and dark. Then, as he turns to head back to the motel, a flicker of light catches his eye. He searches the line of shops opposite, but there's nothing, just darkness. He's thinking it's his imagination, the effects of fatigue and tequila, when he sees it again: a flicker. The wine saloon. He crosses the street, climbs the gutter, peers through the boarded-up window. A candle, a shadow, a glass catching the light. Snouch.

The alleyway is dark; Martin uses the torch app on his phone to navigate past broken bottles and lost newspapers, reaching the side door, turning the knob, hearing the hinges' shrill complaint as he pushes it open. Harley Snouch is not at the bar. He's sitting at a table with a book and a bottle, a kerosene lamp hanging low from an old wire coathanger stretching down from the rafters. He looks up, shielding his eyes from the lamplight, to see who is invading his sanctuary.

'Ah. Hemingway. Welcome, pull up a chair.'

Martin walks into the pool of light, sits at the table. Snouch has shaved off his greying beard and washed his hair, taking years off his appearance. Perhaps it's the flattering softness of the lamplight, but he doesn't look so much older than Martin.

There are two glasses—small tumblers, one full, one empty—and the bottle in its brown paper bag. Snouch pours red wine into the second glass. It looks dark and viscous. 'Have a drink,' says Snouch. 'Thought you might show up sooner or later.'

Martin takes a tentative sip and is surprised to find the wine passable, at least in contrast to Jamie Landers' tequila.

Snouch gives an amused snort. 'What did you expect? Cat's piss?'

'It was last time around. Why the change?' Martin reaches over, extracts the bottle from the bag. Sure enough, Penfolds.

Snouch grins like a naughty schoolboy, stripping more years off. 'Mate, even us derros have standards.'

'Except that you're not really a derro, are you, Harley? I saw your house, remember, before it burnt down.'

Snouch smiles with apparent pleasure. 'I tell you, Martin, some of the greatest bums I've known were loaded. Rich scumbags. My school was full of them.'

'What school was that?'

'Geelong Grammar.'

'That figures. Explains your classy accent and polished turn of phrase.'

Snouch smiles again, taking a healthy slug of his wine.

Martin gets to the point. 'Why aren't you a suspect in the murder of the two backpackers?'

'Because I have a cast-iron alibi.'

'Which is?'

'I was in hospital in Melbourne. For two weeks. Pneumonia. Missed everything. The priest raining holy retribution down on his congregation and some bastard dumping bodies in my dam. Shit timing. Nothing happens for years on end and then when it does, I'm flat on me back in Melbourne. Surrounded by witnesses, covered in documentation.'

'So you say.'

'So the police have established beyond all doubt. If you're trying to work out who killed those girls, I am the last person you should be thinking about.'

'That's nice to hear, but you're not exactly what I'd call a reliable witness.'

'I was a reliable witness last time you were in here. I told you I hadn't done anything wrong. I told you I hadn't gone to prison. And I told you at Springfields that I never raped anyone. And yet you went and published it anyway. Wrote it big and splashed it bigger. You should have listened, but you didn't. Maybe you'll listen now.'

Martin is still, frozen by Snouch's calm words of confrontation. A hollowness has opened in his chest and the wine, pleasant a moment before, has lost its savour. 'What are you going to do?'

Snouch looks him directly in the eye, no longer the derro, more like a predator. 'Well, I'm thinking I might sue the shit out of you, your paper and anyone with the remotest connection to your slander. I'll be drinking fine wine for the rest of my days.'

'Good luck with that,' Martin says, attempting bravado. 'Civil cases don't carry the same burden of proof as criminal trials. Your reputation is already shot. And we have very good lawyers.'

But Snouch scoffs, leaning back with a lupine grin. 'Really? You know as well as I do that won't fly. And even if it did, in some fantastical scenario, it might save the paper but it won't save you. You wrote the story, you got the facts wrong. You're fucked.'

Martin feels like he's wandered into some high-stakes poker game, caught in a pool of lamplight in the old wine saloon. He's dealt himself a shit hand and now he's obliged to table a card. 'Harley, I saved your life—me and Robbie Haus-Jones.'

'Bullshit. I saved yours. That idiot wanted to drive into the dam. I would have survived with or without you.'

'What do you want?'

'I want to reconcile with Mandalay.'

'But you said yourself, out at Springfields, that she's not your daughter.'

'She's not.'

Martin digests that. Snouch's gaze doesn't leave his face. He has the upper hand; he can afford to wait for Martin's next move, knowing he can counter it.

'What about those?' Martin nods at Snouch's hands and their blurred blue prison tattoos.

Snouch smiles indulgently. 'What about them?' He holds his left hand out for Martin to examine. 'You seen anything like this before? Recognise any of the symbols?'

Martin looks. There are squiggles, letters, maybe an omega symbol, but nothing that makes sense. He returns his gaze to Snouch's face.

'You really want to base a court case on those?' asks Snouch.

Martin examines him a moment longer, wondering if he's bluffing, detecting nothing but resolve. 'Okay. What is it you want me to do?'

'Talk to Mandalay for me. Convince her I'm not the monster she thinks I am.'

'Easier said than done. Her mother claimed you raped her and Mandy believes it. How can I overcome that?'

'That's your problem. Convince her otherwise or I'll see you in court.'

Martin leans back, wondering how he might persuade Mandy. He momentarily considers doing the honourable thing: ringing Max, resigning, acknowledging his mistake. But as he looks at Snouch, sees the man's determination, he realises it wouldn't do any good. If Martin can't help engineer a reconciliation, then Snouch will certainly sue; not just for the money, but to offer Mandy some legal proof he's innocent of rape.

'Okay, Harley. I'll try. But tell me, what happened? If you didn't rape her, why was Katherine Blonde so adamant that you did? And why weren't you investigated or charged?'

Snouch tops up Martin's glass, then his own. Martin takes it as a conciliatory gesture, a sign that the conversation has further to go.

'That's better. But I'm serious, Martin: you get results or I sue; I end your career. You understand me? Help me, and I'll be the best friend you ever had.'

Somehow, Martin gets the impression Snouch is not new to this game. 'That sounds like blackmail.'

'Does it? Call it what you like.'

Martin's mouth is dry. He drinks some more wine.

Snouch nods, apparently satisfied he has Martin where he wants him. 'It was a long time ago. Katherine did claim I raped her. The local cop investigated. And he cleared me. Any records, if there were any, were expunged. My father was very wealthy, very powerful. People round here remember him as some sort of patrician benefactor. They don't remember him like that in Melbourne. Tough as mulga root: ruthless in business, callous in person. Treated his staff like shit, belittling the men and groping the women. He didn't give a flying fuck about me, but he wouldn't have the family name tainted. So he pulled the strings; there is no record of even a cursory investigation.'

'And no mention in any of the newspapers? None?'

'Not when he owned the *Crier*. And remember, there was no arrest, no charges, no trial. Because there was no rape. My father's influence didn't get me off the hook, the facts did that. He just kept it out of the media.'

Martin smiles, enjoying a small victory when it offers itself. 'Well, that worked a treat. You're still the town pariah.'

'Katherine was very popular. A lot of people believed her.'

'So what did happen?'

'I'll tell you. But it's not for publication, Martin. You got that? You're already in a hole, don't dig it any deeper.'

'Sure.'

For the first time since Martin's arrival, Snouch breaks eye contact, looking off into the gloom of the saloon instead. 'As I told you before, my family settled Springfields in the 1840s,' he begins, his voice low and resonant. 'We owned it all, thousands of acres of scrub. The worst land in the district, no good for cropping, difficult to clear, no soil to speak of. That's what all the other settlers thought, putting in their crops out on the plain; that's what they thought right up until the first big drought. In practice, Springfields was the best land, because my forebears were smart enough not to impose English agriculture upon it. They got it for nothing, did next to nothing to it. Put on some cattle, used it for grazing, not farming. Didn't even bother with fences; left that to the farmers with bordering properties. They were the ones who needed fences, to keep our cattle off. But there was no wood out on the plain. So we milled it, made fence posts, sold it to them. Mulga wood lasts forever, more durable than steel. So they paid us for the fences to keep our cattle off their land. How good is that? We got rich. And the dam by the house, even in this drought, it's full. You notice that? Spring-fed. Hence the name: Springfields. We always had water.

'By the time I came along, we were the last of the squattocracy, part of the town but not part of it. When I turned ten, I was packed off to Geelong, back sometimes on holidays to ride horses and, when I was older, to piss it up at the pub. It was home, a kind of base, but it wasn't my world. My world was going to be out there, over the horizon, London and New York and running the family company from Melbourne. Springfields meant a lot to my father; he wanted it to mean a lot to me, but it didn't. Riversend was just a way station, a footnote along the way. And then I met a girl. The most beautiful, wonderful girl I had ever met or could ever meet or would ever meet. Katie Blonde. You've met Mandalay. Well, her mum was even more beautiful. Inside and out. She was remarkable.

'We hit it off straight away. I was at uni down in Melbourne. Dad had wanted me to go to Oxford, like he did, but I couldn't see the point. Melbourne was good enough for me. I tell you, Martin, it's a pretty good life being young, wealthy and on the ran-tan. I lived in a college—just like boarding school, except co-ed. No rules, lots of booze, lots of sex. You don't realise how good it is until it's in the past. But once I'd met Katie, I wanted to be with her, and Melbourne was the way station. I'd had girlfriends before, but this was different. Very different. This was love. A short word, a meaningless word, until you experience it. Then there are no other words. It was perfect. *We* were perfect. Made all the more exquisite by these long periods apart. I'd fly to Sydney, hire a car or borrow a car and drive to where Katie was studying at Bathurst for the weekend. We were in love, and then we were engaged, and then—well, then it all turned to shit.'

'What happened?'

'She got pregnant. At first I was excited. Until I did the maths. The timing was wrong. It couldn't have been mine.'

'You sure?'

'Of course I'm sure. She'd been cheating on me.' There is pain in Snouch's voice. And anger.

Martin says nothing, waiting for Snouch to continue.

'I still loved her, still wanted to marry her, but I wanted to know whose kid it was. She wouldn't tell me. For a few days we were at an impasse. Then I got drunk, and then I got angry, and then I lost my temper. It escalated and I delivered her an ultimatum: she had to tell me who the father was or it was all off and I'd let the whole town know she'd been unfaithful. She shouted at me and I shouted back louder. In the end, I called her a slut. And that was that. As soon as I used that word, it was over. Next thing I knew she was accusing me of rape.'

'I'm not sure I believe you,' says Martin.

'Why not?'

'That's an amazingly vindictive thing for her to do, to falsely accuse her fiancé of rape, especially if she was the one who wronged you.'

'That's what you'd think, isn't it? My guess is she was so scared of being exposed, of being branded as promiscuous and unfaithful, that she panicked. I think she wanted me to back down, to marry her, to accept the child as our own and let bygones be bygones. But once she went to the police, that was no longer an option. They cleared me, of course. There was no evidence against me and the police could do their sums as well as anyone else.

'I left town, went back to uni in Melbourne. Tried to put it behind me. I'd never thought much of Riversend to begin with and after that I couldn't stand it. But Katherine stayed on, blackening my name to anyone who'd listen. In the end, my father intervened. He set her up in the bookstore, gave her an allowance, promised to support her and her baby, Mandalay, provided she stopped the allegations. And that was that. I never came back. It was all too much for Mum. Broke her heart. She died a year or two later. After that I only ever saw Dad in Melbourne, never back here.'

'Did you ever marry?'

'After that? No. I never had another relationship that lasted more than three months. I could never properly trust anyone again. You have no idea how much she hurt me, how much she undermined my faith in people. No, I never married, never had kids.'

'So why come back here?'

'Because I couldn't get her out of my mind.'

Snouch sips some more wine. Staring off into the darkness, as if he might still catch a glimpse of her there, his bewitching young fiancée. Martin says nothing, and Snouch eventually speaks again.

'It happens as you get older: the past bears down on you more and more until sometimes you spend more time living there than in the present. And in the night, she'd be in my dreams. Not all the time, but often enough. Every now and then, there she'd be, freed by my subconscious: the Katie I first knew, perfect and golden and glorious, and she'd take my heart once again, so that when I woke I'd know that I was still in love with her. They were the worst days. I'd go out and get ferociously wasted, drive the dreams from every waking thought. Like those poor old soldiers who used to come here to the wine saloon. The walking wounded. But it never worked. So in the end I came back here.

'She wouldn't see me, of course. It ran too deep, it was too entrenched, the petrified loathing. But I found this place, my hideaway. The role of the derro suited me—not that it was such an act; I was halfway there already. It gave people an excuse to ignore me, to leave me alone. I could sit here and occasion-ally I'd see her coming and going. She was older, of course, but not so old. And there is something about old friends, old loves, those who you were young with: when you see them after many years, they don't appear as they are now, but as they were. You can see past the pudginess and wrinkles, past cloudy eyes and sagging jawlines. You can see them as they were when they were young and vital. I would see Katie like that, as she was before it all came apart. She'd walk out the door of her store and in my mind she was twenty again. And then one day—one day I saw the girl, I saw Mandalay, back from uni. Not a girl, though: a woman. She looked just like her mother once had. It took my breath away. I sat here and cried.

'In the end, I did get to talk to her, to Katie. She was in the hospital down in Bellington. Mandalay was there, wouldn't let me in the room, thought I'd upset her mother, but the priest was there, he knew. Later on, he got me in to see her. Katie said to me: "We shan't talk about it, Harley. No talk. Just hold my hand." And so I did. We sat and held hands and looked into each other's eyes. She looked terrible, wasted, but her eyes were just the same. Glowing. And she looked at me fondly, Martin. Fondly. Without recriminations. And a week later she died. I couldn't go to the funeral, but it didn't matter. We'd made our peace. But she never recanted her allegation, not as far as I know, and I am still persona non grata, the town monster.'

He pauses, reflects, drinks some more wine. 'And now I think I really will have to leave. The house is gone, and even when the police clear me, people here will still believe I put those poor young girls in the dam. Pity. Springfields was starting to feel like the home it never was when I was a child. And I like it here in the saloon. I sit here in the dark and I wonder how it might have been different.'

Martin is starting to feel sorry for the old man, but not sorry enough to forget the threat Snouch has made. So when he speaks, he tries to remove any suggestion of sympathy from his voice. 'Why do you want to reconcile with Mandy if she's not your daughter?'

'Because I'm an old man and I have my regrets. The doctors don't like what I've done to my liver. I'm not going to live forever. I sit in here and wonder how it could have been different, if I'd not insisted, if I'd married Katherine and kept her secret. Mandy would have grown up as my daughter, Katie and I could have had our own children, it could have been so very different. Mandy's the last vestige of that left, the only part I might salvage.'

'Harley, I don't see what I can do. She loved her mother. She's not going to take your word or my word or anyone else's word against that.'

'I want you to persuade her to take a DNA test.'

'What?'

'To prove I'm not her father. Tell her if she agrees, regardless of the result, I'll leave Riversend.'

There is silence. Snouch's proposition hangs in the air.

'Have you told anyone else all of this, Harley?'

'No, mate. Not since I came back. Just you. You and Byron Swift.'

'Byron Swift?'

'He was a priest, Martin.'

They sit in silence. Martin finishes his wine, gets to his feet. 'Okay, Harley. I'll see what I can do.'

Martin is almost to the door when the old man, the now not-so-very-old man, speaks. 'Martin, tread carefully. I know she's beautiful, I know she's intelligent. But she's also her mother's daughter. Don't push too hard, too soon. Don't rush it. I've been waiting thirty years; I can wait a bit longer if I have to.'

fifteen SUICIDE

MARTIN SITS ON THE BENCH OUTSIDE THE GENERAL STORE AND STARES AT
The Age. Page five. His article is on page five. Even the *Herald
Sun*'s story is on the front page, and they've got no story at all,
just a jumble of stale facts and fresh conjecture, unsourced
speculation dressed up as the truth that the Germans had been
raped and tortured before being shot. He rereads his copy,
looking for some weakness to explain its banishment to the
inside pages, but finds none. The front page is a grab bag of
second-rate stories. The main story is about Melbourne real
estate, the photo story about a TV celebrity leaving his wife
and family to join a religious cult. Martin recalls the conversation with Max Fuller, the editor assuring him of his trust and
confidence. But Max is the editor of the *Sydney Morning Herald*;
his counterpart at *The Age* is not constrained by personal loyalty.
A pit has opened in Martin's guts. Something is not right.

Back at the Black Dog, he rings Sydney, finally getting through to the editor.

'Martin. Morning.'

'Page five? Really?'

'That's *The Age*. Soft cocks. You're page three in the *Herald*.'

'Is that supposed to make me feel better? It was lead story on all the teevs last night and the *Hun* has splashed with it.'

'Don't you start, Martin. I had to fight to get it in the paper at all.'

'What? Why, Max? What's going on?'

'To be honest, I have no idea. But I'm glad you called. I've got bad news—you're off the story. They want you back in Sydney. They say a week is long enough; they don't want you to overdo it. They're sending Defoe to replace you. *The Age* is sending their own reporter, Morty Lang.'

The words land like a sledgehammer, stunning Martin. An image comes to him of his career, shattered into shards, like splintered glass. Another image: him sitting at a desk at the periphery of the newsroom, a broken man. His anger surges. 'What do you mean "they"? Don't you mean "we"? You're the one taking me off the story and you're the one sending Defoe. At least own the decision.'

'No, Martin, it's not like that—'

'Good. So you'll fight it. You'll insist that the story is mine. You have to.'

'Martin, listen—I'm out as well. They've shafted me. This is my last day. They're replacing me.'

Again the sledgehammer falls. 'What? Why?'

'No idea. It's been seven years. Most editors only last half that time. Circulation's down, advertising's down. Time for renewal.'

'Max, that's bullshit. Circulation and advertising are always down. You can't let them do it. You're the best editor we've ever had.'

'Thanks, Martin, that's good of you to say so. But it's a done deal. I'm out of here. Don't worry: it's the full parachute. Same salary, writer at large. Here and overseas. I'm almost looking forward to it.'

'Jeez, Max. What a loss.'

'Thanks. You'll be looked after too. They want you off reporting for now, but they understand the paper has a duty of care after what happened in Gaza. Plus, you're one of the best writers we have. They're thinking you can write leaders or become the go-to guy for rewrites, plus a training and mentoring role. And some reporting if and when you're ready for it. You'll be okay.'

———

After the phone call Martin sits in his room at the Black Dog. This has been his life: hotel rooms. Grand rooms in grand hotels: suites at The Pierre in New York, the Grand in Rome, the American Colony in Jerusalem. And lousy rooms in lousy hotels: a shack in Brazil with a dirt floor, a brothel in rural Cambodia, an utterly featureless business hotel in The Hague for three weeks. And now here, his last hotel room: a dogbox with a clunking air-conditioner, a mass-produced gum-tree print and water that would give the World Health Organization the trots. After everything—all the adrenaline, all the ambition, all the words, the millions of words—it comes down to this: room six at the Black Dog Motel. He looks at his hands, hands that have shaken the hands of presidents and potentates, pirates and paupers, hands that have worked their magic through dozens of keyboards, hands that have typed out stories both mundane and momentous. Hands soon to be silent, or condemned to shape second-hand words and second-hand thoughts, or to produce nothing more important than inter-office memos. Ultimately, very ordinary hands indeed.

The phone rings: the impatient world, eager to get on, disrespectful of his grief.

'Martin Scarsden! Hello, mate. D'Arcy Defoe. You're every-where. I can't get a word in the paper. I just want to say—'

'D'Arcy. Just a moment.' Martin doesn't hang up. He places the receiver gently on the bed and walks into the bathroom. Time for a shower. He turns the tap, strips off, walks under the dubious water of Riversend.

———

Martin wants to go to the Oasis, unburden himself, tell Mandy what has happened to him, seek solace. In this dying town she is the only friend he has: his lover, hopefully his confidante. And yet he can't bring himself to see her. Instead, he sits in the rotunda in the park, pondering his options. Hanging over him is Snouch's threat: persuade Mandy to take a DNA test or the old man will sue. If Martin refuses, then his career really will be history, any hope of resurrecting it gone. Snouch will take him to the cleaners and the *Herald* will hang him out to dry; the paper could reduce its own culpability by demonstrating it had removed him from the story as soon as it had any inkling that his reporting was inaccurate. It would parade its own good faith by depicting him as a rogue reporter, out for glory and careless of the facts, testifying that it had disciplined him even before the threat to sue. Maybe that's why they've moved so fast to replace him with D'Arcy and Morty: those Mahogany Row lawyers might not know a lot about journalism but they're experts in scapegoating, blame-shifting and arse-covering.

So he considers persuading Mandy to take the DNA test, arguing that the result doesn't matter: either way she'll be rid of Snouch once and for all. But he knows the result will matter. Snouch must be confident of the outcome, or why would he stake so much on it? He must be telling the truth: he isn't her father. And if that is the case, isn't she entitled to know the truth, no matter how painful? Isn't that his duty as a journalist, isn't that what his entire career has been about—telling the truth? To cut through the petty lies, the PR spin and the easy fabrications to deliver the public the truth, no matter how inconvenient or hurtful? How can he in all good conscience not tell her of Snouch's offer?

And yet if she takes the test and it confirms that Snouch is on the level, then what? Her mother will be irretrievably diminished in her eyes, the foundation stone of her life removed. What was it Mandy had said? That Byron Swift and her mother were the only two decent people she had ever known. Swift had revealed himself to be a homicidal psychopath and now here was Martin Scarsden, come to inform her that her mother was a pathological liar, a woman who had not only constructed a fantasy to protect her own reputation, but had destroyed the life of a man she had professed to love in the process. Could he do that? Walk into her bookstore, that shrine to Katherine Blonde, and bring it all crashing down around her?

He looks at his hands, his insipid and useless hands. He doesn't know what to do.

Unable to sit any longer, unable to tolerate his own company any longer, he leaves the park and starts walking. But his thoughts come with him. Maybe he would be doing her a favour. Snouch would be gone, the myth of her mother gone with him. It would hurt her initially, no doubt about that, but it might also free her: from the past and from any obligations to Riversend. She could take Liam and start again somewhere. After all, she's only twenty-nine. She wouldn't need him, wouldn't want him—Snouch's accomplice, a forty-year-old hack, a middle-aged loser with a fading career. But if he's to be brutally honest, that probably wouldn't be such a bad thing for her either.

It seems like a very long time since he was her age. What was he like at twenty-nine? Cocksure, bullet-proof, a handsome heartbreaker. Already a senior correspondent, Max's go-to person for trouble spots, parachuting in, seducing the local women, writing the yarn, returning to the office like a conquering hero. Living the life, living the dream, contemptuous of those pursuing more mundane careers, leading more conventional lives. He'd been arrogant, no doubt about it, not caring tuppence for the opinions of colleagues, the plodders and the office schemers. Maybe now they're exacting their revenge.

He recalls one lad, his contemporary at school, a bright bloke called Scotty with a mop of blond hair and a ready smile. Scotty was intent on dentistry, like his father, explaining how it offered money, plenty of money, and security. Martin recalls his disdain, bordering on pity. But now, approaching forty-one, he wonders about Scotty, where he might be now. He knows the answer: a large home in a leafy suburb, a beautiful wife, two kids going to private schools. There'd be a beach house, skiing holidays, a sizeable share portfolio and, already, planning for retirement. Martin considers Mandy: so young, so beautiful, so vulnerable. What had he been thinking, to sleep with her? He knows he'll be leaving again, leaving her, as he always does. Max's parachute journo, on his last mission, in and out, like a commando. What an arsehole.

He makes a decision. He needs to leave; to get his stuff and check out of the Black Dog. He doesn't want to be here when Defoe arrives. But he also needs to say farewell to Mandy. He can't just slink out of town like a thief in the night. What does he say? *Sorry to be such a predictable middle-aged lech, but thanks for the sex?* Or: *You're starting to mean a lot to me, come to Sydney, let me take you and Liam away from all this. I'm not Scotty, but I've got a one-room apartment in Surry Hills.* Christ, what does he say? What does he say about Harley Snouch?

He's walking along the highway, still wondering what he should do, how he should approach Mandy, when Robbie Haus-Jones pulls up, not bothering with a reverse park but simply swinging the police car in parallel with the kerb, leaving the engine running as he leans out the window. There is an urgency and seriousness to his baritone. 'Martin. Glad I found you.'

'What's up, Robbie?'

'It's Herb Walker. He's killed himself.'

Martin says nothing, just stares with his mouth open.

'In the river, outside Bellington. Drowned himself.'

'Suicide? Are you sure?'

'There's a note. I'm heading down now.'

'Can I come?'

'No, Martin. There's no way you want to be anywhere near this.'

'What? Why not?'

'The note more or less blames you. Your story that he received a tip-off about the bodies in the dam but didn't investigate. He says he always did his duty.'

Martin just stares at Robbie. Walker dead. Suicide. Blaming him. Christ. And he thought the day couldn't get any worse. It's not even 9.30 am.

'I've got to go, Martin, but if I were you, I'd be making myself scarce. No one is going to want to know you after this.'

Martin is still staring as Robbie puts the police car in gear and heads off towards Bellington.

———

Back inside his room at the Black Dog, Martin rings Bethanie Glass in Sydney. She answers her phone with a cheerful: 'Bethanie.' She doesn't know.

'Bethanie, it's Martin.'

'Oh, Martin. I am so sorry. I can't believe you're off the story. They're shits with shit for brains. You absolutely don't deserve any criticism over our coverage.'

'Bethanie, I'm going to get a lot more criticism. You too, probably.'

'What's happened?'

'It's Herb Walker, the sergeant in Bellington. He's killed himself.'

'What? How?'

'Drowned himself in the Murray, not far from Bellington. Apparently he left a note saying it was our story that drove him to it—the one claiming he ignored the tip-off about the bodies in the dam.'

'That story was accurate. He never denied it.'

'Yeah, but he was a smart guy. He must have guessed how you got the story: the top brass throwing him to the wolves, making him the scapegoat. Career over.'

'That's not our fault.'

'I don't think that's the point, Bethanie. We've left the competitors in our wake on this one. Now's their chance. They'll go for the throat. And we can't exactly rely on management to back us up, can we?'

'Shit. What should we do?'

'Well, first thing you need to do is tell Max, or whoever it is that's filling in for him, and explain the shitstorm that's about to engulf us.'

'It's Terri Preswell.'

'Good. She's rock-solid. Tell her as soon as you can. Ask who she wants to write the story.'

'She's in conference.'

'Doesn't matter. Interrupt. They need to know.'

'Of course.'

'Ring me back when you know what's happening. I'm at the Black Dog.'

'Shit, Martin. I feel awful.'

'Well, you shouldn't. You did nothing wrong. You got a genuine story and we ran it. Hold your head high, don't apologise.'

'Thanks, Martin. You too, okay?'

'Sure. Ring me when you know something.'

'Will do. And good luck.'

Forty-five minutes later, Martin still hasn't moved when the phone rings, a shattering, discordant sound, bringing him back from wherever it is his mind has been wandering.

'Martin? Bethanie. Sorry to do this to you, but the cops are holding a presser in Bellington at noon. At the police station. D'Arcy won't get there until tonight. They want you to cover it. Sorry.'

'Christ, talk about eating a shit sandwich. See what I can do.' He tries to keep his voice light, even as he feels a sense of dread descending.

'Good on you, Martin. I'll buy you a drink when you get back. Buy you several.'

'Thanks. I might need a few. I'll call you from Bellington.'

After the call is over, Martin thinks of his advice to Bethanie. *Hold your head high, don't apologise.* Too fucking right. He decides not to check out after all. He puts his phone and laptop on charge to top them up before he leaves for Bellington. The phone will work down there; he can give it extra juice on the drive. No point in getting there early. He fires up the laptop and opens his incomplete feature, RIVERSEND: A YEAR ON. He starts reading, and before long he is typing furiously. The story pulls him in, engulfing him as it so often does, his personal problems temporarily compartmentalised.

Driving towards Bellington he considers Walker's suicide, replaying his last conversation with the sergeant out the back of the Riversend police station. Walker had been aggressive and pissed off, not despondent or distracted. There was absolutely nothing in his demeanour to suggest he was contemplating suicide. On the contrary, he had seemed intent on continuing his investigations into Byron Swift. But Martin realises that doesn't mean anything. Something could have happened in the interim, like some sort of discipline coming down from the executive, a demotion or a public reprimand for not pursuing the tip-off about the bodies in the dam. Walker had been a proud man, ruling his fiefdom with impunity. Perhaps he couldn't bear the thought of the impending humiliation, no matter that it loomed so much larger in his own mind than it ever would among the residents of Bellington. Who knows what dark thoughts and obsessions can take hold in the small hours of the morning, when the mind chases itself down dark passageways and perspective is lost?

Such spectres had haunted Martin often enough in the months after Gaza, when even chemically-induced sleep came reluctantly. The demons had come and he had fought them, but all too often he'd felt as if they were winning, that the fight wasn't worth it. He'd made the mistake of mentioning it to one of his counsellors and red flags had gone up all over the *Herald*. But that had gone on for weeks, the downward spiral and the climb back. Had Walker really gone from defiance and anger to despair and hopelessness in mere hours? Was that likely? Perhaps there were other issues, unknown issues, trapping Walker, and he took the easy way out, making it easier by blaming the *Herald*. Maybe.

An oncoming car rockets past, forcing Martin to concentrate on driving momentarily. The land is flat, a monochrome bone, colour leached by years of drought. Nothing moves. Last night's fresh harvest of roadkill is splayed along the verge. Martin searches for the horizon, but it's an indeterminate blur, the sky melted into the shimmering edges of the earth. For a moment the illusion that he'd forced upon himself a week ago descends uninvited: his car seems stationary and it's the earth that is moving, revolving under him at a hundred and twenty kilometres an hour. He shakes his head, fighting for perspective.

A disturbing thought imposes itself on Martin's consciousness. What if it were his body that had washed up on the banks of the Murray, found by some early-morning jogger or an unfortunate fisherman? It wouldn't need a note: post-traumatic stress from Gaza, a series of incorrect stories, the burden of Walker's death, the humiliation of being taken off reporting. The coroner wouldn't think twice and the police wouldn't think at all. Suicide. Bethanie and Max would co-author a short obituary, D'Arcy would speak eloquently at his wake, and poor Robbie Haus-Jones would wonder who was next. A shiver runs up Martin's spine, defying the heat of the barren plain. At last the first strips of green appear out of the liquid distance. Bellington. Martin is relieved to be leaving the flatlands, almost pleased to arrive and confront whatever awaits him.

There's a dozen media set up outside the Bellington police station, a sturdy red-brick building, purpose built. The camera crews have picked their spot, positioning their tripods in the shade, placing a white card on the ground in the sun to indicate where they want the police to stand. As Martin approaches, the usual banter tapers off into silence. Old Jim Thackery, the wire service journo, has the decency to offer a wry greeting, but no one else wants to talk to him. The *Herald Sun* reporter shakes her head at his lack of wisdom. Doug Thunkleton pretends that he hasn't seen him, but the photographers and camera crews are unapologetic as they fill their lenses with images of their miscreant colleague. *Hold your head high, don't apologise*, he reminds himself silently.

It's not long before the police emerge: Montifore and Lucic, together with Robbie, the young constable frowning when he sees Martin at the back of the media scrum. Montifore is shuffling, getting his position right, asking whether the cameras are recording, when Martin feels a hand on his shoulder. It's Goffing, the ASIO agent. The man smiles grimly and nods, but says nothing. What's that meant to mean? A gesture of support?

'Good morning, ladies and gentlemen,' says Montifore, his delivery stiff and formal before the television cameras. 'I understand the premier and police minister will be commenting in Sydney shortly, so I'll make a brief statement and leave it at that. I won't be taking questions. I will be restricting myself to the facts. At approximately oh-six-hundred and twenty minutes this morning, a local resident spotted what they believed to be a deceased person in the shallows of the Murray River approximately five kilometres north-west of Bellington. That's downstream. We can now confirm the deceased male is Sergeant

Herbert Walker of the New South Wales Police Force. We can confirm there are no suspicious circumstances.

'Sergeant Walker has led policing in the Bellington district for more than twenty years and will be sorely missed by the people of this town and surrounding areas, and by the wider New South Wales police community. Herbert Walker was a very fine policeman, a very fine policeman indeed, and a great servant to his community. During the past few days I have had the privilege of working closely with Sergeant Walker. He was a highly professional officer, dedicated to upholding the rule of law and serving his community.'

Montifore has been looking directly down the barrel of the camera lenses, but now he shifts his eyes slightly to look at Martin. 'Herb Walker gave his all to serving his community at a time of great need. He didn't deserve this.' The policeman's gaze returns to the cameras. 'Thank you. That's all for now. Good morning.'

There's momentary silence among the media as the cameras linger on the backs of the police officers returning to the police station. Then the cameras are off the tripods and are being pushed into Martin's face, catching him unawares, their lenses wide open like hungry mouths, and Doug Thunkleton's booming voice rains down upon him.

'Martin Scarsden, what is your reaction to the death of Sergeant Herb Walker?'

One of the cameras has a light on top, and Martin winces as the cameraman flicks it on.

'I am very sorry for his death. He was a very fine officer.'

'But will you apologise to his family?'

'Apologise? For what, exactly?'

'You have hounded this policeman, driven him to take his own life, and you won't even offer his grieving widow an apology?'

'I'm sorry he's dead. Of course I am.'

'Do you accept you have behaved disgracefully?'

Martin gets it then. Thunkleton has his predetermined angle; he's going to persist until Martin admits some sort of culpability. *Well, fuck that.* 'We didn't do anything wrong. We reported the facts of the story. I am not responsible for Herb Walker's death.'

'The Premier of New South Wales says you are the worst type of journalist, a moral vacuum who'd sell his soul for a headline.'

'Well, in that case, why do you keep interviewing me? You know what you are? A hypocritical parasitic turd.'

As soon as the words are out of his mouth, Martin regrets them. He doesn't need to see the self-satisfied smirk on Thunkleton's face to tell him that. Shit. There are no more questions; Thunkleton has what he wants.

They leave him alone after that. He walks down to the river, sits on a bench in the shade of a line of poplars. The heat is keeping people inside. Thank goodness for that. He should ring Bethanie, he knows he should, but he can't quite bring himself to dial the number. He's almost relieved when his mobile rings, saving him from taking the initiative.

'Martin?' It's Bethanie, her voice subdued, uncertain, concerned.

'Hi, Bethanie.'

'Are you all right?'

'Never better.'

'We've just seen the footage from Bellington.'

'Yes. Perhaps not my finest moment.'

'You appear to be calling Herb Walker a parasitic turd. Please tell me you didn't do that.'

'What? No way. Never. I said I was sorry about his death, that he was a fine officer.'

'So who was the parasitic turd?'

'Doug Thunkleton, that arsehole from Channel Ten.'

There's a sigh of relief at the other end of the phone and a short, if rather forced, laugh. 'Well, you got that one right.'

'Bethanie, keep your head down, okay? I'm going to be the sacrificial lamb on this one. No need for you to cop it as well. You got everything you need? You need any quotes?'

'No, we've got a transcript from the police. Quickest turn-around ever. But you should send through an audio file of your interchange with Thunkleton if you recorded it. We can run it in your defence.'

'Thanks, Bethanie. It's been good working with you.'

After the call, Martin looks out across the river and wonders why he agreed to cover the police doorstop. After all, the tran-script was already out. And he wonders why the *Herald* insisted that he attend, given that he was officially off the story. But what the heck, he isn't ready to become a transcript journalist just yet.

His phone rings again. It's Max.

'Shit, Max. They still don't have the guts to call me themselves?'

'Apparently not. How you coping?'

'Not sure. You see the doorstop?'

'Everyone has seen the doorstop. Sky is playing it on high rotation, courtesy of Channel Ten. I assume you didn't really call that dead cop a parasitic turd.'

'No. Of course not. It was a character reference for that dickhead from Channel Ten, Thunkleton.'

'Well, it's not the way our television brethren are reporting it. Fortunately, Thackery at AAP has put it in perspective and now the ABC have picked it up and are taking the high moral ground. They're having a crack at Ten for sensationalist reporting.'

'So there's hope for me yet.'

'No, Martin, there's not.'

'How's that?'

'That's why I'm calling. You're sacked. Nothing to do with me, I'm just the messenger. You'll be paid your entitlements, but your employment is terminated as of now. I'm sorry, Martin—more sorry than you can ever know.'

For a moment, Martin can't speak. When he does, it's to console his old friend and mentor. 'What a bunch of gutless cunts, Max. Getting you to do this. It's unforgiveable. I won't forget it. I won't forgive them.'

'Thanks, Martin, but don't worry about me, think about yourself. Give me a call when you get back to Sydney. We'll have a drink, discuss options. I've got a few ideas.'

'Thanks, Max. You're a mate.'

'Martin?'

'Yes?'

'Don't do anything silly, okay? Nothing precipitous.'

sixteen FUGITIVE

THE CHANNEL TEN NEWS IS EVEN WORSE THAN MARTIN HAS BEEN EXPECTING. He sits alone in room six at the Black Dog Motel, watching it on the old-fashioned tube television set, the picture snowy. The newsreader wears a look of deep concern: '*There has been a disturbing development in the police investigation into murdered backpackers in the state's south-west. One of the key police investigators is dead—driven to take his own life, allegedly by irresponsible media reporting. Ten's Doug Thunkleton has the story from Riversend.*'

The news package opens with sepia photos of Herb Walker, police hero, accompanied by cello music. There's a brazen EXCLUSIVE dominating the top right corner of the screen. Doug's rich baritone is dripping with sympathy and regret. '*For a town that has already lost so much, there is more loss tonight—the death of policeman and local hero Sergeant Herb Walker.*'

Then a grab of a middle-aged woman identified by the screen super as the mayor of Bellington. '*Herb Walker was one of the kindest, hardest-working men I ever met. He was a pillar of our community.*'

Another grab, this time from Robbie Haus-Jones. '*Yes, I guess in a way he was a mentor to me.*'

Cut to Thunkleton, standing by the banks of the Murray, camera zooming slowly in as he makes his point. '*It was here, last night, that it all got too much for Sergeant Herb Walker. He'd investigated the Riversend massacre and the backpacker murders with courage and integrity, but a note found at the scene suggests he took his own life, unable to come to terms with scurrilous and inaccurate newspaper reporting.*' Cut to a montage of *Herald* and *Age* front pages. Thunkleton's voiceover continues, no longer heavy with grief or sympathy but stepped up into prosecutorial righteousness. '*For three days, the Fairfax press has provided sensationalist and at times inaccurate coverage of Riversend's backpacker murders. It has accused first one man then another of committing the crime—men the police say are demonstrably innocent. Then, yesterday, the paper accused Herb Walker of covering up knowledge of the backpacker murders for almost a year.*'

Cut to the premier, the embodiment of earnestness, standing out the back of parliament, flanked by the police minister, the attorney-general and the police commissioner, all of whom are staring grimly into the back of his neck as they nod their profound endorsement. '*There is no greater defender of free speech than myself and my government. But this is beyond the pale. A good man is dead. All for a grubby headline. All to sell a few extra newspapers.*'

A wide shot of the police doorstop in Bellington, a shot of Thunkleton listening, his voiceover again touched by sympathy: *'Herb Walker's police colleagues are attempting to cope with their loss while continuing their investigation.'*

Montifore: *'Herb Walker gave his all to serving his community at a time of great need. He didn't deserve this.'*

And then the shot of Martin, looking shifty as he begins to walk away, blinking under the glare of the camera lights. Thunkleton homing in for the kill: *'And from the reporter responsible, Martin Scarsden, not a skerrick of remorse.'* Then Martin: *'A hypocritical parasitic turd.'*

'In Riversend, Doug Thunkleton, Ten News.'

Back to the newsreader, forehead creased with the import of the story: *'We are able to report some small consolation for Sergeant Walker's grieving family and the good folk of Bellington; this evening the* Sydney Morning Herald *has published an unreserved apology and sacked the reporter responsible, effective immediately.'*

Martin kills the sound, staring at the glowing set. Charged, tried, convicted, all in a neat two-minute television package. Hung, drawn and quartered. 'Fuck me,' says Martin out loud, almost amused by the absurdity of it all. What now? He's been thinking of getting something to eat and a drink at the club. That's out of the question. Mandy's? No, he would be doing her no favours. Guilt by association would be an ugly phenomenon in such a small town. Best thing would be to check out now and drive somewhere far, far away. The rental car is still on the company account. Perth maybe. Or Darwin.

There's a knock at the door. Who? It sounds too measured for a torch-and-pitchfork mob. Martin eases the door open a whisker, his foot wedged hard in behind it, just in case.

It's Goffing. The ASIO man has a sixpack of stubbies in one hand, a bottle of Scotch in the other. 'Thought you might need a drink.'

Martin opens the door, lets him in.

Goffing looks at the muted TV set, broadcasting the remains of the Channel Ten news. 'So you saw, I take it?'

Martin nods.

Goffing holds the beers up first, then the whisky, offering Martin the choice.

'Beer, thanks.'

Martin sits on the bed; the agent takes the sole chair. They twist off the bottle caps with a gentle fizz and take the first few slugs in silence.

'The police believe it was suicide; I'm not so sure,' says the ASIO man, looking Martin in the eye.

The abruptness of the statement takes Martin by surprise. He doesn't answer immediately as he considers the implications. 'Why's that?'

'Let's just say I have a suspicious mind. Comes with the territory.'

'Well, I certainly hope you're right.'

'Tell me, Martin, do you feel guilty over Herb Walker's death?'

'No,' Martin answers without hesitation, despite the unexpected nature of the question. 'No, I don't. Do you think I should?'

'Not necessarily. What do you feel?'

'Pissed off. Hard done by. A bit despondent. For the life of me, I can't understand exactly what I've done to be in this position.'

Martin pauses, drinks some more beer. It's cold and comforting as it slides down his throat. Why is he confiding in this man, this spy, this exponent of the covert? Because it feels good to unburden himself. And because there is no one else to talk to.

'I accept that we may have been wrong about Byron Swift and Harley Snouch, but they were honest mistakes. You know that. We've been doing our best. And as for Herb Walker, that wasn't even me. My colleague in Sydney got that tip-off from one of her police contacts. I didn't even know about it until I read it in the paper.'

'You were uncomfortable with the story?'

'No. No, I can't claim that. If it was accurate, and it appears to be, he could have checked out the dam a year ago. Why wouldn't we publish that?'

'Because he was one of your sources?'

'No. Being a source doesn't give someone immunity.'

'But I was under the impression you apologised to him when you saw him at the police station yesterday.'

'That's half true. If I'd known what Bethanie had, I would have told him in person, tried to get his side of the story. But I wouldn't have argued against publication. At least, I don't think I would have. And that wasn't the main reason I sought him out yesterday.'

'Yes, so I understand. Mandalay Blonde and Byron Swift's supposed alibi.'

'Supposed?'

'The police aren't convinced. They've sent the diary for forensic analysis.'

'Really? What do you think?'

'Don't know. I'm agnostic on that matter.'

Goffing hands Martin a second beer. Martin hadn't realised he'd finished his first; he twists the top from the stubby.

'Why are you here, Agent Goffing?'

'The name's Jack. And we don't call ourselves "agent"—that's an American thing.'

'So why are you in Riversend, Jack?'

Goffing looks almost sad. 'Sorry, Martin. This is not an information swap. I can't afford to reveal anything more about my purpose here. My superiors are already pissed off at my presence being so spectacularly outed by you on national television. I'm not so ecstatic about it either.'

'So why talk to me now?'

'Herb Walker. You spoke to him yesterday. He was angry with you. You and your paper had fucked him over. He may have been less likely to disguise his state of mind with you than he might have in the presence of his police colleagues. It's not a culture that encourages any sign of emotional fragility.'

'He seemed fine. Angry, but in no way depressed or despairing, if that's what you mean.'

'Resigned?'

'Resigned to what?'

'You know, that his career was over, it was all coming down on top of him, that it was useless to fight back.'

'No. Just the opposite.'

'How so?'

Ah, the rub. Martin takes another suck of his beer. He has to admire the ASIO man's skill, leading him to this point. Does he cooperate? Does he tell him what he knows about Walker? Why not? He's lost his job, Walker is dead, Goffing may be the only person interested in taking the matter any further. He drains more of his beer and talks.

'I don't think he was despondent. He was intrigued by the news of Mandy Blonde's diary. And he remained determined to investigate the events leading up to Byron Swift's massacre at St James.'

Goffing's head is still, face smooth with concentration, eyes fixed on Martin. 'Byron Swift and St James? Do you know anything of his line of inquiry?'

Martin nods. 'I was able to speak to a witness to the shooting. Someone the police didn't interview. He told me that Byron Swift appeared happy and unflustered shortly before the shooting. He'd been outside, talking to some of his parishioners, the early arrivals. Laughing and joking. He even talked to Craig Landers, one of his victims, apparently without rancour. Then he went into the church, presumably to prepare for the service. He came out after five or ten minutes and started shooting.'

'Go on.'

'So what happened inside the church? It occurred to me that Swift either spoke to someone inside the church, or spoke to someone by phone. Herb Walker was trying to find out if there had been any calls made to or from the church that morning.'

Goffing nods. 'Right. And he drew a blank. We know. We checked the same thing. The only calls from the church that morning were Robbie Haus-Jones calling Walker and the ambulance in Bellington after the shooting. So what else?'

'No. Walker said he didn't draw a blank. Yesterday, when I saw him at the police station, he said there had been two other calls, one from the church and one to the church. Before the shooting. He said he was trying to chase down the numbers.'

Goffing doesn't say anything for a good thirty seconds or more. He's looking at Martin, but the ASIO man's thoughts appear to be working away on a different plane.

'Which call was made first? Did he say?'

'No. Perhaps Swift made a call, and then got a call back.'

'Maybe. Anything else? Did Walker mention anything else?'

'No. We weren't exactly on the best of terms by then, if you'll recall.'

'Martin, thank you. What you've told me might prove to be very useful indeed. Very useful. Have you told anyone else of these phone calls? Your colleagues, Mandalay Blonde?'

'You think they're significant?'

'Possibly. When we checked the records, the calls weren't on the database.'

'Someone tampered with the call records?'

'Maybe. It's curious, at the very least. So have you told anyone else about the calls?'

'No. Just you.'

'Very good. Please don't mention this to anybody else, including the police. Especially the police. If I'm going to clear you of responsibility for Walker's suicide, I need to keep this under wraps. Understand?'

Martin feels a surge of adrenaline, of hope. 'Clear me? You think you can do that?'

'I don't know. I shouldn't raise false expectations; it may not be possible. But keep the phone calls to yourself.'

'If you like. But what do I get in return?'

'You mean apart from trying to clear you of Walker's death?' Goffing smiles, then grows more serious. 'There is one thing. Your story in *The Sunday Age*, the one about Swift being a man without a past—it was right on the money.'

'You can confirm that?'

'Yes. Your story is correct. The real Byron Swift was an orphan and a ward of the state in Western Australia. Studied theology at uni in Perth and dropped out. Went to Cambodia, where he worked for a charity delivering development aid up on the Thai–Burma border. Died five years ago of a heroin overdose. All records, most records, redacted. Our Byron Swift assumed his identity.'

'Do you know who he really was? Swift?'

'I do.' Goffing pauses, makes some mental calculation before continuing. 'Martin, I'm going to tell you. It will most likely come out at the inquest.' Goffing again pauses, as if weighing a decision, before speaking. 'You should try to publish it before then but under no circumstances must my name or ASIO be mentioned. Just refer to reliable sources or however you want to phrase it.'

'That's kind of academic; I have nowhere to publish it.'

'You'll find somewhere.'

'All right. Tell me. You have my word I won't reveal where I got it from.'

'His real name was Julian Flynt. He was a fugitive.'

'A fugitive? I thought he was a former soldier.'

'He was. A special forces sniper. Iraq and Afghanistan. By all accounts an amazing soldier: a born leader, fearless and charismatic. Until he was captured by the Taliban and held captive for eight months, during which time he was tortured, degraded and humiliated. Later, after he was freed, he passed all the psychological testing and was cleared for duty. Big mistake. Massive mistake. Seemed fine, everything normal, no sign of damage. Then one day, close to a year later, during a firefight in a Mujahedin compound, he lost it. Two women and their kids, unarmed, arms raised, surrendering. Five of them. He cut them down in cold blood. The army detained him, pending trial. Some wanted to try him for murder; others defended him, citing the fog of war. Those who had authorised his return to the frontline just wanted him to disappear. And he did: he escaped from custody. A warrant was put out for his arrest, for war crimes. There were reports he'd made his way to Iraq, was working as a private bodyguard. When the authorities went looking they were told he'd died in an ambush. That made everyone happy; they closed his file. But as we now know, he wasn't dead. He came back here at some point, not on his own passport. Became Byron Swift.'

'How is that possible?'

'How indeed.'

'Is that what you're doing here? Investigating Byron Swift?'

'I'm not authorised to talk about that, Martin. I'll let you join the dots. But the Julian Flynt story, you think you can get that into the public domain?'

'I guess so. It's not a bad story.'

'Not bad? Do you understand what I've told you? He was an Australian soldier, wanted for war crimes. You reported on the Middle East, you know that story as well as anyone. Have you ever heard of him?'

'No.'

'And why do you think that is?'

'I don't know. You tell me.'

'For starters, the army doesn't want his case publicised, not least because they sent him back into combat when he should have been in care. They were happy to have him forgotten. Next, there's customs and border control. How the hell did he get back into the country? And then the police. He shoots five people dead and they don't bother to find out who he really was? Really? Nobody wants the public to know. Now do you understand the scope of what I'm telling you?'

'So what are you alleging, Jack? Some grand conspiracy?'

'I wish. More likely cock-ups and arse-covering, everyone trying to pass the buck and deny their own culpability.'

'So publish?'

'Yeah. Publish. Let's see if we can flush a few of them out.' A smile passes between the men. And it seems to Martin something else passes between them as well, a kind of understanding. 'You want some whisky?' asks Goffing.

Martin has finished his second beer. 'Shit. Why not?' He locates a couple of grimy tumblers in the bathroom and gives them a good rinse, which does little more than impart the smell of chlorine and decay. When he returns, Goffing has relieved the bottle of its cap and Martin hands him the glasses. Goffing dispenses two healthy shots and the men clink glasses. Martin wonders what significance the gesture holds. He drops back onto the bed and savours the peat and smokiness of the drink. It's been a long time since he's drunk whisky.

'Martin, I really can't tell you anything more about my assignment, you understand, but I can tell you about the police investigation.'

'Why?'

''Cos I think you're owed.'

'Good. I'm all ears.'

'Walker's death looks like a copybook suicide. His body was found in the Murray this morning. He probably died about midnight. He drowned. Filled his pockets with rocks and jumped from a bridge, some way out of Bellington, where he was unlikely to be discovered in the act. He left a note in his car. For the police, the note is always the clincher.'

'What did it say?' Martin takes a gulp of whisky, a little too much, feels it burn at the back of his throat.

'It was short and simple. *I always did my duty. I did nothing wrong. The media are liars. My reputation is everything to me.*'

'That's it?'

'That's it.'

'Shit.' More silence. On the television, some hippies are dancing in a circle, part of a religious cult. 'So why aren't you convinced it was suicide?'

'As I say, suspicious mind.'

The two men drink in silence then, exchanging small talk. Later, they flick the TV over to watch the ABC news at 7 pm. It's politics at the top, the cult and the TV presenter second, with Martin coming in third. The bronze medal. The report is considerably milder, more balanced than Thunkleton's. And more accurate. The confrontation between Martin and Doug Thunkleton is shown from a different, wider angle. '. . . *you are the worst type of journalist, a moral vacuum who'd sell his soul for a headline,*' says Thunkleton. '*Well, in that case, why do you keep interviewing me? You know what you are? A hypocritical parasitic turd,*' responds Martin. Thunkleton looks like a bully, Martin looks like a petulant and uncaring schoolboy, the ABC looks impartial and morally superior to them both. But at least it's clear his turd accusation is directed at the Channel Ten reporter and not the dead cop. Be thankful for small mercies— another of Max's dictums.

After that, Martin kills the box and he and Goffing talk of sport and politics and all those other things that fill the conversational void when other matters are too confronting to be vocalised.

Later, when the sun is setting and the heat has begun to drain off the landscape for another night, they sit outside and Goffing smokes cigarettes. Martin isn't sure, but he might even smoke one himself. At some point Goffing melts away and Martin is left by himself, with only the bottle, the blood moon and the blazing wash of the Milky Way for company.

The whisky does what strong alcohol always does: renders him unconscious the moment his head touches the pillow. And then later, in the early hours of the morning, it brings him back into semiconsciousness, unable to sleep, mind churning repetitively, incapable of properly marshalling his thoughts, so that they eat away at him, anxieties real and imagined. Not that he needs much imagination. Bits of the day come back to trouble him. The confrontation with Thunkleton, seen from three angles: Channel Ten's, the ABC's and his own, none of them pretty. Over and over the scene plays, like a television broadcast of an out-of-form batsman raising his bat to leave a ball pass through to the wicketkeeper, only to see it cannon into the stumps. Different angles, slow motion, fast motion, graphics, and always the same conclusion: the batsman trudging slowly towards the pavilion, eyes downcast, while the bowler pumps his fist and high-fives his teammates. The conversation with Goffing is on repeat too, Herb Walker's demise re-created in his mind, the words of the suicide note echoing, an image of Julian Flynt, soldier, shooting women and children in the dust of Afghanistan.

But at the end of the night, as dawn's light begins to assert itself through the thin curtains and the promise of a headache transmutes into throbbing reality, the phrase that his restless mind has distilled from an entire day of turmoil is a simple one: *The police aren't convinced. They've sent the diary for forensic analysis.* Mandy Blonde. What has she done?

⌒

He gets to the Oasis at seven, well before opening time, makes his way around to the back door and begins beating on it and keeps beating intermittently until finally, some five minutes later, he hears movement inside. Another minute or so and Mandy inches the door open. 'You?'

'Me.'

'Fuck me, Martin, the baby's sleeping.'

'Can I come in?'

She looks pissed off, but she opens the door, lets him come through. 'Jeez, you look like shit.'

'I feel like shit. I drank whisky last night. It doesn't agree with me.'

'Funny that.'

She's wearing a thin silk robe over a t-shirt and boxer shorts. Her hair is tousled and her eyes are still blinking away the vestiges of sleep, but the magic wand of youth has blessed her, rendering her beautiful. He suddenly feels the weight of his fading looks: all the allure of a hessian sack. A hessian sack with halitosis.

'Coffee?' she asks.

'You're a life saver,' he says.

'And you're a mess.'

She puts on coffee, then joins him at the kitchen table. 'So what's so urgent that you come banging on a young girl's door at the crack of dawn?'

'You heard what happened to me?'

'Getting sacked?'

'Yeah.'

'Can't see why it's your fault. That policeman killed himself; you didn't kill him. If people topped themselves every time a newspaper got something wrong, half the cabinet would have gone over the edge.'

Martin can't help smiling. When the whole world is gunning for you, it's good to have someone on your side. Then he remembers Snouch's ultimatum and he stops smiling.

'Is that why you came here? To tell me you've been sacked? You need a shoulder to cry on?'

'No. I came because I was worried about you.'

'About me?'

'Yes. Mandy, you told the police that Byron Swift was with you the night the backpackers were abducted.'

'That's right.'

'Do you think they believe you?'

'Do you?'

'Yes,' says Martin, and in uttering the words, he realises he's lying. During the night, the words of the ASIO man have dripped their poison into his mind, irrigating the seeds of doubt. He wants to believe her, but he's not sure that he does.

'Good to know someone does,' she says. 'But no. I don't think they believe me.'

'Why not? Do you know?'

'Because they're lazy and they're unimaginative. If they pin the murders on Byron, then it's case closed. Homicidal priest takes out another couple of innocents. No need for an arrest, no need for a trial. Everyone goes home happy. Including some psychopath sitting out there rubbing his hands, knowing he's gotten away with murdering those poor girls and whatever else he did to them first. And maybe planning his next little exploit.'

'Mandy, tell me; I want to help. Is the diary authentic? You didn't embellish it, did you?'

She looks at him silently, her green eyes as cold and clear as icicles.

'Was he really here that night, Mandy? All night? Were you?'

Her response, when it comes, is barely a whisper, as dry and as withering as the winds of drought. 'Get out, you arsehole. Get out and never come back.'

seventeen **CHARGED**

Martin checks his watch: twenty past seven. Already the relative cool of night is burning off, the prospect of heat nearly as oppressive as the coming reality. The sky has lost its dawn colours, washed away by the incremental ascendancy of the sun, leaving behind the bleached-out blue of summer. If there are clouds, Martin can't see any.

He sits on a bench in the shade of the shop awnings, challenging the town to respond to his existence, telling himself he will not move until he sees some confirmation of human habitation: a car driving past, a pedestrian, a kid on a bike. The town stares him down: not a stray dog, not a bird. Not the lizard who greeted him when he first arrived. Nothing. Finally, high up in the glowing blue dome, Martin spots the glinting silver of a speeding jet, vapour trail melting away behind it, heading west from Canberra or Sydney towards Adelaide or Perth. But the town remains impassive, conceding nothing.

Martin considers what is left for him here in this sun-blasted vacuum. Not a lot. No job, no purpose. He's successfully alienated Mandy Blonde, the one person he'd established any connection with. Now she's banished him back out into the void. There's Jack Goffing, the ASIO man keen to cultivate him, and Robbie Haus-Jones, a young man facing enough demons for the whole town, and Jamie Landers and Codger Harris, one young, the other old, both of them in mourning. There's Fran Landers, who owes him for saving her son but would prefer him to disappear without a trace, and Harley Snouch, insistent that he help make things right with Mandy. Fat chance of that. He knows them, they know him, but ultimately they're strangers. They may be allies or enemies, but none of them share his burdens. No. Not in this town, not in this life. He is without comrades, devoid of friends.

He looks at his hands, resting limp and purposeless, one on the armrest of the bench, the other on the bench itself. Not agitated, not primed, but dormant, as if they've been switched off by some robotic remote, placed on standby awaiting further instructions. Has that been the big mistake in his life, the essential flaw in his character—that he's always been a loner, slow to make friends, reluctant to make allies, resistant to commitment? There is Max, of course, a mentor and true ally, and perhaps a friend as well. Max, who saw his potential, made him his go-to man, first for out-of-town stories and later for foreign assignments. But what was it that Max saw? A good journo, a good writer, but also an independent unit, someone who didn't want or need the normal support networks of humanity, a reporter at his happiest and his best when he was separated from those he knew, who could parachute into any situation, make acquaintances and recruit sources, and then leave without qualms when the story was done. He'd been perfect for the role. Or so Max had thought, and Martin had thought so too. Now he isn't so sure.

Finally, up on the highway, a truck thunders through, heading east from Bellington, ploughing onwards towards civilisation, not stopping, barely paying Riversend the courtesy of slowing down. Martin glimpses it as it passes through the T-junction at the top of Hay Road. Good enough; Martin stands. His head throbs and his stomach reminds him of last night's excesses. He knows very little, but he knows he doesn't want to be out in the open once the heat turns punitive. He thinks of water and aspirin at the general store, but it won't be open yet. Instead, he crosses the road, making his way towards the wine saloon. Perhaps Snouch is in there, sleeping away his own hangover.

But the wine saloon is lifeless: footprints in the dust, dried wine in the bottom of chipped tumblers, an empty bottle next to a crumpled paper bag. Snouch may have left five minutes ago or on Sunday night or at any time in between; there is no way of telling.

Martin walks to the front of the saloon, to the boarded-up windows where the filtered light from the street penetrates the gloom. There's a stool. He sits and peers out through a viewing crack, looking across the road towards the Oasis. How often did Snouch perch here, spying on his former fiancée and her daughter? What memories ran through his mind, what hopes did he harbour in his heart? Was there a frisson of excitement when at the end of the day she emerged to bring in the outside display bins? Did she ever look up, glance across the road, acknowledge her stalker in his lair? And what happened once she was back inside, the door closed for the night, the lights extinguished? Was it then that he returned to sit at one of the tables, finding comfort in his bottles and conversations with imaginary companions, explaining his motives to the dead veterans?

Martin moves away from the shuttered window and sits himself at the table where he last spoke with Snouch. Martin considers Mandalay Blonde, locked away in the closed bookstore, as inaccessible to him now as her mother ever was to Snouch. She's beautiful, painfully so; no questioning that. She's intelligent too, quick and quirky and independent. And young and troubled, more troubled than she deserves to be. But then again, the troubled are always young; the old are simply pathetic. Grow old and the edges come off: the mind rationalises, the heart concedes, the soul surrenders. We all grow old and frail, inside as well as out. The twists of reaction become entrenched, character traits become permanent: the resentments, the denials, the rationalisations. We learn to live with it. It's so much more troubling when we are young and honest. Maybe Katherine Blonde was onto something when she insisted her daughter lay her demons to rest before she turned thirty.

Martin feels a pang of conscience, a creeping remorse, as he considers the woman shuttered away in the bookstore. Conceived either when her father raped her mother, or when her mother cheated on her fiancé. Growing up wearing the stigma of the rape allegation, bullied by the ignorance of locals, protected by a defiant mother conducting her own silent war. Finally escaping Riversend, but never really escaping it, frittering away her youth in Melbourne, only to be pulled back to the town by her mother's illness. To be preyed upon by Byron Swift, with his looks and his charm and his selfish needs. Byron Swift, slipping between her sheets, between her legs, offering comfort and escape while taking exactly what he wanted. The murderer of Afghanistan, pretending to be someone he was not. Then getting shot, suiciding, and making poor Robbie Haus-Jones wear the guilt. And Mandy, impregnated and abandoned. Left all alone to raise an infant son, having nursed a dying mother. And yet she still loves Swift, despite knowing what he inflicted on her. Loves him well enough to defend him to the police a full year after he died, a pyrrhic display of loyalty if ever there was one. And then what? Him. Martin Scarsden, another thief in the night, a worthy candidate for membership of the wine saloon's lonely company. And what has he given her? Some company, some grief. Some small parcel of companionship in the lonely nights of Riversend.

Martin picks up one of the glasses, absent-mindedly moving it to his lips before realising what he's doing. He puts the glass down, feeling vaguely foolish. But why? There are no witnesses here; there are no ghosts. He offers himself a smile, a twisted sardonic expression, lacking humour, holding sparse compassion. Byron fucking Swift. Homicidal priest, war criminal, sprayer of sperm among the lonely women of the Riverina. Fran Landers, Mandy Blonde, God knows how many down in Bellington, God knows how many before that. A backblocks Rasputin.

Mandy knows he killed the five at the church. Why go to the police with her diary, trying to clear him of the murder of the backpackers? Did she see that as a more heinous crime? That the massacre at St James was some sort of psychotic explosion, conceived and executed in the moment, whereas the abduction, probable rape and murder of the backpackers was premeditated, sadistic and evil? What was she defending: the reputation of her dead lover, her own hesitant faith in him, or the legacy bequeathed to their son, so that one day, when he learnt the truth, he might think slightly better of his father than she thought of hers? *Christ.* Martin looks about. For an instant, despite his aching head, he wouldn't mind spotting an unopened bottle in the dusty gloom.

So what of her allegorical tale, that she'd fallen pregnant in a one-night stand in Melbourne? It seems obvious enough: she didn't want to tell a journalist that she'd been the killer's lover. She didn't want that plastered all over the papers, not for herself and certainly not for their son. She wouldn't want Liam growing up like herself . . . How had she phrased it? The progeny of scandal. But why talk at all? Because she wanted him to find out what she didn't know: who was Byron Swift really? She'd done it deliberately, led him on, hoping he might uncover the past of the priest. What was she seeking? Some unknown vindication of Swift for impregnating her, abandoning her, shooting dead five people in cold blood, bequeathing their son shame and infamy?

Martin thinks of Walker, his discovery that the priest was a man without a past, Martin's article in the Sunday papers, Goffing's revelation of Flynt's war crime. Was that it? Mandy

303

loved Byron Swift but didn't know who it was she loved? She wanted to know his real identity, his story, for herself and her son? Well, Martin knows now. He knows who Swift was, knows his shameful past: that Swift was a war criminal. But can he tell her? And will she listen? And what of Harley Snouch, so confident his DNA test will exonerate him and prove her mother a vindictive liar? How can Martin even broach such possibilities? She would banish him forever.

His stomach churns and his head pounds. He realises he's losing her, that there is little chance of reconciliation, not after his early-morning accusations, not with the information he's carrying around like unexploded bombs. Somewhere, some-time, he'll publish Goffing's story, tell the world that Swift was really the war criminal Julian Flynt, and she'll never speak to him again. And he'll be left with his own doubts about her. Goffing planted the seeds: is the diary genuine, or is it some new manipulation? Is it a fabrication, another allegorical tale? Martin sits in the wine saloon and ponders whether his life has been reduced to an absurdist game show: which does he choose, the money or the box, the story or the girl?

The room brightens suddenly. A shaft of sunlight is carving its way into the saloon, lifting the gloom, sending motes dancing. The sun has risen above the row of stores on the other side of the street, high enough to flush Hay Road with sunshine, yet still low enough to penetrate below the saloon's protective awning. Martin walks over to the cracks in the boarding, angling his point of view to avoid looking directly into the rising sun. But it's no good: the Oasis is obliterated by the dawn's anti-septic flaring. A flash of red, the sound of a car; Fran Landers returning from Bellington with milk and bread and swamp peas. And newspapers. There is life on Mars.

—

But Fran is non-communicative, bustling around her store, restricting herself to the compulsory courtesies, so Martin buys the papers, some water, an iced-coffee-flavoured milk, a Bellington danish and some low-grade painkillers.

He sits out front of the store on the bench, sipping the milk and grimacing at Tuesday's papers. He's gone from *The Age*, banished, all evidence of his existence erased, airbrushed away like a latter-day Trotsky. The story is on page three, by D'Arcy Defoe in Bellington, and listed at the bottom of the copy, like an afterthought: *Additional reporting by Bethanie Glass*. It's a typical Defoe piece, beautifully crafted despite its brevity, sitting under the headline RIVER TOWN MOURNS LOST POLICEMAN. The story refers only obliquely to the circumstances of Herb Walker's death and not at all to the connection with the backpacker murders; there is no mention of Martin Scarsden, Doug Thunkleton or anything else. Rather, it's a eulogy to a fine man, a tough job and desperate times. Defoe has reported the story without reporting it at all; management will be pleased. The story has become a minefield for the paper, and with Defoe here, Fairfax will be in safe hands. He's always admired that in his rival: Defoe never, ever loses perspective. Martin sighs. Time to get out of town.

He's finished the iced-coffee milk and is swallowing some tablets and water when he sees Robbie Haus-Jones and one of the Sydney homicide cops, Lucic, walking purposefully around the corner near the bank, no doubt coming from the police station. They cross the road and walk straight towards him, not talking. For a dread moment his heart accelerates: are they coming to arrest him? What for? They do indeed walk up to him, but not to arrest him.

'Morning, Martin,' says Robbie.

Lucic looks at him with disdain, not even offering a nod of acknowledgement.

'Morning, Robbie. What's up?'

'Nothing concerning you,' says Lucic. He stays standing by Martin as Robbie enters the store. A minute or two later Robbie emerges, accompanied by a concerned-looking Fran Landers.

'Martin,' she says, seeing him sitting there, 'could you do me a favour? Keep an eye on the store? I'll be back in a few minutes.'

'Sure,' says Martin, knowing he has nothing better to do.

He watches the trio walk along the street, disappearing around the corner by the hotel, heading away from the police station, not towards it. He sits outside, waiting. A farmer pulls up in a battered ute, and Martin follows him into the store. The man buys a kilo of bacon, a loaf of white bread, two litres of milk and a pouch of tobacco. The till is locked, so Martin takes the man's cash and sets it next to the register. The transaction is conducted in near silence, the man limiting himself to grunts, speaking only to communicate his preferred brand of tobacco. Martin follows him out of the store, watches him climb into his ute and drive back the way he came.

Not long after, Martin sees the two policemen emerge from a store on the next block. Another surge of dread: the bookstore. Sure enough, as the policemen wait, Mandy joins them, and they cross the road, round the corner in front of the old council building and disappear from sight behind the bank, heading towards the police station. None of the three look at Martin.

He's still sitting there when Fran returns, pushing a stroller. Liam is sucking on a bottle without a care in the world.

'Fran, what's happening?'

'They've taken Mandy in for questioning. I'm looking after Liam. Said they'd likely be a few hours.'

'What are they questioning her over?'

'I don't know, Martin. They didn't tell me.'

'How is she?'

'Okay, I think. Resigned, maybe, as if she was expecting it.'

'Right.'

Martin isn't sure what to do. Leaving town seems like the obvious choice, but how can he? He feels responsible for Mandy. He's slept with her, he's carried her alibi for Byron Swift to Walker, he's returned her affection by more or less accusing her of complicity in murder. And now? Just leave town, wash his hands? Leave her to whatever trouble she finds herself in? A six o'clock execution by Doug Thunkleton, a beautifully written stiletto piece by D'Arcy Defoe, a scapegoat hung out to appease the public by Montifore and the cops?

He walks to the corner, looks towards the police station. The predictable gaggle of cameramen and photographers are already in place. It's not yet nine o'clock. Either his erstwhile colleagues are displaying commendable diligence, driving the forty minutes from Bellington to take up their position, or they've been tipped off by the police for the parade: walk the suspect in, walk her out, parade her for the titillation of the great Australian public, demonstrate that the police are making progress.

It is, he knows full well, growing into a perfect summer story, in the great tradition of Lindy Chamberlain and Schapelle Corby. A heady mixture of murder, religion and sex. And, once news of Mandy's diary is inevitably leaked, a beautiful femme fatale to feed to the cameras, as well as perhaps the most crucial element of all: mystery. Why did Byron Swift open fire? Who did murder the pretty young backpackers? Were they raped and tortured, as alleged by the competition papers? All around Australia, at barbecues and bars, at cafes and canteens, at hairdressers and in taxis, everyone and their dog will be advancing their own half-baked theories of what happened and who was responsible. Talkback radio will be having a field day; the internet will be spawning an equal measure of sick jokes and conspiracy theories, with him featuring in many of them. And yet he can't complain: no one has done more to put the story on the front page, to propel it into the consciousness of the nation, than himself, Martin Scarsden. His stomach lurches at the thought and he needs to sit down. He should never drink whisky.

———

Arriving back at the Black Dog, he feels even worse. There's a television satellite truck parked outside. The story is about to go live, 24/7. And if one network does it, the others are bound to follow. Christ. And he's powerless to do anything about it. He's walking past reception towards his room, considering the gathering media storm, when the woman from behind the counter sticks her head out the door. 'Mr Scarsden? A moment, if you will?' She is back behind the counter by the time Martin enters reception. He sees that she's had her hair cut and dyed, the ragged blonde lengths and their mousy roots replaced by brunette consistency. Bellington chic.

'I'm sorry, Mr Scarsden, but I had a call from your employer. Your former employer. They're stopping the authorisation on your card as of today. They want to transfer your room over to another gentleman. A Mr . . .'

'Defoe.'

'So that's how you pronounce it. Mr Defoe. Is he with you?'

'No.'

'I see. Anyway, if you can vacate, I can get the room ready for him.'

'Look—um, sorry, I've forgotten your name.'

'Felicity Kirby. My husband Gino and I own the Black Dog.'

'Well, Mrs Kirby, I haven't seen Mr Defoe as yet, but I'm inclined to think that he might not stay here. Much of the media are staying down in Bellington. They seem to like it down there by the river.'

'Only because we are booked out here, Mr Scarsden.'

'I'm sure you're right, Mrs Kirby. Nevertheless, in Mr Defoe's case, unless you offer him the penthouse, he's still likely to prefer Bellington.'

'Is that a joke, Mr Scarsden?'

'I'm afraid it is, Mrs Kirby.'

'Really? You're a funny man. Now hand over your key and we can all have a good laugh.'

'Tell you what, Mrs Kirby, perhaps we can come to a more mutually advantageous arrangement.'

'Spit it out, love. I haven't got all day.'

'I keep the room, pay on my personal card.'

'I see. And you're sure this other bloke will be okay with that? I told them I would hold it for him.'

'Trust me. His tastes are a little more elevated.'

'Sounds like a bit of a tosser, Mr Scarsden.'

'Your words, Mrs Kirby, not mine.'

'All right then. It's a week's payment in advance, day by day after that.'

'A week in advance? I've already been here a week.'

'New card, new account.'

Martin shrugs, is about to sign when he notices the rate has increased by thirty dollars a night. 'Inflationary pressures come to Riversend, Mrs Kirby?'

'Textbook economics, Mr Scarsden. Too much money chasing too few assets. Plus it's the school holiday rush.'

Martin starts filling out the credit card authorisation and a new hotel registration form.

'Oh, yes, I almost forgot—your editor rang last night. No, the night before.'

'Thanks. Probably doesn't matter now.'

'He left a message.' She rummages around in her desk, hands Martin a post-it note. There's a phone number on it, a landline. 'He said it was a new number.'

Cripes. Poor Max. They haven't even let him keep his phone number.

Martin smiles as he hands over the paperwork. 'Nice haircut, Mrs Kirby.'

'Why thank you, Mr Scarsden.'

Indecision is waiting in his room, embracing him as he enters, flopping him onto the unmade bed. Has he really just committed himself to another week in this hellhole? More specifically, what should he do now? He's still here because he doesn't want to abandon Mandalay Blonde to her fate, but on the other hand, he's not going to be doing her any favours if he camps outside the police station, providing more grist for the relentless media mill. Moreover, as of this morning, she can't stand the sight of him.

He wonders what she does want, what her desires might be. She had slept with him, it was true. But only the once; it hardly meant she was carrying a torch for him. What had motivated her to take him home that night? Gratitude that Snouch had survived? Gratitude Martin had also escaped death? Guilt for manipulating him? Or perhaps she was just lonely. Or bored. Or she just wanted to share in some of the excitement of the day. She certainly wasn't pining after a man, that much was obvious. She'd only wanted to leave town with Swift after she discovered she was pregnant, but up until then had seemed content to share the priest with Fran, despite claiming to be in love with him. She's certainly made no such declarations towards Martin. And is unlikely to do so, not since his newspaper slurs and his early morning insinuations. What had she said? *Get out and never come back.* He looks at his hands, his pathetic hands, realising he's the one craving an emotional connection, not her. He's the one who needs to help her; she's not the one who needs his help.

So what should he do? Maybe he should return to the general store and wait there with Fran Landers and Liam; it will be the first place Mandy heads to when the police release her. He can speak with her, offer his help, say his goodbyes, leave with a clear conscience. But he delays moving. He doesn't want to be left sitting outside the store for hours on end, like some callow schoolboy. Not with this head, not in this heat. He knows he should be thinking about his future, contemplating what he might do with his life, with his career, now that the *Herald* has cut him adrift, instead of obsessing about an unobtainable young woman. Could he still have any future as a journalist, in a contracting industry experiencing its own financial drought? He should be on the phone, finding someone to take the story about Julian Flynt.

He looks at the paper with Max's new number. Maybe his old editor could suggest someone to take the story? Martin picks up the motel phone, dials, but the call doesn't go through. Instead, he gets a recorded message. '*The number you have called is no longer in service.*' Terrific.

He gets out his mobile phone, reduced by Riversend's lack of service to little more than an electronic Rolodex. He finds Max's mobile number, dials it on the hotel phone.

'Hello, Max Fuller.'

'Max, it's Martin.'

'Martin, good man. Where are you?'

'Still in Riversend. Just tidying up a few loose ends.'

'I see. How can I help?'

'Did you call me here the other night? At the Black Dog? Leave me a phone number?'

'Not me, soldier. What was the number?'

Martin quotes it to him.

'Jeez, Martin, that's not even a Sydney number. It's from down where you are. The first four digits are the same as the phone you're on now.'

Martin looks across at the bedside table where Tommy's takeaway menu lies, red ink on white. *Saigon Asian*, with its phone number. Max is right: the first four digits are the same. Something isn't right. 'Max. I'm an idiot. Sorry to bother you. Crossed wires.'

'Martin, are you okay?'

'Never better. I'll give you a ring when I'm back in Sydney.'

'Make sure you do.'

The call finished, Martin is left staring at the receiver. Was Felicity Kirby mistaken? Who would call him, from somewhere in Riversend or close by, pretending to be his editor? Someone covering their tracks? In order to leave a disconnected phone number? Unless . . . *Holy shit. Walker.* The number from St James. He's still staring at the phone when there's a knock at the door. He feels a surge of panic, unsure whether to answer.

The knock comes again. 'Martin? You there?'

It's Jack Goffing. Martin opens the door, lets the ASIO man enter.

'You look like shit,' says Goffing by way of greeting. 'Glad to see I'm not the only one feeling a bit dusty this morning.'

Martin can detect no evidence of any after-effects on the man's face; his eyes appear as clear and perceptive as ever. Martin sits on the bed; Goffing closes the door and remains standing. There's a smell of cigarettes.

'You know what's happened?'

'What? No.'

'You all right?'

'No, I'm hungover. Thanks to you.'

'They've arrested Mandalay Blonde. They're charging her.'

'With what?'

'Attempting to pervert the course of justice.'

'The diary?'

'The diary.'

'Shit.' Martin pauses. 'Fuck knows why she wanted to come forward with that.'

'Any ideas?'

'Me? No. You?'

'No.'

'So what's wrong with the diary?' asks Martin. 'Is it falsified?'

'Not sure. You understand this conversation is utterly and totally off the record?'

'Like I said, that's academic. I still don't have anywhere to publish it.'

'True. But I don't want you handballing it to your mates. So no tip-offs to D'Arcy Defoe.'

'You have my word.'

'Good. Well, as I understand it, the problem with the diary isn't so much what has been added to it, although the plods suspect at least one line has been written after the fact. The problem is that there are pages missing. She's ripped them out.'

'She's probably just trying to protect her privacy.'

'Maybe. But if that's right, she doesn't know coppers. They'll be like a dog at a bone with this. You can't imagine the sort of pressure that's starting to come down on them to get a result, and then she comes forward and delivers herself on a platter.'

'But it doesn't make any sense. If she were involved in the murders, why would she volunteer the diary? She wasn't a suspect before this, was she?'

'Not that I'm aware of.'

'So they'd have a pretty hard task making a charge against her stick.'

'Don't be so sure. They won't be able to prove involvement with the murder, not without evidence. But the charge of attempting to pervert the course of justice is a good one. The diary details some of the movements of the prime suspect, Byron Swift, in the days surrounding the abduction and murders of the German backpackers and the shooting spree at St James, and she has destroyed possibly vital pieces of evidence. She's in deep shit.'

'Christ, what happens next?'

'That's why I came looking for you. She's applying for bail, wants to look after her kid. The cops are resisting. They're planning to drive her down to Bellington to appear before a magistrate.'

'There's a magistrates court in Bellington?'

'No. Not exactly. They're driving in the bloke from Deniliquin.'

'Why not drive him here?'

'My guess? Because the media has based itself in Bellington.'

'Shit. You're kidding, right?'

'No.'

'So you're telling me this why?'

'Thought you might want to head down. She may need some moral support.'

'From me?'

'From anyone.'

———

It's a long and peculiar caravan that speeds across the baking plain from Riversend to Bellington, a convoy of anticipation and fear, ambition and despair, each vehicle propelled by a different purpose and transporting different emotions. Taking the lead are the police vehicles: Robbie Haus-Jones driving Herb Walker's four-wheel drive; Morris Montifore and Goffing in a rental; a highway patrol car with a garish paint job transporting Mandalay Blonde and Ivan Lucic. Thereafter, the media: 3AW in a tarted-up truck with a colour scheme to rival the highway patrol; a bunch of white rental cars; a couple of personal vehicles; the television networks in their kitted-out station wagons and SUVs. The caravan moves at exactly one hundred and ten kilometres per hour, the police observing the speed limit to the letter, the media not daring to go any faster or any slower, following in perfect formation, seatbelts fastened, cross purposes disguised by uniform velocity, all careering towards Bellington, the river and the next episode in this nation-gripping drama. Halfway across the plain the convoy sweeps past the lumbering satellite truck, not slowing, barely swerving, unimpeded by oncoming traffic, every driver indicating diligently as they pull out, indicating diligently as they pull back in.

Martin's is the last car in the caravan; no longer at the vanguard of the story but in the caboose, not the headline but the footnote. For a moment he considers flooring it, red-lining the rental, sweeping past his former colleagues and the police in a final gesture of defiance, hazard lights flashing, challenging them to respond. But the thought withers; he lacks the psychic capital. And so he resigns himself to his lowly rank and wonders why, at a time when no one else wants to know him, Jack Goffing has sought him out twice in twenty-four hours. To extract information, no doubt, cultivating a source, eliciting facts. What had he said? *This is not an information swap.* And yet that's exactly what it proved to be: Goffing revealed Byron Swift was really Julian Flynt, detailing the soldier's history and his crimes. And the ASIO man volunteered other information: the diary has pages missing, perhaps a line or two added. And he offered an opinion on police motivation. Why? Not because Martin could publish it. Mandy Blonde? That made more sense. Goffing now knows she was intimately involved with Swift and he thinks Martin may be the way to win her trust. Martin smiles at that. Goffing and Snouch, both seeing him as a conduit to Mandy. Chances are, she'll never speak to him again.

He considers whether he should tell Goffing about the phone number. A Riversend phone number. Maybe there is some website that does reverse phone numbers and can tell him who it belongs to. Maybe Bethanie can help. Or maybe he should simply trust Goffing. The man would have the resources to identify the owner of the number, know who it was that Swift phoned from St James in the moments before the shooting started. But if Goffing finds out, would he feel any obligation to share his information with Martin? Yet what choice does Martin have? If Goffing can make any headway on either St James or the backpacker murders, it could spare Mandy a lot of grief. Or provide the evidence to prosecute her. *Jesus.* The permutations start to fuel Martin's headache and he's relieved when the green swathe of Bellington's irrigated orchards emerges from the horizon and the brake lights of the convoy turn red in a chain reaction as the drivers, law-abiding citizens each and every one, slow to the requisite sixty kilometres an hour. By the time Martin drives into the main street, he's made up his mind: he has to tell Goffing about the phone number.

—

The bail hearing is conducted behind closed doors. The magistrate has barricaded himself inside the Bellington police station and ruled that the media must keep their distance. And so the journalists wait, alive with anticipation and speculation. The police have arrested local woman Mandalay Blonde, they report urgently into microphones, their voices deep with gravity. Femme fatale says one, Bonnie and Clyde says another, crime of the century says a third. And soon they are all saying it. Doug Thunkleton booms authoritatively into the eye of a television camera, rewarming old facts and conjuring new ones. The story is breaking across the nation like a wave: the police are making headway, we're awaiting news, stand by, whatever you do, don't miss it, don't change channels, back after the break, must-see TV. And yet, for all the excitement, a momentary hush falls over the mob as they watch Martin walk into the station, before recommencing, eager and urgent, a new buzz-phrase spreading through the pack and out across the nation: *disgraced former journalist Martin Scarsden*.

But today Martin is receiving no privileged access, not this time, and he's asked to wait outside with the media. And so he does, back at the scene of yesterday's train wreck. His former colleagues look either astounded or confused by his presence. Or both. Thackery shakes his head with dismay, but pays him the courtesy of saying hello, saying he's sorry about how it's all ended. An ABC journo requests an interview as if entitled to it, citing how the network had come to his defence on the previous night's news. Martin declines. Doug Thunkleton, live cross complete for the moment, steadfastly refuses to make eye contact, even while his camera crew brazenly film Martin's every movement.

'Martin,' says a voice, deep and self-possessed. It's D'Arcy Defoe. 'Didn't expect to see you here. How you holding up?'

'D'Arcy. Welcome to the circus. Not so bad. What are the police saying?'

'Very little. They've arrested the bookstore owner. Apparently she knew the priest Byron Swift.'

'Yes, she did.'

'Your mate Thunkleton is going in strong. He's saying the police suspect that she and the priest did it together, murdered the backpackers.'

'Listen, D'Arcy, don't report that. Seriously, wait until you hear what the police have to say.'

'So you know differently?'

'I'm not sure what I know. But I've been pushing the envelope on this story and look where it's landed me. Even I wouldn't report that. Not yet.'

D'Arcy is mulling over this information when, from the police station, a thin man in a grey suit and a five o'clock shadow emerges. 'ASIO,' comes the whisper.

Goffing spots Martin, waves him over. He can feel the cameras boring into his back as he joins Goffing and they enter the police station.

'Hope you're cashed up,' says Goffing.

'Why?'

'You may need to post bail.'

The magistrate is sitting at an impressive desk, red in the face, somewhat dishevelled and none too happy. Neither is anyone else: not Montifore, who is looking daggers at the magistrate, not Lucic, who is glaring at Robbie Haus-Jones, and not Robbie, who is avoiding eye contact with the homicide detectives. Mandy is seated, looking small, wearing a white shirt, blue jeans and handcuffs. She looks up at Martin and smiles, eyes hopeful. His heart quickens and he wonders if she might have forgiven him his early-morning accusations.

'Martin Scarsden?' asks the magistrate. His eyes are bloodshot. Martin smells alcohol.

'That's correct.'

'I am informed you may be prepared to go surety for Ms Blonde. Is this correct?'

'Yes, Your Honour.'

The magistrate snorts, sighs and shakes his head. 'I'm a magistrate, not a judge, Mr Scarsden. I am no one's honour.' And he belches, for good measure. 'Pardon me.'

Martin nods. No one is laughing; no one is smiling. The magistrate is drunk, but it's straight faces all around.

The magistrate continues, his voice steady enough, but his hand gestures overly emphatic. 'All right. I'm faced with a dilemma here, Mr Scarsden. A dilemma. Wisdom of Solomon required. On one hand, Detective Inspector Monty here is opposing bail, saying the charge is too serious. On the other hand, the young constable here tells me Ms Blonde is the sole carer for an infant under the age of one. Does that sound right to you?'

'Yes, sir.'

'Very good. Have you ever had gout?'

'No, sir.'

'Very good. Avoid it if you can.' Another belch, the faces of the police officers resolutely serious, although Montifore has closed his eyes. 'So here is what I propose: I will grant bail, provided you post a surety of, what shall we say, fifteen thousand dollars? Yes, that has a good ring to it. Fifteen thousand. Do you have access to that amount of money? And are you prepared to go guarantor?'

Martin looks at Mandy and any doubts he has are erased. Her eyes are on him, filled with concern about Liam. How could he possibly deny her?

'Yes, sir. I can visit my bank here in Bellington.'

'Very good. Here are the conditions. Ms Blonde, you are to report to police in Riversend daily, before noon. You are not permitted to travel more than five kilometres outside the town without informing the police in advance and gaining their permission. And let's see . . . you are not permitted to discuss matters connected to the charge with Mr Scarsden or any other media. However, I do advise you to discuss them with a lawyer. These conditions will remain in force until you face a committal hearing, or the charges are dropped, or I make some other determination. Or something else happens. Do you understand?'

'Yes, sir,' Mandy says softly.

'Mr Scarsden, I am wary about discharging the accused into the care of a reporter. To be honest, I don't think much of you lot. Be that as it may. You will not discuss the charge, Ms Blonde's diary or its contents with her. And you shall not report on matters related to the charge. Do you understand?'

Martin blinks. A gag on reporting. But he looks again at Mandy and the matter is settled. 'Yes,' he tells the magistrate.

'And you are still willing to post bail?'

'I am.'

'All right. Ms Blonde will remain in police custody until she is returned to Riversend. Mr Scarsden, please collect a bank cheque and make your way to the Riversend police station. And Mr Scarsden?'

'Yes, sir?'

'Avoid rich foods if you possibly can. Source of all evil. Now good day to you all.' And he liberates another belch, larger, louder and longer than its predecessors.

eighteen

BAILED

THE CARAVAN HAS LOST ITS COHERENCE; MARTIN FINDS HIMSELF DRIVING BACK to Riversend without another car in sight. He's not alone, though; sitting next to him, having cadged a lift, is Jack Goffing, ASIO investigator. The men drive in silence, occupied by their own thoughts. Martin has been to the bank, organised a bank cheque. It sits in his shirt pocket, weightless, yet heavy with obligation. Martin knows that somewhere ahead of him the purpose of the cheque, Mandy Blonde, is traversing the plain in the back of the highway patrol car, still wearing handcuffs, still a prisoner. Montifore and Lucic will be up ahead as well, planning their next moves. Martin wonders if Robbie Haus-Jones is part of their small convoy or if he's put some distance between himself and his Sydney superiors.

Martin may be trailing the police by some way, but he has a head start on the media, still in Bellington, still filing. Martin can imagine them: Doug Thunkleton talking nonstop down the maw of a camera lens, his observations beamed via the satellite van out across Australia; radio reporters breathlessly describing the scene as Mandy Blonde left the police station in a storm of camera flashes; newspaper reporters making the most of Bellington's functional internet to file online: straight news reporting scant facts, colour pieces conveying the day's drama, opinion pieces bravely asserting what it all means. But regardless of style, and regardless of medium, sitting at the core of each and every report, driving interest across the nation, will be variations of a single image: the young mother, with her ethereal beauty and uncanny green eyes, her wrists bound by handcuffs. Soon the journalists will be done and they too will be on their way across the digital desert to Riversend, eager to report the next instalment of this small-town saga, this tale of murder, religion and illicit love that is suddenly dominating the summer news cycle, this story now revolving around the photogenic couple: Byron Swift, deceased, and Mandalay Blonde, condemned. Halfway to Riversend, the first of the media passes Martin at speed, clocking a hundred and sixty at least: a photographer, having quickly filed his images from outside the police station, thrashing his rental to get a drop on his competitors and position himself for the next episode. Martin watches the car race into the distance, warping and distorting in the heat before dissolving altogether.

Martin tries to concentrate on driving, but there is precious little to concentrate on: the road is flat, straight and devoid of traffic, a bitumen line bisecting an impassive and non-judgemental landscape, like a line of longitude drawn on a map. He wonders what it is he's committing himself to: fifteen thousand dollars is a lot of money for an unemployed journalist, particularly one gagged from reporting Australia's biggest story. It's not the money that bothers him; he doesn't think that Mandy Blonde is about to abscond, but he has no idea what she might do. Or what she has done in the past. He's acted with decency, with chivalry, in securing her release. Or has he? Is it gallantry or is it his desire for reconciliation? Or is it self-interest? Mandy will be in his debt, will surely forgive him, speak with him. Then he'll be able to make the case for Harley Snouch, persuade her to take the DNA test and avert Snouch's defamation threat. Has he been fooling himself; is that his true motivation? Regardless, he'll now be inextricably linked to her in the public mind; if not already, certainly by the time the evening television news stories have delivered their verdict. Her epithet is set: she is now *leading police suspect Mandalay Blonde*, just as he is *disgraced former journalist Martin Scarsden*. And he's stuck here, stuck in Riversend, his fate linked to hers, his fifteen thousand dollars most definitely linked to her. And he's forbidden by the magistrate from writing a word about it. Where it's all heading he has no idea, but his first course of action is clear: he needs to bail out Mandy and then get back on speaking terms with her. A memory comes to mind of her standing in her kitchen wearing nothing more than a loose t-shirt, offering him coffee. He shakes his head, dismissing the recollection.

He looks away to the horizon, shimmering and ill-defined under the harsh sunlight, the sun that should lift all shadows but instead blurs the edges of the world, renders the horizon debatable, so that it's impossible to tell land from sky. Who killed the backpackers? Why did Byron Swift run amok? What was written on the pages Mandy had ripped from the diary? The landscape is blank, the road melts into the distance, the sun beats down.

Jack Goffing breaks the silence. 'Martin, I need your help.'

'I guessed as much.'

'I want to speak to Mandalay Blonde, by herself, away from the police.'

'Is that why you've been cultivating me? To get to her?'

'To be honest, that's a large part of it, yes.'

Martin laughs at that, at Goffing's honesty. 'Right. Let me think about it. What's in it for me?'

'Maybe nothing. But there could be a lot for her. It doesn't make sense, her handing over the diary like that if it implicates her. I might be able to help her get off the charge.'

'So might a lawyer.'

'You won't help?'

'I will. But tell me how you know Swift was really Flynt. And what you're really doing here.'

Goffing doesn't respond straight away. It's something Martin has noticed about the intelligence man: he never seems pressed to respond immediately, taking time if he needs to think through the implications. When he does speak, his voice is serious. 'All right. I'll tell you what I can. This can't appear in the papers. Not yet. Maybe never.'

'If you say so.'

Goffing pauses, again considering his options, before sighing, as if giving in.

'It started more than a year ago. An intelligence operation. You don't need to know the details. Names were mentioned on the periphery: one was Swift, another was Riversend. We thought it was two words: *river's end* or *river send*. Didn't mean anything to us. Then Harley Snouch turned up at ASIO headquarters and exposed Byron Swift, identifying him as Julian Flynt.'

Martin turns, stares at Goffing in disbelief, stares for so long that the car almost runs off the edge of the dead-straight road.

'Say that again.'

'It was Snouch who informed us Swift was really Flynt.'

'I still don't get it. Can you explain how that can even happen?'

'He came up to Canberra a year ago, peddling this story to anyone who would listen that his town priest was a gun-wielding imposter. Not surprisingly, no one would listen. Not the cops, not the media, not us. No one. Eventually he got on to me, only because he mentioned those two names, Swift and Riversend. To be honest, I thought he was a fantasist, that the names were a coincidence. I was just going through the motions. Being thorough. But he was strangely convincing. Once he set it out, it sounded more and more credible. He said Swift liked shooting and that he was former military. Said he had what looked like a scar from a bullet wound and military tattoos.

'I heard him out, then sent him home. But just to be sure, I had an analyst run the name. And bingo: she uncovered the death of Byron Swift in Cambodia. Suddenly we had something. So I got Snouch back in; he was still in Canberra. I sat him down with folios of photographs of former special forces soldiers. He identified Julian Flynt the moment he saw the photo. The name meant nothing to me, but as soon as it went into the system, all sorts of red flags went up: an alleged war criminal, a fugitive, supposedly killed while on the run in Iraq.'

'Shit. So why didn't you arrest him? Swift, I mean.'

'We were too late. That was late Friday afternoon. We convened a crisis meeting on the Sunday morning, hauled all sorts of people into work. We were still deliberating when the news came through: Swift had shot the men at the church and been killed by the local police constable. We were too late.'

'Shit. And Snouch was still in Canberra?'

'Yeah. That's why he's in the clear over the backpacker killings. He was in Canberra that whole week, talking to the police, talking to us. Alibis don't get much better than that.'

'He told me he was in Melbourne. In hospital with pneumonia.'

'Is that right? Convincing, isn't he?'

'So what did he tell you? Why was he so anxious to inform on Swift?'

'Said he was concerned about his stepdaughter.'

'Mandy?'

'Correct. Didn't want her entangled with this bloke he suspected was an imposter and could be dangerous.'

Martin thinks about that; it has the ring of truth to it.

'What about Snouch himself? Did you run a check on his background?'

'Yes, he's a bit of a mystery man. Lot of time out of the country, but nothing extraordinary.'

'Did you find out how he got those markings on his hands? They look like prison tattoos.'

'No. Nothing on that. But he hasn't been in prison, I can tell you that much.'

'So nothing about rape or sexual assault?'

'No. We would have picked up anything like that.'

More silence, the men ponder, the plain rolls by. Snouch had known all along that Swift was Flynt, but he had chosen not to tell Martin. Martin wonders why not, if Snouch was keen to diminish Swift in Mandy's eyes. He'd been quick to repeat allegations of child abuse, so why not tell Martin the truth about Flynt? Because Goffing would know Martin's source and come after him? Or because of Mandy's likely reaction? If she found out Snouch had exposed Swift in the days before the priest's death, then she might hold Snouch responsible for the shooting spree and any hopes of reconciliation would be dashed forever. Is that it? What is Snouch up to?

'Listen, Jack, Byron Swift's dying words to Robbie Haus-Jones were: "Harley Snouch knows everything." Did he somehow know that Snouch was onto him?'

'That's what worries me. And worries the head of ASIO even more. There's nothing concrete, but there's a lingering suspicion that ASIO leaked; somehow Swift found out that Snouch had identified him. We take such suspicions very seriously.'

'But that could be a factor in what made him kill those men.'

'True. But, Martin, you can't write it. Not yet. When the time comes, if the time comes, it's all yours. An exclusive. You have my word.'

Martin smiles at that; the word of a trained liar.

'Listen Jack. There was a woman in the church, in St James, just before the shooting. Could she have alerted Swift? I'm told she was from out of town.'

But Goffing is already shaking his head. 'No. She heard Swift's final words on the step, that's true, but that's all. She doesn't know anything. I've checked her out six ways from Sunday. She's not implicated, just traumatised.'

'Okay. But there is something else.'

'What's that?'

Martin tells the ASIO man about the mysterious phone number passed onto him by the owner of the Black Dog, how he suspects it was left by Herb Walker pretending to be his editor, and that the number might be the one Swift had called from St James just moments before he started shooting.

'Do you have it with you?'

'Sure. In my coat. Take the wheel.'

Goffing reaches across and takes the steering wheel with his right hand. Martin keeps his foot on the accelerator, the car rocketing along, while he reaches into the back seat for his coat and retrieves the number written on the post-it note given to him by Felicity Kirby. He hands it to Goffing and resumes control of the car. In the distance, the tops of Riversend's wheat silos come into view, floating above the heat-distorted plain.

'Can you find out who it belongs to?' asks Martin.

'Sure, piece of piss.'

Martin slows the car, passing the abandoned petrol station and the Black Dog, turning into Hay Road and heading straight to the police station. There's just the one photographer set up outside, the maniac who went tearing past as they left Bellington. The snapper takes a few frames and gives Martin a jovial wave. If he's still the only one there when Martin and Mandy emerge together he'll be more jovial still: the money shot will be his and his alone.

Inside the station, there's little sign of life, just muffled voices in the back somewhere. He gives the counter bell a ring and Montifore's offsider, Lucic, puts his head around the frame of the door. 'Sorry, mate. We can't bail her. We need the constable for that. If he has the guts to show his face.' Lucic offers a malevolent smile and withdraws his head before Martin can reply.

Goffing shrugs in sympathy and heads out to his car, piece of paper in his hand. Martin slumps down on the bench where he was left waiting for Herb Walker two days ago. Everything is the same. The same brochures are in the same slots in the same rack: Neighbourhood Watch, fire permits, how to get your driver's licence. It's as if the world has not moved on, that it's condemned to repeat the same cycles. Riversend, like Brigadoon's evil twin, is locked outside time. Nothing changes. Not even his ageless hands.

Robbie Haus-Jones walks in. 'Hi, Martin.'

'Hi, Robbie.'

'You here to bail Mandy?'

'That's right.'

'Won't be a mo. See what I can do.' The young policeman saunters through to the back of the station, seemingly unperturbed.

But it's an hour before he returns, followed by Mandy and the pretty young constable from Bellington who was there two days before. The hour of waiting vanishes, evaporated by Mandy Blonde's grateful smile, beaming across the counter at Martin.

'Sorry, Martin—had to sort a few things first,' says Robbie. 'I'll need you both to sign some forms, pretty much confirming the conditions set out by the magistrate. Martin, you have the money?'

Martin hands over the cheque. Robbie signs off on a receipt. Other papers are signed. Finally the policewoman—her name is Greevy—removes the handcuffs. 'Free to go.'

Mandy is about to walk out past the counter, but first she turns, takes Robbie's arm and stretches up, planting a sisterly kiss on his cheek. 'Thank you for speaking for me, Robbie. I won't forget it.'

Robbie nods, the faintest hint of a blush softening the seriousness of his expression.

'You ready for this?' asks Martin. Mandy Blonde nods, and they walk out arm in arm, into the blizzard of camera flashes and the storm of yelling reporters. It's the money shot all right, but it's no exclusive.

The photographers and camera operators follow them with the persistence of bush flies, down the road past the bank, past the bronze soldier marking his eternal vigilance, past the shuttered pub. The two of them barely exchange a word. Martin is unable to think of anything beyond banalities amid the mad running, pivoting swarm of cameras. Only as they approach the general store does the media melt away, their appetite for images of the *leading police suspect* and *the disgraced former journalist* finally sated. Inside the general store, there is no one at the counter.

'Fran?' yells Mandy. 'Fran? Are you here?'

Martin follows Mandy through the aisles towards the back of the store, where the shopkeeper might be minding young Liam.

'Fran?'

Fran Landers emerges. She's wearing rubber gloves, a shower cap and an apron. They've disturbed her in the middle of some cleaning task. She looks puzzled. 'Mandy? Thank God you're out. Everything okay?'

'I've come to pick up Liam. Where is he?'

'Oh, not here. Jamie took him back to the Oasis. He said you were back.'

'Oh. Goodo. Thanks. I'll see him there.'

'When was that?' asks Martin.

'An hour or so ago,' says Fran. 'He saw the police cars returning. We heard on the radio that you were getting out.'

'Good,' says Mandy. 'How was he?'

'Liam? Wonderful. You've really got a playful little fellow there.'

'Thanks again, Fran. I owe you one.'

Mandy and Martin walk towards the bookstore, Mandy keen to be reunited with her son. They take the back way, out of sight, down the laneways, figuring Jamie will have let himself into the house. It's Martin who talks. 'You know, Mandy, the magistrate has ordered me not to write any of this down, or not to publish it, but I would really like to know what's been going on.'

And she gives a smile, unaffected and pure. 'Of course, Martin. I'll tell you what I know. But some of it has to remain between you and me.'

They get to the back of the house, but no one's there.

'Maybe they're waiting out the front,' says Mandy.

They make their way down the small side lane, Mandy unlocking the gate, and walk out into Hay Road. Still no sign.

Mandy is looking slightly annoyed. 'Shit,' she says. 'Where are they? Maybe he's taken him to the park.'

'I'll come with you,' says Martin. He's about to speak again when his words are drowned out. The Channel Nine helicopter swoops low over the town, shadowed by the ABC's, before they peel away and head towards their feed points in Bellington or Swan Hill. No prizes for guessing what's making headlines on the evening news.

And that's when he sees the homemade sign, the A4 paper sticky-taped to the light pole, the photograph rapidly fading: MISSING. MR PUSS. REWARD. It stops him dead.

'Shit,' says Martin.

'What?'

'Shit.'

And then he's running, running as fast as he can, running back towards the crossroads, running even as he tries to convince himself it can't possibly be true. Past the blind and useless Anzac, guarding his fading myth, around to the back lane, around to the back of the pub. He stops there, panting despite having run no more than fifty metres, sweat pouring off him in the heat of the afternoon. Mandy is right behind him, younger and possibly fitter, compelled by Martin's urgency to follow. But both stop, halted by a harsh truth: at the bottom of the wooden stairs, half hidden by the car with its deflating tyres, a baby's stroller stands empty and unattended.

Mandy sees it, is about to yell her son's name, when Martin stops her, gesturing frantically, talking in a hoarse whisper: 'Run and get Robbie. Tell him to get here fast. Tell him to bring his gun.'

Mandy stands open-mouthed for a moment, trying to catch up, and then she is gone, sprinting back through the gate, into the lane and out of sight.

'Right, now,' says Martin quietly, summoning courage. He should wait, he knows he should wait, that Robbie is just minutes away. But the empty stroller sits there challenging him, condemning him, compelling him.

He's moving before he makes the decision to move. Past the stroller, to the stairs. Step by step, he climbs. His senses are fine-tuned, the hairs on his neck raised like radar masts, his hands brushing the flaking green paint of the railing as if to vacuum clues, feeling the baking heat rise from the powdery paint. A step creaks under his weight—or is it the plea of a small boy?

He moves more quickly, gaining the top landing, sees the hole punched in the glass window. The door is closed, but unlocked. He swings it open, enters, remembering to avoid as much as possible the shards of glass on the floor, moving away from the cleansing sun into the darkness. Before turning into the main corridor, he pauses to let his eyes adjust. He can hear nothing unusual, see nothing out of place, but deep down his guts are churning out their warning that something is profoundly wrong.

Then he hears it: a cry, a stifled cry. It's not close, not too close. His mind makes the leap, informed by his last visit. He guesses either the guest lounge, with its empty beer cans and bloated ashtrays, or the room of the dead cat. He moves quickly again, into the main corridor, along it, barely pausing to check before turning the right-angle corner to head along the front of the pub. He's creeping forward when he hears something new. He pauses again. Someone singing. A lullaby? Jesus. He gathers his guts, threatening to turn liquid, summons the vestiges of his courage, and walks, purposefully and without pause, down the corridor.

How long does it take him to walk those twenty-five metres? A few short seconds or half a lifetime? It's impossible to say. He passes the stairs leading down into the pub, sees the brass runners on the carpet, notes the watery English light in the fox-hunting picture, sees the blazing Australian light through the French doors leading to the verandah. He sees other things— the ornate yet dusty chandelier hanging above the stairs; the veneer lifting ever so slightly on the antique dresser; a painting of mountains, blue ranges with the anvil clouds of a summer storm above them. Smells come to him: dust and blood and mothballs and cigarettes. And fear. The smell he endured for three days and three nights and an eternity in the boot of a battered yellow Mercedes abandoned somewhere in the Gaza Strip. The smell has followed him across the oceans, seeking him out inside a shuttered hotel in the Riverina. But the smell doesn't stop him. Nothing will stop him. He walks through it, wades through it, pushes through it. The singing is telling him where to go, to the room of the dead cat.

He walks in, treading softly, but not trying to hide. Jamie Landers is sitting on a chair by the window, naked from the waist down. He stops singing. He has a knife in his hand. A long knife, its point wet and red. Liam is on the bed, one arm and the opposite leg tied to the corner posts, a gag in his mouth, eyes wide with terror, tears and snot all over his face. He's naked and there's blood smeared across his tiny torso from a cut to his chest.

'So it's you, reporter man. I wondered who it'd be.'

'Jamie, you can't do this. You have to let him go.'

'It's all right, reporter man. I'll make it quick. They don't last long, you know. Not the little ones. You'll last longer, old man, I promise you. Much longer.'

Martin edges forward, arms wide, as if somehow he might counter a knife thrust. Robbie must be on his way; has to be on his way.

Jamie stands, with a smile splayed across his face. 'You want to watch me do it? Watch the lights go out? It's quite a sight.'

Martin freezes, is frozen, as the blur comes past him on the left. White and blue and so very swift, hitting Jamie Landers in the chest with a force so fast and fearless that the teenager doesn't have time to turn the blade. It's Mandy Blonde, slamming him into the wall, knocking the wind from him, pulling the knife from him.

'Mandy, no.' It's Martin's voice, a distant, disembodied plea, beaming in from some other universe. But it's no good. She's not listening. She glances at her son, struggling and distressed, and then she looks directly into the mad eyes, the face no longer smiling, the smell of fear now filling his nostrils and his alone. She raises the knife, its tip touching his neck. She moves it slowly, drawing blood. 'I'm going to gut you here and now,' she whispers. But his hands are up in surrender, and she hesitates. Robbie Haus-Jones bursts through the door, gun in hand.

nineteen   **WATER UNDER THE BRIDGE**

HOURS PASS AND MARTIN IS STILL AT THE POLICE STATION. THE SAME COUNTER, the same pamphlets, the same useless hands. He looks at them, studies them. The hands of a witness, the hands of a note taker, stained by time but unblemished by achievement.

On some few occasions, in Asia and in the Middle East, he had been present during dramatic events, the stenographer of history, but such heights were rare and, even then, not truly his; they would have unfolded in exactly the same fashion had he been absent. The rest of his career, the rest of his life, he'd been curating history's footnotes, not dictating its narrative. He'd been objective, licensed by his profession to be both present and not present, standing apart, behind the cameras and the head-lines, not in front of them, a voyeur with a notepad, the ghost in the room. That is, until he climbed into the boot of a Mercedes in Gaza and unwittingly became the story and not the conveyor of it; part of events and not just recording them. And now it's happening again: he's involved; profoundly, if unintentionally. He has saved a man—the town leper—from a bushfire, and saved the life of a teenage boy—a killer—in a car crash. He stands accused of driving a policeman to suicide, been pilloried on national television and posted bail for a woman accused of perverting the course of justice. And now he's saved the life of a small child. He has become the antithesis of the dispassionate, objective reporter he once was. Somehow, accidentally, he has inserted himself into the very centre of events, into the vortex of a story sucking in the attention of the nation, pulling in talkback and Twitter and satellite trucks, dragging them in like a tornado across the empty plain.

Max had sent him here to reconcile with his past, to recover from the trauma of Gaza, to rediscover his mojo. But the past has come stalking him: the reality of a life lived on the outskirts, always watching, always recording, never participating. He thinks of a girl, a pretty girl, long ago at university. She had loved him, he realises now, wondering why it has taken twenty years for him to recognise the fact. After all, she had told him so, had said the words, but he had never reciprocated, and they had drifted apart. Where is she now? Happy, no doubt. Married with children; loving and loved. Married to Scotty the dentist, perhaps. And where is Martin? In a one-officer police station in the last town on earth, with no family and no friends and no career. He thinks of Mandy. What passed through his mind, just below the surface, when he first met her in the Oasis: gorgeous, available, transient. Pliable, vulnerable, disposable. He is, he realises, some kind of arsehole, an incomplete man. He came to Riversend to escape his past, but it isn't the past he needs to escape, it's not the present, it's something missing inside of himself. He doesn't need to escape it; he needs to acknowledge it. He looks at his hands: old and young, sullied and innocent.

The interview with the police had started out curt and confrontational, the detectives struggling to assimilate events, scared of being caught out again. 'What the fuck just happened?' Montifore demanded, his face betraying confusion and panic, hope and anger. They'd already heard Robbie's version, how the constable had arrived on the scene to find Mandy preparing to eviscerate Jamie Landers. And so Martin recounted, emotions suppressed, a reliable and seasoned witness, how he and Mandy had gone to collect her son Liam from Frances Landers, how they had then returned to Mandy's place and the bookstore looking for Liam and Jamie Landers, how he had seen the Mr Puss poster and made the intuitive leap to the hotel.

That was when it turned nasty; the police demanding to know why Martin hadn't told them about finding the dead cat. Their intention was clear: they wanted it stated, on the record, that they had been denied vital evidence, that no one could accuse them of overlooking any clue or lead or tip, however obscure, that might have forewarned them of the potential atrocity unfolding a hundred metres from their Riversend headquarters. Martin recognised what was happening and for a moment, the shortest of moments, temptation cast its lure his way: he could lie, say he had told Herb Walker, as he had indeed intended to do. The blame would fall on the dead policeman; Martin would be absolved. But the moment passed, temptation withering. Walker's legacy was already burdened with enough opprobrium and Martin couldn't bring himself to care about his own: the child was safe, the madman was in custody, Mandy had been spared every mother's worst fear. And so he cooperated, accepting culpability, stating he'd intended to tell the police about the tortured cat but had been overtaken by events. His mistake, he confided in them, was that he'd become obsessed with the events of a year before, the shooting at St James, the mystery of Byron Swift and, later, the abduction and murder of the young Germans. Had it not been the same with the police? It hadn't occurred to him that events were still unfolding, that it wasn't the past they needed to worry about but the present.

After that, once he'd exonerated the police, the interrogation became an interview. The questions were no longer accusatory but simply seeking information. He continued his dispassionate narrative, recounting the chain of events at the hotel from the time he and Mandy had arrived and seen the stroller to the moment Robbie Haus-Jones had rushed in the door and arrested Jamie Landers. Martin found he could recall every moment, every word, with startling clarity: the position of the stroller outside the pub, the painting of the fox hunt, the blood on Jamie Landers' dagger. He took them through it, second by second, like a film being played frame by frame. The detectives stopped interjecting, listening. Finally, when he had finished, the silence continued uninterrupted until, eventually, Montifore began to take him back and forth through his evidence.

'From his words and from his gestures, from what you saw, do you have any doubts at all that Jamie Landers was solely responsible for the abduction and captivity of Liam Blonde?'

'No doubts whatsoever.'

'And he had already injured the infant?'

'Yes. There was blood on the boy and blood on the knife.'

'And he intended killing the boy?'

'Without doubt. He invited me to watch, in his words, as the lights went out.'

'And he then intended killing you?'

'Without doubt. He moved towards me, brandishing the knife, saying I would last longer than the child.'

'By which you believed he meant . . .?'

'That he intended to torture and kill me.'

'Like he had done to the two murdered backpackers?'

'Sorry. There was no reference to them, just the suggestion that I would live longer than the child.'

'Do you believe that, through her actions, Mandalay Blonde may have saved you and her son from injury or death? That the minor wound she inflicted on Jamie Landers was justified?'

'Yes, I do. Without a single doubt.'

The meeting had grown more collegiate, Martin more or less a member of the team, invited to assist in locking down the chain of events. It grew even more collegiate when Robbie Haus-Jones interrupted: Landers wanted to make a full confession to the murders of the two backpackers. He wanted to tell it all. Martin observed Montifore's face, the pressure easing out of it, the grin, starting small and contained before spreading out until it covered his face from ear to ear as Robbie conveyed what Landers had already told him. The teenager had lured the backpackers into a car together with his friend Allen Newkirk. They'd tortured them, raped them and then killed them. And then Newkirk had died, his comrade in crime, thrown from the ute out on the highway to Bellington. Landers said he had felt scared and abandoned, all alone. He'd had enough. He knew he was sick in the head. He wanted to die; he wanted to join his mate. But he had wanted to better the priest, to do something truly abhorrent. And the opportunity had presented itself to him, as if by fate. He claimed he hadn't sought out Liam Blonde; the child had been delivered to him. He'd killed a cat, shot some cows out in the Scrublands, some kind of pagan tribute to his dead friend and the fun they'd had with the German girls. Taking Liam had seemed preordained and perfect.

With grim objectivity, Martin then recognised a sense of euphoria among the police. The murder case captivating the nation, the one that had seemed so intractable just that morning, the one that had funnelled pressure down onto Montifore's team—starting from the premier, flowing down through the police commissioner and the head of homicide—that case had been blown right open. They had the killer, the investigation was now all about tying up loose ends and preparing a brief.

'It still doesn't explain why Byron Swift went on his rampage,' Martin interposed.

Montifore looked at him sadly, shaking his head. 'True. But who gives a shit? That's not why we're here.'

'What about Mandy Blonde? Can I see her?'

'We'll be releasing her soon enough. She's with her son and the doctor. She'll be free to go once the kid is patched up.'

'What about the diary and perverting the course of justice?'

'Forget it. Water under the bridge, mate. Landers and Newkirk killed the backpackers, not Byron Swift. It's all water under the bridge.'

Martin is still waiting by the reception counter of the Riversend police station for Mandy Blonde to be released. His mind is not entirely his own; unbidden, it keeps replaying incidents from earlier in the day: the confrontation upstairs at the pub, with Jamie Landers gloating and mad one moment, terrified and pleading the next; Mandy and himself searching for Liam and Jamie, oblivious to what was unfolding upstairs in the Commercial Hotel; driving across the endless plain to stand outside the Bellington police station, the site of his on-air execution. It's all mixed up, all shuffled together, his mind throwing up scenes at random, as if independently trying to make sense of the day. He doesn't understand why he's feeling so disorientated; nothing truly terrible has happened, the boy is safe, the murderer in custody.

Pretty young Constable Greevy from Bellington has been bringing him cups of hot tea and comforting words. Her name is Sarah, it transpires. To help distract him, she flicks on the television mounted on the wall next to the counter. There's a game show on. Martin can't follow it; the rules seem too complex, there are too many flashing lights, too many glaring teeth. Nevertheless he's transfixed by the screen, even as his mind drifts away, sifting again and again through the events of the day.

It's snapped back abruptly to the here and now by Doug Thunkleton's matinee-idol face, mellifluous voice and earnest tone. The game show has finished and the news has begun. Martin hadn't noticed the transition. Thunkleton is standing outside Bellington police station. Martin catches the end of his introductory blurb: '. . . *in dramatic scenes outside the magistrate's hearing here in Bellington.*' The screen wipes to Thunkleton's package, starting with Mandy entering the building that morning, the camera jostling for position, the voiceover urgent: '*She's been dubbed the suicide blonde. Mandalay Blonde—charged with perverting the course of justice, now a prime suspect in the murders of German backpackers Heidi Schmeikle and Anna Brün.*'

The voiceover stops; the camera continues to fight for position as Robbie Haus-Jones tries to clear a way through the media pack. Thunkleton is leaning over Mandy's shoulder, thrusting a microphone the size of a turkey drumstick, painted in the garish livery of Channel Ten, under her nose while he bellows in her ear: '*What do you have to say to Herb Walker's widow?*' The story doesn't wait for her response, instead cutting to a still photograph of her, captured as she stares into the camera lens.

Thunkleton's voiceover resumes. '*Mandalay Susan Blonde is formally charged with perverting the course of justice, accused of destroying evidence linking homicidal priest Byron Swift with the abduction and murders of the innocent backpackers.*' There's a slow, almost imperceptible zoom into the photograph, into her eyes; there the viewer can see whatever they wish to see: confusion, or guilt, or madness, or whatever else Thunkleton's voiceover might suggest.

The story cuts back to the reporter, standing beside the Murray River. '*Channel Ten can now exclusively reveal that Blonde is being linked to another death—that of respected Bellington police sergeant Herb Walker.*' On the screen now is a middle-aged woman, grey hair tinged with blue, identified by an onscreen title bar as *Belinda Walker—Hero's Widow.* '*He always said she was trouble—that no good would come of her.'* Another cut, this time to a new voice of authority, D'Arcy Defoe, as self-confident and smooth as ever: *'She is the femme fatale of this story. I can't reveal too much as yet, but suffice to say Mandalay Blonde lies at the very epicentre of police inquiries.'* Cut now to the scene of Mandy and Martin leaving the Riversend police station arm in arm, pushing through the media scrum. *'It's suggested that Mandalay Blonde has also been manipulating this man, disgraced former journalist Martin Scarsden, the same way she once manipulated homicidal priest Byron Swift.'* The story finishes with a close-up of Mandy, played in slow motion, as the voice signs off, redolent with gravitas: *'In Riversend, this is Doug Thunkleton, Ten News.'*

Martin hears wild laughter echoing from further inside the police station, but there's more. The glamorous newsreader is back on screen. The image behind her is of drug paraphernalia stamped with the words ICE EPIDEMIC. She turns to camera, frowning: *'The drug plague sweeping rural Australia shortly, but first we understand there has been a major breakthrough in the backpacker murders. We cross live to our reporter Doug Thunkleton in the Riverina with the latest news.'*

Thunkleton appears, hair perfect as always, but his tie is askew and his face is shiny and flushed. His voice is deep and rich, but his diction is ever so slightly slurred. *'Thanks, Megan. Yes, Ten News can confirm that police believe—our sources confirm there has been a major breakthrough. We believe an arrest is imminent. However, for legal reasons, we cannot at this point reveal the identity of the accused. But we do understand it is not, I repeat not, Mandalay Blonde. Her role in the affair is still to be explained. Just repeating, there has been a major breakthrough in the Riversend backpacker murders, with police expected to make at least one arrest in the near future.'*

Megan is looking serious and professional, but there is a hint of poison in her follow-up question. *'Thanks, Doug. And how does that fit with allegations against the woman you've branded the suicide blonde?'*

Thunkleton shifts balance from one leg to the other. Perhaps it's the lag on the satellite, but for a moment he looks like he's been frozen by a roo shooter's spotlight. His comeback is good, though. *'Megan, I think it's safe to say that as the details of this case, this extraordinary case, come to light, we'll be able to see how these and other factors are all inextricerr . . . how they are all interlinked. As Fairfax reporter D'Arcy Defoe said earlier, Mandalay Blonde is at the very epicentre of these events.'*

The newsreader nods, lips pursed. *'Doug Thunkleton in the Riverina, thanks for bringing us up to date.'*

There is more laughter from inside the police station, then Robbie Haus-Jones emerges, smiling broadly. He looks up at the television. 'Did you see that idiot?'

Martin nods.

'Use the phone on the counter if you like. Ring that ex-colleague of yours in Sydney. Bethanie what's-her-face. She can report the facts for once.'

'What about the magistrate's orders? I'm not meant to be reporting, remember.'

'I wouldn't worry too much about him. He's been pulled over for drink-driving in Corowa. We've thrown him in the can. Here.' Robbie holds out a piece of folded paper.

'What's this?'

'Your bank cheque. For God's sake, don't lose it.'

Martin rings Bethanie from the phone behind the counter. She answers with a barked hello, clearly under the pump.

'Bethanie, it's Martin.'

'Martin? Where are you?'

'Riversend.'

'Good. Do you know what the fuck is going on? The ABC are promoting a big breakthrough to be revealed on their seven o'clock news. The commercials seem to be clueless. Terri Preswell is screaming her tits off at me but my contacts aren't answering. Defoe claims he's across it, but won't tell me what it is and now he's not answering his phone.'

Slowly, methodically, Martin sets out the facts: that it was Jamie Landers and his mate Allen Newkirk who killed the backpackers, that Landers has confessed and is in detention. He's not denying anything. Martin tells her that Mandy Blonde is in the clear, to ignore the commercial television reports, that the young mother nearly lost her child in horrifying circumstances, almost murdered by Landers.

Bethanie is all ears, only interposing questions for clarification, respecting Martin's ability to order the facts. Only at the end does she seek advice on how to frame the story.

'Martin, I should give you a by-line. What do you think?'

'No. You'll only antagonise management. Don't refer to me at all, or call me a reliable source if you need to, but no names. And do yourself a favour: file before seven so people know it's all your work—but after Defoe sees the ABC and files, share the by-line with him. You'll want to keep him onside in future; don't humiliate him.'

There's a pause on the other end of the phone. 'Martin, that sucks.'

'Tell me about it. Now get moving, it's already six-thirty.'

'Absolutely. And, Martin, thanks.'

Martin sits alone in the foyer of the country police station, imagining the frenetic scene back in the Sydney newsroom: Bethanie yelling that she's got it, the editors crowding around, the front page being remade. It will be a corker, one of his best, certainly one of his biggest, even though his name will be nowhere to be seen.

He'll miss it, he knows he will. In the whole confused and confusing day, the whole confused and confusing week, the only periods of clarity and purpose had come when he was reporting events he'd witnessed, first to the paper, then to the police and now to Bethanie. The old thrill, one last time. He's still sitting there when the ABC news comes on at 7 pm. It's a national broadcast out of Sydney, all states receiving the same signal, that's how big the story has become. The newsreader is grim, urgent and professional. *'The ABC can reveal a major breakthrough . . .'*

The report says police have arrested a suspect, a Riversend local, a teenage boy, and are expected to charge him this evening with the murders of the two German backpackers. There is no mention of Allen Newkirk, no mention of Liam Blonde, no mention of the confrontation in the Commercial Hotel. The new facts, sparse and lacking context, are at the top of the package, the remainder a rehash of the day's events,

Mandy and himself again caught in the storm of camera flashes even as the voiceover exonerates Mandy of any guilt. But there's a sting in the tail, just before the reporter signs off: *'It's believed the police may have been denied vital information, delaying this evening's arrest.'* That's it then; the police are already preparing to hang him out to dry.

He's still sitting there an hour later when Mandy emerges. She looks frail, exhausted. She is clutching Liam to her, soothing him even as he sleeps. Mandy turns to Martin then, and there is no barrier, no pretence in her eyes; he sees her anguish and he sees her relief.

'Martin,' she whispers, reaching out, taking his hand. 'Thank you. Thank you so much.' And then she smiles: a smile so pure, so free of calculation, that it takes his breath away. 'I need to look after this little one tonight, but come and see me tomorrow. Say you will.'

'Of course I will. If you'll see me.'

And another smile, more illumination lighting his soul. 'Of course.' And quickly, still holding her son, she kisses him. A weight lifts from his shoulders and he feels, for the first time in a very long time, that things are turning for the better.

He's about to offer to walk her home when Jack Goffing comes back through the door, urgency plain on his face. The evening isn't over yet.

twenty **GRAVEROBBERS**

GOFFING WAITS UNTIL MANDY AND LIAM ARE OUT THE DOOR, ESCORTED BY Constable Greevy, before speaking, his voice low and urgent. 'The phone number, Martin. It's disconnected, but I got an address here in Riversend. Hay Road. Registered to someone called Avery Foster.'

'The publican.'

'How do you know that?'

'His name's written above the door. It's on the licence sign.'

'Isn't he dead, though?'

'Yes. Suicide. Six months ago.'

'Fuck,' says Goffing, losing some of his urgency. 'He won't be telling us much, then. Bugger it.'

'Listen, Jack. Maybe there is something.' Martin explains his first visit to the Commercial Hotel, seeing the locked room at the end of the corridor with its gold-painted sign: PRIVATE. 'Should we take a look?'

'Absolutely.'

'The door is locked. Two or three locks.'

'I'll bring my picks.'

'You can do that? Pick locks?'

Goffing looks at him like he's an idiot. 'I'm ASIO, remember. We do it in basic training.'

Night is almost complete as the two men leave the police station. The western horizon is rimmed with blood and the scarlet moon hangs above it; there is the smell of wood smoke and desolation. Three large moths circle the POLICE sign, but they seem lethargic; having survived the heat of another day they can barely raise the energy to circle their blue-and-white beacon. There's no such lethargy among the gaggle of journalists who also flitter around the police station, lured back across the plain by news of the arrest. They buzz with energy, desperate to report on the police breakthrough, the story that has somehow eluded them and arrived independently into the newsrooms of the capital cities. Alerted by the ABC news, they have come dashing from Bellington, breaking speed limits and playing Russian roulette with kangaroos but, now they're here, there's little for them to do: recording pieces to camera and filming guilty buildings. Montifore and his team will spend hours grilling Landers, teasing out every last detail while the young man remains willing to talk and before any lawyer can counsel him otherwise. For now, feeding the media will be a very low priority. Carrie, the Fairfax photographer, captures a couple of frames of Martin and Goffing as they leave, her camera flash abrupt and insistent. She shrugs apologetically and takes a couple more shots. Martin can see a few locals have joined the media but, away from the police station, the town is closed for the day, slowly surrendering its pent-up heat into the clear night skies.

The hotel looks little different; only the crime scene tape draped across the entrance to the back laneway suggests anything amiss. Goffing doesn't hesitate, lifting it, passing under it, holding it for Martin to follow. He has a torch in one hand and is carrying a small backpack in the other. Martin is using the flashlight on his phone, leading the way up the outside stairs and into the darkened interior. The glass from the broken door pane crunches under their feet. The air is unchanged, laden in the enclosed space with the smells of the afternoon: dust and neglect and residual fear. Martin's muscles tighten, the hairs on his neck lift once again, he reminds himself to breathe. He shines his light down the corridor, towards the corner of the pub, but there is nothing to see, only darkness.

'This way,' he says, almost a whisper, despite knowing he and Jack Goffing are alone in the abandoned building. He guides Goffing to the locked apartment, holding both lights as the ASIO man picks first one lock and then another and then another, taking remarkably little time to do it.

'Like riding a bike,' says Goffing, his voice clear. If Martin is tense, Goffing almost seems to be enjoying himself. 'Here, put these on.' He hands Martin some latex gloves and retrieves a second pair for himself from the backpack.

Inside, the apartment is like a tomb, the air still and bone-dry. The absence of moisture has mummified its contents:

a budgerigar lies desiccated at the bottom of its cage, like one of Horrie Grosvenor's trophies, feathers intact, beak open; a half-eaten bowl of spaghetti sits on a coffee table, the pasta returned to its original pre-cooked state; slices of bread sit brittle and dehydrated next to it, no sign of mould or decay. There's a pot plant, now nothing more than bare stalks, surrounded on the windowsill by a ring of brown leaves. By the light of Martin's phone, Jack Goffing looks like Howard Carter, come to raid Tutankhamun's burial chamber. Martin feels a strong sense of trespass: they have entered the dead man's domain, uninvited, like graverobbers in the Valley of the Kings.

'Jesus,' says Goffing. 'It's untouched.'

The men explore further: a kitchenette with unwashed dishes, a bedroom with an unmade bed, a bathroom with underwear on the floor. A study, papers strewn across the desk, chair pushed back, as if the person working there has gone to get a cup of tea and will be back at any moment.

'Look,' says Martin. On the wall, framed and mounted, is a certificate recognising the service and dedication of Captain Avery Foster, 1RAR, Afghanistan. 'He was there. Infantry, not special forces. But he was there.' Next to it hangs another framed certificate, this one from the Central Orphanage Kabul, thanking Avery Foster for his support and generosity.

'Interesting,' says Goffing, examining it.

'What does it mean?'

'Not sure yet.'

The desktop reveals invoices and orders, demands for payment and bills, booking calendars and bank statements. Goffing takes a seat and starts sifting through the papers, dividing them into two piles: the mundane and the noteworthy.

He pauses. 'You say he suicided?'

'That's what I was told.'

'Curious. It must have been very spur of the moment by the look of this place. Do you know why he did it?'

'I was told money problems—the pub was sinking under debt.'

'Who told you that? Police?'

'No, just a local, an old bloke called Codger Harris. He was probably just repeating the accepted wisdom. He told me Foster shot himself.'

'Did he say where?'

'No, not that I recall.'

'Well, I'm not sure about the money problems. Here, look.' Goffing hands Martin a bank statement for Riverina Hotels and Food Pty Ltd. The balance is eight thousand dollars; not a fortune, but not scraping the bottom.

The men keep searching, Goffing at the desk, Martin returning to the small lounge. There's a bookcase, its shelves containing little fiction, just an airport thriller or two. Most of the books are history and biography, some military books and a few textbooks. Psychology and sociology. And on the bottom shelf, a series of photo albums. The most imposing is a professionally produced wedding album bound in burgundy leather. Martin flicks through, the feeling of transgression strong. A handsome young man, hair dark and eyes shining; a beautiful young woman, lustrous smile and a face luminous with self-belief. The couple look at Martin out of the photo, out of the past, dressed in their wedding finery, confident of themselves and their future. In the first photos it's just the two of them, standing at the shores of a lake, the foliage green and the water blue and expansive. So much water. There are more images, with the best man and maid of honour, the parents, siblings, children with flowers. There are pages of the ceremony itself, the ring, the celebratory kiss, smiles and goodwill. And on the last page of the album, preserved for posterity, an invitation, *requesting the pleasure of your company at the wedding of Avery Foster and Dianne Webber*. The card is white, the edges gold, the writing raised black cursive. Martin flicks back to the first photos. Avery Foster, before life went awry.

He extracts another, more utilitarian album. Memories from the military. The same man, a younger man, Avery Foster, graduating in dress uniform. In camouflage, face blackened, an assault rifle at the ready, but the smile revealing this is an exercise, not combat. Photos in Australia, photos overseas. And then the familiar colours: brown and beige, the palette of Afghanistan, interspersed with the greenery of the valleys. Foster in camp, Foster with colleagues. Foster in uniform, his arm around a colleague, both smiling at the camera. Martin notices small variations in their uniforms, looks closely at their identifying tags. Is the man on the right Julian Flynt?

He carries the album into the study to show Goffing. The ASIO man is still sitting at the desk, leaning back. In his hand is a roll of banknotes, hundred-dollar bills. He looks up at Martin. 'About five thousand dollars. It was taped under the desk. If Avery Foster killed himself, it wasn't for lack of money. And look at this.' He hands Martin a receipt. 'It's for a headstone. The week after Swift died.'

'I've seen it,' says Martin. 'He's buried in Bellington. The inscription is *Known unto God*, the one used for soldiers who can't be identified. And check this out.' Martin shows Goffing the photo album, open at the page with the image of the two soldiers. 'The man on the left is Avery Foster. Looks like Afghanistan.'

'And the man on the right is Julian Flynt,' says Jack Goffing without hesitation.

'They were comrades in Afghanistan. So what does that add up to? Do you think it was Foster who smuggled Flynt back into Australia, who set him up with a false identity and a bolthole in Bellington?'

Goffing says nothing, not for a long while, before nodding in affirmation. 'Sounds as plausible as anything else.'

'And on the day of the St James shooting, Swift is preparing to leave the district for good. He calls Foster from the church and sometime later Foster calls him back. Then Swift goes out and starts shooting.'

'And six months later Foster kills himself.'

The men are still, speculation running unfettered through Martin's mind. Nothing moves in the rooms of the dead publican.

'What time is it in Afghanistan?' asks Goffing eventually.

Martin checks his watch, does the calculation in his mind. 'Early afternoon.'

'Good. Let's go. I've got some calls to make.'

twenty-one   **OUTLAWS**

MARTIN IS BACK IN THE BOOT OF THE MERCEDES ON THE GAZA STRIP, BUT HE'S no longer so perturbed. He knows help is on its way; it won't be too long now and he'll be rescued. He can hear the clanking tanks, the rumble of activity. A helicopter passes benignly overhead. So he lies in the darkness, enjoying his last moments of respite before the boot is opened and a new day begins. And right on cue, the hammering comes, not ordnance, not mortar shells, but someone pounding on the door of room six of the Black Dog Motel. He opens his eyes, fully conscious, gets up and opens the door.

'Martin. Mate. Talk about a scoop machine.' It's Doug Thunkleton.

'Fuck off, Doug.'

'But you are the story. Make the most of it, do an interview. Salvation awaits!'

'Just fuck off and die, will you,' he says, not even bothering to raise his voice, and shuts the door in the face of the television hyena.

He's emerging from the shower when another knock comes. 'Martin? Are you in there? Martin?' It's Jack Goffing. Martin lets him in, scanning the car park for media as he does so.

'It's okay,' says Goffing. 'I told them Montifore is doing a doorstop. They've all scurried off to the police station.'

'Is he?'

'Bound to be sooner or later.' Goffing is smiling. 'They've got their man; they'll want their credit.'

Martin smiles as well. Both men can feel it: progress, momentum. They're getting closer.

'Finish getting dressed,' says Goffing. 'I'll have a smoke.'

—

Outside, Riversend's clear night skies have drained off much of the car park's heat, but the morning's light is already so intense that Martin needs his sunglasses. He can feel the power of the sun on the bare skin of his arms. It will be another ferocious day.

'Any news?'

'Plenty. I rang our people in Kabul last night. They called back this morning; I've just got off the phone to them.' He takes a drag of his smoke, looking as if he's relishing it. 'Get this. Avery Foster didn't just know Julian Flynt in Afghanistan: he treated him. He was an army chaplain and a qualified psychologist. He was the one who gave Flynt the clean bill of health to return to active service after he'd been held captive by the Taliban.'

'That's it, Jack—it's starting to come together. Foster felt responsible for what happened, Flynt killing those women and children.'

'That's what I'm thinking. I don't know if he helped Flynt escape Afghanistan, or if he helped him get back into Australia, but I know for certain that he helped him get ordained and placed in Bellington.'

'For certain?'

'Yep, I've spoken to the Bishop of Albury. He says Foster, a former chaplain, was a major sponsor of Swift and backed him for ordination.'

'You have been busy.'

'Not me so much, but the team in Kabul have been outstanding. They also checked out the orphanage. It's the real deal; does good works, cares for about sixty kids. It presents as secular, which is only sensible, but the Kabul office reckon its key staff are all Christians. The woman running it says she knew Foster; he was very supportive while he was in country. And get this: it was receiving anonymous donations from Australia. About a year ago, the flow of money started to slow, then stopped altogether about six months later.'

'Right,' says Martin. 'Swift died a year ago, Foster six months later. They were sending money.'

'Looks like it.'

Goffing takes a long, satisfied drag on his cigarette. The men look into the distance, thoughts racing through Martin's mind, connections being made, theories advanced and rejected.

The silence is broken by the jagged ringing of the phone in Goffing's room. He stamps out his cigarette and raises his eyebrows at Martin, communicating his expectations: watch this space.

Goffing closes the door behind him and Martin considers what he knows. Jamie Landers and Allen Newkirk abducted and killed the two backpackers. Swift was with Mandy Blonde at the time of the abduction and probably had nothing to do with the crime. Swift may have seen some evidence left by Landers and Newkirk out in the Scrublands, but that's the only likely link between the deaths of the German girls and the shooting at St James. They were probably distinct crimes, connected only by their proximity in time and location. But that still leaves a lot Martin doesn't know. Swift and Foster were acting in concert, sending money to Afghanistan, but where were they getting money from in the middle of a drought, rolls of hundred-dollar notes? Someone had accused Swift of abusing children and Herb Walker reckoned he'd had it verified by two Riversend victims. Who made the allegations and were they true? And did they explain why Swift shot the five members of the Bellington Anglers Club?

The moment Goffing emerges from his motel room, Martin knows something is wrong. The spring has gone from the man's step, a veil has come down over his eyes. He slumps into the plastic chair, reaches for a cigarette and lights it without looking, a man on automatic pilot. When he draws in his first toke, there is no enjoyment, or even awareness that he's smoking.

'What's wrong? What's happened?'

'Something bad.'

'You want to tell me about it?'

Goffing looks at Martin, examining him. Martin can see the calculation in the intelligence officer's eyes. To confide or not to confide. The camaraderie is gone; the guile is back. Eventually, Goffing sighs. 'I asked Canberra to run checks on Foster's phone for the morning of the shooting. It's not good.'

'You have recordings?'

'No. Of course not. No content. It's just billing data. Metadata. Which number called which number at what time and for how long. The telcos are required to keep the metadata for two years.' A drag on his cigarette, another calculation. 'At ten forty-five on the morning of the shooting, a call was made from St James to Avery Foster's apartment at the Commercial Hotel. The call lasted about a minute. At ten fifty-four Foster called the church back. Same thing: about a minute. After the second call—it must have been almost immediately after the second call—Swift went out and started shooting.'

'Yes,' says Martin. 'That's more or less what we knew from Walker's information: Swift called someone and then that person rang back. It was Avery Foster.'

'Yes,' says Goffing. 'But that's not all. Between the two calls with St James, Foster received another call.'

'Really? From whom?'

'No specific number. It came through a switchboard. Russell Hill, in Canberra.'

'Russell Hill . . . the Defence Department?'

'No. More likely ASIO.'

'ASIO?'

'Snouch had identified Swift on the Friday. That Sunday morning we were gathered, a crisis team of about eight people, at ASIO headquarters. The cops were there, so was Attorney-General's, and a liaison officer from Defence. Someone called Foster and warned him.'

'So it's true: ASIO leaked.'

'Looks like it. Everyone in that room was security cleared, but one of them called Foster.' He shakes his head, still coming to terms with the information. 'You don't understand, Martin. This'll go off like a hand grenade when I tell the boss. There'll be all sorts of internal investigations. A veritable witch-hunt. A mole-hunt. And if they don't find out who was responsible, every person in that room, including me, will carry a question mark on their CV for all time, a very nasty and sinister question mark.' Goffing finishes his cigarette, grinds it into the car park gravel, grinds it so thoroughly that it disintegrates beneath his shoe.

'The Defence liaison officer? Could it have been him?'

'Her. That'd be my guess.'

'Hang on. Jack, where was Harley Snouch?' asks Martin.

'Snouch? Outside the meeting, in case we needed him.'

'Well, don't you see? It was Snouch who called Foster. ASIO didn't leak. Snouch rang Foster and then Foster called Swift back. Remember Swift's dying words to Robbie Haus-Jones: "Harley Snouch knows everything." It must have been him; you're in the clear.'

But there's no relief on the face of Jack Goffing. He's shaking his head, a portrait of dismay. 'Fuck. You could be right. That's even worse.'

'Worse? How?'

'Don't you see? If you're right, he played me. He played ASIO. He didn't come to Canberra to provide information—he came to gather it. He came because he knew we could identify Flynt for him. The identity of SAS soldiers, past and present, is classified. You're a journo; you must know that. He never intended to help us.' Goffing has his head in his hands, shoulders slumped. 'Fuck, Martin. This is career-ending.'

'Maybe. But we're not dead yet.'

'Easy for you to say. It's not your career on the line.'

'No, mine's already fucked, thanks very much.'

This time Goffing has no comeback.

'Good. So let's think it through. Why would Snouch call Foster and why would it have any impact? Foster already knew Swift was really Flynt; Snouch wasn't telling him anything new.'

Goffing grimaces, re-engaging. 'I see where you're coming from. Snouch was exerting some sort of leverage. He says, "I know Swift is Flynt; I know he's a fugitive and a war criminal. Do what I want or I expose him." No, that's no good; he'd already exposed him.'

Martin nods. 'Maybe he's been telling us the truth. Maybe he just wanted to get Swift out of town, away from Mandy. So he rings Foster and says, "Get him out of town." Maybe he was doing Foster a favour, keeping him out of the firing line.'

Goffing is frowning. 'But Swift was already leaving, wasn't he?'

'Yes. But Snouch didn't know that. He'd been in Canberra the whole time and missed Walker launching his child abuse probe.'

'That's ironic. Swift was going anyway.' Another grimace. 'Doesn't help me, though.'

'And it doesn't explain why Swift opened fire, either.'

'Jesus Christ. Every time I think we're getting somewhere, it slips through our fingers. You get that feeling?'

'I do,' says Martin. 'But listen. How does this play? Snouch rings Foster, tells him ASIO is onto Swift, that he has to go. But Snouch says he can keep Foster's name out of it.'

'Blackmail?'

'Blackmail. Snouch tried something similar with me.'

'What was that?'

'He's threatening to sue me for defamation unless I help him reconcile with Mandy.'

Goffing takes his time before responding. 'He played me, he's blackmailing you, he coerced Avery Foster. The guy's a ratfucker.'

'And a good one. Foster's name *was* kept out of it. Until last night, I'd never connected him to Swift. Had you?'

'No. So he acceded to Snouch's demands? But what was Snouch demanding?'

'Money. Rolls of hundred-dollar bills would be my guess.'

'Snouch never struck me as someone with money,' Goffing objects. 'More like a derro.'

'He was restoring the old family homestead. He was getting money from somewhere. My guess is from Foster.'

'But what money? Where could Foster find money in this shithole?' Goffing stands, gestures around him, emphasising the absurdity of hidden wealth in Riversend.

'Listen, Jack, I've lost my job, you're about to lose yours. Let's say we put it all on the table. No secrets. We've got nothing to lose.'

Goffing looks at him: assessing, calculating, deciding. He shrugs. 'Okay. What do you want to know?'

'What you're doing here. Why you came down with the cops, even before the bodies in the dam were identified.'

Goffing shrugs again. 'Sure. It's not such a big deal.' He sits back down, reaches for another cigarette, thinks better of it. 'A lot of what we do nowadays is terrorism-related. Back in the day, during the Cold War, it was all counterespionage and keeping an eye on the commies. We still do the anti-spy stuff, lots of cybersecurity and so forth, but terrorism is the growth area. My unit is involved with monitoring communications between Australian extremists and jihadis in the Middle East, in particular the movement of foreign fighters and Australian money. In the months before St James, we picked up a trail of money being sent from Australia to Dubai and then disappearing. We suspected it was being funnelled to Islamic State or the Taliban or any one of a number of other extremist groups. There were a couple of key words picked out of the ether: Swift was one, Riversend was another. I mentioned this before; it's why, when Snouch turned up, I gave him the time of day.'

'I see,' says Martin. 'Except instead of going to Muslim extremists, the money was probably going to a Christian orphanage.'

'Yeah, looks like it now.' Another shrug. 'We all make mistakes.'

'But why come down here a year later when the bodies turned up at Springfields?'

'Snouch rang me at the same time he called the coppers. After he found the bodies. Don't know why. Probably wanted me to vouch for him. I immediately thought there might be a connection with Swift's shooting spree, that it might have to do with the money flow. I half expected the bodies in the dam to be young Muslim hotheads, or informants, or God knows who. Not German fruit-pickers, that's for sure.' The men sit in silence, pondering. 'I think we need to go after Snouch,' says Goffing. 'He's the key.'

'I agree. But how can we?'

'What do you mean?'

'Well, he has you over a barrel for letting him use ASIO resources to identify a former special forces soldier. And he's threatening to sue me for defamation and destroy what's left of my career.'

Goffing shakes his head. 'He's up to his eyeballs in something. I wish I knew what it was—that way we could threaten him straight back.'

'I swear those are prison tattoos on his hands, but we've both run checks. Mandy's mother accused him of rape, but there's nothing. No records, no evidence.'

There's little left to say. The two men are immobilised, their frustration mounting with the arc of the sun. It's getting hotter; soon the car park will be unbearable. Goffing lights another cigarette. Half-a-dozen cockatoos fly over, screeching raucously, complaining at the injustice of another day without rain, another baking day in western New South Wales. And now, into the silence left by the cockatoos, a new sound, a vibration felt before it's heard, the guttural roar of approaching thunder.

'What's that?' asks Goffing.

'Motorbikes,' says Martin.

The noise comes closer and the two men stand and watch as four bikies, riding two abreast, ease by along the highway. The four horsemen of the apocalypse, vacationing in the Riverina. The noise bounces this way and that, filling the town with its presence. Martin and Jack Goffing watch them pass, and then follow their progress by sound alone as they change down gears and turn into Hay Road, the growl of the engines reverberating this way and that off the shopfronts. The sound is retreating when Goffing speaks. 'Bikies. Here. They look like the real deal.'

'Yeah, I've seen them before. They pass through now and then.'

'Seriously? Out here? The most boring landscape in the world to ride a motorbike. Why?'

'How would I know?'

'You've seen them before, you say. Do you know who they are?'

'I haven't spoken to them, if that's what you mean. They're the Rebels or the Reapers or something. Here, I took a snap.' Martin searches through his phone, finding the blurry shots of the bikies riding down Hay Road. 'Here.'

'Reapers. Well, fuck me.'

'What's so significant about a few scruffy blokes on motorbikes?'

Goffing is shaking his head. 'No, Martin. The Reapers aren't a few scruffy blokes on motorbikes; they're serious shit. An outlaw gang, more like organised crime. Based in Adelaide. Drugs, extortion, armed robbery. What are they doing here? Do you know where they stay?'

'No. Don't know if they do stay. The only bloke who looks anything like a bikie around here is a vet named Jason who lives out in the Scrublands. Has the bike and the look, but I didn't see any colours.'

'You know his surname?'

'No idea. Has a girlfriend called Shazza. Sharon. Why, what is it?'

'Don't know. Give me an hour or two. I need to make some calls.'

Jack Goffing returns to his room and closes the door behind him. Martin is left standing alone, listening to the distant hum of motorbikes. He's still standing there when the phone in his own room rings, a jangling discordant sound.

He answers it. 'Martin Scarsden,' he says tentatively.

'Martin, it's me, Mandy. Can you come round to the bookstore? I need your help. It's kind of urgent.'

twenty-two   **THIRTY**

MARTIN AVOIDS HAY ROAD, TAKING THE BACK LANE BETWEEN THE ABANDONED supermarket and the petrol station to reach the Oasis. He's greeted at the back door by Mandalay Blonde, her smile radiant. She's holding Liam as she answers the door, but places the boy gently at her feet before reaching out to Martin, kissing and holding him.

'Martin, thank you so much. You saved his life. You know that, don't you?'

Martin is unsure how to respond: is it gratitude or affection? 'I saved Jamie Landers as well.'

'Hush. That's neither here nor there.'

'How is he? Liam?'

'Remarkably good. Tough little fellow. The cuts were super-ficial, thank God. No stitches. Just need to stop him pulling off the dressing.'

On the floor, the boy has pushed across to Martin's feet and has begun pulling at his shoelaces, fascinated by their complexity. Mandy bends and lifts him up. 'Come through, there's someone I want you to meet.'

She leads the way through the house and into the bookstore. She's happy, he can see that, her feet almost floating above the floor. It makes him feel glad.

In the bookstore, sitting in one of the armchairs near the Japanese screen, sipping a cup of tea, is a rather proper-looking woman. She looks almost elderly, possibly in her seventies, but her dress is professional, her hair is dyed and her posture is erect. Half-moon glasses give her some of the appearance of a librarian, except the frames look too expensive.

'Martin, this is Winifred Barbicombe. She's a lawyer.'

'Pleased to meet you, Mr Scarsden,' the woman says, shaking hands but remaining seated. 'Please take a seat. We'd like you to witness some documents, if you'd be so kind.'

Martin looks to Mandy for guidance and receives a glowing smile in return. He takes a seat, as does Mandy, the boy on her lap.

'I'm a partner in a Melbourne law firm, Wright, Douglas and Fenning. For as long as I can remember, which is quite some time, and for as long as anyone can remember, which is even longer, Wright, Douglas and Fenning have provided legal advice to the Snouch family of Springfields. We first acted for them in the nineteenth century.'

'I see,' says Martin, though he doesn't.

The lawyer continues. 'In a few short weeks, Mandalay will turn thirty years old, at which time she will inherit Springfields and a considerable portfolio of investments, including shares, bonds and property—including many properties in Riversend, such as this one. A considerable fortune, in fact.'

Mandy shrugs, expressing her own surprise at this turn of events, her eyes alight at her change in fortune.

'Would you be willing to witness some documents for her?' asks Winifred Barbicombe.

'Yes. Of course,' says Martin. 'So who has bequeathed all this? Eric Snouch?'

'That's correct.' The lawyer places the first of a series of papers on the coffee table between them, and Martin signs and dates it with Winifred's elegant fountain pen.

'What about Harley Snouch? He's Eric's son, isn't he?'

The lawyer's expression is impenetrable. 'He will receive an allowance. Generous enough; considerably more than unemployment benefits.'

She places more papers on the table, but Martin leans back, pen in hand, his curiosity alive. 'Did Katherine Blonde know Mandy would inherit? Mandy says she urged her to have her house in order by the time she reached thirty. She must have known something.' Martin glances at Mandy; her smile has been replaced by the stillness of concentration.

'Well, not from us,' says Winifred. 'Eric Snouch was adamant about that: he wanted it kept secret. But perhaps he said something to Katherine before he died. I simply don't know.'

'He remade his will shortly before he died?'

'That's right.'

'But why keep it secret?'

'I don't know. Perhaps he was worried Mandalay was still

too young and too wild to be informed she was coming into money. Perhaps he didn't want Harley to know.'

'But Harley must have asked—I mean, when his father died. Didn't he ask you, your firm, what was happening with the estate?'

'Constantly.'

'And what did you tell him?'

'Nothing.'

Mandy has lost her serenity. She's holding Liam close. 'Ms Barbicombe—Winifred—is it true? Is Harley Snouch my father? Did he rape my mother?'

For a moment, the professional facade falls from Winifred Barbicombe's face, exposing some of the human underneath, sympathy written in her eyes. But only in her eyes; her voice retains its professionalism. 'I'm sorry, my dear. We acted on behalf of Eric Snouch and his family on a number of matters that are protected by lawyer–client confidentiality. I can't comment on such matters.'

'So I'll never know?' Mandy whispers.

The lawyer seems unsure how to respond; instead it's Martin who intercedes, seizing this unexpected opening. 'Mandy, I haven't mentioned this before, but I spoke to Harley Snouch. He denies paternity. And rape. He wants you both to undertake a DNA test to establish the truth once and for all.'

Mandy looks at him, looks to Winifred Barbicombe, seeking advice. Martin feels annoyed with himself. Is he trying to help Mandy, or is he trying to appease Snouch and assuage his threat of defamation? He really needs to think more before he speaks, weigh his words, like Jack Goffing.

Winifred Barbicombe responds. 'I'm not sure what I can advise. But rest assured, no matter what such a test of DNA might reveal, it will not alter the effect of Eric Snouch's will or provide Harley Snouch with grounds to challenge it. Springfields, and all that goes with it, is yours. If you wish to go ahead with the test, that is entirely up to you.'

Mandy nods her understanding.

'Now, there are more papers to sign. Mandalay first, then Martin.' There is silence as the paperwork is completed, the earlier lightness of mood weighed down by the spectre of Harley Snouch. Martin knows he needs to warn Mandy about Snouch, his duplicitous nature, but that can wait until the lawyer has left. The last paper signed authorises Winifred Barbicombe and Wright, Douglas and Fenning to act on behalf of Mandalay Susan Blonde, soon to be mistress of Springfields and sole owner of the Snouch family fortune.

Winifred Barbicombe gathers the papers, snaps the cap back on her fountain pen and places them into a slim leather briefcase. She stands, shaking hands formally with Martin and more warmly with Mandy. 'It is a pleasure to meet you and an honour to represent you, my dear. If we can help in any way, call me. And if Harley Snouch should menace you, tell me straight away. I'll have a restraining order slapped on him before he knows what hit him.'

Mandy looks uncertain, still coming to terms with her new status.

Martin takes the opportunity to ask a question. 'Listen, before you go, can you tell me how Harley Snouch got the markings on his hands? They look like the sort of tattoos prisoners give each other.'

The solicitor looks grave as she responds. 'As I said, we have acted for the Snouch family for many years. There is no statute of limitations on lawyer–client privilege. However, I can inform you that Harley Snouch has never been convicted of any crime in any Australian court.'

'I see,' says Martin, feeling deflated. 'Thanks.'

'Nevertheless, you are a journalist, are you not?' the lawyer continues, the suggestion of a smile on her lips.

'That's right.'

'There's a fascinating story you should look into when you have a spare moment. A court case. A conman named Terrence Michael McGill, convicted and imprisoned in Western Australia some time back. Released just two years ago.' The smile has extended to her eyes, twinkling above her half-moon glasses. 'Now I must be getting along. A pleasure to meet you both.'

It's left to Martin to show Winifred Barbicombe out. Mandy remains rooted to the spot, the joy of her windfall gone, replaced by a look of anguish. Martin moves to her. On the floor, Liam recommences his exploration of Martin's shoelaces.

'You were right. I thought there must have been a mistake.' There's a quaver in her voice. 'He was never convicted. He didn't go to jail.'

Martin reaches out, places a hand gently on her shoulder. 'No. It doesn't mean it didn't happen, just that he didn't go to prison.'

'But Mum said he did.' Martin can see the pain in her eyes, knows she's doubting her beloved mother, questioning Katherine's motives. 'What should I do?' she asks.

'You should think about taking the DNA test.'

She doesn't say anything, just bends down and lifts Liam, holding the boy close.

'Can I use the phone?' asks Martin.

She nods, thoughts elsewhere.

Bethanie Glass answers her mobile immediately. 'Martin, is that you?'

'Yes, how's it going?'

'Great. Did you see the front page? We killed it. Thanks to you. I even got a herogram.'

'That's great. Well deserved.'

'Have you got something new?'

'No, not exactly. Actually, I'm ringing to ask a favour.'

'Anything. I owe you big time.'

'Can you search the archives for me? I'm looking for anything you can find on a Terrence Michael McGill convicted in Western Australia in the past ten years or so. Released from prison about two years ago.'

'Sure. Who is he?'

'I'm not sure. But if there's a story in it, I'll see you get a slice of it.'

'That's good enough for me. What's the best number to get you on?'

'This one or the Black Dog. And email me any clippings.'

When he emerges from the office, Mandy and Liam have returned to the kitchen. She walks across and kisses him. 'Thanks Martin.'

'For what?'

'For being halfway decent.'

He's not sure how to respond. The old Martin would have gone with the moment but, then, the old Martin was not halfway decent.

'I'm going to take the test,' she says.

'That's probably for the best. But please don't trust Harley Snouch. Check the DNA if you want to, but he's more than just a harmless derro.'

'What is it? What have you found out?'

Martin tries to think it through before he responds, trying to find an easy way of telling her about Julian Flynt, his murderous record and Harley Snouch's role in exposing him. But before he can formulate an answer, there's a knock at the kitchen door, hard and insistent.

'Jesus,' says Martin. 'It's probably some journo trying to cadge an interview.'

But when he opens the door a crack, it's no journalist; it's Jack Goffing, despondency gone, urgency back.

twenty-three **THE CELL**

one to witness their conversation.

'It's the Reapers,' Goffing states baldly.

'The bikies?'

'Yep. The federal coppers didn't have anything, or weren't telling me if they did. Same with the state plods. Don't know nothing about nothing. But the Australian Criminal Intelligence Commission does. I got lucky, talked to the right person. The ACIC has been running a long-term surveillance operation targeting the Reapers, probing their criminal structure. I was right: organised crime.'

'But what's the Reapers' connection with Riversend?'

'Don't know. Yet. One of their senior investigators, a bloke called Claus Vandenbruk, is on his way down to liaise with us; he's chartered a light plane to get him into Bellington.'

Martin blinks, trying to keep up. Such sensitive information, obtained so quickly. 'They're running a covert surveillance operation? Into a bikie-run crime syndicate? And he tells you about it over the phone?'

'Well, I've got clearance. That's a start. But here's the thing: thirty-five years ago, Claus Vandenbruk and Herb Walker were at the police academy in Goulburn together. And later, best men at each other's weddings. Lifelong mates.'

'Shit. Do you think that's where Walker got the information on the phone calls?'

'Vandenbruk isn't saying.'

'And Vandenbruk now feels responsible for his death? That's why he's willing to help?'

'He's not saying.'

'He doesn't have to. Great. When does he get here? When can we talk to him?'

Goffing places his hand on Martin's shoulder, as if to restrain him. 'Listen, Martin. On that score, it's probably not a good idea for you to meet him.'

'Why's that?'

'Because Vandenbruk, like everyone else in law enforcement, thinks you drove his best mate to suicide. And you're a journalist. It's surprising enough he's willing to trust ASIO, even with my clearance. He's only talking because he thinks I might be able to tell him something useful.'

'You didn't tell him we were working together?'

'I certainly did not, and neither should you. I'm going to drive down to Bellington and pick him up. If we run into you, don't be too familiar with me, okay?'

Martin has little choice but to agree, grateful that Goffing is keeping him in the loop; he could easily have kept Vandenbruk and this new information to himself. Martin wonders why he hasn't. 'I guess that makes sense.'

'Good. Now while I'm gone, there's something you can do to help.'

'What's that?'

'Jamie Landers. He wants to talk to you.'

'Landers? Why? Is he still here?'

'Yeah, they're driving him out this afternoon, after they take him out to the Scrublands and film him recreating what happened. Don't know what he wants to talk to you about—maybe he just needs to get it off his chest.'

'And Montifore, the police, they're happy with that? He's been charged; it's sub judice. If I published it could threaten a fair trial, undermine their case.'

'Yes, you'd be done for contempt. So don't publish, not until after he's convicted. That's what they want. He's going to plead guilty, probably won't take the stand. This way, once he's put away, they can get it on the public record, just how depraved he and his mate were, what a great job they did to catch him. It's a way for them to thank you and to help me. And to get the acknowledgement they want.'

The cell is cool, relatively cool, one of two holding cells connected as an afterthought to the back of the Riversend police station, like a converted garage. The brickwork of the interior walls has been rendered smooth by multiple coats of green enamel paint; the concrete floor is bare. There's a cantilevered bed with a thin mattress and a scratchy blanket, a stainless-steel toilet with no seat and a matching washbasin. The ceiling is high, too high to reach even standing on the bed, with an indestructible light fitting. Its glow is supplemented by natural light filtering in from a grille high in one wall.

Jamie Landers is sitting in the middle of the bed, staring at the opposite wall, when Martin is escorted in by Robbie Haus-Jones. Landers turns and looks at Martin blankly, but doesn't speak. Robbie tells Martin to yell if he needs anything and locks the door behind him as he leaves. A flash of memory comes to Martin—Jamie advancing, knife in hand, murder in his eyes. Suddenly the cell feels very small.

'Hi, Jamie. You wanted to speak to me?'

'I guess.' Landers' face is expressionless. If any emotions are playing out inside his mind, none are evident to Martin. Perhaps he's been medicated. Martin hopes so.

There's nowhere for Martin to sit, not unless he wants to sit next to Landers or perch on the rim of the toilet. Instead, he eases himself down onto the hard concrete floor. His eyes are below those of Landers. He feels uncomfortable, at the mercy of the killer, but hopes his submissive position may put Landers more at ease. He swallows with difficulty, reassuring himself that Robbie is listening outside, that the constable is just a cry away. He has his notebook and pen; the police haven't allowed him his phone.

'I'm told you confessed,' says Martin.

Landers nods. 'Yep.'

'That's a good thing to do, Jamie. It makes it easier for the families.'

'Have you seen my mum?' Jamie looks up, his eyes suddenly focused.

'No. Not yet.'

'Tell her I'm sorry, will you? That I didn't mean to hurt her. I'd never hurt her.'

'Is that why you wanted to see me?'

'They won't let her see me. Can you help? Help her in to see me?' The numbness has gone from Landers; Martin can hear the pent-up emotion in his voice. He transcribes the words. He wasn't expecting this: compassion from a psychopath.

'I'll see what I can do. Ask for you. But you know it's not up to me.'

'I know. Thanks for trying, though.'

Martin can see the anguish on the teenager's face. He's not sure what to make of it.

'What happened, Jamie? Why did you do it?'

'We didn't mean to. We didn't plan to. It just happened.'

'How?'

Landers looks into space again, eyes losing their focus, emotion dissipating, the impression of numbness returning. When he speaks, his voice has a faraway quality. 'Allen had his Ps, so we went driving. Didn't plan to go far, but we did. Just kept going. All the way to Swan Hill. No real reason, we just drove. We had some bourbon, some tequila; we ended up drinking by the river. The river there is so big. Just looking at it makes you feel cooler. It's a good place to drink. I knew we shouldn't be drinking, 'cos Allen needed to drive back. You can't drink if you're on your Ps. We met the girls there, by the river. They were pretty and fun. They tried the drink, but didn't like it. Then they left.'

Jamie is no longer looking at the wall; instead, his eyes are cast down, looking at the floor.

'Later, when we were drunk, we drove into town for some food. We saw them walking, offered them a lift, they got in. That was it.'

'That was it? You killed them?'

'We weren't planning to. I told you that. We stopped by the river again, to drink, but they wanted to go to their hostel. Then it went bad. They'd been to university. They started laughing at us when they found out we left school at fifteen, like we were idiots or something. Then they were teasing Allen, because he'd never seen the ocean. So I hit one of them in the face, to stop her laughing. I splatted her good. She stopped laughing. The other one screamed, so Allen punched her. It just kept going after that. We didn't know how to stop.'

'You brought them back here? To the Scrublands?'

'We didn't know what else to do. They were going to dob on us, tell the police. They promised not to, but I knew they would.' Landers looks up, meets Martin's eyes, gaze unflinching. 'And you know what? It felt good. I liked scaring them. I liked being the one doing the hitting for once. It felt good. That's sick, isn't it?'

'So you killed them?'

'Yeah. We killed them.'

'You raped them first?'

'Yeah. We raped them.'

There are no tears in Jamie Landers' eyes; no tears for the dead girls, no tears for himself. No remorse. Martin knows he should probe further, extract the awful details, the timeline of depravity, the abominations that occurred in the Scrublands. Landers is ready to tell him, wants to tell him, and he knows the readers will want it too: a glimpse inside the mind of a teenage killer. It's what journalists do, even if many of the details are too abhorrent to publish. It's part of the job: witness the worst the world has to offer, then sanitise it for public consumption, make the events somehow explicable and twice-removed. But Martin feels sick in the stomach.

He takes a deep breath, considers why he's interviewing Landers. He's fallen so easily back into the habits of the journalist, homing in on the confessional. He knows his former colleagues would give their eyeteeth to secure it, but feeding the news cycle is no longer his priority. The girls are dead, Newkirk is dead, Jamie Landers is fucked in the head. Does he really want to wallow in such evil? It's not going to help him and Jack Goffing—an exploration of Jamie Landers' twisted mind will do nothing to advance their investigations.

So he changes tack. 'Jamie, the priest, Reverend Swift—did you and Allen tell Sergeant Walker that he had abused you?'

Landers' face lights up. A smile. 'Yes. Ha. That was me. I made that up.'

'You made it up? It wasn't true?'

'Shit no.' A look of contempt. 'As if Allen and me would let him touch us. No fucking way.'

'And he didn't abuse anyone else? Any kids?'

'Not that I know of. But you know, he was a priest. They do that sort of shit.'

'So why make the allegation? Did it have something to do with the girls?'

Landers nods. 'Yeah, that's it. You're smarter than you look. He found them, or he found something. He was suspicious, but not of us. He warned us not to go out to the Scrublands, said something bad had happened out there. To be careful.'

'He warned you?'

'Yeah.'

'So what was the idea? Were you going to frame him for the murders?'

'Nah. We were going to kill him.'

Martin stares at the young man, struggling to comprehend this new horror, but Landers merely smiles back, as if he's just said something very witty.

'Can you explain that?' asks Martin.

'I tell you, it was my idea. Allen was never that smart.'

'What were you planning?'

'Isn't it obvious? We'd set the scene, told the cops he'd abused us. We were going to lure him somewhere and shoot him. With one of his own guns. Then we'd tell the police he'd tried to molest us again, that we fired in self-defence. That way, if they found the bodies in the dam, they'd think it was him as well. We'd be home free. Beautiful, hey?' The boy is smiling again, proud of his scheming.

'You think anyone would have believed that?'

'Everyone would have believed it. He was a priest.'

Martin considers that claim for a moment and surprises himself by concluding the scheme might well have worked. He continues, 'There was a call to the police, Jamie. An anonymous call, to Crime Stoppers a year ago, not long after you killed the German girls. It was a tip-off that there were bodies in the dam at Springfields. The story was in the paper the other day. I thought it must have been Swift.'

'Nah, that was us. Part of the set-up. Although we didn't say the dam, just that the girls were dead and their bodies were somewhere in the Scrublands.'

'Shit,' says Martin, not knowing what else to say.

But Jamie is on a roll now, happy to talk, happy to boast, happy they've moved on from the torture and murder of the girls. 'In the end, we didn't need to do anything. He went mental, mad cunt, and killed everyone at the church. Then his copper chum shot him. So we let it go. We figured the longer the bodies were in the dam, the better. Less evidence. And if they did get found, then they'd blame him, or that old rapist, or both. We told ourselves we were in the clear.'

'That's pretty amazing,' says Martin, feeding the kid's ego.

'Pretty cool, hey?'

'Yeah,' says Martin. 'Pretty cool. But listen, you told Sergeant Walker that Swift molested you—is it true he told your dad and your dad believed it?'

'Yeah. Dumb and dumber.'

'You saw him, didn't you, the morning he died, before he went to St James?'

'My dad? Yeah, I did.'

'What happened?'

'He was in a fucking flap, I tell you, him and his mates, but especially him. Spitting chips. Funniest thing you ever saw. He was ranting on about killing the priest. Allen and me were cacking ourselves.'

'But he didn't really intend to kill him, did he? They didn't take guns to the church.'

'No. Mum turned up. I think she'd been to see him, to see Swift. Said he was leaving town, that Dad didn't have to do anything. He calmed down a bit after that. He pulled me aside, demanded I tell him the truth, whether Swift had abused us or not.'

'What did you say?'

'I told him it was bullshit. That Allen and I were just getting back at him.'

'For what?'

Landers doesn't respond, doesn't seem to want to.

'For what, Jamie?'

'For being a superior cunt, for thinking he was better than us.' The assertion has the ring of truth to it, at least part of the truth. Martin lets it go.

'Okay. So what happened then? With your dad?'

'Well, he calmed down. I thought they were going to go hunting and that was the end of it. Allen was going with them, to make sure they didn't go anywhere near where we'd finished the Krauts or near the dam at Springfields. But then, I don't know, Dad got kind of happy, started laughing. He said something to Mum, I don't know what, but he was laughing and she was crying. The prick. And then Dad and his mates went to the church anyway.'

Martin considers this. Why did Landers go to the church? His wife Fran had told him Swift was leaving, his son Jamie had told him Swift had not abused him after all. So why go? Martin looks at Landers; he can't think of any reason the boy wouldn't be telling the truth. 'You're worried about your mum, hey?'

That brings Landers back to earth. He deflates, eyes cast downwards. 'Yeah. She doesn't deserve this.'

'What about your father, Jamie? Swift killed him.'

'Best thing he ever did.'

'Kill your father?'

'Too right.'

'Why?'

'You don't need to know.' Landers gets to his feet, starts pacing, suddenly menacing. Sitting on the floor, Martin feels vulnerable, Landers stalking the cell above him. He starts to get up, finds it difficult. One of his legs has fallen asleep, pins and needles running down his thigh and into his calf; his stance is unsteady. He recalls what Jamie said about the Germans: *I liked being the one doing the hitting for once.*

'Was he violent, Jamie? Did he hit you? Did he hit your mum?'

Landers' eyes turn volcanic. His fist comes from nowhere, Martin swaying his head at the last moment, turning it into a glancing blow. But it's enough for his knees to buckle. 'Robbie!' he calls as he falls. 'Help! Robbie!' Landers is standing over him, seething, fists clenched, but not moving, not lashing out. The cell door opens and Martin is pulled up and out.

'You all right?' asks Robbie, leading him back into the main station, into the kitchen.

'Yeah, I think so. He blindsided me.' Martin touches his left cheek where Landers connected. It's tender to the touch and beginning to swell.

'Let me take a look at it,' says Robbie, sitting Martin down. 'It's not cut, but you'll have a decent bruise. I'll get you some ice. You want to press charges?'

Martin shakes his head. 'What's the point? Rape and murder. He'll be inside for years.'

Robbie gets some ice cubes from the freezer, wraps them in a tea towel.

'You heard?' asks Martin.

'I was listening,' says Robbie.

'He lost it, hit me when I suggested his father had been abusive. Is that true?'

Robbie nods, eyes more sad than angry. 'Ask any country cop. Domestic violence is half of what we do. It's endemic.'

'So he was violent? Craig?'

'Sure. Drought like this, times like this, heat like this. The pressure builds up; throw in a bit of grog and tempers become hair-trigger. I'm not excusing it, but that's life for a lot of women. In the bush and in the city. Craig Landers beat his wife from time to time when he was in his cups. So do a lot of men.'

'Did you intervene?'

'I locked him up a couple of times. Talked to him. But after that, you really need to be guided by the women. No good going further if they don't want you to; it might achieve nothing more than inciting another beating.'

'Jesus.'

'Welcome to my world.'

'And Jamie? Did Craig beat him as well?'

'Couldn't say. Jamie never said anything; Fran never said anything. But that doesn't mean it didn't happen.'

'Well, something fucked him up, that's for sure. Did you hear what he said in there? About the backpackers?'

'That's nothing. You should hear the full confession. What they put those girls through. It's not human, makes your skin crawl. Montifore is insisting on counselling for the lot of us.'

Robbie pauses and Martin takes the opportunity to change subject. 'Hey, there are a few other things I'd like you to help me with. Off the record.'

Robbie shrugs affably. 'Sure. Montifore's commandeered my office, but we can talk here.'

'Remember that first time we met, when I interviewed you at the police station. You said that you and Byron Swift had been friends. You remember that?'

'Sure.'

'You just heard what Jamie said, that Swift warned him and Allen that something bad had happened out in the Scrublands. Did Swift ever say anything to you?'

Robbie is unable to meet Martin's gaze, staring at his hands as he picks at his nails. 'No. No he didn't.'

'Any idea why not?'

'Not really. I guess he didn't want it made public for some reason.'

'Walker told you his theory, didn't he? That Swift was an imposter. It wasn't his real name.'

Robbie looks at him then, eyes intense. 'Is it true?'

'I think so, yes.'

'Who was he then? Do you know?'

'A former soldier. He was wanted by the authorities. I'm guessing that's why he didn't tell you. He knew you'd arrest him.'

Robbie nods, as if endorsing Martin's interpretation. 'And you intend publishing this?'

'I do, as soon as I find someone who'll run the story.'

Robbie stares at him, hesitating before speaking again. 'Did Harley Snouch know? Byron's last words. Was that what he was trying to tell me?'

'I think maybe it was.'

Robbie just shakes his head, as if in disbelief. Or in despair. 'Shit. Harley Snouch knew, Herb Walker worked it out. Just poor dumb Robbie Haus-Jones left in the dark, sucked in and spat out.' He shakes his head again. 'I'm going to look the right fool when your story comes out. Fuck me.' A third shake of his head. 'But thanks, Martin. Thanks for telling me. For warning me.'

'Sorry. There are a couple of other matters. I keep seeing bikies riding through town. What's the story with them?'

'The Reapers? No idea. They stay down in Bellington. There's a pub there they like, owned by a former member.'

'So not around here?'

'No. No bikies around here.'

'What about Jason, out in the Scrublands?'

'Jason? He's not a bikie. He's an invalid with a Yamaha.'

Martin nods. 'The publican—Avery Foster. You knew him?'

Robbie frowns, looking confused by Martin's question. 'Sure. Everyone knew him. He served behind the bar most lunchtimes, most nights. Can't say I knew him well, though. He was a pleasant bloke, but quiet for a publican. Not prone to banter.'

'Accepted by the community?'

'Oh yeah. People were happy someone was trying to make a go of the pub.'

'Was he mates with Byron Swift?'

The frown deepens. 'No. Not particularly. I don't think Byron went to the pub much. He wasn't up here that often. But maybe he did. I know Foster donated some money to our youth group, so they must have known each other somehow. Byron organised that. Either that or Avery got wind of what we were doing and decided to help off his own bat.'

'He killed himself; am I right?'

'Yes. It wasn't good. Put a shotgun in his mouth and pulled the trigger. Down by the river. One hell of a mess. I should tell Montifore's counsellors about that while I'm at it.'

'Do you know why he did it? Did he leave a note?'

'No, no note. But the reasons were pretty clear. His wife had left him. She'd never liked it here, never fitted in. The week after the shooting at St James, she packed up and headed back to the city. You can understand why. And he was out of money, so they say. The drought. It's tough times, Martin. Desperate times.'

'What happened to his body? His affairs?'

'Why are you so interested in Foster?'

'I think he may have known Swift's real identity.'

'What? How?'

'They were in the military together.'

'How do you know that?'

'Jack Goffing and I, we broke into his apartment over at the Commercial.'

'But the pub's empty. The wife cleared everything out.'

'Not everything. Goffing's on his way to Bellington to pick up a criminal investigator.'

twenty-four **THE CORPSE**

OUTSIDE THE POLICE STATION THE DAY GROWS HOTTER. A HIGH-PRESSURE system suspended above eastern Australia like a spiteful god, banishing clouds and forbidding moisture. Martin can feel the sun on his bare skin like a physical assault, as if the hairs on his arms might catch fire like the mulga of the Scrublands. The temperature must be approaching forty. He's been here for more than a week and he's yet to experience a cool day, yet to see a cloud. The only variation is the wind: too much and there's the risk of fire, too little and there's no relief whatsoever. Today is windless.

Across the road, in the shade of a tree, the gaggle of media, beaten down by the heat, come alert at the sight of him. A couple of photographers notch up some lazy frames, more out of boredom than interest: he's yesterday's story. The media will get a doorstop with Montifore, then the spectacle of Landers at the Scrublands crime scene, recounting his atrocities. Then they can be on their way, the story that drew them to Riversend, the murder of the backpackers, resolved.

A thin figure of a man, wearing moleskins, riding boots and a light linen shirt, breaks away from the group and makes his way towards Martin. D'Arcy Defoe, dressed the part.

'Martin.'

'D'Arcy.'

They shake hands.

'Looks like I got here in time to turn around and go back again,' says D'Arcy.

'Sorry to inconvenience you.'

Defoe laughs. 'Yeah. I reckon you did it on purpose.'

Martin smiles. His rival has always possessed an easy line in banter.

'For what it's worth, Martin, I think you have been most shabbily treated. Most shabbily. Our management is a disgrace— but you already know that.'

'Thanks, D'Arcy. I appreciate it.'

Defoe flicks his head in the direction of the police station. 'Any developments?'

'No, not a lot. Jamie Landers has confessed to everything. He isn't holding back. It's not going to be much of a trial; very open and shut, I should think. The coppers are going to drive him out to the bush to film him taking them through it.'

'I know. They want a media pool.'

'You going out?'

'Yeah. I don't think there's any news left to wring out of the yarn, but that could provide some useful colour. If I can hack the heat. Is it always this hot?'

'Yep.'

'Listen, Martin, if you don't mind me asking, what are you still doing here?'

'Not sure I know myself. Just want to see it through to a conclusion, I guess. My last story, and all that.'

D'Arcy nods, his manner sincere. 'Listen, you should give Wellington Smith a ring. You know him? Editor of *This Month*. I'm sure they'd go for a longer piece on what you've seen here. Be a shame to waste what you've got.'

'Thanks, D'Arcy. That's not a bad idea.'

'Just a moment.' D'Arcy has his phone out, writes down the number of the editor of the monthly news magazine. 'Here. And give me a ring if there's anything else I can do, okay?'

'Sure. Thanks.' Martin watches D'Arcy return to the media fold. The two have long been competitors, their rivalry at times intense, but now he's no longer in the contest, that all seems petty. Typical of D'Arcy to be alive to the new reality; Martin has always been slower on the uptake. He looks at the number his former colleague has given him. D'Arcy is right: it is a good idea. He already has the makings of a great story, a compelling long read: everything from Robbie's initial interview, through Julian Flynt hiding out as Byron Swift, to his own role in saving Liam Blonde and flushing out the backpacker killers. Plus an exclusive interview with Landers, erratic and lost to himself. Maybe he's selling himself short: surely he's got the makings of a book. A small surge of excitement runs through him; he's not dead yet. Instead of returning to wait for Goffing at the Black Dog, he decides to make his way out to the Scrublands with the others; the sight of Jamie Landers at the murder scene may yet prove useful for a longer narrative.

By the time he collects his car from the Black Dog and returns to the police station, Montifore is finishing a door-stop interview and the media are preparing to drive to the Scrublands. There's the sudden snarl of camera shutters; Jamie Landers is being led out wearing handcuffs and assisted into the back of a car, but not before the police are sure the cameras have had their fill.

⏤

Once more, Martin finds himself driving the last car in the media convoy. He's debating whether the trip is worth it. D'Arcy's suggestion of a longer piece for *This Month* is a good one, but the closer Martin gets to the murder scene, the less likely it appears he will learn anything useful traipsing around in the searing heat. Defoe is no slouch, he'll milk the moment for all it's worth, and he's always been the more evocative writer of the two of them. And the cops won't let them get within cooee: it's a job for the photographers, television crews and telephoto lenses. There'll be precious little left for any *This Month* piece. Perhaps Martin would have been better off staying in town, waiting for Goffing. Or going to see Mandy. He's yet to tell her what he's learnt about Swift. She won't take it well, he knows that, the revelation that her lover was a fraud, a war criminal, a murderer of innocents. Is that why he's driven out here? To avoid her? To delay? To savour this morning's kiss a little longer? At least now he'll be able to tell her that Defoe's allegation was false; Swift was no paedophile—Jamie Landers has cleared him of that slander, at least. He wonders how much of an impact learning of Swift's past will have on her. She had looked so happy; her son is alive, her charges have been dropped, she has inherited a fortune. For a moment he wonders if he needs to tell her about Swift at all. Why threaten her new-found equilibrium? But he knows the answer to that: she can't learn about it from the papers, certainly not from a magazine article with his name attached to it. He has to tell her.

He reaches the turn-off into the Scrublands, the same circle of gravel where Errol Ryding and his fire crew had waited a week before. The police continue, followed by the media. Martin stops the car, leaving the engine running, the air-conditioning not so much cooling the car as making it less hot. Gradually the cloud of dust and ash from the departed cars falls from the air around him, hardly drifting at all in the windless day. He cuts the engine and feels the heat surrounding him, like the ocean around a diving bell, the pressure pushing inwards. Across the clearing he can see the array of letterboxes, rusted paint tins and painted boxes, mounted on poles, bearing RMB numbers. He thinks of Harley Snouch, tempted to confront him but knowing he shouldn't. Instead, he decides to visit Jason and see if the motorbike-riding veteran knows anything about the Reapers.

Martin gets out of the car, into the silence. Somewhere, off in the distance, there is some sort of buzzing, some insect life impervious to the heat but serving only to emphasise the stillness of the day. He walks to the letterboxes, but most don't have names, just the numbers. He realises he has no idea where Jason and his girlfriend live, which path might lead him there. Nothing would be more futile than driving around the Scrublands hoping to chance upon them. Except breaking down in the middle of nowhere. He thinks of Codger Harris; the old man could give him directions. And Martin knows the way to his shanty.

He finds it spared from complete destruction. The same fluky winds that left one cow skull untouched and the other incinerated at his fence line have played the same game of Russian roulette with his buildings. The house has survived, but the sawmill and garage are gone, the old Dodge a blackened shell. Martin wonders what happened to the bitch and her puppies; he hopes they escaped alive. A ten-year-old Toyota, covered in dust and ash, looks somehow modern sitting amid the frontier architecture of the yard. Codger, wearing a battered hat, boots and nothing else, emerges from the house, his skin like lizard leather.

'Martin. Didn't expect to see you out here. Come in. Enjoy some terroir,' he says, giving his scrotum a tug.

Martin follows him in, but with no wind coming through the gaps in its wall, the corrugated-iron shack is an oven, super-heated by the sun. Martin accepts some water but suggests they find some shade outside.

'Any news?' asks Codger.

'Quite a lot.' And Martin recounts the arrest and confession of Jamie Landers while Codger nods, eyes downcast, face solemn.

'It's a merciless world, all right,' is all the old man has to say in response. 'I guess it was him shooting me cows. So what brings you out here? Not to tell me that, I'd guess.'

'Can you tell me how to get to Jason's place? The vet with the motorbike?'

'I could, but you'd get lost. The tracks over there go every which way.' The old man again scratches his balls, as if it helps him think. Martin wonders if he has lice. 'But I can take you if you like.'

'Would you? You sure?'

'What else have I got to do? This place is like *Waiting for Godot*. Without the conversation. Give us a tick and I'll find some clothes.'

———

By the time they get to Jason's bush block, Martin is comprehensively lost. Codger has guided him through back paths and short cuts, across dry creek beds and over rocky ridges; past trees destroyed by fire, past trees devastated by drought. On two occasions, the men pull fallen branches from the track; on another, Martin narrowly escapes getting bogged in a drift of windblown sand. The landscape is lifeless, the lack of wind denying even a false sense of animation. The world has stopped turning; it is dead still.

Jason's gate, made of steel, survives among the ashes, adorned with various signs forbidding entry: TRESPASSERS PROSECUTED and PRIVATE LAND—KEEP OUT!, joined by a red-and-white sign pilfered from some distant freeway: WRONG WAY—GO BACK. But the signs have lost their authority; the gate is wide open and off its hinges.

Martin proceeds cautiously. He sees tyre marks in the ash; someone has been here recently, may still be here. It occurs to him that seeking out Jason may not be wise. But there is no room to turn around without risking getting bogged and he's come too far to reverse all the way out. He looks at Codger, who appears utterly unconcerned. The track leads on, through the blackened skeletons of trees.

They come over a small rise and arrive at what must have been Jason's home. A pot-bellied stove stands on its brick hearth surrounded by ruination. Out of the car, Martin can see the house was small, but no bush shack; the brick pilings suggest a more thoughtful and complete structure. None of which matters now; there is nothing left. Codger has joined him, shaking his head at the sight.

Martin walks around the clearing, checking the ground as he does so. The tyre marks are easy to follow in the ash: blurry parallel lines created by a car, better defined impressions left more recently by motorbikes. He follows them, trying to work out if they've been left by Jason's bike alone or if he's had company. Company, he concludes; anywhere between two and four bikes. He imagines the scene: the Reapers arriving, gunning their engines as they slowly circled, full of menace. There are footprints as well, four sets, all made by boots, leading away into the bush. Leading where? How recently?

Martin follows the footprints and Codger follows Martin, past a clump of burnt-out trees, up and over a slight incline. Another burnt-out building, a large machinery shed, steel frame and metal sheeting unable to withstand the power of the fire. It lies like a gutted corpse, the aftermath of autopsy, exposed for examination. Its steel trusses twist upwards like blackened ribs, the sheeting peeled back to expose the innards. But the

innards are gone, incinerated. The footprints stop short of the
building, the people who left them having seen enough. But
Martin persists, walking through the ash and into the corpse.

There is little to see; if this was a machinery shed, it housed
no machinery; there are no burnt-out tractors, no incinerated
drill-presses, no blackened ploughshares. Martin looks at the
detritus, sifting through its patterns with his mind, trying to
visualise what was here. Slowly, the corpse begins to give up
its secrets. Martin sees the twisted metal poles, aligned in rows:
the remnants of table legs. He scrapes through the ashes with
his shoe: a piece of yellow metal. He bends down, picks it up:
a brass fitting, like something from a garden hose. He looks
up again. Along the remains of one wall, piles of long rect-
angular ceramic pots, blackened but impervious to the fire's
heat. He's walking across to examine them when something
unexpected seizes his attention: a dark stain on the ground. He
crouches, places his palm against the soil. It's not his imagination: the ground is damp and cool to the touch. Water. Water
out here, where there is no water. And against the darkness of
the moist ground, something new, the luminous green shoots
of tiny plants.

'Hey, Codger. Take a look at this.'

The old man shuffles over.

'Are these what I think they are?'

'Looks like it, young fellow. Baby dope plants.'

Martin stands, surveys the remains of the shed around him.
A hydroponic operation, PVC pipes incinerated, together with
wooden tables and rubber hoses. The shed must be thirty metres
by twenty: a lot of plants, a lot of money. And a lot of water.

'Did you know about this?'

'Not me, young fella.' The old man's face is guileless, hiding nothing.

'Where does he get water from out here? Are there bores?'

'Nah. Only one place that has water out here: Springfields.'

'Harley Snouch's place?'

'That's right. It's a fair way along the tracks, but only a kilometre or two as the crow flies.'

'So Snouch has been supplying water? Selling it, or taking a cut from profits.' A sense of elation is welling inside him: Snouch is part of a hydroponic drug operation; his threat of defamation against Martin evaporates, as empty as Riversend's river. 'Gotcha,' he says aloud.

'Don't be so sure, Martin. Young Jason could've just stolen the water.'

'Stolen? How?'

'We all do it. Snouch's dam is spring-fed, never runs dry. It feeds water out to troughs in the scrub, water for the bush cattle. Pretty easy to tap into it, feed some water into our own troughs. We started doing it back when the drought began. Old Eric turned a blind eye, and once he was gone and the place was empty, it was open slather.'

'What about Harley?'

'He ripped out the obvious taps, the bastard. Soon as he arrived. So most of us put in more discreet ones. Not so hard to do.'

Martin looks about him. *Gotcha* starts to lose its certainty. He thinks of the day of the fire, he and Robbie and Snouch retreating through the blazing homestead. There had come a point when Snouch's hose had failed, when the fire reached the pump house. 'But an operation like this, that's a lot of water. Wouldn't he hear his pump working overtime?'

Codger shrugs. 'Maybe. And his electricity bill must have been a beauty.'

Martin is alerted by a sound, the crunching of a footstep on metal sheeting. The men turn.

Jason's petite girlfriend is standing before them, but there is nothing petite about the shotgun she's wielding. It's pointed at Martin. 'What do you cunts want?' she hisses. She looks a mess: face dirty and blackened, eyes bloodshot, clothes torn and filthy. She's wearing a black singlet, ripped jeans, boots, tattoos on her arms. An extra from a post-apocalyptic blockbuster.

'It's okay, Shazza—we don't want trouble,' says Codger, his arms spread in a non-threatening gesture.

'Who's he?'

'Martin. You remember, from the fire. He's not a cop.'

She considers this for a moment. 'You got any water?'

Martin can hear the need in her voice, see her cracked lips. 'Sure. In the car. In the back.'

'Lead the way,' she says.

Martin and Codger leave the shed, returning towards the car, arms raised. Codger falls behind Martin, dropping back towards the woman with the gun. 'You don't need the gun, love. We're unarmed, don't mean any harm. We want to help.' His voice is calm, measured, reassuring.

'Don't be a dickhead, Codger. No one's going to help us.'

'Where's Jase?'

Behind him, Martin hears a stifled sob. He stops walking, tenses, fearing the blast of the shotgun. But there is no response

404

from behind, no insistence that he walk on. He turns slowly, arms held high. Shazza has stopped, the gun lowered, a tremor moving through her.

'Let's get some water, love,' says Codger. 'And you can tell us all about it.'

At the car, the woman still grips the gun but no longer points it at Martin. He springs the boot and Codger reaches in, takes a one-litre bottle, opens it and offers it to Shazza. She takes it, gulping greedily. Codger gets another bottle, drinks some himself, hands the bottle to Martin. He drinks too. The three of them, drinking water together amid the ruins. And without prompting, the woman starts talking.

'We came back after the fire, saw there was nothing left. Came back again last Sunday, with a tent and some supplies, to see what we could salvage. But there was nothing left. Nothing. We didn't know what to do. Jase said we'd just have to start again, borrow some money to build a little shack. Take it from there, a day at a time.'

'You don't have any money?' asks Martin, thinking of the hydroponic operation.

She shakes her head. 'Fuck all. Not since the priest died. But Jase thought he could borrow some, get an advance. He had a half-bottle of bourbon. We were toasting the future when the cop arrived and it all went to shit.'

Martin's breath catches; he can hardly speak. 'Cop? What cop?'

'Not Robbie. That arsehole from Bellington, the fat one.'

'Herb Walker? What did he want?'

'He had a gun. Arsehole. Made us take him to the shed, what's left of it. I was scared he was going to shoot us.'

'What happened?'

'The Reapers got him. Him and Jase. Took them away in the cop car. Came back later for their bikes. Took Jason's as well.'

Martin's mind is leaping from one fact to another. *Dope. The priest. The Reapers. Last Sunday. Walker.*

'You've been here by yourself since Sunday?' asks Codger. 'You poor thing.'

She nods. 'Ran out of water yesterday. I was about to walk to Snouch's. But I didn't want to leave in case . . .' She sobs, fighting tears. 'In case he comes back, in case they let them go.'

Martin looks at Codger, sees the concern writ large on the old man's face. He looks at Shazza, sees her stubborn hope. 'Shazza, listen: Walker is dead. They think he committed suicide. That same night. Sunday. But there's no news about Jason. He could be okay.'

But the news about Walker is too much for the woman. She breaks down completely, openly weeping, despairing for the fate of her partner.

Gently, moving slowly, Codger goes to her, takes the shotgun, breaks it open, removes the shells and lays it on the ground. He holds his arms wide and Shazza falls into them, like a child comforted by her grandfather. Martin watches this unfold without seeing; his mind is throwing up scenarios one after the other, trying to find one that makes sense. Jason growing dope but not making any money. Swift implicated; giving money to Jason. The Reapers, abducting Walker and Jason. Driving Walker to suicide? Killing him outright? *Holy shit.*

Into the silence, emphasised by Shazza's weeping, another sound insinuates itself: a car. A car coming closer. Martin walks around to the side of his rental, picks up the shotgun. What did Codger do with the shells? Never mind. He snaps it shut, thinking maybe he can use it as a bluff.

A final wave of sound and the car comes over the rise into the broken yard. Jack Goffing is driving. He and two other men get out, one in his fifties, the other in his twenties, in the telltale dress of plainclothes policemen. The younger man is holding a handgun, out of its holster, pointing at the ground. He looks like he means business. Martin carefully puts the shotgun down, raises his hands, leaving no room for mistakes.

'Are you Sharon Young?' asks the older man, ignoring Martin and Codger.

Shazza nods.

'Good. My name is Claus Vandenbruk. I'm a police officer. Your partner Jason Moore is helping us with our inquiries. He wants you to know he is alive and well.'

Shazza says nothing, surrendering entirely to tears, Codger supporting her.

'You Scarsden?' the cop barks, looking bluntly at Martin.

'That's me.'

'You been over there?' The policeman tips his head in the direction of the burnt-out dope shed, not taking his gaze from Martin as he does so.

'Yeah. I had a look.'

'What'd you see?'

'A burnt-out machinery shed.'

The cop smiles menacingly. 'Good for you. You work out what's been going on?'

'Yeah. Marijuana. Must have been quite a crop. Tapping into the water from Springfields.'

'Clever lad. You thinking of publishing that?'

Next to Vandenbruk, Goffing is shaking his head, signalling to Martin to say no.

'Any reason why I shouldn't?'

'Hundreds. Including being charged with obstructing a police inquiry. Your choice.'

'Then I won't. Not a word. Not yet. But when the time comes, when you bust open the Reapers, I want the inside running. Agreed?'

A flash of anger passes across the policeman's face, and one of dismay across Jack Goffing's. 'Who said anything about the Reapers?'

'I did. What do you think I'm doing out here? Do we have a deal or not?'

The young policeman, standing off to one side, places his handgun in its holster, reaches behind him and removes some handcuffs from his belt. 'You want me to cuff him, boss?'

But Vandenbruk shakes his head, eyes still boring into Martin's, looking as if nothing would please him more than wading into the reporter, boots and all. 'No,' he says eventually. 'Here's the deal, Scarsden. You tell me everything you know. Everything. In return, I don't arrest you here and now. And if it suits me, if it suits the investigation, we'll tell you what's happening. When the time comes.'

'Fair enough,' says Martin.

'Goodo then. Was Herb Walker your source?'

'It's okay, Martin,' interjects Jack Goffing. 'Claus knows you weren't responsible for Walker's death.'

Martin shakes his head. 'I don't reveal my sources. Including you—when the time comes,' he says, parroting the policeman's words. 'What do you know about Herb's death?'

The policeman's face is hard to read, not because it's devoid of emotion, but because there are so many to see: anger and amusement, disgust and grief, eddying back and forth, one after the other. Finally, disgust wins out.

'He didn't suicide. The Reapers killed him. Waterboarded him, but fucked it up. He had a heart attack, so they drowned him. Stupid cunts.' And he spits into the ashes at his feet.

'How do you know that?'

'That's for me to know, not you.'

'And the Reapers? You'll arrest them?'

'Arrest them? They have no idea the amount of shit that is about to come down upon them. Forget the rest; they killed a cop. We're setting the raids up now with the feds and state coppers. They're fucked six ways to Sunday.'

'I can report that? When it happens?' asks Martin.

'Mate, the whole world will be reporting that particular shit-storm. But you breathe a word about it before we're done, and you'll be as sorry as Sisyphus. I'll see to it myself. And breathe a word about Jason Moore—ever—and you risk having his blood on your hands. Got that? Ever.'

'So why tell me?'

Vandenbruk pauses. Another emotional squall passes over his face, leaving him more subdued. 'Because you're here, because you know. And Herb trusted you. Stupid bastard. Now let's get out of here; I don't want to be around if any of those bike-riding bastards show up. We'll take your car, Jack. Sharon can come with us. You okay riding back with Scarsden?'

Goffing nods, looking somewhat taken aback by the policeman's presumption.

Codger helps Shazza over to Goffing's commandeered rental. Before she gets into the car, she takes one last look around her devastated property. But in her eyes there are signs of hope; her man is alive.

The car pulls away, leaving the three of them to watch it go.

'We haven't met,' Goffing says to Codger. 'I'm Jack Goffing.'

'Hello, Jack. Everyone calls me Codger. Codger Harris.'

'Pleased to meet you, Codger. Do you mind giving Martin and me a moment in private?'

'No worries,' says Codger and he shuffles away towards the ruins of the house.

Martin waits until he is out of earshot. 'What did Vandenbruk have to say?'

'The Criminal Intelligence Commission has been running surveillance on the Reapers for almost two years. The bikies are Adelaide-based, but have been extending their influence into the east coast. They're moving members into Canberra, setting up a chapter; the anti-consorting laws are weaker there. Meanwhile, they're putting drugs into country Victoria and New South Wales, carving out new territory. Crystal meth, ecstasy, dope. They've been using Riversend as a staging point. Byron Swift was in on it. That and growing dope out here. That's why he put a phone line into St James: to coordinate it.'

'So that's where he and Avery Foster were getting the money for the orphanage? Marijuana?'

'Looks like it. Spend a bit of time in Afghanistan and hashish becomes a non-issue very quickly. It's nothing compared to the rest of the shit going down over there.'

'Dope maybe. But ice? That's no laughing matter.'

'You're telling me. But that's what Vandenbruk said. Swift put the phone line in. Maybe it was just intended to sell the dope, but the Reapers definitely started using the church as a staging point for hard drugs. The ACIC has been monitoring the number, running surveillance on the dope shed, the lot.'

'So that's where Herb Walker got Avery's phone number? From Vandenbruk?'

'That has to be right. But go easy there. Vandenbruk is like a grenade with the pin out. He reckons he got his best mate killed; he seriously wants to do some damage to someone. Make sure it's the Reapers, not you.'

'And the Reapers? How come Jason Moore has no money if he's growing dope for them?'

'Because they're ruthless. Utterly ruthless. My guess is that Flynt could hold his own, with his guns and his military training, but once he was gone, the bikies sidelined Avery Foster and took over the operation. Any money the orphanage or anyone here was getting would have dried up pretty quickly.'

'What a bunch of charmers. Sounds like they're going to get what's coming to them. Anything else?'

'Yeah—here,' says Goffing, pulling an envelope from a pocket and handing it over.

'What's this?'

'It's from your girlfriend. Mandy. Said your *Herald* colleague Bethanie rang, told her you needed to see it.'

'Did you open it?'

'Of course I did. I'm ASIO.'

Martin opens the envelope, extracts a single sheet of A4 paper. It's a newspaper clipping. The headline reads: CONMAN GETS FIVE YEARS. He scans the lead paragraph.

The master forger behind one of Western Australia's most brazen corporate frauds, Terrence Michael McGill, has been sentenced to five years prison with a three-year non-parole period . . .

Next to the copy is a small head-and-shoulders photograph of a man, his identity blurred by the low quality of the print-out. But there's a red circle drawn around it, together with a handwritten note: *Harley Snouch, beyond doubt—Mandy.*

'Let's pay him a visit,' says Martin, feeling his emotions stir, a mixture of satisfaction and indignation and something altogether more volatile.

twenty-five **WIRED**

'Turn right here,' interjects Codger from the back seat.

'Actually, pull up here first,' says Goffing.

Martin complies.

'Listen, this stuff about McGill. That and the dope growing. Snouch can no longer blackmail you. If he threatens to sue, you can just throw it back at him. You're out from under. But I'm not. He still has me by the balls for letting him into ASIO. I'll wait in the car.'

'You don't want to hear for yourself?'

'I do. I want you to wear a wire. I want to hear and I want to record.'

'A wire. Are you serious? Lock picks, latex gloves, wires; what else do you carry around in that bag of tricks of yours?'

'Oh, you know, the usual. Tracking devices, X-ray specs, truth serum.'

'Very fucking funny.'

———

Some minutes later, Martin drives into Springfields, with Codger next to him in the front seat and Goffing lying low in the back. The wireless transmitter is pinned under his collar, a thin wire circling behind his neck. There is no sign of life, but in the stillness of the day, there's the low hum of a generator. Snouch must be about somewhere. Martin's mouth is dry. He drinks some water and pauses to compose himself, to put the events at Jason's behind him. He drinks more water before leaving the car, but the dryness remains. He gets a sixpack of bottles from the boot.

He crosses the yard, enters the gloom of the machinery shed. Three fans hang rotating from the roof, pushing air around the space. The shed is not cool, but the concrete slab has retained some of the overnight chill and, combined with the fans, it's not the oven of Codger's shanty. Martin walks further in, spotting Harley Snouch seated at the far end of the workbench, concentrating over some work. Martin calls out. 'Harley.'

Snouch looks up, alert, springing to his feet and coming over. 'What do you want?'

'Thought I'd bring you out some water.' Martin holds up the bottles in their cling wrap.

'Thanks,' says Snouch, moving forward and taking the bottles. 'Thanks. That's good of you.' He's wearing khaki shorts, a singlet and sandals. He's also clean: his face is washed, his hands are spotless, his eyes are clear. And wary.

'Mandalay says she'll do the DNA test,' says Martin. 'Thought I'd come and tell you.'

'Is that right?'

'Yeah. I persuaded her it was a good idea. Didn't take much persuading.'

Snouch smiles, relaxes a little. 'Excellent.'

'How does it work?' asks Martin. 'The test?'

'I ordered a kit. Got it here somewhere. She takes a swab from inside her cheek, I do the same, we send them off and the lab compares them. Easy for them to tell if I'm her father or not. It'll take a week or so. I can give you her vial, if you like. She can take the swab and you can drop it back.'

'Okay. But why don't you take your swab here, she can do hers back in town and I can post them off for you both?'

Snouch smiles, as if recognising something familiar. 'That's an excellent idea. Let me get the kit. You can be my witness. Wait here.' Snouch walks deeper into the shed, past the old Mercedes, its tyres now pumped up and the paintwork freshly washed, to the far corner of the workbench. Now Martin's eyes have adjusted to the dim light of the interior, he can see that the far end of the bench is more like a desk, with a laptop, a printer and an angle-poise lamp. Snouch returns with two small styrofoam boxes, each containing a clear plastic vial shaped like a miniature test tube, with a screw lid. Snouch cracks the lid open on one of the vials. Attached to it is a thin shaft, like a cotton bud. Snouch guides the shaft into his mouth, running the end around the inside of his cheek, then carefully inserts the shaft back into the vial and tightens the lid.

'There you go, nothing to it. She rubs it around the inside of her cheek, same as me, then seals it back in the tube. Label it, put it in the box and post them as soon as you can. Keep them in the fridge until you can send them, just to make sure. There's some paperwork that needs to go in the box too. I've done my bit; she'll need to do the same.'

Snouch has a form. He's already filled in his name; now he signs it, passing it to Martin to witness. Martin prints his name in black letters, signing and dating the form in the required place. While he does so, he wonders at Snouch's confidence. He had all the paperwork ready to go, the two DNA test kits, everything. He must have been sure that Martin would comply with his wishes, sure that Mandy would agree. The thought irks Martin: does Snouch believe him to be so pliable?

Snouch hands him another piece of paper. 'Here's Mandy's form. You can witness that too. I've already spoken to the lab and I've also written a covering letter, setting out what we're seeking. You and Mandy can read it if you like. I've signed it. She can sign it as well, but it's not necessary. I'll pay the bill, or we can go halves if she can spare the money. It's five hundred bucks all up.'

Martin takes the boxes and forms. 'You seem very confident of the result.'

Snouch smiles, betraying just a hint of indignation. 'Of course I am. I was there, remember. I know what happened.'

'Okay. I'll see she gets it. And this means we're square, right? No more defamation threats?'

'I guess. But no more about me in the paper, okay? Nothing. Good, bad or indifferent, I don't want to see my name in your shit sheet again.'

'And not your photo either,' says Martin.

Snouch's eyes bore into him, the alertness back. 'What does that mean?'

'Well, someone might recognise you. Terry.'

Snouch smiles knowingly, not thrown off balance in the way Martin might have expected; instead a sly grin concedes the point. 'Very clever, Martin, very clever.'

'So tell me, Harley: why did you ring Avery Foster from ASIO headquarters and tell him you knew that Byron Swift was really Julian Flynt?'

Snouch blinks at that, as if calculating how much more Martin might know. But when he replies, he does so with confidence. 'That prick Goffing been telling tales out of school, has he? You should tell him to back off, or I'll let his boss know what happened.'

'Fine by me,' bluffs Martin. 'Do what you like to Goffing; he's not my concern. But I still want to know why you rang Foster.'

'Or what?'

'Or I tell Mandy Blonde all about Terry McGill. And it becomes the next cover story for *This Month*.'

Snouch shrugs, as if unbothered by the threat. 'Mate, I've got nothing to hide. I rang Foster to get Swift to back off, to leave town before the spooks and the coppers got him. I wanted him away from Mandy.'

'Why?'

Snouch's voice loses its untroubled tone and turns earnest; Martin hears an undercurrent of passion. 'You know the answer to that—the guy was a predator. He was rooting her, he was rooting Fran Landers, he was into a widow down in Bellington and was grooming more. Mandy might not be my daughter, but her mum once meant a great deal to me. I wanted him out of town and out of her hair.' He pauses, shakes his head. 'But I was too late, wasn't I? That boy of hers, Liam; he's Swift's, isn't he?'

It's Martin's turn to smile. 'But you didn't need to ring Foster. You knew who Flynt was, what he'd done. And thanks to you, so did the authorities. The police would have arrested him soon enough.'

'Don't be so sure. We're talking Canberra here. Bureaucrats and arse-covering. They'd already convened a meeting to work out how to minimise the damage. I wanted to make sure.'

'No. I think you wanted to make sure Swift was gone, but the dope-growing operation wasn't endangered. You wanted Swift gone, Foster compromised and the money still flowing. That's how I see it.'

Snouch pauses, but doesn't deny the allegation. 'Who cares how you see it? It hardly matters now.'

'Listen, Harley, I don't know if you realise this, but you're a great story. A cracker. The conman who conned ASIO, even as he helped run a hydroponic dope operation. That's a yarn for the ages. It's also a yarn that would make life very difficult for you, so you don't want to piss me off.' Martin scrutinises his adversary's face, seeing residual defiance but also comprehension: Martin has him where he wants him. 'But it doesn't have to be like that. We can help each other.'

Snouch is receptive. 'Go on.'

'I'll see Mandy undertakes the DNA test. But I want some information in return. First, was Swift a paedophile? You told me he was. You followed him around, spied on him, knew he was sleeping with Mandy and Fran and some widow in Bellington. Is the child abuse allegation accurate?'

Snouch considers his options before replying. 'No. I didn't see any evidence of that. Make no mistake, I wanted the guy gone, I wanted him away from Mandy, so I've got no reason to defend him. But I saw no evidence of that.'

Martin thinks it has the ring of truth to it. He knows the conman wouldn't hesitate to lie if it helped his cause, but also that lying would be risky when Martin has him at such a disadvantage.

Now he and Landers have both exonerated Swift.

'One more thing. You were the invisible man; you saw things others didn't. Do you know why Swift shot the men at the church?'

Snouch shakes his head. 'That I can't tell you. I never saw it coming. It's batshit crazy. But he did the same thing in Afghanistan, you must know that by now. Sometimes things don't need a reason; they just happen.'

He smiles and offers his hand. Without thinking, Martin shakes it.

'Thanks for coming, Martin. I know you don't like me, I know you don't trust me, but believe me, I have Mandalay's best interests at heart. Whatever I'm doing, I'm doing for her. Please don't publish what you know; it could end up hurting her more than it hurts me.'

'What does that mean?'

'Trust me, Martin. When the DNA results come back, when she learns I didn't rape her mother, she won't want me turned into fodder for your shit sheet. Let it go.'

Martin nods, but looking past Snouch, the angle-poise lamp catches his attention. It seems somehow incongruous, here in the machinery shed. The desk, the computer, Harley Snouch's spotless hands. *Terrence Michael McGill. Five years. Master forger.* 'What's on the desk, Harley?'

'House plans. Some rough ideas about rebuilding.'

'Great. Mind if I have a look? Mandy might be interested.'

'No, mate. They're just rough ideas. I'll give her a look when I've got something more concrete.'

'Oh come on, Harley. Don't be bashful.' Martin walks past him towards the desk. And as he does so, he sees for the first time a flash in the man's eyes: a flash of panic. It brings a small grin to his own face, some satisfaction; in the game of verbal brinksmanship he has somehow come out on top.

'Hey, Martin?'

Martin turns, but the retort forming on his lips is stillborn. Harley Snouch is holding a shotgun, and he's pointing it at Martin's chest. Dread falls like a guillotine, the smugness draining from Martin, leaving his guts hollow and filling with fear. The muzzle of the gun is just metres away, black and full of menace. Snouch's grip is steady, his eyes determined; there is nothing of the shakes or desperation of Shazza Young. He's three metres away, now he steps closer; he can't miss, the barrel a cobra poised to strike. All he has to do is pull the trigger and Martin will be shredded, reduced to ragged flesh, blood and terminal pain. 'Maybe you don't need to look at the desk, Martin.' His voice is measured, almost serene. 'This is my property, and you're trespassing.'

A thought comes to Martin through the paralysing fear. He remembers the wire, Jack Goffing listening in from the car. Do ASIO officers carry guns? 'A shotgun, Harley? Really? What are you planning to do, shoot me?' Even to his own ears, his voice sounds thin, a threadbare attempt at bravado.

'Why not? There's a sign on the gate warning trespassers of exactly that. I'm within my rights.'

'No you're not. This isn't America. Besides, I'm not alone. Jack Goffing is in the car.'

'What's he doing there?'

'He didn't want to come in. Reckons he can't stand the sight of you.'

Snouch smiles. 'I bet he can't, the idiot. I've got him by the short and curlies.' He pauses to think momentarily, reassessing the situation. 'Maybe I don't have to shoot you after all; maybe we can come to an arrangement.' Martin nods, keeping his focus on Snouch, even as he catches movement behind the man out of the corner of his eye. Martin desperately wants to look, to see if Goffing is armed, but he knows that Snouch is watching him, that he will see Martin's eyes shift, that he will turn and shoot. And if he kills the ASIO man, he will certainly kill any witnesses.

'So what *is* on the desk?' asks Martin, trying to hold Snouch's attention. 'What's so sensitive?'

Behind Snouch the figure of a man moves closer, into focus, but it's not Jack Goffing. It's Codger Harris, armed with Shazza

Young's shotgun. Martin's knees threaten to buckle, his bladder to release, even as he fights to keep control, to match Snouch's gaze and hold his attention, even as his mind is screaming fight or flight, even as the adrenaline pumps out through his bloodstream. Someone is about to die, and there's a good chance it's going to be him: three men, two shotguns, and he's the one without a weapon. Even if Codger has reloaded Shazza's shotgun. *Where the fuck is Goffing?* Still Martin maintains eye contact with Snouch, searches for something to say to keep the gunman looking at him. Codger keeps advancing, calm and assured, deftly flipping the weapon around so he's holding it by the barrel with both hands.

Snouch, sensing trouble, reading more than fear in Martin's face, begins to turn. But he's too late. Codger has already begun swinging the gun, a scything arc. The stock crashes into the side of Harley Snouch's head. The impact is sickening; he collapses. Martin cringes, fearing a shotgun blast, but the gun hits the floor without discharging.

'I've been waiting thirty years to do that,' says Codger Harris.

Martin rushes forward. Harley Snouch is alive, breathing steadily. A lump the size of a golf ball is growing low down on the back of his skull, but there's no blood. Martin gingerly moves the shotgun away before turning him over, pushing him into the recovery position on his side. 'Jesus, Codger. You could have killed him.'

'And he could have killed you.' There is nothing even approaching regret in the old man's voice.

'What the fuck was all that?' demands Jack Goffing, rushing up to them, a coiled earpiece still hanging from his collar. 'He had a gun?'

'That one there,' replies Martin.

Goffing picks up Snouch's shotgun and disarms it. 'Is he okay?'

'Who knows? Concussion for sure. Lasting damage, maybe. But for now, he seems fine. Breathing and pulse are okay.' As if to confirm this diagnosis, Snouch groans.

'I think he's coming round,' says Goffing. 'Let's tie the arsehole up.'

They drag Snouch into a sitting position, and Martin ties him, hands secured behind his back, to the workbench.

'Let's have a look at this desk,' says Goffing, leaving Codger to watch over Snouch.

It's not really a desk as such. It's a clean piece of laminated board, attached by counter-sunk screws to the top of the workbench: a large clean space for Snouch to work under the light of the angle-poise lamp. Martin and Goffing don't have to look far; the evidence is laid out before them. There's a letter from a firm, Excelsior Genealogy, confirming it's able to conduct DNA testing. It says it can certainly compare two samples for paternity and includes two testing kits and a return address. The letter is written on the company's letterhead, russet branding within a green logo representing a family tree.

And next to it, on the desk, is a second letter, on identical letterhead.

Dear Mr Snouch and Ms Blonde,

Thank you for availing yourselves of the services of Excelsior Genealogy. We are pleased to report that our technicians were able to extract robust samples of DNA from the two specimens provided and were able to make the comparison requested.

We can confirm, with a 99.8% degree of confidence, that Mr Harley Snouch is NOT the father of Ms Mandalay Blonde.

However, after further investigation, we can also confirm you are closely related. With a 98.5% degree of confidence, we can report Mr Snouch and Ms Blonde are half-brother and half-sister, sharing a common father and different mothers.

We trust this information is useful to you both. Please don't hesitate to contact us if you require any further inform-ation or testing.

Yours sincerely,

Arthur Montgomery

Chief Analyst

Excelsior Genealogy

The letter is not yet signed. There is a blue fountain pen on the desk beside it. Snouch must have been preparing to deliver the coup de grace when they interrupted him.

The men read the forgery again, Martin trying to imagine the effect it would have had on Mandy.

Goffing speaks first. 'Pretty impressive. But half-brother and half-sister?'

'Yes. Perfect. Not only clears Snouch of raping the mother, Katherine, it frames his father, Eric. The father who, Mandy and I were informed just this morning, disinherited Snouch and bequeathed Springfields to Mandy. Reading this, Mandy would think old Eric was a bastard and most likely raped her mother. Sweet revenge for Harley; even as he shifts the blame, he creates a scapegoat. And Mandy would feel sorry for him, perhaps feel a sibling bond—maybe cut him a share of the inheritance. Like I said: perfect.'

Snouch groans. Martin moves back towards the door, rips a bottle of mineral water from the cling wrap, returns, and empties it over the forger's head. It has the desired effect: Snouch groans again, coughs and opens his eyes.

Martin crouches down, his face just inches away from Snouch's. He waits until he's sure Snouch is fully conscious, fully aware that he's tied up and at their mercy. Martin holds the forged letter where Snouch can see it. 'I have your handiwork, Harley, which I'm going to show to Mandy. I have your DNA sample, which we are going to test. For real. And I have news: your father's lawyers—Wright, Douglas and Fenning—have confirmed Mandy is the sole heir to Springfields and all that goes with it.' He can see the comprehension in the conman's eyes, the bitterness and rising bile. 'I'm going to tell the police where to find you. They'll want you to testify against the Reapers and their drug operation. Unless the Reapers find you first. Sounds like fun. My advice? Fuck off while you still can and never come back.'

'Should we untie him?' asks Goffing.

'Fuck that,' says Codger Harris. 'Let the coppers have him.'

twenty-six **BONFIRE**

THE THREE MEN DRIVE IN SILENCE, LOST IN THOUGHT, NOT EXHILARATED BY the unravelling of Harley Snouch, but turned reflective by his demise. Behind the wheel, Martin ponders the prodigal son despoiling his own heritage. He imagines Snouch enduring prison in Perth, dreaming of better days ahead, being released, shedding his assumed identity, learning of his father's death, anticipating his inheritance—only to receive nothing; the lawyers at Wright, Douglas and Fenning tight-lipped and duty-bound, telling him he'd been disowned and nothing more. He'd been let go, set adrift, no longer his father's son. Winifred Barbicombe had known of the conviction in Perth; the will had been redrawn shortly before Eric Snouch's death. Perhaps the jail sentence for fraud had been the last straw.

And so Harley Snouch had left prison with nothing. He returned to Springfields, only to find his erstwhile birthright deserted and vandalised, left open to the elements, his neighbours pilfering water. And so he squatted, lost for a time in despair and self-pity, drinking too much and growing increasingly embittered. In truth, a derelict. And yet he must have retained some hope, some ambition. He closed the doors, cleaned the house, stopped his neighbours siphoning water. And then they came to him, the priest and the publican, offering money for water. The money was welcome: money to live and money to restore the house. And something else; the implicit acknowledgement of title, that possession equalled ownership. They gave him money because they believed the water was his. It was the acknowledgement he needed. Gradually the derelict became more of an act and less of a reality.

Martin is aware this is nothing more than speculation; he can never know the inner workings of Snouch's mind. But that makes it all the more fascinating. He wonders what Snouch felt when he first saw Katherine again after all those years. Remorse? Hope? Love? Or something altogether more calculating? And then one day, peering out from the wine saloon, Harley Snouch saw the daughter, his daughter, Mandalay Blonde, a woman now, back to care for her dying mother. Did he somehow learn the truth of his father's will or was he simply smart enough to work it out? The money from the dope was useful, but nothing compared with the accumulated wealth of the Snouch dynasty.

And so the plan evolved, following the death of Katherine Blonde. Everyone who had known the truth, everyone who had lived through the events three decades before, was dead: Eric Snouch, Katherine Blonde, Herb Walker's predecessor. He'd outlived them all; he alone knew the truth. And from that seed grew his audacious plan. He spent his marijuana money on repairing Springfields, a gift to Mandy, a symbol of his devotion, even as he schemed to win it back. But she rejected him, repelled him, resolutely taking the side of her mother. And worse was to follow: the priest made his move on her, with his good looks and callous charms. Snouch watched it unfold: Mandy falling for Byron Swift, confiding in him, alerting him. Snouch needed Swift gone, and so he spied, learning his secrets, seeking out leverage, looking for a weakness—and finding it.

Martin wonders why he didn't simply inform on the drug operation, get rid of Swift that way. But no, that would have destroyed his only source of income, risked his own arrest as an accessory and invited reprisal from the Reapers. Instead, he worked out that Swift was an imposter, a wolf in sheep's clothing. And so the trip to Canberra, to tell the authorities. Martin thinks of how audacious it was to walk into ASIO with his far-fetched story of a soldier impersonating a priest. Had he been surprised by its success, that the intelligence service believed him? Maybe, maybe not. For if he were a conman, a confidence trickster, a man used to acting, to performing fiction on the stage of real life, then such a gambit would not be beyond him. It was brazen, yet he had little to lose and everything to gain. The worst the authorities could do was kick him out without listening; he wasn't risking arrest or violent retribution. Audacious, but wasn't that the hallmark of all great conmen: selling the Harbour Bridge, impersonating royalty, salting goldmines? And it had worked; ASIO was co-opted, the priest was exposed. And it was the same with the DNA ploy: if the cards had fallen only slightly differently, then it too would have succeeded.

Martin is brought back to the here and now. They drive into Codger's property, entering across the cattle grid, past the remaining cow's skull on its pole, the smell of the dead cattle appalling in the still air, and on to the house. Codger taps him on the shoulder before climbing out. 'Good show, young fellow. You've sorted him out once and for all.' Martin smiles, wishing him well.

Goffing gets out too, has a few quiet words to Codger, no doubt emphasising the need for discretion, at least for a day or two. Martin sees Goffing hand him something. Money, most likely. Goffing and Codger shake hands, and then the ASIO man climbs back into the front seat. Martin puts the car into drive and swings it around, the track back to the main road now familiar to him. And as he drives, he thinks.

The bodies in the dam must have come as a shock to Snouch, threatening to derail his plans. Had he been tempted to leave them undisturbed while he worked towards conning Mandy? His opportunity was approaching; the window was opening. The destruction of the homestead must have been devastating, but it spawned an unexpected outcome: something had softened in Mandy after the fire; perhaps news came to Snouch that she was relieved he had survived, the first tentative sign of a possible reconciliation. So he created a new character: concerned citizen. He called Goffing and the police, reported the bodies, perhaps hoping to win credit from the authorities—and credit from Mandy. Surely she would feel even more compassion for him: first his home burnt down, then the horror of finding the bodies.

Martin smiles. The plot was good but Martin hadn't read the script. His wildly inaccurate reporting in the Fairfax press all but accused Snouch of murder at a time when he might have expected praise. Mandy's opinion of him grew worse, not better. Snouch must have been furious: held in custody, questioned by police, as Doug Thunkleton and his colleagues gleefully repeated Martin's calumny. Snouch could indeed have sued Fairfax for defamation, sued and won. But the process would be slow, too slow. He must have suspected the inheritance could be settled before the case was resolved; Mandy could have sold up and moved on before the case even went to court. And Fairfax has good lawyers—they could destroy him, revisiting the rape allegations, uncovering his past as Terrence McGill, arguing he has little reputation left to slander. That would hardly win over Mandalay Blonde. So instead of suing Martin, he coerced him into helping. He could see Martin was becoming close to Mandy; he probably knew they had slept together. Martin nods to himself as he drives: Snouch had determined he was the best chance to get to her.

So Snouch acted, as quickly as he dared, manipulating Martin, rolling the dice; the conman stepping onto the stage once more, a bravura performance, the audience in raptures. The DNA testing was a brilliant idea, a plot device to rewrite the narrative. The lab was no doubt genuine, the tests real, but the results would be posted to him. He'd destroy them and present the forgery to Mandy, exacting revenge on his father at the same time. It would have had no legal standing, couldn't be used in court, couldn't alter Eric Snouch's will. But it didn't need to. Martin considers Mandy's likely reaction and decides it would have worked: she was too generous in spirit, too willing to believe the best in people, too desperate to discover some decency in this world. Too eager for her childhood dream of reconciliation to come true. Martin shakes his head; the melodrama would have played out, the curtain falling, the audience cheering for more.

'Martin?' says Goffing, gaining his attention. 'Thanks.'

'For what?'

'Snouch.'

'What do you mean?'

'You know what I mean.'

And Martin does. They should have brought Snouch in, handed him over to the police. They'd caught him perpetrating a fraud. Moreover, he was a beneficiary of the drug operation and potentially a valuable witness as Claus Vandenbruk and the police built their case against the Reapers. But instead Martin had warned him off, told him to flee. Snouch no longer threatened him, but he could still destroy Goffing's career.

'Don't mention it,' says Martin.

'I owe you one,' says Goffing. 'You tied the knots. How long before he works his way free?'

'Probably already has.'

The sun is setting as they leave the crooked dirt tracks of the Scrublands, emerging into the clearing, past the letterboxes and out onto the bitumen highway, the straight black line from Hay to Riversend. The headlights are on, already taking effect in the fading light. The scrub, untouched by fire this close to town, rushes past as Martin accelerates, glad of the speed after the slow going of the Scrublands. They crack open the windows, the car's velocity gifting some coolness to the warm air. The trees come to an end and they drop ever so slightly, down onto the flood plain, the sky open, the first stars evident. And then Martin sees it: a glowing aura, like a second sunset.

'What's that?' he asks, arousing Goffing from his own reverie.

'Fire,' says Goffing.

The Commercial Hotel is well alight by the time they make it back to town. Half the top storey is on fire, flames spewing out of windows, the verandah a swirling blaze of orange, smoke and embers spiralling skywards; a bonfire gone awry. Martin slews the car into the kerb on the far side of the road, niceties of reverse parking forgotten. The pub is screaming its distress: shrieking metal, exploding glass, roaring flames. The smoke is tainted: not the clean eucalypt-scented destruction of bushfire, but the industrial exhalation of an incinerator, stinging his eyes and clouding his vision.

Errol Ryding is there with his volunteers, their tanker gleaming in the firelight, water streaming from two hoses into the building. Townspeople are gawking from a safe distance, pointing and muttering; the media are pressing closer, camera crews and photographers lost in the moment, in thrall to the flames and the imagery, careless of their own safety.

Martin rushes over to Errol, standing stoic beneath the bronze Anzac. The statue is uncaring, back to the conflagration, reflected flames rippling across its back like flexing muscles. 'Errol, what happened?'

'Who knows? Just went up.'

'Can you save it?'

A shake of the head. 'Doubt it. There's no wind, so we might salvage something. Main thing is to stop it spreading. Give Luigi a hand, will you? Same as the other day.'

Martin nods, moves to the young man struggling to keep his hose trained on the fire. Martin taps him on the shoulder; Luigi turns, acknowledges his presence. Martin takes up the hose a few metres behind the nozzle man, helping him to wrangle it when he moves. Slowly the two men crawl right, Martin following Luigi's lead. The local pours water into one window, then moves along to its neighbour. The tanker is at the inter-section; Luigi is moving them around the corner, opposite Jennings. The fire is upstairs, concentrated on the corner and the rooms above Somerset Street, but with the verandah alight, the whole top storey is threatened.

Behind them, a man pulls up in a farm tanker: good for grass fires, not something on this scale. He looks at the pub, gives Martin a thumbs-up, then turns his attention to Jennings, spraying the untouched shopfront with his hose, then the roof, protecting it from embers.

There's the slow scream of metal; Martin turns back to the pub, watches as the verandah starts to peel away from the front of the building, Errol striding before it, signalling for the crowd to get back, for the photographers to make themselves safe in case the verandah comes down. Where's Robbie? Why isn't he controlling the crowd? Martin begins to feel faint. The heat is intense, the day has been so very hot, the night too young to bring relief, the fire amplifying the temperature, draining the energy from him.

Fran Landers emerges from the bedlam; she's walking through the crowd, blinking in the smoke, handing bottles of water to the firefighters and media. For half a second, their eyes meet. She takes the top from a bottle, hands it to him, leaves another by his feet. Moves on. Some water goes down his throat, some goes over his head. Relief. Then, through his other arm, wrapped around the canvas hose, he can feel the pressure dropping. They're running out of water. He looks to the truck; men are attaching a feeder line to a hydrant. Errol is with them.

'Two minutes and we'll be back on. Take a break—these other blokes can take over.'

Martin and Luigi hand over the hose. Luigi walks to the far side of the road and slumps down on the gutter. Fran gives him water. Martin looks at the fire. It's gaining territory. The crew is holding the line along Hay Road but the back half of the pub is beyond saving. It must have started there, close by the rear of the building, near Avery Foster's apartment.

Martin walks around past the pumper just as it starts up again, twin hoses blasting water into the hotel, the focus now trying to prevent the verandah collapsing into the street. He looks at the door to the staircase. Images come to him: the fox hunt, the chandelier, the painting of the summer storm. He's still looking as the door bursts open. Claus Vandenbruk is pushing out through the smoke, clearing the way for two younger, fitter officers, who are half carrying Robbie Haus-Jones, his arms around their necks. The constable is coughing uncontrollably, body racked, his face black with smoke, his clothes singed, his hands a red mess, swollen and ugly. They get him onto the street, out to safety. Sit him down.

Martin is frozen to the spot, watching. Doug Thunkleton's camera crew, all the camera crews, swarm about, Carrie the photographer pushing her lens within centimetres of the policeman's face, shutter firing like a machine gun, his rescuers standing, breathing in the air, looking at each other in disbelief. And Martin sees D'Arcy Defoe, thin frame silhouetted against the fire, standing slightly back from the throng, taking it all in, writing notes, dispassionate, removed, professional. Like a shadow of a person, like an echo of Martin Scarsden. There's something in the stance, something in the concentration, the focus, that takes him back. Martin in battlefields, in refugee camps, in field hospitals: present but not present, viewing events through a reporter's eyes, witnessing the suffering, but not feeling it. It's D'Arcy Defoe's silhouette, but it's himself he sees.

Something explodes deep within the hotel, and as if in answer, the front section of the verandah tears away and starts to fall: slowly at first, then accelerating, like a sinking ship, breaking apart and crashing into the street, embers flying, the crowd retreating. He sees her then, across the road, in front of the bank—Mandy, holding Liam. He moves towards her, but she sees him coming, shakes her head. Her face is wet with tears, shining orange and red in the fire's reflected glow.

twenty-seven — THE BRIDGE

THE PHONE WAKES HIM. THE DISCORDANT JANGLE OF THE BLACK DOG'S OUTDATED technology. His sleep has been deep, but not long. Yet the phone won't let him slumber; it won't let him be. It persists. He lets it ring out once, only for it to start again a moment later. He lifts the receiver, if just to stop it ringing. 'Martin Scarsden.'

'Martin, Wellington Smith. How are you? Trust I didn't wake you.'

'No. Of course not.' He glances at his watch. Six forty-five? What sort of newspaperman is Wellington Smith?

'Martin, I've been thinking. This story you've got. It's massive. Fucking huge. I want the magazine piece, the first bite, but I want a book as well. This is going to make your career. You, mate, are going to be a legend.'

'Right,' says Martin, unsure what to say. Not that he needs to say anything; for a full ten minutes Smith speaks nonstop, promising Martin a lot of money and a lot of everything else as well: recognition, salvation, awards, status, fame, television rights and groupies. Everything. Smith talks so quickly, so effusively, that he doesn't appear to draw a breath, like a didgeridoo player on repeat. Finally Smith pauses long enough for Martin to thank him and end the call. He should be enthusiastic, he knows he should; he should be grateful, he just doesn't feel it.

He tries to go back to sleep but it's no longer possible. Now he's awake and aware, he can smell himself; he stinks of smoke and sweat. Reluctantly he abandons his bed for the shower. The water pressure seems even weaker than usual, as if fighting the fire has all but depleted the water supply. Who knows? Maybe it has.

Leaving the motel, he enters a wounded town. Hay Road is a mess. The tanker stands guard across from the burnt-out shell of the Commercial Hotel, splintered pieces of verandah littering the street. A couple of locals, belatedly dressed in high-vis overalls, stand guard by the side of the truck. They offer a mumbled 'g'day' as he surveys the damage. Errol and the crew have done their job well; the damage has been restricted to the hotel. The building's bottom half is still standing, largely intact, although the smoke and water damage will have ruined it. The second storey is another matter. At the corner overlooking the intersection, the roof has collapsed and the verandah gone, part of the outer wall crumbling in. The windows are blackened sockets. There is little left of Avery Foster's apartment; the windows are blown out, the verandah is a remnant, only a small section of the roof hangs from the end wall. Smoke is still swirling upwards, grey tendrils from a thousand coals, but not enough to justify further dousing. The hotel is beyond saving; it requires demolition.

The general store is closed. Of course it's closed. After the arrest of Jamie Landers, will it ever reopen? Martin walks back towards the T-junction. There's no sign of life at the Oasis Bookstore and Cafe, none at the wine saloon, none anywhere else. It's Thursday, but it's still too early for Riversend's surviving stores to open. At least the service station on the highway is trading, offering newspapers and an approximation of coffee: Nescafé self-serve, the granules rattling as Martin spoons them into a white foam cup, filling it with boiling water from an urn, milk from a two-litre container. It tastes the same way he feels: ordinary.

He sits on a white plastic chair at a white plastic table, cheap outdoor furniture brought inside for the summer. Inevitably Riversend is on the front page again: Carrie O'Brien's long-lens photo of Jamie Landers at the crime scene in the Scrublands. BLUE-EYED PSYCHOPATH says the headline. Martin reads D'Arcy's stories dispassionately, the news report supplying the facts, the colour piece supplying the emotion. D'Arcy does them both well, but it all seems like a very long time ago, not yesterday afternoon. Riversend has experienced new dramas since then; new questions have emerged. Martin looks up from the papers, as if trying to spot an answer lurking in the petrol station.

Instead, through the door barges Doug Thunkleton. 'Hi, Martin. Fancy seeing you here. How are you?'

'Oh, you know. Disgraced.'

'Huh?'

'Never mind.'

'Oh, right. I get it. Listen, Martin, about that—I want to apologise. You know, what happened in Bellington. It wasn't my angle; the chief of staff pushed it.'

'Right.'

'Angie Hester. Sounds like you know her.'

Angie? An image of a dark-eyed woman comes to Martin, the memory of a brief assignation, but nothing more.

'Don't know what you did, but she sure has it in for you. The news director is apoplectic. Reckons it will take forever for our reputation to recover. He's sacked her.'

Martin feels a barb of guilt: guilt for whatever it was he'd done to the woman, and guilt for not remembering what it was. 'What about you?' he asks Thunkleton.

'I went along with it, so I have to wear some of the grief. But I'll survive. I just wanted to say sorry.'

There's contrition in Thunkleton's manner and Martin finds himself offering solidarity of a sort. 'I saw the suicide blonde story. You get shit-canned by your editors?'

'Did I what. Bunch of fucking desk jockeys. Not that I didn't deserve it. Some of it. But I won't be getting a pay rise this year, put it that way.'

The two men sit in silence; Martin suspects it's an unusual experience for Thunkleton. He's right; the television reporter stands up, nods his apologies again and leaves.

A moment later he's back. 'Thought you might want to see these. Late editions.' He hands Martin the latest Melbourne newspapers, *The Age* and the *Herald Sun*. The front page of *The Age* is given over entirely to another of Carrie O'Brien's photographs, taken as Vandenbruk's officers helped Robbie

Haus-Jones from the inferno of the Commercial Hotel. The men are in silhouette, rimmed by fire, the flames brought closer by the length of the lens. There is something vaguely Christ-like in the posture of Robbie, his arms draped across the shoulders of his rescuers, his legs buckling beneath him. The headline is emblazoned onto the photo: DEATH TOWN HERO SAVED, with only enough room for the first few paragraphs of D'Arcy's story.

> The hero of Riversend, Constable Robert Haus-Jones, has been saved from a fiery death as yet another remarkable day of high drama unfolded in the embattled Riverina town.
>
> The young police officer, who saved countless lives when he shot dead homicidal priest Byron Swift close to a year ago, again put his life on the line, rushing into the town's burning hotel to ensure no one was trapped inside.
>
> Haus-Jones was saved by fellow officers after he became disorientated and affected by smoke as the fire tore through the century-old landmark.
>
> The dramatic rescue came just 24 hours after Robert Haus-Jones saved the life of a young child moments before alleged backpacker murderer James Arnold Landers allegedly attempted to butcher the boy.
>
> The fire, believed to have been caused either by an electrical fault or deliberately set by vandals, moved through the structure at astonishing speed, trapping Haus-Jones.

The story continues inside but Martin doesn't bother turning the page. D'Arcy would have been racing against time to get the story to print, only just making the late edition. But that doesn't save it from being wrong: there was no one in the Commercial Hotel; there was no one to save. Just a fire, upstairs, engulfing the apartment of Avery Foster. Not caused by an electrical fault, not when the power was disconnected months ago; not caused by vandals, not with Allen Newkirk dead, Jamie Landers in custody and the place wrapped in crime scene tape.

Martin remembers Robbie's face; he remembers his hands. And he remembers telling the young policeman about the undisturbed flat. What had Robbie imagined up until that point? That Foster's widow had cleared out all the records? Not an unreasonable assumption if she had known what her former husband was up to. Not an unreasonable assumption if Robbie Haus-Jones had known what her former husband was up to. If he had known . . .

Fuck. Robbie. What an idiot.

———

Back at the Black Dog, Jack Goffing is sitting outside his room, smoking a cigarette. They nod to each other, but don't speak. Martin hands Goffing the papers, eliciting a wry grin.

'So he's a hero, is he?'

'Apparently.'

'You told him about what we found?'

'Enough. Yesterday, after I talked with Jamie Landers.'

'You going to publish the truth?'

'You think I should? There's a bloke wants me to write a book. Offering hard cash and easy redemption.'

'Sounds promising.'

'Yes. I'm filled with enthusiasm.'

Goffing smiles at the ironic turn of phrase. Martin offers him tea, makes them a cup each in his room and brings them outside.

'So where is he?' Martin asks. 'Robbie?'

'Down in Melbourne. Burns like that need specialist care.'

'Will they charge him?'

Goffing shrugs. 'Montifore's gone, taken Landers back to Sydney. Homicide have their man; they won't give a shit about Robbie. And the brass like the idea of having a hero. They don't have that many.'

'What about Vandenbruk?'

'That's a different story. He probably hasn't worked it out yet, but he will. If Robbie knew about the drugs, if he was taking backhanders, if he didn't tell Herb Walker what he knew, then Vandenbruk will crucify him. You can ask Vandenbruk yourself. He's down at the cop shop but he'll be back in a moment. He wants you in the loop.'

'Me? Why?'

'They're raiding the Reapers. Started before dawn. Here, there, everywhere. Adelaide, Melbourne, Canberra. Half the towns in between. They're wrapping it up, pulling in the Mr Bigs. Robbie's heroics will be washed away by lunchtime. The media's been tipped off; they're all over it.'

'So why does he want to talk to us?'

'Not sure. It's not his show. He's senior, but not in charge. I think he wants to know why Walker died.'

'He's blaming himself?'

'I would, if I were him.'

Martin sits next to Goffing, sipping his tea and looking up at the sky. He knows that somewhere in the world there must be clouds; there have to be. Somewhere it is raining; somewhere it is pelting down. There will be floods and landslides and hurricanes and monsoons. Somewhere. More water than you can imagine, more water than you could ever want. Somewhere, but not here. Here there are no clouds and no rain. The drought can't last forever; he knows it, everyone knows it. It's just become hard to believe.

Claus Vandenbruk arrives, ushering them into Goffing's room, bringing his surly manner with him, shutting it in with them when he closes the door. Martin finds it hard to imagine Vandenbruk and Walker were ever best mates: Walker was always laughing, patting his belly with satisfaction; the ACIC investigator is a man without a smile, a hair's breadth from rage.

'Okay. The raids are going well. We've got just about everyone we want and the evidence already looks compelling, but I need to tie up loose ends here. So, Martin, I need to know everything you know. Dick me around, and you won't believe how much shit I can drop you in. Help me, though, and I'll help you.'

'How can you help me?' asks Martin, trying not to sound intimidated.

'I have the telephone intercepts from the church—on the day of the shooting.'

'You have recordings?' Martin doesn't hesitate. 'What do you want to know?'

'The dope operation. The shed out in the bush there. Tell me all you know.'

'I thought Jason Moore was helping with inquiries?'

Vandenbruk pauses; he appears to be counting to ten. 'Right. Listen carefully. Jason Moore is a protected witness. He's going to put a lot of very nasty people behind bars. So you must never, not in this world and not in the next, mention his name. Never. Not to anyone. Not in print, not at the pub, not to the love of your life. He's a no-go zone, okay?' He pauses for effect before continuing. 'But I do need to corroborate what he's been telling us, so talk.'

'Okay, here's how I see it,' says Martin. 'Jason was growing a few plants. Most people living out there in the scrub do. Then the drought came, there was less water, less money. So he started stealing water. There's a big old homestead out there called Springfields—at least there was until the bushfire last week. It has a dam, spring-fed. Doesn't run dry, even in a drought as bad as this. Jason was stealing water from it for his plants. It's the same dam where the bodies of the backpackers were found, but that's coincidental. You following?'

Vandenbruk nods.

'Good. So back to Jason. A few years ago, the owner of Springfields, a man called Eric Snouch, died and the place became vacant. His son Harley was in prison in Western Australia under a false name, Terrence Michael McGill, so the place was empty and there was an opportunity to steal even more water. With impunity. Open slather.'

Vandenbruk has his hand up, signalling Martin to stop. 'Is this true?' he asks Goffing. 'In prison under a false name?'

Goffing nods. 'Yep.'

'What a bunch of plods,' says Vandenbruk, shaking his head. 'Okay, go on.'

'My impression is that it was still a pretty small-time oper-ation. Then Byron Swift turned up, and he and the publican, a bloke called Avery Foster, bankrolled a big shed with a hydroponic operation and started supplying the Reapers. Jason was getting some money and, once he showed up, so was Harley Snouch, who claimed he was the owner of Springfields. But most of the profits were being sent offshore, to an orphanage in Afghanistan.'

Vandenbruk, who has been nodding, ticking off a mental checklist, looks to Goffing again. 'Jack? Is this right?'

'Yeah. Remember? I told you on the drive from Bellington. Swift was an alias. His real name was Julian Flynt, a wanted war criminal. From what Martin and I have uncovered, Flynt knew Foster from Afghanistan. They were sending money to the orphanage.'

'How do you know this?'

'We found evidence in Foster's flat. Upstairs in the pub.'

'Upstairs? Where the fire was?'

'That's right. We were there the night before last.'

'Fuck. Really?' It takes Vandenbruk a moment to consider the implications of that, a moment more for the penny to drop. 'Did either of you tell Haus-Jones about the flat?'

Martin hesitates, but Goffing has no such qualms. 'Yeah, he knew.'

To Martin, it's like watching a fuse burn down. He looks on as Vandenbruk fights for control, his face swelling red with anger, before he rises to his feet, pacing, detonation imminent, starting to vocalise, filling the air with expletives. And abruptly lashing out: the explosion, a single punch, driving his fist through the Black Dog's thin plasterboard wall, driving it through up to his elbow. 'Fuck,' he says a final time, investing the word with all his pent-up venom and fury. Martin and Jack exchange a glance. Vandenbruk withdraws his arm, brushing off white flakes of plaster, then turns to them, his temper coming back under control. 'Did you find any evidence in the flat that Haus-Jones was involved with the drug op?'

'No,' says Goffing. 'None.'

Vandenbruk nurses his hand, takes a deep breath. 'My men risked their lives getting him out.' He reflects on this, his fury slowly subsiding. Eventually he calms down enough to resume his seat, giving his head one last shake, more from sorrow than anger. 'You think he was trying to suicide? Take the evidence with him?'

The thought hadn't occurred to Martin. He exchanges another look with Goffing. 'Sorry. No idea.'

'Okay. Go on then, Martin. You were talking about the drug operation.'

'Sure. It seems everything was travelling along smoothly until this time last year. Then Swift shot five people dead and got killed by Robbie Haus-Jones. Swift, or should I say Flynt, was former special forces and not easily intimidated. But once he'd gone, the Reapers saw an opportunity and moved in, squeezing out Avery Foster. He was still getting some money but probably not all that much; the Reapers were taking the lion's share.'

'Okay, you two saw Foster's flat. Jack, was there any evidence he was planning to kill himself?'

'Not that we saw. On the contrary: the place looked like he'd just walked out for a minute. There was no note, nothing like that. His dinner was still on the table.'

'So you think the Reapers killed him?' asks Martin.

'Don't know,' says Vandenbruk. 'But we'll definitely be adding it to the list. Who decided it was suicide, then? Constable Haus-Jones?'

Goffing looks to Martin. 'I guess so.'

'Okay. What else can you tell me about the dope operation?'

'Not a lot; I think that just about covers it,' says Martin.

'Good,' says Vandenbruk, leaning back, appearing to come off the boil for the first time. 'There's a couple of things you should know. First, like I told you earlier, Herb Walker didn't commit suicide; the Reapers killed him after they found him at Jason's. You need to correct that when the time comes. Second thing, that story you ran in the *Sydney Morning Herald*, that he had ignored the tip-off about the bodies in the dam, he was outraged. Fucking furious. You know why?'

Martin looks contrite, nods. 'Jamie Landers told me yesterday. Said it was he and Allen Newkirk who rang Crime Stoppers. But he said they didn't mention the dam, just said the girls were dead and their bodies dumped in the Scrublands. That's hundreds of square kilometres.'

'Correct. And even then, Herb didn't ignore it. It wasn't his patch. Scrublands is north-west of Riversend; Bellington is forty minutes south of Riversend. He asked Constable Haus-Jones to check it out.'

'He told you that?'

'He did. The day he ended up dead. The day I gave him the phone number Swift had called.'

'Avery Foster's number?'

'That's right. So, Martin, when you revisit this story, I want you to set the record straight; Herb Walker didn't suicide and he didn't neglect his duty.'

Martin agrees, chastened. 'Of course. It's the least I can do. But you should know, my colleague, Bethanie Glass, she was told the Crime Stoppers tip-off specifically referred to the dam. It wasn't us who made him the scapegoat.'

Now there is no temper visible on Vandenbruk's face, just a steely gaze. 'Who was her source?'

'She doesn't know. It came through police PR. From somewhere high up.'

'Jesus wept,' says Vandenbruk, shaking his head in a mixture of disbelief and disgust. 'They do that to him, shaft him, then when he turns up dead a day or two later, they eulogise him, call him a hero.' Now the temper is returning, the fuse reset. 'Well, fuck me, Martin, you make sure you put that in print.'

'You have my word.'

'Good,' says Vandenbruk. 'Now here's the deal. I'm going to keep Jack's little fuck-up out of the investigation—the bit where he got played by Snouch in Canberra. No one needs be the wiser.'

Martin glances at Goffing. The ASIO agent is staring at Vandenbruk, his face white.

'You know?' Goffing asks.

'I worked it out. After I heard the intercepts, I checked out the metadata on Avery Foster's phone. Just like you did. It was Snouch who called Foster from Russell Hill.'

'Who else has figured it out?'

'No one, as far as I'm aware. Why would they? Only a few others know Snouch was the one who fingered Swift, who revealed he was really Julian Flynt, and they all think he was motivated by altruism. Unless they heard the St James intercepts, they'd have no reason to think he was really trying to eliminate Swift and get a bigger share of the drug operation.'

'That wasn't what was motivating him,' interjects Martin, and then realises too late he's played into the policeman's hands, essentially confirming that Snouch had indeed conned Goffing. Jack gives him a withering look.

Vandenbruk smiles without warmth and turns to Martin. 'I'm going to play you the tape from the church and possibly feed you a bit of information on the Reapers, if you need it. But there are things I need in return, guarantees. I don't want to be mentioned. I don't want people to know I gave the telephone number to Herb and I don't want it known that the ACIC tampered with Telstra's database. Okay?'

Martin says nothing, Goffing says nothing, but Martin can see by the look on the ASIO man's face they're both thinking the same thing. *He's arse-covering.*

Martin asks, 'Why did the Commission tamper with the database?'

Another flash of temper and another pause to control it, fuse sputtering. 'Because we were in the middle of a major intelligence operation, involving hundreds of investigators and years of work. We didn't want it derailed by a random shooting by a deranged priest. If homicide got wind of it, the whole force would have known, and if the whole force knew then the whole world would know. The operation could have come crashing down.'

Martin sees an opportunity to probe further. 'Protecting the operation must have seemed pretty important. Your old mate, Herb Walker . . . He put Byron Swift in a cell after allegations of paedophilia were levelled at him, but someone in Sydney ordered him released. Was that you?'

Vandenbruk is back on his feet, fuse alight, again threatening to explode. The effort to control himself has him hissing his response. 'No, it fucking well was not. It was someone on the task force, I now know that much, and if I ever find who it was, I'll break their fucking neck. Now, you want to hear the tapes or not?'

'Sure,' says Martin, again taken aback by Vandenbruk's hairtrigger temperament.

'So we have a deal?'

Martin looks at Goffing, but the ASIO man is staring at the floor. Vandenbruk has them where he wants them. 'Yes. We have a deal,' says Martin.

'Good.'

Vandenbruk pulls out his phone. 'I can't give you a copy, so listen carefully.'

There's the sound of a phone ringing, a crackle as it's answered.

'Avery, it's Byron. This is fucked. I need to take Mandy with me.'

'Byron, slow down, slow down.'

'I can't slow down. She comes with me, okay?'

'Look, we talked it through. You agreed. What's changed?'

'Craig Landers. It was him.'

'The guy from the general store? What do you mean it was him?'

'Him and his gang. That crime scene out in the Scrublands, that one I told you about, the blood and the women's underwear, it must have been him. And his mates. Not the Reapers.'

'What? How do you know this?'

'His wife warned me they were gunning for me. She came here in a panic, saying they were animals. Then he shows up—Craig—as good as admits it. Came to the church. Said he knew I was leaving. Said once I was gone, he'd be coming after Mandy and his wife and anyone else he fancied. I can't leave her here. You didn't see what I saw in the Scrublands. He's deranged. They're animals. She's pregnant.'

'Pregnant? To you?'

'Yes, to me. Who else?'

'For fuck's sake, Julian. Some fucking priest you are.'

'So can I take her with me or not?'

'Yes. Take her with you. Get her out of harm's way. But remember who you really are and what's at stake. I've put my neck on the chopping block for you, you know.'

'All I want is to get her and the kid to safety. After that, they're on their own. They don't have to know anything else.'

'Okay. Well get going then.'

'I will. After church.'

A crackle. The recording ends.

Martin looks at Goffing; the ASIO man returns his gaze. There's not a lot to say.

'Okay, here's the second one, a few minutes later. But remember, in between the two, Foster has received a call from Russell Hill. We have the metadata, but we were tapping the church phone, not Foster's, so there's no recording.'

Goffing nods, reliving his ignominy. 'It was Snouch. He called Foster.'

'Right. And this is Foster calling Swift.'

The sound of a phone ringing.

'*St James.*'

'*Byron, it's Avery. We're busted.*'

'*What?*'

'*I just got a call from Harley Snouch. He knows who you are, what you did.*'

'*Snouch? That cunt. What does he want? More money?*'

'*Nothing. He's told the cops and he's told ASIO. They're on their way.*'

'*What? Why's he done that?*'

'*It doesn't matter. Leave. Leave now. Forget the girl, forget the church service. Just go. Take your guns and go.*'

'*I can't. I can't just leave her. Landers is an animal.*'

'*For fuck's sake, Julian, you can't help her, not anymore. Get the fuck out of there. Now. Leave Landers to me.*'

A burst of static and the line is dead.

———

The heat is rising although it's still only nine-thirty in the morning and the sun is a long way from its zenith. A light southerly has come up, bringing some small respite, but Martin isn't fooled. The temperature, already in the high twenties, will climb much higher. He might be acclimatising to the dry heat, but no one acclimatises to forty degrees.

A group of locals stand across from the hotel, pointing and muttering, their faces creased with disbelief. Martin sees Luke

McIntyre with a couple of other lads around the same age. He gives the boy a wave.

A late-model SUV glides past, a BMW with Victorian plates. It pulls in to the kerb, front in, ignoring the signs. A well-dressed couple get out, the man with a bulky camera. He starts taking photos while his wife collects selfies on her phone. *Christ*, thinks Martin, *sightseers. Come to witness the town of death, collect happy snaps and anecdotes for their next dinner party.*

The locals look askance, melt away into the smattering of stores that have opened.

Inside the Oasis, there are more tourists at the counter, ordering coffees and asking directions to St James. Mandy is taciturn, working the machine, her brow furrowed and her lips pursed. Martin wonders why she bothers, the heiress to Springfields. She sees him and offers a guarded smile, but behind the welcome he can see the concern in her eyes. She makes him a coffee without his asking and hands it to him.

He takes a seat, amusing himself and Liam while he waits, reaching through the bars of the playpen, building towers from multi-coloured blocks for the boy to destroy with sweeping arms and chortling joy. Such simple pleasures. Eventually the inter-lopers leave and they're on their own, just the three of them.

'Martin, what is it? Has something else happened?'

Martin raises his eyebrows, admiring her perceptiveness; she already knows him well enough to read his mood. There is no easy way to say what comes next, so he doesn't try to embellish it. 'I know who Byron Swift was, Mandy—who he really was.'

The weight of his words stops her for a moment. Then she moves to the door, locks it, turns the sign to CLOSED. She returns to her coffee machine, begins to make herself a cup, giving her hands something to do before finally responding. 'So was your article true? He was in Afghanistan? A soldier?'

'Yes. His name was Julian Flynt.'

'Julian?' she says. 'Julian,' she repeats, testing it aloud. 'Julian. Julian Flynt.'

'Mandy, it's not good.'

'Tell me.'

And so he does. First the good: the elite soldier, the leader of men; then the bad: the captive of the Taliban, the traumatised survivor; and finally the ugly: the rogue soldier, the killer, the war criminal. The fugitive. Mandy listens without comment, without movement. Only a quiver in her lip betrays her feelings.

'He was a killer?' she asks. 'He was always a killer,' she says, answering her own question.

Martin wants to go to her, to comfort her. But not yet. 'There's more, Mandy. Avery Foster, the publican—he knew Flynt in Afghanistan. He was a chaplain there. He probably helped get him out, hide him here.'

Mandy leaves the machine, coffee unfinished, and takes a seat, her perfect features troubled, like ripples in water. 'It was an act? Being a priest was an act? I can't believe it. He was too . . . I don't know . . . too good at it.'

'He was a priest. He was ordained—under a false name, but he was ordained. And I don't think it was an act. He and Foster were sending money to Afghanistan, to an orphanage. I think they were trying to make amends, an act of atonement.'

Mandy is blinking, her distress seeping out. 'You're going to write all this, aren't you?'

Martin nods. 'I will. And if I don't, someone else will. The authorities know. It will come out at the inquest, probably before.'

'I trusted him, Martin. I loved him.' She's looking directly at him, directly into his eyes. 'Is that why he killed those men? Because they discovered who he was? Was he that evil?'

'No, Mandy. I don't think they had any idea he was Julian Flynt.'

'Then why?'

'I'm close. I think I might get there. But I need your help.'

'My help? How?'

'The diary.'

'Oh, Martin.' She seems to collapse then, as if a weight has come down upon her. She no longer meets his gaze, but looks at the ground and then, after some time, at Liam, lying on his back, playing with a block and mouthing noises to himself. Martin stands, moves across to her, crouches down and takes her hands. Finally she looks at him and speaks. 'The diary proves that Byron was with me, here, the night the backpackers were taken. The police needed to know. They thought he'd killed them. But I knew it wasn't him, that the real killer was still out there, that he might kill again. I needed to show them.'

Martin squeezes her hand. 'It was the right thing to do, Mandy. The right thing. The police were wrong; you were right. It was Jamie Landers.' He pauses, but then presses on. 'But why rip out the pages? What were you hoping to protect him from?'

She looks a little surprised. 'Byron? I wasn't protecting him. He was dead. It couldn't hurt him.'

'Who then?'

'Robbie.'

'Robbie Haus-Jones?'

'Robbie.'

Martin thinks of the young constable, hands red, face blackened. 'Why, Mandy? What did you write in the diary?'

She closes her eyes, bites her lips, bracing herself. 'Robbie worshipped Byron. He was kind of infatuated with him, maybe in love with him. Byron and I used to joke about it. If the police had read that, their ridicule would have been merciless.'

'True. But that's not all, is it? Maybe it's enough to rip out the pages, but it's not enough to get arrested over, to risk prison, to risk separation from Liam. There must have been more.'

Mandy's eyes are locked on his. 'Byron told me. Not that he was Julian Flynt, he never told me that, not about being in Afghanistan, but other things. He said people were growing drugs out in the Scrublands, selling them to a bikie gang. He was helping them, acting as an intermediary, stopping the bikies from robbing them. And that last time I saw him, before he went to the church, when he said he was leaving and couldn't take me with him, he told me that if there was any trouble after he left, I should go to Robbie. He told me Robbie knew what he was doing. Robbie was shielding Byron. That's what I ripped out.'

'You were protecting Robbie?'

'It wasn't his fault, Martin. He loved Byron; he believed in him. He was defending him. Robbie wasn't taking any money. It wasn't corruption; it was love.'

Martin can see the sorrow written on her face, yet he persists. 'Who else knew?'

'I don't think anyone knew the details of how it worked, not even Robbie. But we all knew there was money. For the footy team, for the youth group, for families that were doing it tough. To help with the fire brigade, with the services club. We were in it together—the drought was getting worse, closing in—we didn't ask questions.'

Then she stands and he holds her fully, holds her close. He needs to tell her that Byron was more than an intermediary. And he needs to tell her about Harley Snouch, offer her the DNA kit, but for now that can wait.

⁓

The day is hot and the day is dry and the day is barren. The morning's breeze has died and the sun hangs over Riversend like a sentencing judge. The shops, having opened ever so briefly, have closed again, shut for the week or shut forever: the bank, the art gallery, the op shop, the real estate agent, the hair salon. The wine saloon sits in shuttered anonymity, its ghosts back in sole possession. Smoke still drifts skywards from the ruins of the pub, and journalists roam the streets like jackals. At the crossroads, the soldier stands unmoving on his plinth, keeping his head down, observing the same moment's silence he's been observing for the best part of a century. Next to the pub, unscathed by fire, the general store remains locked, its bottled water inaccessible. After ten days, the town has grown familiar; Martin feels he knows every building, every fixture, that he knows every person, by name or face. And now he knows their tawdry secret. He knows the town, the town knows him, and he knows it's time to leave. There is nothing left for him here. Wellington Smith is waiting with his money and his promises and his enthusiasm.

In the end, they'd argued. There'd been a moment there, with her in his arms, when he'd hoped for more, believed he might be embracing the future. But then he ruined it. He hadn't fully appreciated what she'd endured: left grieving by her mother, deceived by Swift, betrayed by Snouch. Martin hadn't anticipated how much his revelations would wound her. She now knew the priest hadn't trusted her, hadn't disclosed who he really was, even as he'd professed his love for her. Even as he'd impregnated her. He'd perpetrated his fraud upon her just as he'd perpetrated it upon everyone else. So when Martin suggested that Swift's final act—the murder of the five men— might have been a misguided attempt to protect her, this did not placate her. Her anger flared, directed at Swift and directed at Martin. How dare the priest, this violent man with his violent past, kill in *her* defence, as if she were incapable of defending herself against the predations of Craig Landers and his ilk? Landers hadn't left her pregnant, Swift had.

And then Martin, compounding her anger and despair, revealed the true nature of her father, Harley Snouch, dashing her scarcely acknowledged hopes for all time. Thirty years after he had violated her mother, there was no remorse. None. He'd schemed to win her affection, pretending to be her half-brother, plotting to deceive her while manoeuvring to steal her inheritance, the inheritance of Liam, his own grandson. She cried then, really cried: cried for everything she'd lost, everything she'd never had. She cried for herself and she cried for her son and she cried for his future, when he would learn the truth of his father and his grandfather. And in comforting her, Martin offered himself to her, with the implicit promise that he was different, that he was genuine, that he was not deceiving her. And for a moment she believed it and so did he, believed that he was a better man. She believed it long enough to stop crying, long enough to take him to bed and weep a different quality of tear.

But the pretence didn't last; the story got in the way, his need to tell the world. For as they lay there, planning their escape, planning their future, he told her of Wellington Smith's promise of salvation, of his reputation restored, of how he intended to write a book, to set the record straight, to reveal to the great Australian public the truth, to expose the secrets and reveal the lies of Riversend. He presented it as a wonderful opportunity: they could go anywhere, live anywhere. She had her wealth; he could write the book as they built a new life together. She fell silent then, saying nothing. Her silence should have warned him, but he'd prattled on, oblivious.

In that moment she saw him as he was, as he'd always been: the journalist, putting his vocation before all else, a secular priest worshipping at the shrine of truth, careless of who might get hurt in its telling. And eventually she spoke, in a voice soft and cautious. She wanted to know, quietly demanded to know, if he intended to write it all, without exception, to set down everything he knew. Not just condemning Byron Swift and Harley Snouch, but exposing all those people who had helped Martin: Robbie Haus-Jones and Fran Landers and Errol Ryding. And herself. The entire town. Were they all expendable, all to be sacrificed on the altar of journalism? 'It's what I do,' he said. And when her temper flared again, he responded in kind, demanding to know how she could possibly judge him, she who'd manipulated him into uncovering Swift's ugly past, all the time hiding her knowledge of the drug operation and Robbie's involvement. He accused her of lies and deceit; she accused him of selfishness and thoughtless disregard for others. They fought; he yelled, Liam cried, she threw him out.

Martin gets to Thames Street, the end of the shops, the end of the shade. He steps out into the cauldron, the heat bleeding into him, as he continues up Hay Road, up onto the old wooden bridge, oblivious to the temperature. As if it could hurt him now. Finally he pauses, places his hands on the rail, feels the burning heat of the wood, leaves them there. The riverbed is still dry and broken; the fridge still sits there, offering the mirage of beer.

When he first crossed this bridge ten days ago, he'd come to recover, to put his demons behind him, to come to terms with spending his fortieth birthday locked in the boot of a Mercedes-Benz in the Gaza Strip. Max Fuller had sent him, hoping that being back on the road, covering a story away from head office, might help restore him to the journalist he'd once been. But standing on the bridge, Martin realises he'll never again be that journalist, never again be that person. Heraclitus's dictum comes to him: that a man cannot step into the same river twice. He regards the empty riverbed. Does it hold for waterless rivers? It had always puzzled him, even through the hours of counselling, why being abandoned in the Mercedes had had such a profound impact on him. It was accumulated stress, they told him, that he had seen and heard too much, and the experience in Gaza had tipped him over the edge. After all, he had witnessed far worse things: prisoners executed by machine gun, their families forced to watch; the deaths of babies in refugee camps, their mothers ululating with grief; the hollow eyes of survivors, their loved ones erased by ethnic cleansing. What was being shut in the boot of a car for a few days compared to that?

He knows now. He saw it last night, when he watched D'Arcy Defoe standing unmoved and unmoving as the flames of the Commercial Hotel roared before him, taking notes, recording the spectacle, observing the reactions of others, impervious to reality, unblinking as Robbie Haus-Jones was dragged from the inferno barely alive. Martin saw himself then, as he had been before Gaza, removed from events. Max Fuller's go-to man, travelling light: taking nothing of himself into the story, leaving nothing of himself behind. For the story was something that happened to other people; he was just there to report, an observer. And that all changed in Gaza. He became the story; it was happening to him. He was involved; he had no God-given leave pass, no right to stand apart from the story, apart from life. He was a participant, like it or not. Things no longer happened only to other people; some small part of their grief, or their joy, or their hollowness wore off on him, became part of him. How had he ever thought otherwise?

Standing on the bridge, he realises the old Martin Scarsden is gone now, gone forever. A week or so shy of his forty-first birthday he's being reborn, like it or not. But it's coming too late. Mandy is back in the bookstore and she never wants to see him again. After a lifetime alone, he's still alone and probably always will be, the go-to journo gone for all money. And now it hurts; he's no longer impervious. For the first time, he's brought himself to the story and now he's condemned to leave large parts of himself behind. A tear comes to his eye, surprising him. He can't remember ever crying, not as an adult, not as a teenager, not on any of his assignments, no matter how harrowing, not since he was eight years old. There were times when all around him had wept and he alone had remained dry-eyed. He wonders why. And the tear runs down his cheek, falls towards the parched riverbed. He smiles at its futility.

He returns to town, following the road down from the levee bank. Indecision has him, but the heat is insistent; he can no more ignore it than he can ignore life itself. Looking along Thames Street, in the distance he recognises a red station wagon parked outside St James. He walks to the church, unsure of what he's about to do. The building appears as anonymous and as uncaring as ever, inured to the assault of the sun, sitting aloof above its short flight of steps. Today, its double doors are ajar. Perhaps the tourists have prised them open. Inside, it's cooler, darker, but there are no gawkers, only one person, up by the altar, kneeling in prayer. The owner of the red car—Fran Landers. He waits quietly up the back until she's finished.

'Oh. It's you, Martin. I wondered if you'd be back.'

'Hello, Fran. You okay?'

'Not so good. Awful, really. How can I help?'

'I spoke to Jamie yesterday, in his cell, before they took him away. He was concerned about you. He said to tell you he was sorry, that he didn't mean to hurt you. I'm sure he meant it.'

It's too much for Fran. She sits, almost collapsing onto a nearby pew, head bowed, and starts, almost imperceptibly, to weep.

Martin sits down next to her, giving her time before speaking. 'I'm thinking of writing something, Fran. To explain what has really happened.'

'And you want to speak with me?' It's more a statement than a question.

'I do.'

And she nods in resignation.

There's a stillness about the building, a sanctuary from the heat and glare pounding down outside. Martin opens the voice recorder app on his phone. He waits for her to compose herself before beginning.

'Fran, the day of the shooting, you told me you came here to the church. That you warned Byron Swift that your husband and his friends were threatening violence.'

'I did. I told him they had guns, that he should leave. He told me he was already going, straight after the service. He told me to wait at Blackfellas Lagoon for him.'

Martin pauses, lets her words settle before challenging them. 'No, he didn't, Fran. He told you the same thing he told Mandy Blonde: that he had to go alone. We know that, from Mandy and from phone calls he made from the church. He planned to leave by himself. That's right, isn't it?'

'He loved us. He cared for us.'

'I believe he did. He must have wanted to take you with him. But that's not what he said, is it? He said it wasn't possible.'

Fran doesn't move for a long moment, then nods her affirmation, her voice a whisper. 'Yes. It was me. I said I'd wait for him at the lagoon. I was hoping he'd come. He never said he would, but I hoped he might.'

'So did you go to Blackfellas? Jamie said he saw you at home.'

'Both. I went home. Then I went out to Blackfellas. In case he came. And just to be there.'

'And when you went home, you saw Craig, didn't you?'

Fran looks up with eyes of pain. But she must see the resolve in Martin's eyes, and drops her head again. 'It doesn't matter now, does it? Craig is dead. Byron is dead. Jamie is as good as dead. None of it matters.'

'So tell me what happened, Fran. What did you tell Craig?'

'I told him that Byron was leaving. There was no need to confront him, no need for guns, no need for violence. He was leaving. But Craig went anyway.'

'But not with his gun. The men were unarmed.'

'Jamie was at home. He'd calmed Craig down somehow.'

'I know. Jamie has told me about it. He told Craig that Byron had never abused him, that Herb Walker was wrong, that he and Allen would never have allowed it.'

'Is that how it happened? I see.'

'Jamie said that before Craig left for the church, he said something to you. It made you cry.'

Fran again appears to be on the brink of tears. 'Craig wanted revenge.'

'Revenge?'

'He hated Byron. He knew Byron had slept with me, made me happy. You have no idea how much that angered Craig, how much it ate away at him, me being happy. He wanted revenge.'

'And Byron had beaten him up, humiliated him.'

'You know about that?'

'I do. And I know why. Byron was warning him off, telling Craig to stop hitting you. You and Jamie.'

Fran lets out a sob; Martin is surprised by its unexpected power. It comes from somewhere deep inside, racking her chest before escaping, the release of something long suppressed. She keeps her eyes down but her body is betraying her.

'Fran? What did Craig say he was going to do?'

She looks up. 'He said he was going to fuck with his mind.'

'What does that mean?'

'He went there to gloat, to inflict pain. He knew Byron was a decent man, a caring man. He told me what he was going to say, because he wanted to hurt me just as he intended to hurt Byron.' Another sob escapes, shaking her body.

'What was he going to say?'

'That once Byron was gone, I was his again, his property, his plaything. He would do whatever he liked with me, treat me however he liked. Like a dog. And not just me. Mandy too. We would both be his. And any other woman Byron had been with. That's why I went out to Blackfellas. After Craig told me that, if Byron didn't come for me, I was going to kill myself.'

'Jesus, Fran.'

'But I didn't. I couldn't leave Jamie to face him alone. He was a monster.' Another sob, a deep wave, wells up and escapes, her body trembling as it passes. 'I'm glad he's dead, Martin. I'm so glad Byron shot him. I celebrate it every day. I come here and give thanks. I'm sorry about the others, Alf and Thom and the others, I truly am, but not about him.'

Martin hesitates, uncertain whether to push on, to further distress this fragile woman. But he feels he has no option; the need to find the truth remains, insistent and unwavering, however uncomfortable he now feels about it.

'Fran, the police have a recording of Byron talking on the phone from St James to Avery Foster. After you'd visited Byron, shortly before he started shooting. You understand?'

Martin can see in her eyes that she does. He sees confirmation and he sees torment and he sees trepidation. 'Byron told Foster that Craig was an animal—but not just him, his hunting buddies as well. Is that what you told Byron, when you were pleading with him to meet you at Blackfellas, to save yourself from Craig? You were so desperate to get away from your husband, for Byron to save you, that you also accused his friends of violent abuse with no evidence to support it?'

Fran Landers says nothing; she doesn't have to. Her eyes make her confession for her. And then the sobbing takes her over; she loses the last vestiges of self-control, no longer able to meet Martin's gaze, the church no longer a sanctuary.

Martin doesn't know whether to condemn her or comfort her. So he does both: condemning her with his mind as he comforts her with his words. This woman who had suffered so much for so long, trapped in a loveless marriage with a vicious husband. And yet had that desperate lie, accusing not just Craig but also his friends, been the sliver on the scales of Byron Swift's unbalanced mind that had tipped him into murder? How can Martin forgive her? How can he not?

———

Later, out on the fateful steps, Martin stands in the blazing sun, stands where the priest was standing when he had opened fire. He looks out to where Swift's congregation had milled beneath him, looks over to where Fran Landers' red station wagon is parked in the shade of the trees, where Gerry Torlini and Allen Newkirk had sat in the fruit-grower's truck, where Torlini had died and the boy had cowered. He looks across to the levee bank where Luke McIntyre had witnessed the massacre. And, at last, Martin believes he knows why Swift did it. Standing on the church steps, he tries to put himself in the priest's shoes, to see the world as he did in those last moments of his life.

Swift arrived at church planning to conduct one last service before leaving the district, taking his guns with him. Walker, misled by Jamie Landers and Allen Newkirk, had unjustly accused him of child abuse and locked him in a cell. The allegations were false, but that didn't mean they would go away; the Bellington sergeant would most likely investigate his past, possibly discover his true identity. The policeman might also discover the drugs growing in the Scrublands, Avery Foster's involvement, Robbie's concealment. And there were signs an awful crime had been perpetrated in the Scrublands. He needed to be gone.

So before arriving at the church, Swift had visited Mandy to say goodbye. She'd told him she was pregnant with their child, asked to go with him. But he'd refused. Because he wasn't really

Byron Swift, he was Julian Flynt, a war criminal and a fugitive. He would be doing her no favours taking her with him. He'd told her about the drugs, about Robbie Haus-Jones, but he'd never revealed the truth about himself. Martin can understand why: growing marijuana is one thing, killing women and children in cold blood is another.

Swift had left Mandy and gone to the church. Fran Landers arrived in a panic, warning him that her husband and his friends were coming to kill him. He laughed at the thought of Landers, a demonstrable coward, posing any threat to him. Swift had beaten him up before, he could beat him up again; if Landers brought a gun, he would fetch one of his own from the vestry. He told her not to worry, that he was leaving town anyway, leaving that very day.

That was the first she knew of his imminent departure, so she pleaded her own case. Swift would be abandoning her and her son Jamie to the violence of her husband; he should take them with him. And when that failed to move him, she not just accused Craig, but also implicated his friends. Yet Swift remained unmoved, unable to help, unwilling to meet her at Blackfellas Lagoon.

And then the shape of the morning changed again. Fran returned home, tried to pacify her husband, told him Swift was leaving, that there was no need for violence. Jamie Landers then convinced his father that the abuse allegations were unfounded. And in that moment, Craig, the violent husband and father, saw the opportunity for petty revenge. He came to the church, enlisting the unknowing support of his hunting companions, to wreak vengeance on the man who had cuckolded him, beaten him and humiliated him. Martin considers this, just how intensely Craig Landers must have hated Byron Swift— and how badly he misjudged him.

Craig arrived at church, unarmed, outwardly civil, shaking the priest's hand and smiling benignly. And delivering a message of hate. What did he say, what phrasing did he use to fuck with Swift's mind? If Fran was right, he told the priest that he was going to enslave her and Mandy, unleash his depravities upon them. That the town belonged to him. Martin recalls what Swift said in his phone call to Foster: *'Him and his gang. That crime scene out in the Scrublands, that one I told you about, the blood and the women's underwear, it must have been him. And his mates. Not the Reapers.'* Martin thinks about that. Landers couldn't have alluded to the killings of the backpackers; he was ignorant of that. If the hunters had discovered the crime scene, they would have reported it. But in Swift's imagination, Craig's guilt must have seemed undeniable; he had become the embodiment of evil, the devil incarnate, a violent sexual predator, depraved and Godless, leading a gang of dark apostles.

Believing Craig's false claims and stated intentions, believing Fran's unfounded smear against the Bellington Anglers Club, believing his own fevered imaginings, Swift went to the vestry. He used the phone, the one he'd installed to communicate with the Reapers, and called Avery Foster. Martin recalls the recording. Swift told his confidant that he needed to take Mandy with him, to get her away from Landers' clutches. Foster had agreed. At that point Swift was still planning on leaving, perhaps even picking up Fran on the way after all, perhaps sending for her later.

But while he was getting changed, preparing to conduct his last service, Harley Snouch, prosecuting a deception of his own and unaware of what was happening at the church, rang Foster, telling him he knew that Byron Swift was an imposter, that he was the war criminal Julian Flynt. Foster called Swift immediately, told him to leave, told him to abandon Mandy.

Martin imagines the priest, sitting in the vestry, crucifix in hand, considering his options. Swift could still flee, but the police would be after him now that they knew he was Flynt. It was unlikely he could run for long. Taking Mandy, newly pregnant and ignorant of his past, was no longer an option: in the short term it would endanger her life; in the long term it would stain her with complicity. But how could he flee and leave her in Riversend, her and their baby, and Fran, leave them here to be preyed upon by Landers and his followers?

Swift sat there in the vestry, the priest in his cassock, amid his guns, and realised he couldn't go and he couldn't stay. So he walked out here, to where Martin is standing on the steps, and shot them one by one, methodically. He made Riversend safe, the future safe, for Fran, for Mandy, for his unborn child. But he was wrong, so very wrong. None of the men were rapists and none of them were murderers, except for Allen Newkirk, whose life he spared. None of them had committed any crime whatsoever, except for Craig Landers. And even Landers, a wife beater and a son basher, didn't deserve to be summarily executed. Nor was it inevitable that his threats would be carried out. As Mandy had so forcefully reminded Martin, the fact that Landers had abused his wife in the past didn't mean Mandy was about to submit to the same treatment.

Martin considers all of this as he stands at the door of the church. Was it possible that the priest, driven by decent if misguided motives, committed a heinous and unforgiveable crime? And Martin decides that is exactly what the evidence suggests.

And then what? The priest sat here with his gun, where Martin is now standing. He'd killed the five men, believing he'd rid the town of evil. He could run, but the police would catch him soon enough. They'd spare no expense, no resource: he was a mass murderer twice over. Did he consider suicide? Probably. Put a gun in his mouth, pull the trigger. So why didn't he? Religious conviction? Or because it would still leave them all exposed, the people he cared for: Avery and Robbie and Jason, all the people he had persuaded to help him, all the townspeople who had benefited from the drug money? He was the one who'd killed those innocents in Afghanistan; he was the one who needed to make amends. Or the police would find them and punish them too, punish them for his crimes.

And then Robbie appeared, sweet foolish Robbie, and the solution presented itself. If he had to die, then he could make it a worthwhile death. A sacrifice, dying for all their sins. What better death for a man of the cloth? For if Robbie killed him, then the constable would be a hero, above reproach; no one would suspect him of aiding and abetting the drug operation. And Robbie could protect Avery, and in turn Avery could shield Jason and Shazza. So Swift had fired at Robbie, fired and missed, slowly, deliberately, forcing Robbie to kill him. But not before warning him: 'Harley Snouch knows everything.' Mandy had suggested Robbie loved Byron Swift; perhaps at the end, Byron recognised that love and did what he could to protect it.

Martin sits down where the priest sat and died almost a year ago. The concrete is griddle-hot, burning him through his trousers. It will make a remarkable book; Wellington Smith will be ecstatic. Four different crimes, all taking place in and around the same drought-ravaged town, all separate but all interlinked, driven by greed and hate, guilt and hope: the drug operation, an instrument of atonement co-opted by bikies; the murder of the Germans, abuse spawning abuse; the shooting at St James, innocents murdered with the best intentions; and Harley Snouch, attempting to expunge rape with fraud. Four crimes, all seeded by violence from the recent or distant past. He considers all that he has uncovered. Yet Martin feels no joy at all at the prospect of writing it.

twenty-eight LIFE

MARTIN IS REPEATING HIMSELF. THE SAME FLIGHT FROM SYDNEY TO WAGGA Wagga, the same car rental place, perhaps even the same car. But two weeks on, he is, he decides, a different Martin Scarsden. The hands gripping the steering wheel are his hands, familiar once again, in no way special but in no way alien. On the seat next to him sit advance copies of *This Month*, their red covers dominated by the face of Julian Flynt, caught in the moment he became Byron Swift. It's a freeze-frame from the video cameras monitoring immigration control at Sydney Airport, courtesy of Jack Goffing, capturing the moment Flynt offered Byron Swift's doctored passport as his own. He'd glanced up at the camera, just for an instant, aware of its surveillance, and it had recorded the faraway quality of his gaze.

Wellington Smith has ordered twice the normal print run and is sending embargoed copies to the mainstream media ahead of publication. It will be the definitive account of the story of the summer, perhaps of the year. Martin glances down at it once again, Flynt's face turned two-tone by the graphic artists, black on red, superimposed on a picture of St James. The headline is simple: THE TRUTH. And underneath it: *The war criminal, the drug syndicate and the cover-up—the truth behind Australia's most notorious mass murder. By Martin Scarsden.* Disgraced former journalist no longer.

The article revolves around Byron Swift. At six thousand words, it's long for Australia, even for *This Month*, but there is still much to reveal in his planned book. Avery Foster's role is detailed, for his part was central and there's little point in protecting the dead. The Reapers are well referenced too, but Jason Moore is nowhere to be found or even hinted at. Herb Walker is exonerated, of both suicide and negligence. ASIO emerges looking good, as the agency that finally picked up on the failures of Customs and Immigration; Jack Goffing isn't mentioned by name. Harley Snouch doesn't rate a mention either, but Martin hasn't so much spared him as saved him for later: next month's cover story and an entire chapter in the book.

At first, it was a difficult article to write. Old habits die hard. He'd wanted to tell it all; the impulse was ingrained and not easy to shake. It was certainly compelling enough. But the image of Mandy, screaming and in tears, branding him a sociopath, had returned again and again. He sought counsel from Max, but that had only deepened his disquiet. His old editor had been hardline: 'Protect your sources; everything else goes in. If it's newsworthy, the public has a right to know,' he preached. 'We're not here to play God.' In the end, Martin didn't listen, turning apostate, spurning his mentor's advice. He spared Mandy and he spared Fran; he spared Jack and he spared Claus; and, most of all, he spared the townsfolk of Riversend: the footy team and the youth group and the fire brigade, Errol Ryding and the rest of them, the recipients of money they'd never questioned. He didn't lie, except by omission. He told the truth about Byron Swift and Craig Landers and Jamie Landers. With some regret, he told the truth about Robbie Haus-Jones: how he'd fallen under Byron Swift's spell and had turned a blind eye—not from self-interest but from compassion—to the drug trade; how he had reported Avery Foster's death was a suicide when he must have at least suspected it wasn't; how he had failed to report the drug operation even after Swift and Foster were dead. And with some joy, Martin told the truth about Horrie Grosvenor, the Newkirk brothers and Gerry Torlini: how they were indeed all innocent victims, beyond reproach. And when it was done, when it was filed, he felt good about the article and better about himself.

But that's not why he feels so good today, driving across the vast plain from Hay, heading towards the Scrublands, the flood plain and Riversend. He'd rung Mandy, trying to do the right thing, leaving a message for her, warning her the article was coming, emailing her a PDF. It was, he decided, all he could do in the circumstances. He didn't expect any response, let alone her phone call. He'd sent the DNA results through a week earlier, confirming Snouch's paternity; he'd heard nothing from her then and he expected nothing now. Yet she called him back, almost as soon as she'd finished reading the article. She told him she was leaving Riversend: packing up her mother's bookstore, taking her life and her boy elsewhere. She thought Martin might like to give her a hand. He couldn't believe his luck, the change in his fortune. Her voice was light and her laughter like a blessing. And so he is on his way, heart in his mouth.

The plain runs on forever, the sun omnipotent, the air dry, but today is different. For marching across the horizon, as if painted onto the blue backdrop of the sky, is a front of clouds, dark and purposeful, a rare low-pressure system penetrating Australia's interior for once, instead of scuttling across south of the mainland. The horizon is sharply defined, a clear blond line against the grey clouds. From his right, the Scrublands emerge, at first nothing more than a khaki stain on his consciousness, then coming closer, and closer still, the smudge turning into clumps of vegetation, then individual trees, spindly and malnourished. The muted grey-green turns monochrome, then back again, as he passes through the wake of the bushfire. The flood plain arrives, the noisome bridge and then Riversend itself, silos sentinel in the distance, glowing gold against the blackening sky. He drives down into a main street looking much the same as he'd left it. The pub has stopped smouldering and the detritus has been swept from the street, but the soldier still stands, unbent and unaffected. The dead are still dead; the survivors still grieve.

He parks his rental with practised ease, its bumper mere centimetres from the gutter. He enters the bookstore; here there is change, if not what he's anticipated. The books are still on their shelves, the armchairs and occasional tables await customers at the front of the store, the roof fan rotates slowly and water tinkles from slate to slate in the miniature fountain on the counter. But the Japanese screen has been removed and the curtains opened; the shop is filled with light.

Mandy emerges through the swing doors, Liam in a new backpack, fingers in her hair and mischief in his eyes.

'Hello, mister.' Not bothering to remove the backpack, she stretches up, clasps her hands behind Martin's neck and kisses him with power and intent and longing. The kiss lasts forever, the kiss of Martin Scarsden's life. 'Welcome back.'

Martin is momentarily speechless.

'Coffee?' she asks.

'Absolutely.'

She smiles again, eyes playful, dimples teasing. She floats past him, busies herself at the machine.

'Still working then, the machine?' he says, regaining his voice. 'And what's with the books? I thought you were shutting it down, packing up.'

'Change of plan. I got a manager.'

'Really?'

'Sure. I own the place now. Remember? I own half of Riversend for that matter. No one's going to buy it, no one's going to rent it, so why not?'

'Who's the manager?'

'Me.' A head bobs up from behind a shelf: Codger Harris. He's been lurking there the whole time.

———

Later the four of them sit together in the armchairs at the front of the store, Martin holding Liam on his lap, feeling the boy's weight, sensing impending responsibility. Codger is reading his article in *This Month*. Mandy is smiling, alternately amused and indulgent, as if she likes what she sees. She tells Martin of her plans. She'll keep the bookstore; Codger need pay no rent and can keep any profits. She'll also keep Springfields, clearing out the dam and installing a cistern to feed water, clear and pure, into the town. Errol Ryding is helping to push approval through council; it will pay for the water and the profits will go to a certain orphanage in Kabul. While she talks, Codger continues reading, harrumphing as he goes. He looks transformed: clean and clean-shaven, clothed and bespectacled, his hair cut and remaining teeth polished. He finishes, nods slowly.

'All right?' asks Martin.

'Very good, young fellow, as far as it goes.'

Martin smiles. 'I know. There are things better left out.'

'And there are things you don't know.'

And that's when he tells them, the story he hasn't told anyone, not for thirty years, looking at Mandy as he recounts it, his voice reverential.

'The day my family died, the day the truck went off the road in Bellington, was the day my life stopped. The truck killed my wife Jessica and it killed my boy Jonty. And it killed me inside. It still hurts; thirty years on it still hurts.'

'Codger?' says Mandy, her voice laden with concern.

'I should have been with them, of course. But I wasn't. I was with your mother, Mandy. I was with Katherine.'

'With Mum?' Mandy asks, confused.

He smiles then, fondly. 'No, it wasn't like that. I was in love with my wife, and your mother was in no condition to be romanced. I was the bank manager in Bellington. She'd come to me for money. She wanted to leave, to get away, but she had no money. He'd turned violent, started hitting her, treating her as his possession. She'd confided in Jess. My wife was her old schoolteacher. Katherine was already pregnant by then, pregnant with you, and she feared for her safety and for yours. She had nothing, of course. No savings, no collateral. Her father was totally unsympathetic, wanted his daughter married into the Snouch dynasty at any cost. Awful to say, but there it is. The rules at the bank were strict, but we were trying to work out how to help. And then my family was killed, and I was no use to anyone, not even to myself. I felt so guilty, being with her, trying to help someone I barely knew, when I should have been with them.'

'But Codger, what could you have done?' asks Mandy. 'No one could have prevented what happened.'

'I could have died with them.'

'Oh, Codger.'

'That's what I thought for years. Drove me mad, put me in the funny farm. Drugs. Electric shock therapy. Suicide attempts. I don't recommend it, I really don't. But that's a long time ago now; that's in the past. I learnt to think of other things, not to dwell on it. Eventually I got back here, with my busted mind and my busted soul. And the first person to help me was Eric Snouch. A true gentleman; a heart of gold. He gave me the land out in the Scrublands, my own little piece of sanity, my own little piece of solitude. And in return, I hurt him. I told him the truth about his son: that Harley had indeed bashed Katherine, bashed her and raped her, that my wife and I both knew it, that Jessica had seen the bruises. Funny way to repay

Telling him his son was a brute.

his kindness, wasn't it? Telling him his son was a brute. Up until then he'd backed Harley, got the charges dismissed, hushed it all up. Given him the benefit of the doubt. But after I told him, he no longer deluded himself. He had it out with Harley, ended up disowning him, sending him into exile. Eric tried reaching out to Katherine, I know that, tried to apologise for not believing her previously. He offered to make amends. But she was proud, said she didn't need help, not from a Snouch. So he helped her without her knowing.'

'The bookstore and the house?' asks Martin.

'Yes. Errol Ryding was the mayor, back when we had a mayor. Eric convinced him that when the library closed, Katherine should have the books. Errol told her the shop and the house were council-owned, apologised that they couldn't pay her a salary, but she could keep the profits instead and not pay any rent. Same arrangement you have with me. I think she believed it, at least at first. By the end, I'm not sure.'

'Did you ever see her, Codger? Did she remember you? I can't remember you at all, not when I was a kid,' says Mandy.

'No, you wouldn't. I was a hermit. I lived in the Scrublands, didn't have a car back then. I didn't want to see anyone. And I was pretty disreputable. But I would see her; she was almost the only one. I was always glad to see her. She would come out once a week or so. Bring me food, bring me books, while you were at school. She'd pull up and blow her horn, warning me to get some clothes on. Most times she'd just drop me stuff and leave, but sometimes she'd stay and chat. We never talked about what had happened in the past, though. Never. But she was a wonderful woman, Mandalay. Wonderful.'

'Oh, Codger,' says Mandy again, hand stretched out, holding his.

There's silence for a long moment. And then the sound begins, a gentle drumming on the tin roof—but it's the scream from outside that grabs their attention, cranking Martin's senses up to maximum. The scream comes again, but now he identifies it more accurately: not a scream, but a squeal of delight. Then, through the recently revealed windows, he sees the spattering rain, light at first, then approaching up the street in a grey wall. A great peal of thunder breaks across the town, shaking the windows and reverberating in their bellies. They're on their feet then, rushing out the door, out into the street, joining the people already there, dancing in circles, laughing, arms outspread, catching the drops. Mandy is swirling, holding Liam close, the boy alive to the joy of the moment. Martin feels the impact, large drops, stinging as they hit. Thunder rolls across Riversend once again, like a church bell. And for a few glorious minutes it pours down, the sky emptying itself. And then it ends, as abruptly as it began, having lasted no more than five minutes. It leaves the road steaming and the people elated. Shafts of sun angle down, cleaving the cleansed air, golden against the darkened sky. Martin takes deep breaths, sucking in the taste of it. Life. At long last.

AUTHOR'S NOTE

THE SETTING FOR *SCRUBLANDS* EMERGED FROM MY TRAVELS IN THE SUMMER of 2008–09 at the height of the millennium drought, as I researched my non-fiction book *The River*. However, the towns of Riversend and Bellington are entirely fictitious, as are their inhabitants. Riversend borrows bits and pieces from various country towns but comes mostly from the imagination.

The crimes in the book are not based on real events and all the characters are entirely fictitious. The *Sydney Morning Herald*, *The Age*, Channel Ten and various other news outlets are real media organisations, but none of the characters in these pages are based on real people. Moreover, the questionable journalistic standards portrayed at times in *Scrublands* are not intended in anyway to reflect the real-life standards upheld by those organisations.

ACKNOWLEDGEMENTS

WRITING IS A SOLITARY PURSUIT, UNTIL IT ISN'T. AT SOME STAGE, THE manuscript needs to see the light of day. The first to read an early draft of *Scrublands* were those mighty journalists and close friends Michael Brissenden, Katharine Murphy, Paul Daley and Jeremy Thompson. They all provided insightful feedback. Next was Benjamin Stevenson at Curtis Brown, who politely pointed out some major deficiencies. Thanks Ben! And then Grace Heifetz at Curtis Brown, who liked it well enough to become my agent. Grace has done the most phenomenal job in representing the book and myself, garnering interest from publishers near and far.

A huge thanks to all those at Allen & Unwin: Jane Palfreyman, Tom Gilliatt, Christa Munns, Ali Lavau, Kate Goldsworthy and the whole impressive team. And thanks to Alex Potočnik for his brilliant map.

In the UK, thanks to Felicity Blunt and Kate Cooper at Curtis Brown and to Kate Stephenson at Wildfire/Headline. In the US, gratitude to Faye Bender at The Book Group and Tara Parsons at Touchstone/Simon & Schuster. There are plenty of other people I should be thanking—all those working so hard behind the scenes to give this book its best chance of success. Thank you.

I'm grateful for a grant from the ACT Government's Arts Fund early in the life of this work. Such grants are vital in providing support to aspiring writers.

Finally, and most importantly, my love and thanks to my wife Tomoko, our children Cameron and Elena, and our wider family.